NAN'S CHILDREN

Stella Cullip

Cromwell Publishers

First published in 1999 by
Cromwell Publishers
Eagle Court Concord Business Park
Threapwood Road Manchester M22 0RR

Printed in Great Britain by
In-House Printing, Huddersfield

Bound in Great Britain by
J E Ingle & Son Ltd, Leeds

Paperback ISBN 1 901679 16 0

With love and gratitude to:

My husband, Richard, for his patient criticism and unfailing
support through all the rejections,

and

my mother, Anne, who introduced me to the joys of
reading and shared with me her own love of books.

To Chris,
A dear schoolfriend who shares so
many memories.
With love and admiration
from Stella

In loving memory of:

My grandmother, who first inspired "Nan"

and Sylvia, my dear friend and "sister" who is still missed
so much

ENGLAND 1918

"Nan! Nan Fisher! You'd best hurry home, love. I saw the telegram boy knockin' at your door a few minutes back. If it's bad news your Mum'll be needin' you."

The words momentarily stilled the thin figure in the shabby grey coat and battered felt hat. The keen April wind cut through the cheap material and her aching body was crying out for warmth and rest. But as the full import of Mrs Flint's words alerted Nan's weary brain, she was galvanised into action by an awful foreboding.

She pelted unseeingly down Holgate's drab high street whose shops were becoming shabbier by the month: the haberdasher's window bare, save for a few black or grey items of clothing; food shops even emptier. Past the one-legged paperseller in his faded army uniform on the corner, Nan reached Holfield Terrace. Oblivious to the stitch in her side, feet swollen from hours of cooking and cleaning since five that morning, breath rasping in a dry throat, she finally clattered down the steps to the basement of number thirty.

Before she had closed the door behind her, the sound of her mother's wailing confirmed her worst fears. Entering the kitchen she found a scene of domestic tragedy which was occurring daily in homes across Europe, in that year of 1918. Emily Fisher was huddled in the creaking armchair beside the range, head in hands, her body rocking with grief.

Gazing down at her, granite face devoid of expression, the flimsy slip of paper still grasped in his fingers, her husband stood, making no attempt to offer any comfort.

Leaning against the table, which she had partially laid for their evening meal, Nan's younger sister, Ruby, was twisting a damp handkerchief through agitated fingers. Her usual air of bored and tawdry glamour, which she tried so hard to cultivate in an endeavour to belie her sixteen years and grim surroundings, was for once absent.

She looked what she was – a bewildered child terrified at the sudden and total collapse of her rock-like mother who customarily dealt with all adversity, but was now shattered by this long-dreaded announcement.

"Mum, Mum? Tell me, is it the boys?" Nan crouched beside the rocking figure in the faded blouse and dark serge skirt, the grief-stricken face buried in the familiar white apron. On gaining no response, she looked up at her other parent, who silently passed her the telegram.

"War Office ... regret to inform ... Private John Fisher ... died on active service ... the Somme."

Whilst her eyes perused the words, her brain rejected their meaning. Not Private John Fisher, but Jack, their Jack, like countless others, would never come home again. He had been abandoned for ever in that infamous, unimaginable hell called the Somme.

Pictures of his cheerful smile unreeled in her head. The idolised friend and companion, who from his four years' seniority had protected and teased, comforted and supported her since Nan's earliest memories. The fishing expeditions to Alexandra Palace after school, when she had been graciously allowed to tag along, bearing jam jar and makeshift rod, in the excited hope of tiddlers in the lake: the conversations sitting in the back yard on hot summer nights, poring over tattered books from the penny library at the corner shop. Jack was the only one in the family who shared Nan's love of reading, a trait much ridiculed by his builder father, and a source of vague wonderment to his ever-practical mother.

Later, when Nan had to leave school at fourteen and in spite of her obvious ability, take the first skivvying job that came along, to assist the family finances, Jack was the one who offered a shoulder to cry on at the end of those first weary days.

He understood the pain and humiliation in Nan's soul at her dismissive treatment by the lady of the house, the high and mighty Mrs Leigh. He was there to bring a bowl of hot water and a towel warmed by the range, when Nan's feet were throbbing from hours of labour, sandwiched between the long walk to and from home, because there were no extra pennies to spare for the tram.

He had been among the first to enlist, proudly marching away in his ill-fitting uniform, whistling *Keep The Home Fires Burning*, with a jaunty wave as he turned the corner. There had been smudged letters written from unnamed camps and a brief embarkation leave before he was shipped off to France. After that the news was even scantier and Nan guessed he wrote so briefly because he was reluctant to harrow them with descriptions of the horrors around him. But now the ultimate horror was upon them.

She automatically folded the paper and placed it behind the clock on the mantelpiece. Then she said quietly to Ruby, "Make a cup of tea for Mum. She ought to have something stronger for the shock, but that'll have to do."

Uncharacteristically docile, Ruby moved into the scullery to fill the kettle and Nan put her arms about the sobbing woman. "Come on, Mum, let's get you up to bed. I'll get you a hot water bottle – that'll stop your shivering."

Emily blindly held out her hand in a mute plea for comfort, but seemed unable to gather the strength to stand up. Her husband wordlessly bent and lifted her out of the chair. Still sobbing she was carried up the flight of dark stairs with their worn linoleum to the front bedroom above.

Like everywhere else in the dingy terraced house, apart from the kitchen which was heated by the range, the air was dank and icy. There were fireplaces in all the bedrooms, but no-one could remember the last time there had been money to buy fuel for them. Now of course all fuel was rationed anyway.

Unceremoniously Will Fisher deposited his wife on the double bed which had seen the conception and birth of all four of their children. If asked, probably neither he nor his wife could have remembered when it had last witnessed any loving communication between them. Their marriage had suffered like so many others in that poverty-stricken neighbourhood.

Years of making-do, scrimping and saving to keep a roof over their heads, clothes on their backs and food in their mouths, had gradually eroded their relationship. Only rarely having enough money for treats such as a day at Southend or a visit to the Finsbury Park Empire, they were slowly ground down by the gloom and depression of the mean little house in that north London slum.

There were damp patches on the walls and mice ran riot below the floors and above the ceilings. Rooms were freezing in winter with endless draughts from ill-fitting doors and windows, but unbearably hot in summer, with hissing gas mantles to provide the light, and the kitchen range which had to burn throughout the year as their only source of cooking and hot water.

Above all, there was the endless depression of the unremitting drabness of their surroundings – floor and wall coverings, curtains and bedclothes alike. Materials were so old and much-washed they had faded to a uniform greyness, with the original colours almost indiscernible. Small wonder any romance in their relationship had long dwindled away, stifled for one hint of colour or cheer.

Nan gently helped her mother undress and don her thick flannel night-gown. She filled an old stone ginger beer bottle with hot water and tucked it in beside Emily. Ruby brought up the tea and Nan clasped her mother's shaking hands round the cup and helped her drink. They did not speak – there was nothing to say. Besides, Nan and Emily had never enjoyed a close relationship.

Emily had been a good mother according to her own standards. The four children had been fed and washed and brought up to respect their parents and the law. But tenderness had not been part of the equation – particularly with her daughters. The two boys were different.

Fred was born prematurely and because he had needed extra care, Emily had always regarded him with a certain softness. It had been very hard when he had followed his older brother and enlisted a month ago, when he had reached eighteen. Emily prayed that his time at training camp would be prolonged. The thought of sacrificing a second son in the muddy nightmare of the trenches was not to be contemplated.

Jack, as her eldest, came first in her affections. She had relished his sturdy independence and enjoyed looking up at his six foot figure towering over her. Especially she was thankful for his cheeky humour when life was particularly hard. She had been almost bursting with love and pride when she saw him in his uniform. His few letters she would read again and again, her lips soundlessly spelling out the words.

Now there would no longer be the happy lifting of her spirits when the postman delivered the envelope with the familiar handwriting, which would immediately brighten her day. Jack, her lovely boy, was lost and the grinding depression and poverty of her life stretched out, unrelieved.

Waiting till the sobs had finally died away and her mother's eyes had closed in exhaustion, Nan went downstairs. Ruby and Will were sitting at the kitchen table; plates of thin stew, whose main ingredient appeared to be a few vegetables, were set before them, along with a slice each of tasteless bread made with potato flour.

"I've left yours in the saucepan with Mum's. I didn't know how long you'd be." Ruby bent once more over her plate and Nan felt a wave of nausea at the thought of food. She moved to sit beside the range, numbed with grief and shock. Will stolidly finished his portion, then stood up.

"I'm off out. I'm on early shift fire-watching tonight. Don't forget to lock up after me." He reached for his tattered jacket with its Specials armband, swathed his neck in a thick muffler and pulled down a greasy cap over his eyes. Without one word of comfort or comment on the death of their brother, he slammed the front door and marched up the area steps.

10

He was hard, their Dad, no argument about that, thought Nan wearily as she finally took off her cracked boots and thankfully wriggled her numbed feet before the range.

"You can wash up, can't you, Nan? Only I promised Vi next door I'd go round and help her sort out that pattern for the dress she's altering. I think she's got some mauve ribbon, so I'll ask if I can have some to make an armband. Might as well show we've lost someone at the front, eh?"

Too tired to argue that she had been cooking and cleaning in another woman's house since first light and it was hardly fair to expect her to start again when she came home, Nan silently nodded. Knowing her younger sister so well, she was not really surprised at her lack of grief over Jack's death. Ruby was nothing if not self-absorbed, which she amply demonstrated on this night of all nights. Looking in the mirror above the range, she carefully applied powder to her cheeks and rearranged her hair, before pulling a cardigan over her green jumper and flared skirt.

Ruby was undoubtedly the beauty of the family, thought Nan. Her auburn hair was naturally curly and she was forever experimenting with different styles. She had threatened to have it bobbed like so many fashionable young ladies, but her natural vanity had so far prevented it.

She had worked in a local café since leaving school but was always complaining about the boredom and low pay. She was tempted to become a conductress on the trams, where she would have enjoyed showing off her slim figure in the masculine uniform which would have allowed her to wear trousers, but Emily was not in favour! She longed to work in a really high-class dress shop in the West End, but there seemed little chance of this whilst the war lasted.

New clothes were rarely purchased these days. Even among the gentry it was considered unpatriotic to appear in new gowns. Women in all classes had become experts in redesigning and making over their old garments. One of Ruby's most treasured possessions was a Frister and Rossman sewing machine which Will had acquired from the establishment of a German tailor who had been interned at Alexandra Palace. She would spend hours with her bosom pal Vi, poring over patterns, unstitching seams and recreating dresses.

However, Will and Emily were both very strait-laced in their moral attitudes so there was a limit to how short Ruby might wear her skirts and although powder was permissible, rouge and smoking were frowned on, being the prerogative of "fast" girls. "We may be poor, but we can still have standards," was a favourite saying of Emily's, which her children might laugh about behind her back, but were in no doubt must be adhered to, whilst they lived under her roof. Even the boys would never dream of swearing in their parents' hearing.

Nan closed her eyes and leant back in the armchair. Alone now, her grief overcame her. Suddenly life seemed too much to bear. What did the future hold for her? At least before she had looked forward to the end of the war and Jack returning to bring a little fun and affection into her daily existence. But what now?

She hated the ugly home, which seemed meaner than ever since she had been working in Mrs Leigh's Muswell Hill mansion. She knew now at first hand what it would be like to have lovely furniture, attractive rooms, a beautiful garden. But what chance had she of accomplishing such a life?

Not given to personal vanity, when she sometimes watched Ruby primping before the glass in their shared bedroom, she would wryly compare her own features. Medium brown hair, dead straight and usually strained back into a neat bun out of her way beneath her housemaid's cap, made her look older than her twenty-four years. Her face was thin and sallow from spending little time in the open air, with prominent cheekbones and large brown eyes that gave it a hungry look. Her best feature she supposed was her skin, which was very smooth and quite unblemished, save for the dark shadows that appeared beneath her eyes at the end of a particularly exhausting day.

She was of medium height – not short enough to be petite like Ruby, and not tall enough to appear elegant, as she would wryly tell herself. Ruby, in spite of the poor diet they all existed upon, had definitely feminine curves in all the right places, (no doubt the odd left-overs at the café helped a little with this) but Nan was, in her own words "flat as a board" and in her own eyes utterly unattractive.

Most of the time she was untroubled by her personal shortcomings. Six days a week her labours at Mrs Leigh's were so wearing she was simply thankful to accomplish them with as little criticism as possible from her employer, and come home to lose herself for a short while in her current library book, before sinking into exhausted oblivion.

On Sundays she would sometimes give Emily a help with domestic chores, clean up her bedroom, (Ruby rarely did a hand's turn in that direction) and if the weather was fine she would go for a walk through the grounds of Alexandra Palace. This had been a place of refuge ever since early childhood. Its undulating parkland, with views across miles of north London; the picturesque lake; the grey terraces in front of the palace itself; it had an air of formal grandeur that had inspired her youthful imagination.

Now of course it had been taken over as a depot for internees and would probably never be the same again. But for Nan it had always represented an escape from her daily squalor to a place of beauty and clean fresh air. But even that would be spoiled in future, because she would hear Jack's laughter as he raced her to the top of a slope or teasingly with-held the ice-cream he'd bought her from the street vendor's tricycle.

Would she remain forever in this depressing house, taking care of her parents as they grew old and infirm? There was no doubt Ruby would marry young and probably move away to something better if she had her way. But that night, Nan's life truly seemed a gloomy prospect and the loss of Jack underlined the bleakness of her future.

The next months dragged by, full of news of defeats in France where the Germans were mounting a second offensive on the Somme. The age of conscription had been raised to fifty and Will only narrowly missed being called up.

Fred came home briefly on leave and was silent most of the time. Nan found him sitting in the yard late one night, crying softly as he hugged an old jacket that had belonged to Jack. Emily with her usual practical streak had simply altered any of Jack's remaining clothes to fit her second son.

"Nan, I know I always had his cast-offs when we were nippers, but it don't seem right somehow, taking his things after he's gone," his voice broke and he buried his head in the patched old garment.

"I know, love, I know. But Jack would have been glad for you to have his things. You know how generous he always was – if he ever had a shilling in his pocket, us kids always got a Saturday penny, didn't we? Why he'd have given you the shirt off his back ..." her voice trailed away as she realised the awful truth of what she had said. Then they were both clinging together, crying softly for fear that Emily or Will might overhear and condemn this open display of grief.

Emily had reverted to type the morning after they had received the telegram. She rose and dressed at her customary time and went about her work as usual. Her only concession to losing her son was to put his black-bordered photograph in the front window, next to the card which had shown his and Fred's names as being members of the family "doing their bit".

Will was busy with his building job – like many other labourers he had found the Zeppelin bombing of London had brought the blessing of extra work – and he stood his shifts as a Special Constable. Jack's name did not pass his lips.

So Fred and Nan seemed alone in their grief, for Ruby, as usual, was far too preoccupied with her own affairs. The highlight of her week was a visit to the local cinema with Vi from next door.

So it was a relief for Nan to cry out her pain to Fred and comfort him in his. When he whispered, so quietly she had to strain to hear the words, "I'm scared Nan, I'm so scared it'll be me next," she felt as though her heart would break for him. But what could she do other than rock him in her arms and murmur soothingly?

Watching him walk away that last morning, knowing he was bound for France and its waiting horrors, Nan struggled to keep her agony to herself. Of course Emily must have been feeling badly, she knew, but she seemed able to cope as usual through practicalities.

"You have packed that helmet I've knitted for you under your gas cape, haven't you, Fred? And that waistcoat in case the nights are cold … and I've done some mittens, though I don't suppose you'll need them at this time of year. Please God it'll all be over before winter. They say with all the lads from the Empire joining in, it can't be much longer."

Unable to watch Fred's trembling lips as he desperately held on to his final shreds of courage, Nan had preceded him up the area steps to the street. Mrs Flint along at number twenty-six thankfully lightened that last dreadful moment, calling out loudly, "Good luck lad. Watch yourself over there. An' I mean the French trollops, not the German cannon!" So they were all able to have a moment of shared laughter before he hugged Nan and his mother and walked away without a backward glance.

Now it was June. The weather was humid and Mrs Leigh was being more demanding than ever. Some of the work Nan really enjoyed, and would have taken even more pleasure in it, if she had been left uninterrupted. But one of the tiny row of bells on the wall in the kitchen would inevitably summon her at Mrs Leigh's slightest whim.

On some occasions her employer went off with other middle-class women friends to the "Tipperary Club" which had been formed to aid soldiers' wives, organise canteens and generally help out with the morale of the wounded in the overflowing hospitals. Nan was then content to methodically empty the contents of one of the ornate chiffoniers in the drawing or dining rooms and lovingly clean the glasses and ornaments.

Sometimes she would be instructed to carefully polish the silver-backed brushes and mirrors on Mrs Leigh's dressing table or in her husband's dressing room. He was a figure that Nan rarely saw. A big, bluff man, red-faced and inclined to corpulence, she understood he had been "something in the city" and was now much involved with supplies to the war office. Although Nan had been sent to do the shopping bearing the Leighs' ration cards, she often saw evidence of extra provisions in the larder, which she was loftily informed were gifts donated by friends "from the country".

On this particular morning she found that Mrs Leigh was still in bed and obviously suffering from early cold symptoms, but in view of the world-wide Spanish flu epidemic which was causing so much panic, she had decided to cosset herself even more than usual.

"I'm certainly not setting foot out of bed, feeling like this. It's probably too late and I've already picked up this ghastly flu but perhaps if I take great care it may not develop into anything really serious. You'll have to go to the cottage hospital this afternoon in my place. I'm supposed to take along all the bandages my ladies circle have rolled and there may be some patients who need letters written for them. I take it your writing is legible enough for that?"

Nan flushed angrily. Of course Mrs Leigh knew that her handwriting was perfectly neat, probably she had a better hand than her mistress, but it was the usual attempt to put her down and make her feel an "inferior", which was how Mrs Leigh regarded all the servant class.

"I'll be glad to do what I can at the hospital, Ma'am. Shall I go straight after I've given you your lunch?"

"Yes, I suppose so. Though heaven knows I certainly don't fancy anything to eat in my state. But I suppose I must keep up my strength."

It was quite a treat for Nan to leave the house in the early afternoon. The sun was very strong and she wished she might take off her hat and unfasten the short jacket, worn over her long-sleeved blouse, with its tightly buttoned cuffs and high-collar. Mrs Leigh had given her money to catch the tram which went past the hospital, but had not bothered to include fare for the return journey.

"Mean cow!" muttered Nan to herself and wondered whether it would be better to save the fare to travel home, when she would probably feel more tired. The appearance round the corner of a tram which went right past the hospital made the decision for her, and she hastily mounted the platform.

Sinking back thankfully, she allowed herself to relax for the first time since she had entered her workplace that morning. Running up and down stairs with trays for Mrs Leigh, as well as trying to fit in all her usual jobs, had been quite exhausting in the June heat. Her eyelids began to droop and then as they went over a rut in the road, she hastily jerked herself awake, settling her old straw boater more firmly in position.

As she did so, she was aware of being watched. The soldier in uniform sitting opposite was grinning appreciatively at her, obviously having seen how nearly she had fallen asleep. Embarrassed, Nan felt her cheeks redden and she looked hastily out of the window to avoid his gaze. She was glad when the tram stopped outside the hospital and she was able to descend. In her eagerness to get out, she stumbled in her ill-fitting cracked boots and narrow skirt and would have measured her length on the pavement had a strong hand not grabbed her round the waist and held her whilst she regained her balance.

Of course it was the grinning soldier. At close quarters Nan had to admit he was a handsome devil. His skin was rather swarthy looking but went well with the dark curly hair, which he revealed immediately by whipping off his cap. The eyes were very dark brown and had a disconcerting expression as they gazed so closely into hers. Nan had a fleeting ridiculous impression that he was looking straight into her soul and reading her every secret thought.

The uppermost thought in her mind at that precise moment was how warm and firm his hand felt at her waist. It gave an impression that his tall, muscular body would also be very warm and very hard as it fleetingly brushed against her until she hastily pulled herself upright.

"Careful, Miss, you could've had a nasty fall. All right now?" Even white teeth grinned engagingly, as Nan hastily moved away from his steadying arm.

"Yes. Thanks for your help." She turned to walk through the hospital gates and was disconcerted when he fell into step beside her.

"Lovely afternoon, Miss. Going visiting are you? Bring a bit of comfort to the troops eh?" There was an underlying innuendo of something not quite proper behind the innocuous words. Feeling more and more flushed at his continuing proximity and appreciative stare, Nan strove to regain her composure and take command of the situation.

"Yes, as a matter of fact I am. Not that it's any of your business. And I really don't need an escort, thank you very much, so I'll say good afternoon." Head in air, Nan hastened away towards the main building, though speed was not easy in her hobble skirt and uncomfortably tight boots, encasing feet that had swollen in the heat.

"Right you are, Miss. Far be it from me to thrust myself unwanted on a young lady!" He gave her a mock salute and another cheeky grin, to accompany words that once again left an impression of double meaning. But she was aware of his gaze until she had entered the reception hall.

Having delivered her parcel from the ladies of Mrs Leigh's club, Nan offered her services to visit any of the patients who needed company. The sister on duty eyed her sharply, taking in the shabby clothes and menial status.

"Usually we have ladies such as your mistress to visit the wounded. We can't have them disturbed by giggling young servant girls. Still, we do have several that can't

20

write their own letters and need it done for them. You can write, I take it?"

"'Course I can write! Where do I go? I'll be glad to help the poor blokes. 'Specially as I've recently lost my own brother on the Somme, and have another one out there as well. Least I can do." She fixed the sister with an intrepid stare, and the latter had the grace to redden slightly.

"Oh, well, in that case ... Go to ward three, down that passage. Ask the nurse which patients need your help. When you've finished there, go to hut five, out in the grounds."

"Right, Sister. Thank you."

Nan found her way to the ward and passed through the swing doors with a slight feeling of trepidation. She was not queasy at the sight of blood. Living in Holgate she had grown up among the victims of Saturday night pub brawls, or domestic arguments, which had resulted in the odd knifing as well as fist fights. But she was worried as to her emotional reaction at being among the wounded soldiers. Would she picture Fred's face instead of theirs? Would she regret that Jack was not amongst them, instead of decaying somewhere in the french mud?

But once she was inside and sitting by the first bed, her fears evaporated and Nan's inherent good sense asserted itself. Although she had a strongly sensitive and romantic streak, which had been nurtured by her choice of reading over the years, there was enough of Emily's practicality in her make-up to enable her to get on with the job in hand, rather than dissolve emotionally at the sights around her.

This ward seemed to consist of patients recovering from surgery, so there were many amputees, some hopping around on crutches, but others confined to bed. Some had faces swathed in bandages and had obviously been blinded and it was amongst these that Nan spent most of the time.

Those that could see called cheerful greetings as she passed, and gave cheeky descriptions of her charms to their blind comrades who were availing themselves of her services. Nan was easily at home with their harmless banter and gave as good as she got. She spent an hour in the ward and then set off for the hut in the grounds.

It was almost at the boundary fence and partially surrounded by thick shrubs. The cottage hospital had obviously once been a grand manor house, that had been taken over when the owners fell on hard times. As more beds were needed during the course of the war, huts had been built to accommodate the extra patients. When she entered number five she quickly realised it was very different from the previous ward.

Here the men were mostly silent. Some were dressed and lying on their beds or sitting staring listlessly into space. Some between the sheets had their eyes closed, but occasionally would break into strange little whimpers or moans. Nan hesitated, wondering if she was in the right place, but then the ward sister bustled up.

"Have you come to write letters for those that can't do it themselves? There are only one or two. The rest are in no state to think clearly about anything, let alone compose a letter to their families!"

"What's the matter with them? Why are they all so quiet?" Nan looked round uneasily. The ward had an odd, almost sinister atmosphere about it. Although there were some bandages in evidence, many of the patients had no obvious injuries at all.

"These men are all suffering from some form of shell shock. Some have forgotten who they are; some have forgotten what happened to them before they left France; some appear quite normal for hours at a time and then have panic fits; a lot of them can instantly lose control at a sudden loud noise that reminds them of the sounds at the Front." She looked at Nan, grim-faced.

"Frankly, I'd rather nurse a blind man or a man with no legs any day. At least you know what the problems are and how to deal with them. With these cases you don't know how they're likely to react from one minute to the next.

"Now the chap I want you to help is over in the corner. Most of the time he's quite coherent – you see he's reading a paper – but as you'll notice, he's got no control over his body. His hands won't stop shaking, so he has to be helped with every little thing such as eating and dressing, and of course he can't handle a pen. But he really wants to write to his mother and his girlfriend, so he'll be glad to dictate to you."

"Yes, Sister." Nan swallowed hard and forced a bright smile to her lips as she walked over to the shaking figure who was bent over an open newspaper, his head jerking from side to side as he tried to read.

"Hello, soldier. Found any cheerful news, have you? 'Cos if you have you'd better share it with the rest of this lot!"

The sky was clouding over when Nan finally left the hut. Private Johnson had been pathetically grateful for her assistance, both with his letter-writing and his afternoon mug of tea. Nan felt emotionally drained as she moved away through the shrubbery. Somehow these mentally damaged patients had been more upsetting than those who had lost an arm or a leg.

There was a metallic glitter to the light and it was obvious that a storm was imminent. At least it might clear the air a bit, she thought, but hoped she wouldn't be soaked whilst walking home. Should have saved my tram fare, after all. But there was no way she was going to spend any of her own pennies. Her budget was far too tight for the luxury of an extra tram ride! Suddenly a brilliant flash of lightning zigzagged across the blackening heavens and was followed immediately by an ear-splitting thunderbolt, practically overhead.

The sudden noise made Nan give a strangled gasp, which became a scream as a wild figure suddenly burst out of the rhododendrons fringing the path and flung her to the ground.

"Down, down, you little fool! Once they've got you in their sights they'll keep on firing. Which way's the dugout? These bushes are no cover, they'll all be scorched away in no time! The captain should have ordered a proper trench to be dug before we advanced!"

As this crazed apparition in khaki pinned her down, the weight of his solid physique temporarily winded her and she could only gasp for air as she struggled to throw him off.

"Keep still! Keep still! If you move they'll mow you down, just like my friend Pete. I couldn't recognise him when they brought him back – the bits that were left of him.

"We should never have gone over the top. We knew they were waiting for us. We heard them shouting in the night across No Man's Land. But they don't care. At HQ they don't care. We're just acceptable casualties to them, you see. They don't care." The mad, high-pitched monotone continued as his hot, stale breath fanned Nan's hair across her neck.

Although it was obvious that in his mind he was reliving some terrible experience in France, the hands that had grabbed her were now roughly exploring her body trapped beneath him. Nan was terrified that his madness was escalating as the violent scenes were being replayed in his head.

When she attempted to wriggle away, he pushed her further into the ground and it was clear she was helpless against his frenzied strength. Another flash of light and a crack of thunder seemed to drive him beyond all bounds of reason. With the scream of a terrified animal he began to tear wildly at Nan's clothes.

"Help me! Help me! Don't let me die! Make it stop! Make it stop!"

Nan realised the remembered panic and fear were somehow becoming confused with an animal arousal produced by the feel of her body beneath his own. Back in France the battle-weary would seek forgetfulness for a time in the arms of the women in the brothels. Now in the same way he was desperately striving for oblivion by using Nan to slake his sexual craving, which was the only force strong enough to blot out the awful terror that was controlling him.

Nan's own panic was rising swiftly to keep pace with his. Although she had grown up among the poorest class in a rough background, where the basics of life and death were rarely hidden, she had been schooled by Emily in a strict code of morals.

Her encounters with the opposite sex had been limited to the occasional kiss at a Christmas party, and she had never been out with boys. Unlike Ruby, they held no fascination for her. She had seen enough of the drudgery in her mother's life and those in the streets around her, to have no eagerness to get married and raise a family in such poverty-stricken conditions.

To Nan, any fantasising about sex came from the romantic novels she devoured so assiduously. Her practical nature accepted that it was unlikely a knight would ride into her world and carry her away to a life of ease and plenty, but she was still not eager to accept the common-sense alternative. She had never met a boy who had aroused her sexually, and the whole idea of physical love was one she had rarely considered.

So she was filled with abject horror at the intimate assault on her person by this gibbering wreck. His hands were tearing at her skirt, the nails scraping the skin on her legs through her thin stockings, his bulk forcing her face down into the dry, dusty earth, so that she feared it would choke her nostrils and fill her open, panting mouth.

She managed one despairing scream, but then a rough hand squeezed her throat as the agonised voice throbbed in her ear. "Shut up, shut up! They'll hear you between the guns. Oh, don't let me die, don't let me die!" He seemed to reach a greater paroxysm of pure terror as the thunder crashed again, and his hands became ever wilder as her petticoat was ripped and he groped savagely at her knickers.

As Nan's own grip on reality began to fade, the blackness of the earth beneath her eyes started to whirl into a deeper and darker vortex, which threatened to suck her away. As all coherent thought left her, she was conscious of the crushing burden shifting suddenly off her and in its place a stinging bombardment of violent hailstones.

She lay immobile on the wet earth, too traumatised to even attempt to rearrange her tattered skirt and petticoat. Above the sound of the man's continuing crazed monologue, which soared to fresh peaks of terror at each crash of thunder, she heard another voice.

The tones were loud but steady, and they conveyed a kind firmness, which gradually filtered through to Nan's consciousness and that of her attacker.

"Come on then, mate. The raid's over for today. Didn't you hear the Captain's whistle? Back to the dugout for us, eh? The guns are getting fainter. Hear that? Expect they've got some other poor devils in their sights, eh? Let's get you inside and have a nice brew-up. Then you can have some shut-eye. You'll need it after this little lot, I shouldn't wonder."

The voices faded away and so did the storm. Nan lay still. It had all happened so swiftly and shockingly, she could scarcely believe it. Feebly she put out a hand to rearrange her clothes and oblivious to the mud around her, curled into a foetal position which seemed somehow comforting beneath the steady onslaught of the elements. As her tears mingled with the rain, which had now succeeded the hail on her cheeks, she felt she would never have the strength to move again. She simply wanted to relish the utter peace after the terrible violence.

Her eyes were tightly shut and she kept them so when gentle hands placed a mackintosh cape over her body and lifted her upright.

"Come on then, Miss, you're all right now. He's safely back in the ward again. Should never have got out. But they can't watch 'em every minute, I s'pose."

She was effortlessly lifted off her feet and carried through the shrubs and back to the hut. The sister stood in the doorway, a look of concern on her face.

"Bring her into my office. She's soaked through. I'll find her something to wear. Here's a towel, my dear. Give your hair a rub with that. Soldier, pour her out a cup of tea. The kitchen's next door."

"Right you are, Sister."

Eyes downcast, Nan took the rough towel and with shaking hands removed the last few pins from her hair, which had collapsed from its neat bun into a wild, soaking mass. She felt so shamed and horrified by what had happened, it seemed impossible to look anyone in the face.

But a tiny voice, deep inside, was reminding her, that bad as it was, it could have been even worse. She definitely had her rescuer to thank for that. Another few seconds ... She shuddered violently at the thought of the ultimate violation that she had narrowly escaped.

"Drink your tea, Miss, whilst it's nice and hot. I've put plenty of sugar in – they say it's good for shock, don't they?" The khaki-clad legs stopped before her and the thick china mug was proffered. Slowly, reluctantly, Nan met his eyes, which were filled with sympathy.

"Thank you. Thank you for what you did." The whispered words choked in her throat as she tried to control the tears. She was frightened that if she started to cry, all last vestiges of control would be gone. So she gulped down the strong, syrupy, brew.

"A nasty business, right enough. Must have given you a terrible fright. I was just walking back to my ward when I heard you scream. Seem fated to come to your rescue today, don't I?" He grinned disarmingly and Nan suddenly realised it was the same cheeky soldier who had caught her earlier, when she had tripped off the tram.

The sister hurried in with an armful of dry clothes. "Here you are, dear. You can bring them back another day. I'm so sorry you've had such a fright. Corporal Dobson has been so calm the last few days, I really thought he was recovering.

"But it's always the same, a car back-firing or someone dropping a tray in the kitchen and it sets them off. Of course he shouldn't have been out on his own, but we've been rushed off our feet this afternoon with new admissions. Really, we just haven't enough staff to watch them all the time. You are all right, aren't you? I mean he didn't ... actually ...?"

"No. No. I'm just a bit shocked, that's all. Thanks to Private ...?"

"Stuart, Miss, Charlie Stuart."

"Well that's all right then. I think the rain has stopped now, so I expect you'd like to get off home. I'll leave you to finish your tea and get changed. Perhaps Private Stuart will walk you to the main gate?"

"Be a pleasure, Sister. I'll wait outside while you change, Miss. I'll make sure no-one comes in." He smiled reassuringly and followed the sister out. Nan stripped off her sopping jacket and dress and put on the faded but clean garments the sister had brought.

She brushed her hair back with still-shaking fingers, wondering fleetingly what had happened to her hat. Probably somewhere amongst the bushes and covered in mud. There was no mirror, and since she didn't carry one in her bag, she had to leave her hair hanging loose around her shoulders. She rolled her own wet garments into a bundle and went outside to the waiting soldier.

He quietly took her arm and continued to hold it as they walked down the steps from the hut and through the shrubbery. It was fragrant after the heavy rain, which was now steaming from the hot earth. The air was still warm but with a crisp freshness about it after the storm. It was hard to imagine the noise and violence that had been enacted so recently amongst the bushes.

Nan's legs still felt shaky and she was grateful for the sturdy support of Charlie's arm as they made their way to the gate. The impending walk home to Holgate seemed interminable and Nan decided that for once she must spare the money for the tram fare. She need not have worried, however, for when they reached the entrance, Charlie continued beside her and then paused when they reached the tram stop.

"If it's all the same to you, Miss, I'll see you to your door. You've had a nasty experience and I wouldn't like to think of you passing out on your way home."

"Oh, I don't want to put you to all that trouble. It's a fair distance to Holgate, where I live." She had noticed as they walked side by side that he had quite a pronounced limp. "Shouldn't you be back in the hospital? You are a patient, aren't you?"

"I am, but not for much longer." He nodded down at his leg. "Lucky I was, and copped a Blighty one. Bit of shrapnel lodged in there and I'll always have a limp, but at least they can't send be back to that hell-hole. Begging your pardon, Miss."

"That's all right. I can only begin to imagine what sort of hell it must really be – judging by what it's done to that poor bloke, and the rest of the others in that ward like him."

Charlie's habitual cheekiness was missing as he held her gaze and said seriously, "You don't want to imagine it. It's a living nightmare and when you come home you have to believe that's what it was – a nightmare. If you think of all those other poor devils, still enduring it, day after day, night after night, then you end up like that madman this afternoon. So don't even try and imagine it, Miss ... Here, I can't keep on calling you 'Miss' – what's your name then?"

"I'm Nan, Nan Fisher," she held out her hand. "Pleased to meet you, Charlie."

"Likewise, I'm sure!" He tucked her hand back through his arm. "Now where's this tram, then? Anyone'd think there was a war on, the service you get these days!"

In spite of her aching body and the stinging of the scratches on her legs and the shaking inside that was still unabated, Nan couldn't resist a watery smile at his cheerful humour and was rewarded with a wink and a squeeze of her arm, which was somehow very warming and made her feel reassuringly safe.

So she got her tram ride home, for which Charlie of course insisted on paying. He then walked her to the door of number thirty. She wanted to invite him in, but suddenly dreaded the thought of the explanations and fuss that his appearance and the description of the afternoon's events would cause.

When she hesitatingly asked, "Would you like to come in for a cup of tea? I expect your leg could do with a rest," he seemed to understand her dilemma.

"That's all right. I've got all the evening to sit still. A bit of exercise is good for it. Besides, I ought to get back. The nurses on my ward'll be pining for me! And I help some of the blokes with their suppers, ones who can't manage properly, so I'd better go."

"Well, thanks again for what you did. I can't bear to think about what would have happened otherwise ..." Nan's voice broke and she bit her lip hard.

Charlie patted her arm. "Don't give it another thought, girl. You get yourself indoors and have a good cry on your mum's shoulder. That's what you need now. But before you go – will you come and have a cup of tea with me soon? There's a nice café near the hospital gate. What about Saturday afternoon?"

"Well, I work till three, but I suppose I could come after that. I'll have to take these clothes back to the hospital anyway." Her heart was beating faster as she realised that Charlie was actually looking at her with real eagerness in his gaze. Could he find her attractive? Perhaps he was just being kind? As she hesitated, he nodded and gave her a beaming smile.

"That'll be just fine. Three thirty by the hospital gate, and perhaps we'll go for a walk in the park before our tea. Mustn't forget to exercise me old dodgy leg, must I?" With a mock salute he turned and strolled away down the road, whistling a cheerful version of *If You Were The Only Girl In The World*, which brought a blush to Nan's cheeks as she went down the basement steps to face the family.

She would have preferred to keep the whole episode quiet, but there was no way she could avoid an explanation about the strange clothes she was wearing and her generally dishevelled appearance. Not to mention the missing hat.

Their individual reactions were very predictable. Emily sat her down in the armchair and bustled about making a cup of tea. Then she took the damp and muddy clothes to be washed, after saying with a searching look straight at Nan, "This mad soldier, he didn't do you any real harm did he? The other one came along in time, did he?"

"Yes, I told you, Mum. I'm just a bit bruised and shaken up, that's all. Though if Charlie hadn't been there ..."

Ruby gasped, wide-eyed, "D'you mean he'd have raped you, the loony one?"

"That's enough of that sort of talk, girl!" Will looked up from his paper, which had appeared to be reading throughout Nan's story. "Give your mother a hand with the supper. And keep your mouth shut if you can only open it to talk dirty!"

Ruby shrugged and made a face as she flounced into the scullery, but she was too frightened of Will to answer him back. Nan knew, however, that she would have to undergo a merciless cross-questioning when the two of them retired to bed that night.

She was none the worse for her experience and in looking forward to her meeting with Charlie, managed to put the unpleasant business to the back of her mind. She took her "best" navy costume and clean white blouse to work with her on the Saturday, and Ruby generously offered the loan of her own straw hat with a freshly washed navy ribbon round it.

When she had finished her duties, Nan washed herself scrupulously in the sink in Mrs Leigh's scullery and brushed her brown hair till it gleamed, before carefully redoing her neat bun. She had a fleeting urge to leave it hanging round her shoulders, but it made her appear in her own eyes, "a bit flighty", so she carefully restored it to its usual sensible style.

Catching sight of her hands which were roughened and red from so much scrubbing and cleaning, she sighed ruefully. Then she took from her bag a tiny bottle of cheap cologne that had been a Christmas present from Ruby, and sprinkled a few drops on her clean hankie. Then, greatly daring, she patted a little behind each ear and on the inside of her wrists. Catching sight of herself in the fly-spotted mirror above the sink, she shook her head laughingly.

"I don't know what's got into you, Nan Fisher. Acting like a silly girl off to meet her beau. You're no beauty that's certain, and a handsome chap like Charlie Stuart can take his pick! He's just a kind bloke who wanted to cheer you up, and asked to see you again to take your mind off what happened. So don't start getting any romantic ideas about him!"

But for all her sensible talk, Nan's spirits lifted in happy anticipation as she set off briskly along the road towards the hospital. She had already returned the borrowed clothes whilst taking an evening stroll with her best friend, Phoebe Flint, who lived next door but one. Although she had secretly hoped to encounter Charlie, he was nowhere about.

But this afternoon he was already lounging outside the hospital gate, boots polished, uniform brushed and a welcoming smile on his lips.

"Well, you're a sight for sore eyes and no mistake! Pretty as a picture in that hat, you are!" He gave her an impudent wink and tucked her hand in his arm. "That scent's a knock-out too, if I may make so bold! I can see I shall have to keep a strict check on myself this afternoon. A lovely lady like you could go straight to a bloke's head!"

"Oh, Charlie, you do go on!" But Nan was blushing and laughing delightedly in a manner that would have done her younger sister credit, and amazed her family if they could have seen her.

That afternoon and evening passed in a wonderful atmosphere of gaiety and irresponsibility. Somehow with Charlie, Nan shed all her serious, practical, common sense and revelled in his jokes and admiring glances.

They spent an hour wandering through the park near the hospital and then had tea in a café. It was an unheard of treat for Nan to be waited on by someone else, and Charlie plied her with sandwiches and the few cakes available. Throughout the meal he regaled her with hilarious stories of his mates in the army and the other patients in his hospital ward, and the terrible pranks they played on the young nurses.

"Not Sister, though! Worse than my old sergeant she is, and as for Matron ...! Wouldn't like to meet her on a dark night – a finer moustache than my Captain's, she's got!"

Giggling at his non-stop anecdotes, Nan was aware that she had never felt so relaxed or carefree in the company of any other person in her whole life. The horrors of war and the daily drudgery of her home and work seemed to magically vanish before the onslaught of Charlie's irrepressible humour.

After they had finished tea, Charlie suggested a visit to the local cinema. "If we see the next performance, you won't be late getting home. And I won't be too late back in the ward. I told them I was visiting friends, so they won't expect me for supper."

"I don't know Charlie ..." Having tea with a man she hardly knew was one thing, but sitting in the dark intimacy of a cinema with him could encourage all sorts of ideas. But she was sorely tempted. She loved the wonderful escapism of moving pictures, and rarely had the money to treat herself.

"Don't worry, you'll be quite safe with yours truly. No sitting in the back row, and I promise I'll keep my hands in my pockets if you like!"

Unable to resist his impudence and the unerring habit he had of reading her thoughts, she smilingly agreed and allowed him to lead her into the foyer of the cinema. It was a wonderful romantic film and she was quite lost in the vicissitudes and triumphs of the heroine. The time went all too quickly and then they were coming out into the warmth of the still-light summer evening.

Charlie took her home, right to the doorstep and then shook hands, but retaining hers in both of his he said, suddenly serious, "You will come out with me, again, won't you Nan? I've really enjoyed your company."

"Thanks, Charlie. Yes, I'd like that. I've had a lovely time."

"Right, that's settled then. How about a walk round Alexandra Palace tomorrow evening? I'll meet you at the gates at seven. All right?"

"All right, Charlie." Nan hesitated, wondering half-hopefully, if he would kiss her. But he just squeezed her hand, saluted and marched away whistling as usual. Feeling light as a thistle, Nan floated down the steps to the basement door. She was humming beneath her breath as she wandered into the kitchen.

Emily was occupied with her interminable mending, sitting in the open doorway looking out on the back yard. Will had spread a sheet of paper on the kitchen table and was painstakingly polishing his boots. Ruby was out of course, it being Saturday night.

"Hello, Mum. Dad." Nan carefully removed her best hat and then stood beside her mother, trying to get a breath of fresh air. Will ignored her, but Emily asked quietly, "Had a good time did you?"

"Yes thanks. We had a walk round the park near the hospital and then had tea in ever such a nice café. Then he took me to see a lovely film. Real tearjerker, it was!"

"You should have brought him in for a cup of tea. I think we could have managed that – it's not rationed yet," Emily said stiffly, and Nan realised that her mother's pride was ready to be hurt. Ever since Nan had been working in Muswell Hill and brought home tales of the grand lifestyle that the Leigh family enjoyed, Emily was always ready to take umbrage.

Although she enjoyed hearing about the beautiful furnishings and the rich food in their larder, she would use the Leighs as a means of irritating Nan. Referring to them as "your fine employers" or "that toffee-nosed madam," she would insinuate that Nan had become stuck-up and too full of airs and graces to live at number thirty since associating with "the gentry".

Both Emily and Nan knew that this was all nonsense, but when she was in a bad mood, it was simply Emily's way of provoking Nan. She was well aware that Nan found her relationship with Mrs Leigh very irksome and would dearly love to work elsewhere. Nan had thought of taking on war work, perhaps in a munitions factory, or even helping on the land, but Emily was against her moving away from home. Besides, there were such dreadful accidents in the factories, it seemed best to remain in service.

Feeling so elated after her wonderful time with Charlie, Nan was determined not to be drawn by her mother's carping manner. Although she said little, Emily must still be mourning Jack. In the past Nan had rarely gone out, so at least she gave her mother some company. Now she had a male admirer, it was probably underlining Emily's own loveless marriage and humdrum lifestyle.

So Nan said cheerfully, "I never thought to ask him, Mum. But we're going for a walk to Ally Pally tomorrow, so perhaps he'll come and meet you then."

"You want to watch yourself, my girl." Will glared at Nan across his shining footwear. "These young blokes are all the same, and the soldiers are the worst of the lot! You make sure he keeps his hands to himself. Stick to the road and no wandering off in the bushes!"

"Don't worry, Dad, I can look after myself. Anyway, Charlie's a proper gentleman. Very respectful towards me, he is." Nan blushed as she thought of her own disappointment when Charlie had not attempted to kiss her goodnight. Not that she would have allowed him any liberties of course! No, but a nice, chaste kiss would have been quite acceptable and very … pleasant.

At that moment Ruby came in from her evening round at her friend Vi's house. Beside her bright pink blouse and flower trimmed hat, although both were cheap and tawdry, Nan felt suddenly drab and no longer young and carefree.

"Hello Nan, how did you get on with your young man, then? Give you a nice time did he? Hope you behaved yourselves. Didn't take you in the back row at the cinema, did he?"

"Yes, we had a lovely time, thanks. And no, not that it's any of your business, we did not sit in the back row!" Nan could feel her elation slipping away as the usual family bickering and depressing surroundings blotted out the innocent frivolity of her time with Charlie. Suddenly hot and tired, she forced herself back to grim reality and put on the kettle for a cup of tea.

But next day the sun was shining again, it was Sunday and there was no long trek to Muswell Hill, with a nagging Mrs Leigh at the end of it. Today she was free to spend her time as she wished and there was the exciting prospect of an evening with Charlie to anticipate. Ruby as usual had her Sunday "lie-in" till nearly mid-day, but Nan got up and washed a few items of underwear and pegged them out in the back yard, under the blazing sun.

Mrs Flint, next door but one, was sitting outside peeling potatoes and waved across the fences. "Another scorcher, Nan. Soon dry your smalls in this, eh?"

"Yes, it's lovely weather. Think I'll have to water our tomatoes again." She looked at a few plants that Will had grown in one corner of the yard, along with some lettuce and onions. Like many other town dwellers, he had taken to growing some of their food to combat the shortages that had worsened with the passing war years.

"Hear there's talk of another Big Push at the front. Wonder how many more poor devils are going to die before it's all finished? Expect your Mum's worried out of her life about your Fred. Especially since losing Jack?"

"Yes, it doesn't bear thinking about really." Nan wished absurdly, and guiltily, that she had not been reminded of her brother's awful situation on this particular morning. But that was appallingly selfish – wanting to hug her little bit of happiness to herself, unspoilt, whilst he was out there enduring goodness knows what horrors and dangers! After Mrs Flint had gone indoors, she determined to write another letter to Fred that afternoon, in an effort to salve her conscience.

But in spite of herself, as the afternoon waned and it was time to prepare for her meeting with Charlie, her heart lifted and tiny quivers of excitement surged through her. Painstakingly she heated a large pan of water and then filled the enamel bowl in the bedroom. She drew the curtains and stripped off her underwear, before scrupulously washing from head to foot. In the dimness she suddenly caught sight of her reflection in the fly-speckled mirror which rested above the chest of drawers she shared with Ruby.

Nan had little personal vanity and rarely dwelt on her own body, but suddenly she was fascinated by its normally hidden contours. It was painfully thin, with none of Ruby's youthful roundness. But the long legs with shapely ankles and slender thighs gleamed white and unblemished, in stark contrast to the shadowy mass of curly hair, that crowned the cleft where they merged with her lean torso.

Although the hips were too pronounced and bony for Nan's liking, the tiny waist was a source of shy pride and the small breasts, rising firmly with their darkened tips, suddenly proclaimed a dormant femininity that once Nan would have feared, but now welcomed with a sense of glowing excitement. Before her was the shadowy image of a woman, whose body she would not be ashamed to reveal before Charlie.

A door slamming below brought her back to reality and she hastily reached for her clean underwear. When Ruby entered the room she was wearing her petticoat.

"Getting ready for a night out? Meeting your soldier boy, again? What's he like then, Nan? Ever so dashing and handsome, is he?" Ruby sat on the bed and eyed her older sister. Nan had always been so serious and ready to criticise Ruby for her preoccupation with boys and clothes, it was a revelation for the younger girl to see Nan in this new light. Suddenly she felt more like one of Ruby's own girlfriends, when they giggled together over the latest boys who had caught their fancy.

Nan smiled as she smoothed the folds of her navy skirt over her hips, and buttoned up the long-sleeved, matching basque-style jacket. It was quite old, but she had shortened the skirt, to make it more fashionable. "Yes, he is handsome I suppose. He's got lovely dark, curly hair and his eyes are always laughing. In fact he's a real joker. Hardly ever serious. I think that's why I like him. He's really good company, Ruby. When I'm with him I can forget about the war and Fred, and never having enough money and always making do ..." she trailed off as she noticed the surprise in Ruby's eyes.

"Blimey! You have got it bad, haven't you? I never imagined you getting so carried away by a bloke, Nan. You'd better watch it. You'll be thinking of wedding bells next!"

"Oh, don't be daft!" Nan busied herself buttoning her bar shoes. "He's just a nice man and I enjoy his company. There's nothing more to it than that."

"Just as well. After all, if he's a soldier, and nearly fit, I expect he'll be leaving the hospital soon and going home, won't he? Where does he come from?"

"I don't know. He hasn't said much about his family. I think he was born in Scotland – he's in one of the Scottish regiments – but he doesn't have much of an accent." Nan was suddenly shocked by Ruby's words. Of course, Charlie would be moving away soon. He would be discharged now that he was unfit to serve. The thought of Charlie leaving Holgate caused a sinking sensation in Nan's stomach. The day was spoilt.

But as soon as she saw him, waiting beside the entrance to Alexandra Palace, Nan's face broke into a smile and she hurried towards him. As they met he clasped both her hands tightly for a moment and beamed down at her.

"It's good to see you, girl. It's been such a long time. I've been counting the hours, I can tell you."

"Charlie, you are a fool! It was only last night we went out."

"Only last night! D'you know how many minutes that is since I last looked at your funny little nose – you've got freckles – been sunbathing have you? And I'm sure your eyes have changed colour whilst we've been apart. I could've sworn they were brown, but now I reckon they're green!"

"Oh, Charlie!" Nan smiled radiantly at him and it seemed the most natural thing in the world when he slipped an arm around her waist and held her closely beside him, so that their hips brushed together as they strolled up the slope through the Palace grounds.

The evening sped past as they talked and walked and finally settled on the grass which was still warm from the day's heat. Charlie told her more about himself and what he revealed gave Nan a different picture of this jovial, wise-cracking soldier.

He was a foundling. He had been discovered on the doorstep of a Glasgow orphanage and brought up there. He looked back on his childhood with great bitterness. It was another side to his character that he showed Nan only briefly, but the bleak look in his eyes and the grim twist to his lips made her realise that the scars were indelible.

"We had enough to eat, barely, and we had clothes on our backs, but that was about all we had. They never showed any care for our thoughts or feelings, Nan. We were totally dependent on their charity and we had to be grateful. Yes, gratitude was a word we learned early! Gratitude and obedience. They were the mottoes by which we lived. God help us if we forgot! There was no sparing the rod in that place, I can tell you! They wanted to stifle every last whimper of rebellion in me, but they didn't succeed."

The dark eyes gazed sightlessly across the rooftops of London spread out below them, and Nan knew that he was seeing again that loveless boy filled with anger and loneliness.

"As soon as I'd grown tall enough to lie about my age, I ran away. I lived by my wits and made my way south. I slept in barns and ditches. Sometimes I begged, and sometimes I stole – I'm not ashamed to admit it. Finally I ended up in Liverpool and I worked the docks for a while. It was a grim life, Nan, but at least I was free and I learnt to be tough. I used my fists when I had to – my boots as well sometimes – and I survived."

He smiled at her, the old sparkle back in his eyes again. "Didn't know you were keeping company with a gaol bird and a street fighter, did you, Miss Fisher?"

"You actually did time in prison, Charlie?" Nan was shocked, but so great was her sympathy for the pathetic orphan she had pictured from his description, she was unable to feel too much censure for his misdemeanours.

"Yes, I served three months for pinching off a street barrow at one time, and I came close to facing a longer sentence for getting into fights with some of the dockers, but I usually showed a clean pair of heels when the coppers appeared on the scene."

"So did you stay in Liverpool till the war started? You don't sound like a Scouse."

"No, I left the 'Pool years ago. I decided I wanted to see the world, and unloading cargoes from all those far-off places gave me itchy feet. So I joined a merchant ship. Been all round the world I have, several times over!"

"That must have been a wonderful experience – all that travelling," Nan said wistfully. Some of her reading had given her a deep longing to visit other countries, which she knew was never likely to be satisfied.

"I don't know about wonderful, girl. Most places were hot and dirty and full of beggars of one sort or another. One port is much like another for a sailor who wants to spend his pay and forget his lonely weeks at sea. You never put down any roots and you never call any place home. You become hardened after a while, it takes all the softness out of you, Nan.

"Maybe it's not so bad for those that have families waiting for them at the end of a voyage, but when you've no-one anywhere to care if you come back safe or not, well …" he shrugged and then gave a rueful grin. "Here! What's the matter with me then? Lovely young lady to entertain and all I do is moan about my murky past. Fine evening this is turning into. I want shooting, I do!"

"It's all right, Charlie. I'm glad to listen if you want to tell me about yourself. It makes me feel as though we really know each other." She hesitated shyly and there was silence between them as their eyes met for a long moment. Nan could feel the colour rising in her cheeks at the expressive look on Charlie's face, and to break the awkward moment she said, "How long did you stay at sea?"

"Till war broke out. I'd had more than enough by then anyway. Life at sea is pretty tough and I didn't fancy making it worse getting blown up by the German navy! So I decided to try my luck in the army. I reckoned I was as capable of taking care of myself as the next man – I'd certainly had enough experience!"

"So then you were at the Front and eventually wounded?"

"That's right. I was lucky and finally copped a Blighty one and ended up in Holgate cottage hospital, where I was fortunate enough to rescue a beautiful maiden in distress, first from breaking her ankle and then from a fate worse than death!"

The serious atmosphere lightened as Charlie had obviously intended it should, and as Nan retaliated with a playful push against his chest, replying in a scoffing tone, "My hero!", he caught her hand and lifted it towards his face.

She thought he would kiss it, but instead he turned it over and looked tenderly at the work-roughened palm. Suddenly embarrassed, she attempted to pull it away, but Charlie shook his head and said softly, "No, girl, don't be ashamed. Your hand is what you are, Nan, a strong, hard-working, honest woman. Nothing soft and pampered about these fingers, is there?" And very slowly and delicately he brushed each finger-tip in turn with a butterfly touch of his lips.

Nan sat mesmerised. Each touch of his mouth sent shivers of heat throughout her body and imperceptibly her reclining figure swayed towards him. With infinite eroticism his lips travelled the length of each finger, lingered on the pad of flesh at the base of her thumb, and eventually paused on the sensitive pulse on the inside of her wrist.

Involuntarily her other hand lifted and she gently stroked the crisp curls on the downcast head. At her touch, he slowly looked up and then his fingers gently traced the outline of her parted lips, through which her breath was sighing in tiny gasps. Eyes trapped in the black depths of his, which held hers unblinkingly in their gaze, Nan was aware only of a simultaneous assault on all her senses: the faint tang of some hidden masculine aroma which blended with the comfortingly familiar odour of carbolic soap; the touch of his fingers, exploring her face or entwined with her own, which like the rest of her body were paradoxically drained of all energy and yet tinglingly alive, in a way that she had never experienced before.

In her ears came the whispering of their intermingled breaths as his mouth enclosed hers, and her tastebuds

47

encountered the alien sweetness of his exploring tongue which performed a strange caressing ballet with her own, as it probed her parted lips.

Minutes passed but might have been hours. New sensations crowded in upon Nan's body and soul from the incredible power of Charlie's hands and mouth to evoke responses that she had never dreamed existed. As he revealed the tiny areas of exquisite sensitivity among the contours of her face and throat, and an electric arousal was produced by his probing tongue on its voyage of moist discovery, Nan was transported to another universe.

She was oblivious to the hard ground beneath her, as gradually Charlie lowered her down on to the grass, although the smell of the crushed stems was strong in her nostrils. The faint voices of other strolling lovers made no impact on her thoughts, and the gradually darkening sky was not noticed, as her lids closed tightly the better to absorb the wonderful sensuality that Charlie was unleashing.

She rejoiced in the weight of his hard body pressed full-length against hers. As he lay half on top of her, his animal heat almost scorched her quivering skin through the thin cotton of her skirt and petticoat.

Then, like a douche of iced water, reality rudely invaded this dream world with the sound of the bell that signalled the imminent closure of the Palace gates.

Reluctantly, Charlie drew away from her and smiling down at her dazed looking face, he painstakingly removed some dead grasses from her hair, which had come loose from its restricting bun. Her skin was flushed, her eyes were soft and bemused, gleaming with a shining happiness, and Charlie thought she looked quite beautiful.

"Time to go home, girl. Unless you fancy climbing over the wall when the gates are closed? I'm quite happy to stay if you are?"

"Oh, Charlie! Of course I must go! I'd no idea it was that late." Nan scrambled to her feet and energetically began to brush down her clothes. Charlie grinned, as he handed her the straw hat that had long ago been abandoned, and then very gently refastened the top two buttons at the neck of her jacket, which she had not even noticed had been undone.

The flush in her cheeks became a deep scarlet and Charlie laughed out loud, as he cupped her chin in his hand and kissed her soundly, till she was once again breathless.

"You're blushing, my girl! No need to feel embarrassed because you've discovered you're made of flesh and blood you know! The most natural thing in the world – and the most enjoyable, eh?"

"Charlie, please don't tease me. It's just I've never been like this … felt like this … I don't know what's happening to me." Nan looked suddenly very vulnerable and almost child-like – her usual, sensible, competent self a million miles away.

Charlie's smile faded and he wrapped his arms gently round her as he said softly, "Tell you the truth, girl, I've never felt quite like this before either. Oh, I'll not pretend I haven't had some fun in times gone by – don't expect you'd believe me if I told you different, with my past – but with you, Nan, it's something a bit special. Now then, Miss Fisher, time to get you home. You've got work in the morning and I've got a ward sister who'll expect me to be nicely tucked up in my sick bed before lights out!"

The weeks of summer sped by and Nan floated through life on two different planes. One part of her was still the sane, hard-working skivvy who carried out her duties for Mrs Leigh as efficiently as ever. She wrote her regular letters to Fred, helped out Emily where she could, fended off Ruby's meaningful queries about Charlie, and put up with the hardships of life at number thirty.

But for the new Nan, life was lived in a different world during the hours spent with Charlie. The weather was kind and they spent their evenings walking in the park or, mostly, Alexandra Palace. Invariably they would find a secluded spot amongst the shrubs and lay entwined on the grass. Nan found the responses invoked in her body by Charlie a constant source of wonderment. The old Nan would have been horrified and scared by the utter abandonment she experienced, indeed a small warning voice sometimes still murmured in her subconscious, but her passion for Charlie had become so overwhelming, nothing really mattered beside it.

Charlie guessed how sexually unaware Nan had been, and was careful to treat her gently and progress slowly in their love-making. But as the weeks passed, both their feelings were swiftly escalating. When she was apart from him, Nan was afraid at the thought of total physical love-making, and the attendant risk of pregnancy, but when she was with Charlie, any cautious thought was swamped by her body's demands. Although she was frightened at the thought of losing her virginity – indoctrinated by Emily's upbringing that "nice girls don't" before they had a wedding band on their finger – nothing mattered except her feelings for Charlie, when his fingers were urgently unbuttoning her bodice and she could feel the hardness of his body against hers.

There was still enough of Emily's teaching in Nan for her to be appalled at the thought of making love in a public place, where they could be discovered by passers-by at any moment, so perhaps caution might have won. But then fate intervened when the Leighs departed for their annual holiday in Scotland, leaving Nan in charge of the house. Coupled with this was Charlie's announcement that the hospital had told him he was fit enough to be discharged. After that it was just a matter of formalities before he was invalided out of the army, as the leg injury made him permanently unfit for duty.

Nan's mind was in a whirl the morning after the Leighs had departed. Charlie had been passionate in his declarations of love towards her, but he had never mentioned the future. Actually Nan had been so absorbed in the wonder and excitement of their present relationship, and the incredible revelations of her own sensuality, she had barely given it a thought herself.

Now she was faced with the prospect of Charlie moving away. What would he do without the army? Where would he live? What sort of job would he get? Most important, would his plans include her?

That afternoon she had just finished polishing the furniture in Mrs Leigh's bedroom when she heard a rapping at the back door. It was an opportunity to give the house a thorough going-over while they were away, and her employer had left a list of extra cleaning jobs to ensure that Nan would not take advantage of their absence to idle away her days.

She hurried through the kitchen and to her amazement saw Charlie waiting outside. Brushing back the straggling wisps of hair from her sweating forehead, she hastily unlocked the door.

"Charlie, whatever are you doing here?"

"Hello, Sweetheart. Thought I'd come and walk you home. You said the old dragon was away, so I knew the coast would be clear. How about entertaining a wounded soldier to a cup of tea in her ladyship's drawing room, then?"

"Come in quick, before anyone sees! You'll get me the sack if any of the neighbours tell her when she gets back!" Nan pulled him inside, laughing in spite of herself at his typical effrontery. "As it happens, I've just about finished for the day. I was going to have a wash and make myself a cuppa before I leave, so you're in luck. But you'll drink your tea in the kitchen, like me! If I let you loose in the drawing room you'd probably smash her best Crown Derby!"

She made the tea and they sat relaxed at the kitchen table. Charlie as usual made her laugh with his tales of the hospital ward and the men's antics in the constant battle with Sister. After a while, Nan asked hesitantly, "Do you know what you'll do after your discharge? Have you made any plans yet?"

Charlie grinned as he reached for her hand across the table. "Counting the days till you get rid of me, are you?"

"No, of course not! I just wondered, that's all."

52

"Well I suppose I'll have to look round for a job. Though I don't reckon that'll be too easy. I've always fancied getting away from town life you know – perhaps working on a farm somewhere in the country ..." he lapsed into silence and Nan could see he was lost in some fantasy.

She had a momentary picture herself of his muscular body stripped to the waist wielding a pitchfork or driving a plough in some golden, sun-drenched field in the middle of nowhere. She would be waiting for him in a spotless farmhouse kitchen, with freshly gathered eggs frying in a pan with rashers of home-cured bacon ...

"Penny for 'em girl?" Charlie jumped up and pulled her to her feet and with a quick jerk gathered her tightly against his chest. All daydreams vanished in the immediate rising passion that his demanding mouth instantly produced in her melting body. All thought of the future vanished as she revelled in the exciting present.

The kitchen grew dimmer as the sun moved round and they remained engrossed in the storm of sensuality they were mutually arousing. By the time that Charlie took her hand and drew her out of the room and slowly upstairs, halting on each step to inflame her senses with deeper and more intimate caresses, Nan had lost every vestige of reasoning thought or caution. It all seemed right and totally inevitable. Even Charlie's natural audacity that somehow guided him to open the door of Mrs Leigh's own bedroom and lead them both across to her newly made bed was all part of the dreamlike experience.

Nan felt no fear and no shame at what followed. She was content to abandon herself to her own passionate responses and Charlie's needs. She was too naïve to appreciate that she was fortunate to have a lover experienced enough to ensure that her enjoyment of her own sexuality outstripped any physical discomfort at the moment of losing her virginity.

An hour passed in a series of magical tableaux. Recalling that afternoon in later years, even in spite of the events that would give her cause to hate Charlie Stuart, and scar her for life, Nan, with hindsight, was grateful to him. That episode of pure passion was the kind that some people are destined never to experience in their entire lifetime. On that afternoon and those that followed during the Leighs' absence, Nan discovered a deeply sensual side to her own nature, which, coupled with her burgeoning love for Charlie, made their passionate encounters almost incandescent in their power.

Her love for Charlie now verged on adoration. It was compounded of so many factors. Apart from his physical attraction, he replaced the companionship and masculine humour she had lost when Jack died. He also aroused feelings of deep pity and maternal sympathy as he allowed her to see into the bitterness and pain that he still harboured from his childhood. With him Nan could be all things, mistress, companion and mother.

For her part, he made her feel loved, appreciated and admired. His obvious physical need for her, gave Nan for the first time a real confidence in herself as a woman. Suddenly she felt feminine. In response her skin had a glow, her eyes sparkled with life and her body imperceptibly rounded to a new, womanly shape. Nan had discovered love and sexuality and they suited her.

Those fourteen days sped past and the Leighs were due back. On their last evening, Charlie walked her home under a star-filled sky. Nan felt emotionally exhausted as she strove to accept that the idyll was over. Charlie was leaving hospital in two days, she knew. But she had not asked again what he intended to do and he had not vouchsafed any information. She had pushed it away while they had their special time together at the Leighs', but now it was over and real life was waiting.

Charlie smiled down into her sad, tired eyes as they stopped before number thirty. "Worn you out, have I girl? Better not let your mum see you looking like that or she'll put two and two together, eh?"

"Don't Charlie, please. It's hard enough facing them anyway, without you joking." Nan's voice choked and she suddenly wanted to cry. The glory and passion were over. Charlie would go away and she would be left, alone with the memories. And she would miss him – how she would miss him!

"Come on, why the long face? Anyone would think I was going away and we'll never meet again! Just because I'm getting my discharge it doesn't mean you're seeing the back of me, girl."

"I didn't know ... you've not said ... I didn't like to ask ... in case you thought I was trying to push you into staying." Nan swallowed and looked up at him, hope gradually dawning as he smiled his special, tender smile, that he reserved for moments of genuine closeness between them – so different from his usual impudent grin.

"As a matter of fact I've got a job at the local pub. Old Jarman knows me well – I've often been in there with the walking wounded from the hospital – and his youngest boy has just gone off to enlist, so he needs a full-time cellar-man. He's getting too old to hump the barrels about himself. There's an empty attic room as well, so I'm in clover, girl!"

"Charlie, that's wonderful!" Nan gazed up at him, her heart in her eyes. "You're really staying in Holgate? I can't believe it! I was so sure you'd leave." Nan smiled radiantly, all tiredness miraculously disappeared.

"You didn't really think I'd go, did you?" Charlie was serious now. "I thought you realised how I feel about you, Nan. I've shown you often enough! I can't imagine a future without you and me together, girl. I thought you felt the same?"

"Oh, I do, Charlie, I do!" Oblivious of any peering eyes behind neighbouring curtains, she flung her arms around his neck and clung tightly as their lips met in a long, hard kiss.

"Well, excuse me! Mind if I come past, please?" Ruby's brittle tones brought Nan back to reality with a shock and she went to guiltily pull away, but Charlie's arm held her tightly against him as he raised his cap and said with a faintly mocking humility, "Sorry I'm sure, Miss. Have I the pleasure of addressing Miss Ruby Fisher? A privilege to meet my girl's lovely sister."

"Charmed, I'm sure!" Ruby bridled as she eyed him with the usual flirtatious pout she reserved for any attractive male. She had been intrigued about Nan's ongoing relationship with the wounded soldier and peered at him from behind the bedroom curtain on several occasions.

In spite of heavy hints from Emily, dour and sarcastic comments from Will and endless questioning from Ruby, Nan had so far avoided introducing Charlie. He was such a wonderful phenomenon in her life, she was not anxious to make him part of her home surroundings, which would inevitably bring him into the real world.

Also she still felt extremely guilty about the sexual nature of their meetings, knowing how horrified her parents would be if they discovered Nan's behaviour. It was difficult enough to answer questions about how they spent their evenings together, but if she had to actually stand before them with Charlie, she was convinced that some sort of aura would emanate from their bodies that would immediately proclaim the passionate activities they had mutually enjoyed.

Now, of course, Ruby was insisting that Charlie come inside. "I don't know where your manners are, Nan! Fancy not inviting your young man in to meet Mum and Dad. Him a wounded hero too!"

Somehow Nan found herself following the other two down the basement steps and through to the kitchen. It was Ruby who loudly performed the introductions and Nan found herself standing silent in the doorway as Charlie shook hands firmly with first Emily, then Will. Ruby had called him, Nan's "young man" and it was on this that Will pounced immediately.

"So, you're Nan's young man, are you? First we've heard of it."

"Never mind that, Will. Let the young chap sit down. Got a bad leg, Nan says. Is that right?" Emily pushed forward a chair and then bustled to put the kettle on.

"Yes, that's right. Copped a Blighty one on the Somme so that's me unfit to serve. Can't say I'm sorry either. Nan told me you lost your own son out there recently, Mrs Fisher. Please accept my sympathy."

"Thanks, lad. Did she tell you we've another boy out there, Fred, that is?"

"She did. It's hard on all you mothers, I reckon. Sometimes I'm not sorry I never knew my own mother. At least I didn't have to think of her worrying over me back home, and try to write cheerful letters from that hell-hole. Begging your pardon."

"I reckon that's a fair description, lad. So you have no family then? No-one at all?" Emily laid out cups and saucers and fetched milk from the safe in the scullery.

"That's right. I was brought up in an orphanage in Glasgow, so I learned early on to fend for myself. Probably a good training for the army, that was!" He looked round the dingy, but clean kitchen. "Makes a nice change to be in a proper family kitchen like this one. It's a credit to you Mrs Fisher."

Emily gave one of her rare smiles and passed his cup of tea and Nan realised thankfully that he had somehow won over her parents by his natural charm. Will was scrutinising him in silence, but at least he was not making any of his sarcastic comments, with which he often embarrassed them in front of visitors.

Ruby had seated herself opposite Charlie and now proceeded to question him about his exploits in the war and his experiences in the French towns. She was giving him the full battery of fluttering eyelashes, knowing smiles and wide-eyed stares, which usually proved very effective

58

with the male sex. Nan could feel her own resentment rising at this "taking over" of Charlie by her younger sister. She was unaware that it was the primitive emotion of sexual jealousy that was suddenly twisting her stomach with fear and tightening her forehead with tension.

She remained standing awkwardly in the doorway until Charlie suddenly interrupted Ruby's description of a film she had recently seen at the local cinema. "Come and sit here Nan, or are you standing there hoping to grow good – you're good enough already, aren't you?" He grinned and pulled out a chair beside his own at the table.

Blushing, but absurdly happy that he had noticed her in spite of Ruby's flirtatious overtures, Nan sat down thankfully and glowed as his arm draped casually around her waist and stayed there quite boldly for all to see. Suddenly she knew that she was "his girl". Charlie loved her, he wanted her family and all the world to know that. He was proud to claim her as his!

The next few weeks passed uneventfully. Charlie settled into his job at The Crown and his cheeky humour soon made him popular with the customers. His working hours meant that the time he could spend with Nan was very limited, and Sundays were the highlight of her week. He would come into the house to collect her for their outings and seemed to have been accepted by Emily, and more grudgingly, by Will. Ruby continued to flirt with him, to which he responded cheerfully, but Nan was sure he regarded Ruby very much as a younger sister to be humoured.

The war news was much more optimistic. Empire troops from Canada and Australia joined the British in a massive attack on the Germans near Amiens, leading to a very decisive retreat of the enemy. Fred's letters were few and far between. One came from a field hospital where he was recovering from a gas attack. But it was not serious enough to have him shipped home. Sometimes Nan almost wished he would cop a "Blighty one" like Charlie had done. A bit of shrapnel lodged permanently in your leg was a small price to pay for your life, as Charlie always insisted, when customers sympathised about his limp.

By September the Germans were retreating in earnest and everywhere optimistic talk related that this year the war really would be over by Christmas. Everyone's hearts were lighter and plans were made for when the "boys come home". Thankful though she was at the prospect of Fred's deliverance, Nan had other things on her mind.

Emily looked at her sharply one evening as she sank, white with exhaustion, into a chair after walking home from work. "You look done in, my girl. Not sickening for that dratted flu, are you?" The terrifying epidemic had claimed horrifying fatalities and many public places had been sprayed with disinfectant and schools even closed. After the years of wartime diets the poverty stricken slums were the perfect breeding ground for the fast-spreading virus.

"No, Mum, I'm all right. Just a bit tired that's all. Mrs Leigh had me washing curtains today and beating carpets and nothing I did was right!"

Emily said no more, but she kept a wary eye on Nan over the next few days. When Charlie appeared on Sunday after lunch to take Nan out for their usual walk, she waylaid him as he walked through the passage.

"I want a word with you, my lad."

"Hello, Mrs Fisher. What's up?"

Emily made no reply, but she marched him into the front room, which was musty and dim, as the curtains were partially drawn to protect the furniture from the sun. It was never used except on very special occasions such as Christmas, and had an air of being shut up.

"Wait there." Emily went out and returned pushing Nan before her. "Now then, I want some answers from you two, and I want the truth."

Nan shrank beside Charlie in front of the empty fireplace. Emily confronted them sternly, hands on hips, and accusation in her eyes. Nan could feel a tide of scarlet sweeping over her face and neck and was thankful for the dim light that partly hid her shame.

Charlie appeared simply bewildered as he looked from one woman to the other. "What's all this then? Nan what's going on?"

"Oh, Charlie, I've wanted to tell you ... I hoped I might be wrong ..." She buried her face despairingly in her hands and sobbed quietly. All the growing terror of the last few weeks poured out of her and Charlie put his arms round her automatically as he gazed at Emily, who was now nodding her head, her face black with condemnation.

"You may weep, lady. It's a bit late for that now! How could you let yourself down like it, Nan? If it had been Ruby, I wouldn't have been surprised! But you. I always thought you had some sense in your head, let alone a few morals! After all I've taught you, how could you behave like such a slut?"

61

"Here wait a minute, Mrs Fisher! You can't talk to her like that! Nan's not a slut and I won't listen to you calling her names!" Charlie's embrace tightened about Nan as her sobs increased during her mother's diatribe.

"You won't listen? What right have you got to argue with me? You – the cause of her shame! Well, I presume she hasn't any other fancy man hidden away? I take it you are the father of the little bundle she's carrying?"

"Yes, he is! Of course there's no-one else! How dare you say that, Mum! I'm sorry, ever so sorry for what we've done. I know it was wrong and I never meant to shame you, but we love each other and you're not going to make it all seem dirty! It was wonderful and I'm not sorry it happened and you can't take that away, for all your ranting and raving." Nan's tears were drying on cheeks now red with anger as she lifted her head proudly and faced her mother with her hand in Charlie's.

"Very well, then. Now we know where we stand and it's all out in the open. Perhaps you'll tell me what you intend to do about it? Is he going to do the right thing by you, or are we going to have the shame of an unmarried daughter with a fatherless grandchild living in the house? For you've nowhere else to go, that I do know!"

Charlie, who had been listening to this exchange with a blank expression now roused himself. Shoulders back, voice firm, he said, "Yes, Mrs Fisher, of course we shall be getting married. If Nan will have me, I shall be proud to make her my wife. I'm in regular employment, and we'll manage. You don't have to worry that there'll be any shame brought on your house by us."

Emily nodded bleakly. "In that case you'd better get a wedding date fixed as quickly as you can. You can leave me to break the news to Mr Fisher. I'll pick my moment, so that he has time to calm down before he sees you again. Otherwise we might see murder done!" and she walked out of the room, closing the door quietly behind her.

Charlie pulled Nan down on the hard, horsehair couch and held her tightly as he asked, "Why didn't you tell me, girl? How long have you known? You must have been going through hell with worry."

"I wanted to say something, Charlie, but I kept hoping I might be wrong. I'm not always regular each month, so I thought perhaps it was nothing. Then the last few days I've been feeling really awful and I've been sick in the mornings. I expect Mum heard me and guessed. Oh, Charlie, I've been so scared to tell you, and her and Dad!"

"It's about time you started trusting me, girl!" Charlie gave her a tiny shake as he laughed into her swimming eyes. "You know I love you and you know we planned to stay together, so what were you frightened of? Did you think the prospect of being a father would send me running?

"You're a silly little girl at times, Nan. So we didn't plan it to happen this quickly – a proper place of our own would have been nice before we started a family – but we'll manage and we'll do it without help from anyone! Now give us a kiss, then dry your eyes and we'll go and see the vicar!"

Nan found the next days very contradictory. It was hard having to explain to other people that she and Charlie were getting married within a matter of weeks. No-one asked outright about the hasty arrangements, but their eyes took on a slightly amused, knowing expression, which would make Nan's cheeks flush and her words become hurried.

Mrs Leigh was her usual disagreeable self, offering no congratulations, but merely stipulating that Nan's work must not suffer simply because she had a husband and a home of her own to look after.

"Of course if you decide to start a family then I hope you will have the courtesy to advise me so that I can find a replacement before you have to leave." Her eyes swept up and down Nan's still thin figure and her eyebrows raised a fraction, whilst her lips turned down in a sneering smile, that conveyed she had her suspicions and time would tell!

But Nan's romantic streak was thrilled at the prospect of her imminent wedding, although it would all be very penny-pinching and lacking in style. Mrs Flint along the road had kindly offered the loan of her married daughter's dress and jacket with a smart little veiled hat, which had been packed in mothballs since the beginning of the war.

"'Course hers was a rush do as well, love. But in her case it was because they wanted to get married before her Harry was shipped out to France. There wasn't any hint they had to get married!"

Nan was glad to take up the offer of the outfit, so she bit her tongue. Mrs Flint was really a harmless old woman, with a heart of gold, and couldn't help being tactless, she thought.

Ruby would be bridesmaid of course, in a made-over party frock from before the war. She was the only one who seemed really thrilled about the wedding. Probably because she loved dressing up and was sure her own good looks would outshine the bride's.

The real problem was somewhere to live. The landlord of The Crown refused when Charlie requested that Nan share his room there. They searched locally, but there was no way they could afford to rent even a small flat on Charlie's earnings. "You see, it's a live-in job, so they don't pay me that much. If I want to live out, that's my choice, but I can't expect them to put my wages up," he explained as they sat in the bus shelter one evening a week before the wedding.

"Yes, I understand that, Charlie, but I don't see what we can do. We might manage the rent for a place of our own whilst I'm working, but what about when I have to stop, before the baby's born?"

"Reckon I'll have to find another job, girl. Either one that's better paid, or one where we can both live in. In the meantime, I suppose we could ask your mum and dad if I could stay at your place. You've got the room, haven't you?"

"Well, yes, there's the room that Jack and Fred shared, or the little room at the top of the house that used to be my Gran's before she died. But I don't know, Charlie. I can't see them making it easy for us. You know how badly they feel about the baby and everything." Nan bit her lip, remembering the atmosphere that existed at number thirty these days.

Emily was very bitter at the way Nan had let them down, by forgetting the moral standards she almost imbibed with Emily's own milk. Apart from her own disappointment, Emily had to endure Will's fury and act as a buffer between him and Nan, and especially Charlie. Will had a violent temper that she was terrified might lead to a physical confrontation with Charlie, so she was handling her husband with kid gloves these days. This made her even more irritable with Nan.

"I'm afraid the alternative is you sleeping in your bed and me in mine, half a mile away, and that doesn't sound like much fun to me!" Charlie squeezed her waist tightly allowing his fingers to brush the underside of her breast, which was extra tender with her pregnancy. A shiver swept through Nan as pictures of those precious hours spent in the Leighs' bed flashed before her. At that moment any embarrassment or ill-feeling with her parents appeared a small price to pay for a nightly reunion with Charlie.

"I'll speak to them, Charlie. Maybe it will be all right."

Nan tackled her parents the following evening after supper. Will looked fit to explode with fury, but Emily forestalled him. "Is he going to want feeding or just a bed to share with you? Because if he expects his meals here, I'll expect some rent from him."

"No, he's fed at the pub. He'll come back after work and leave in the morning. If it's all right with you, I thought we could use Gran's old room. I can give it a good clean and he can put his things in her old wardrobe. He is looking for a better job, so that we can afford a place of our own. So it'll only be a temporary arrangement."

"You'd better make sure it is! I tell you now, lady, I don't want your squalling brat underfoot in a few months' time. I've had my share of yelling kids and dirty nappies with four of my own. Much good have they done me!"

Will glared at her and flung out of the door to feed the chickens he had recently installed in the back yard.

"He's going to make a lovely grandad, isn't he?" said Ruby sarcastically, adjusting her hat before the mirror. Although girlishly excited by the talk of the wedding, she often adopted a superior manner towards Nan, implying that she would never do anything so stupid as being caught with an unwanted pregnancy. Like so many other humiliations, Nan suffered it in silence, trying to obliterate everything in thoughts of Charlie and the warm security of his often-declared passion.

"There's no need for you to take that tone, madam!" Emily glared at her younger daughter. "Time enough for you to be so hoity toity when you're safely married with a home of your own and no little ones on the way before they're welcome! The way I hear you've been seen giggling and carrying on at street corners some nights, you'll be lucky to go to the altar wearing white and know you're still entitled!"

Grateful and touched by this unexpected support, Nan said softly, "Thanks, Mum, for letting Charlie come. I promise he'll be no trouble and we'll find a place of our own as soon as we can." She looked pleadingly into Emily's eyes, willing her mother to show some softening and compassion. She longed to speak to her, woman to woman, confiding her own worries about the future and the responsibilities of motherhood, but Emily merely pursed her lips and followed Will outside.

The last days before the wedding passed in a whirl of preparations. Of course there would be no proper reception, because of food shortages, even if the Fishers had been able to afford a big send-off for Nan. But Emily was determined that no-one should have cause to turn up their noses and say that she and Will had not done right by their elder daughter.

So a few close friends and neighbours were invited back to number thirty after the church ceremony to have a cup of tea and something to eat. Emily had managed to find the ingredients to make a few scones and biscuits, as well as piles of sandwiches.

A home-made sponge, with eggs from their own hens, did duty as a wedding cake. There was no icing as this was forbidden by the wartime restrictions, but Ruby cut out a paper "lace" frill to go around it and the local baker lent a tiny bride and groom to sit on the top. Nan picked a few marguerites from Emily's flower bed in the back yard, and used them to decorate the table.

The night before the wedding, Mr Johnson, who lived three doors away, and worked on a stall in Wood Green, brought in some left-over flowers that were going for a few pence. With these and some white ribbon, Nan fashioned herself a tiny posy and made button holes for Emily and Ruby.

Friends had rallied round with such small gifts as they could find, when money was scarce and the shops were practically empty. Many were second-hand items, such as Mrs Flint's crocheted table cloth, or home-made such as the tea tray carved by Charlie's Best Man – one of the walking wounded from his old ward at the hospital.

It was a golden September day and Nan felt the luckiest woman in the world as she paced slowly down the aisle on Will's arm, with Charlie's loving smile to greet her.

Beneath a matching jacket, her cream georgette dress with its floating skirt, moved about her in a beam of sunlight and behind the tiny polka-dotted veil on the pill-box hat, her eyes glowed with love as she reached his side. At that moment she would not have changed places with a countess being married in Westminster Abbey.

Charlie looked absolutely magnificent. He had borrowed the full highland dress, which he felt entitled to wear as an ex-member of a Scottish regiment. His own uniform was so worn and his civilian clothes were even worse, but he had been determined to make Nan proud of him, and also make Emily and Will take notice.

As they walked back down the aisle they made a very handsome couple. Even Emily, resplendent in her Sunday-best coat, the neck embellished by an old fox fur she had unearthed in her mother's old trunk, felt a stirring of pride in her two daughters. Nan the dignified bride (fortunately showing no embarrassing bulge as yet!) and behind her, Ruby, in her powder blue crepe dress and home-dyed matching hat, for once looking restrained and elegant on this solemn occasion.

The party went on at number thirty till late that night. Charlie's boss had sent along some bottles of beer and stout as his contribution and Mrs Leigh had even donated a bottle of port, as well as a silver cake plate which she no longer used. Mr Flint brought along his piano accordion and they had a sing-song in the front room and then the younger ones danced. As the rooms grew hotter the back door was opened and Nan and Charlie slipped outside for some fresh air.

"Happy, girl?" he whispered as he pulled her tightly against him.

"Oh, Charlie, you wouldn't believe how happy!" she told him. All the worries of the last few weeks had vanished and at that moment she was positive that life held nothing but good things in store for them.

Sadly that blissful optimism rapidly dissipated in the ensuing weeks. Charlie spent every spare minute searching for a job that would improve their situation, but nothing was forthcoming. Nan would brood for hours in the evenings, whilst he was working at the pub, as she knitted away at clothes for the baby. She dreaded that matters would be so much worse when it was born if it had to share their tiny room.

It was in November that their own troubles were briefly forgotten in the national euphoria as the war finally ended. The whole country went wild with relief and thanksgiving. The street organised a tea-party for the children and in the evening there was a huge bonfire, with dancing and singing. Even Will managed to smile, and joked with Charlie once or twice. Emily and Nan confessed to each other how thankful they were that Fred had survived and shed tears over Jack who had not. Ruby was in her element dancing with everyone in trousers and tossing her hair in the firelight.

But the brief period of cheer soon passed and the atmosphere of gloom and tension descended once more on number thirty. Nan was more and more aware of a sense of claustrophobia under the accusing glare of Will as her pregnancy gradually became apparent, and every move that Charlie made whilst in the house tightened her nerves as she waited for him to commit some misdemeanour in her parents' eyes. She was aware that Charlie himself was becoming more depressed by the situation and even his chirpy good humour gradually disappeared.

Then one Sunday he dropped his bombshell. She woke early to find him sitting by the window staring out into the back yard.

"Charlie, what's wrong? You're never up this early on a Sunday."

"I've been thinking, girl. Something I've been turning over for the last few days, something important."

Nan pulled herself upright on the pillow. The bedroom was icy in the November morning and she tugged the blankets and quilt up round her shoulders. As she tightened the covers, she could see the tiny bump that was becoming more noticeable each week. She would soon have to tell Mrs Leigh, she knew.

Charlie was dressed, but he came and lay beside her on top of the bedclothes and put his arm about her shoulders, so that she snuggled into him for warmth.

"I met an old mate in the pub recently, Nan. He was a Canadian that was in hospital with me when I first came back from France. Don Rogers his name is. He's a good bloke and we get on well together. He likes a laugh, same as me, but I reckon he's a hard worker too."

"That was nice for you Charlie, meeting up again. Is he going back to Canada now the war's over?"

"That's right, Nan, he is. He's been telling me all about his plans. He's like me, no family and he wants to make a new life for himself. He wants to get a place out in the

71

country, a small-holding or even a farm. It's just what I've always dreamed of, Nan."

"But that would cost a lot of money, wouldn't it? Buying a place like that, Charlie?"

"That's just it, Nan. Don was telling me he plans to go to this place called Welland, near Niagara Falls. They're building a new canal there. It's a really big job and they need a big work force. He reckons he'll have no difficulty getting a job and whilst he works on the canal he can look round in the countryside for a place to settle. He says there are places to rent from farmers, where you work their land and gain the experience. Then you can save some money for a deposit and buy a place of your own. The rents are cheap, and you can grow most of your own food so it's easy to save. What d'you think, Nan?"

"Sounds as though he's thought it all out, Charlie. Good luck to him. Will he keep in touch and let you know how he gets on, d'you suppose?"

"That's what I'm coming to, Nan. How would you feel about going out there with him? We're good mates – I think you'd like him – and we could find somewhere sooner if we went into partnership together. Be cheaper than each getting a place of our own. What d'you say?"

Nan gaped at him, hardly able to grasp what she was hearing. "Canada, Charlie. You mean emigrate – to Canada?"

"That's right, girl. It's a great country. I called there a few times when I was on the boats. Lovely clean fresh air and plenty of space. Room to breathe. Wonderful place to bring up the little 'un as well!"

"But Charlie, it's such a long way. A strange country, leaving all our family behind. I'd be scared to travel all that way. I don't think I could do it, Charlie." Nan fixed worried eyes on his as her voice became higher and faster in panic as she saw from his expression that this was not some idle fancy on his part.

"Look Nan, think about it sensibly for a bit." Charlie stroked her hair back on her forehead and spoke long and earnestly. "What chance have we got of really making a go of things here? The atmosphere with your folks is miserable most of the time and we both know it'll be a sight worse when the baby comes. With Fred coming home from France this place will be even more crowded.

"I know we talk about a place of our own, but what chance have we really got? When you have to stop work, we'll only have my wages, and jobs are not easy to find now. And they'll be even worse when all the blokes come home from the forces and want work in civvy street. It seems to me we're trapped as we are and if we stay, our kid will be no better off. I want more for our family than that.

"I've always dreamed of living in the country and I know you'd love it. It's a chance to make something of our lives and build something for our kids in their turn. I know it's a long way and frightening to think about, especially with you being pregnant and all, but we'd be together and settled by the time the baby comes. What d'you say, Nan? Will you trust me and take this chance with me? I won't let you down, I swear."

Nan looked at his sincere and pleading eyes. She knew he meant every word, and the picture he painted of a fresh

73

start in a clean spacious country with room to breathe and healthy surroundings for their future family made an attractive prospect. As she hesitated, torn by her own natural caution and the desperate longing in his face like a little boy who sees the chance to obtain a longed-for toy and is afraid it will be snatched away, she felt an odd sensation in her midriff.

She looked down and then slowly smiled. Was it an omen? Was this Charlie junior putting in his two pennyworth? "How soon would we have to leave, Charlie?"

"Don says we can get a passage with him on a vessel sailing at the end of December. I could sign on working as part of the crew, so we'd only have to find your passage. We'd be starting a new life at the beginning of a new year, girl. Think of it, you'd leave the winter behind and see spring in Niagara Falls. Don has friends in Welland and they run a boarding house, so we could live with them while we find our own place."

As he sensed her weakening, his voice bubbled with enthusiasm and she could hear the faint Scottish intonation that occasionally surfaced in moments of excitement or passion.

"Say you'll do it, Nan! Say you'll come with me to Canada!" His dark eyes laughed into hers as one hand slipped beneath the bed clothes and caressed the small bulge before sliding up to cup one breast that pushed above her cotton night-gown.

Shivering as usual at his familiar touch, she whispered joyfully, "Yes, Charlie, yes, I'll come to Canada!"

CANADA 1919 – 1922

"How are you feeling, lassie? It's a biting cold wind out there, and no mistake." Jessie Campbell bustled into the steamy kitchen bringing a draught of freezing cold air with her. As usual she was swathed in shawls and scarves against the rigours of the Canadian weather, and Nan suspected that if all her outer layers were unpeeled, she would have quite a petite figure underneath.

"You're looking worn out my girl. In your condition you should be taking more care. Sit yourself down and I'll put on the kettle for a nice hot brew."

"I must finish off this basket of ironing. Mrs Johnson was promised it for this afternoon." Nan paused to straighten her aching back and push a strand of limp hair off her forehead. Her feet were throbbing and she knew that she would have to make another trip to the closet out in the backyard. Not a pleasant prospect in the icy March winds. Unfortunately her advanced pregnancy was having a pronounced effect on her bladder, so she put the heavy black iron back on the stove top to heat up, dragged a thick shawl over head and shoulders and battled her way across the yard.

When she returned, Jessie had made the pot of tea, set out the crockery and was working her way through the remaining pile of ironing.

"Oh, Jessie, you shouldn't be doing that. You must be tired yourself after your cleaning job. Come and sit down for a minute."

"Nay, lassie, this won't take me long. Then I'll drop it off at old Ma Johnson's on my way. You shouldn't be carrying such a heavy load in your state. Where's your man, anyway? Has he found himself a place at last?"

Nan flushed as she poured out their tea. "It's not easy for him, Jessie. Ever since he had that ... bother with the labouring boss on the canal, he's found it hard to get anything. Especially with his bad leg. As soon as they see him limping they think he's not very fit. It's hard for his pride – being turned down so often. But he keeps looking."

"And meantime you slave away taking in washing and ironing and mending to pay for your board and lodging. You can't carry on like this much longer, lassie. You're worn to a frazzle and apart from your bump, you look like a bag of bones!"

Nan laughed. Jessie's broad Scottish humour always cheered her up. They had met on the long voyage over from England. Conditions in the third class had been cramped and Spartan, to say the least. Charlie had signed on to work his passage as a stoker, so she had seen nothing of him at all.

It would have been a lonely, frightening time without Jessie. The winter weather had been dreadful – fog and icebergs a constant hazard – and along with the nausea produced by her pregnancy, Nan had suffered horribly from sea-sickness. Jessie had been like a mother to her throughout, and continued to be a tower of strength.

The two months since their arrival had been gruelling in themselves. The golden vision that Nan and Charlie had shared of all the wonderful opportunities in a new country had not been realised at all.

Charlie's friend, Don Rogers, had taken them straight to Welland when they had disembarked in Toronto. The countryside was cloaked with snow and Nan felt she would never be warm again. They had moved into a small lodging house in a mean area of the town. Most of the lodgers were men working on the construction of the Welland Canal, which ran from Lake Ontario to Lake Eyrie. Nan and Charlie rented one room high under the roof, which was about the cheapest on offer, and were allowed the use of the back kitchen.

Charlie had signed on as a labourer straight away. After paying for Nan's passage, there was little left from Charlie's wages at the end of the voyage. He had planned to work only a short time on the construction site, whilst he looked around for somewhere in the country. They both longed to have a place of their own in which to bring up the new baby.

Planning to boost their meagre finances, Nan immediately looked for some work to do herself, just until the baby arrived. Mrs Wilson who ran the lodging house suggested she might do the household laundry and anyone else's she could take in. The back kitchen was not frequented by any of the other lodgers, so the landlady was happy to let Nan use it, paying her a pittance for the work that she did.

A matter of weeks after they arrived Charlie got into a fight with a group of other labourers and since they were native Canadians, the boss dismissed him out of hand. It was a bleak day for Nan, although she tried hard to make allowances for Charlie. She was discovering that he might show his cheerful, irrepressible self most of the time, but occasionally a different personality would emerge.

He would descend into black moods when his childhood memories assailed him, along with the horrors of all the months endured in the trenches. Then he would pour out his grievances to Nan. All the world was against him and he would take comfort in a glass or two of beer or whisky.

After Jessie had left her, having insisted on finishing the ironing and taking it away for delivery, Nan allowed herself time to reflect miserably on the flaws she was discovering in Charlie's character.

The first time she saw him drunk had not been too bad. It was Don's birthday and he carried Charlie off to the local pub for a drink after work. Nan had expected him back for his supper after an hour or so, but he did not appear. Anxiously she checked his food that was gradually spoiling, as she kept it warm above a saucepan simmering on the range. The kitchen clock ticked away whilst Nan strained her eyes in the dim light, bending over the skirt that she was altering for Mrs Davis. The hypnotic flaring of the gas lamp gradually lulled her senses and her head drooped with tiredness. Her eyes must have closed briefly and she was jerked awake with a heart-stopping shock as the front door slammed shatteringly.

A drunken male duet bellowed noisily *Don't dilly dally on the way*, as they burst into the room. It was obvious at a glance that although both were the worse for drink, it was Don who was supporting Charlie, whose legs threatened to collapse beneath him.

"'Allo then, my lovely girlie. 'Ow's the light of me life then? Look at 'er, mate, what a ravishing sight to come

'ome to! And not only pretty as a picture, but workin' as well! See that! Workin' her fingers to the bone for her loving husband, eh? Where would I be without 'er? Give us a kiss, Nan. I need something to warm me up after walkin' back from the pub. Freeze yer whatsits off, it would!"

He pushed away Don's supporting arm and lurched towards Nan. Tripping over his own feet, as he found it harder than usual to control his limping gait, he measured his length on the floor beside the fire, narrowly missing the fender and ending up by catching Nan a glancing blow with his flailing arm and sending her needlework into the dirty cinders of the grate.

"Oh, Charlie, look what you've done! Mrs Davis's skirt will be ruined! How could you come home in this state? Your dinner's ruined and I've been so worried. I thought you must have had an accident. Do you know how late it is?"

"My fault! My fault, Nan my dear!" Don hauled Charlie upright and deposited him in a chair. "I must confess it was me that tempted him off the straight and narrow and into the Welland Arms. I begged him to join me in a short or two to celebrate my birthday, you see. But one thing led to another – or should I say one drink led to another? Some old comrades from the trenches came and joined us and I fear the result was ..." he waved his hand towards the now snoring Charlie. "As you see, dear lady, as you see."

"You should be ashamed of yourself, Don, you know he can't afford to go out drinking like this. And how will he get himself up for work tomorrow? He finds it hard enough as it is, with his leg giving him gyp in this cold weather."

"Please accept my heartfelt apologies!" Don swept her a theatrical bow and nearly overbalanced himself in the process. "I will help him up to bed and don't worry about the money he spent on the booze. Most of it he won back in a game of cards!"

Poor Nan! If she had only known it, that night was to set the pattern for so many to follow. As Charlie found it harder and harder to keep physically active, labouring in the cold weather and suffering a nagging ache in his leg, Nan struggled to budget their money to ensure he ate enough to keep him fit.

Most of the other labourers were single men who would happily go off each pay day and spend their hard-earned wages in cheap booze and, when the fancy took them, the company of cheap women. As with any large construction site, the Welland Canal had attracted all the usual camp followers, eager to make money out of the huge labour force employed. But Charlie of course had Nan and he would tell himself he was lucky to find her waiting for him with a hot meal, as nourishing as her purse permitted, always ready on the table.

But soon the joys of married bliss began to pale for Charlie. Nan's face became thinner and lines of worry were etched upon it as she strove desperately to make ends meet. The physical toll of living in such Spartan conditions, in the midst of the rigours of the unaccustomed Canadian winter, was almost unbearable with the general strain on her health of the swiftly advancing pregnancy.

Charlie's previous good humour gradually disappeared as he failed to come to terms with his own physical inadequacy, alongside the brawn and brute strength of the other men. The foreman joked once too often about "dot and carry one" as Charlie limped awkwardly along behind a barrow-load of mud. He was tired, freezing and in constant pain with the twinges in his leg. So he had hurled the barrow down the slope towards his tormentor and thrown a nearby shovel after it.

Fortunately there was no serious injury inflicted, just a few bruises and a gash above the eye, but Charlie was lucky to escape retribution from the law. Instead, he was dismissed on the spot and black-listed amongst all the other labour gangs. Each day he would set out looking for work, and invariably ended up in a pub. For a while, as his charm and good humour entertained the other drinkers, he would forget the grim reality of a pregnant wife who was now the sole breadwinner.

Basking in the good fellowship and accepting a friendly drink in return for his endless funny stories or lively sing-songs, he would leave at closing time, unsteady on his feet and at peace with the world. Nan would be waiting, exhausted from the day's labours, washing, ironing, mending and cleaning. Her back was aching, her feet throbbing as shiveringly she crouched beside the kitchen stove, whose fire sank lower while she desperately tried to eke out their dwindling store of fuel.

But in spite of all the problems, she could not find it in her heart to blame Charlie. She loved him so much, she could only pity his physical infirmity that must be such a source of frustration and shame, as he forced himself to compete for jobs with the fit and tough workmen that swarmed through Welland. She readily understood the desperation that drove him to seek a brief oblivion in drink, before coming home to face her and his own inadequacy as a breadwinner.

How are we to manage when I have the baby? Nan moved restlessly, trying to find a more comfortable position as she felt the infant kicking energetically in the womb. It would only be a matter of weeks, maybe days, if it should come early. Their landlady had no softness in her dealings with a pregnant woman, so a new-born, noisy baby was hardly likely to melt her heart sufficiently to ignore unpaid rent. Nan had no illusions. If she was unable to do the usual laundry and cleaning about the boarding house, as payment for their room, out she and Charlie would go.

That evening, when they had finished their meal of thin soup, containing the odd scrap of stringy mutton, Nan voiced her fears. She had been trying hard not to sound critical, but she was so frightened of what the future might hold, she desperately needed some comfort and reassurance.

"Oh, Charlie, I'm so worried about when the baby comes! How will we manage if you can't find any work? Suppose she turns us out on the street? I'm at my wits' end thinking about it." Her voice choked and she stared into the embers of the fire which were suddenly blurred in her sight.

He came and crouched beside her. For once he had not paid a visit to the pub and the dark eyes looking up into her face were filled with shamed bitterness. "I've not proved much of a husband, have I girl? Bringing you half across the world to this snow-covered hell, after so many fine promises. Oh, Nan, I didn't mean it to be like this!"

His arms encircled her and he buried his face against her swollen stomach as her hands automatically reached to cradle the curly, dark head. Even in the midst of her fears and physical discomfort the warmth of his touch and his very closeness were enough to send a quiver of desire through her.

"It's not your fault, my dear. You couldn't have known how it would turn out. If anyone's to blame it's Don, filling your head with all those dreams of a place in the country, and never telling you how bad the winter would be. Sometimes I think I'll never stop shivering!" Charlie's arms tightened about her and they clung together for comfort and warmth. It seemed then that physical closeness was the only consolation in the face of all their problems.

But the next day it appeared that an answer had been found. The barman at Charlie's favourite pub had slipped on the ice and broken his leg, and for once Charlie was in the right place at the right time. When the barman failed to arrive for his shift, Charlie cheerfully stepped behind the bar and the landlord offered him the temporary job.

"So you are looking at a member of the working classes again, Mrs Stuart! Not only that, they'll give me my supper whilst I'm working in the evening, so that'll save money on food for me. Which means, my girl, that you can spend a bit extra on some proper grub for yourself. It's no fun going to bed with a bag of bones! And once the little 'un has arrived, I expect to have my wicked way with you again! Got some time to make up in that direction, haven't we?" He reached round her as she bent over the pan she was stirring on the range, his body pressed meaningly against hers, and slipped his hand between the buttons of her blouse, that was gaping taut across her swollen breasts.

"Oh, Charlie, you are dreadful!" But as usual she was unable to resist the powerful physical attraction he exerted and turned into his embrace, despite her awkward bulk.

After that life improved for the next few weeks. Charlie enjoyed himself as the life and soul of the pub, although it meant he came home very late each night after closing time, so Nan saw little of him. It was such a relief to know that a regular wage was coming in, and that she was no longer the sole breadwinner, so she was able to slow down a little. Added to that, the snow was finally disappearing and April was at last bringing a breath of spring warmth to the air.

Nan awoke one morning to bright sunshine and a sudden urge to be up and doing. Charlie lay as usual comatose beside her after his late night working. She knew that he still enjoyed a pint or two, but since he was actually employed in the pub, she had not seen him drunk. His old confidence had returned with the job, and she dreaded what would happen when his predecessor was fit to return to work.

No good thinking about that, girl, she told herself as she dressed quietly. Try and be like Charlie, and let the future take care of itself. He was fond of teasing her out of a worried mood by chucking her under the chin and uttering one of his favourite clichés, such as "Cheer up, it may never happen!" or "Lost a bob and found a tanner?" And when he winked and pulled some ridiculous face, Nan could never resist the urge to smile and forget her problems.

But on this particular morning it wasn't hard to feel optimistic. The sight of the sun was such a treat that she longed to feel the rays on her face. She wrapped a shawl over her long coat and decided to walk to the market. There was a stall that sold second-hand clothes and Nan had been promising herself that she would spend the few carefully hoarded coins, in the old tea caddy on the mantelpiece, on some items for the baby.

It seemed to have settled lower this morning and the urge to visit the closet outside was very frequent. Still, she should be all right if she went immediately before setting out shopping. When she returned she would get the second hand purchases washed and ironed – you never knew what germs they might harbour from a previous owner, and Nan was determined to take no chances with her son or daughter.

Charlie was convinced it would be a boy and was always weaving fantasies about teaching the lad to box and play football, but Nan truthfully said she would be quite happy with whatever arrived, so long as it was healthy with ten fingers and toes!

It was like stepping into another world to be outside without the snow on the sidewalks, and to feel the warmth of the sun was quite wonderful. Of course the melted snow had created great piles of slush and filthy puddles everywhere so that passing carts and other traffic had soon covered the hem of her skirts with mud. But that was a small price for being outside and actually strolling slowly along enjoying the sights, instead of rushing about with head down against the freezing wind, anxious to get through her errands as quickly as possible, and back in the warmth of the house.

Nan browsed happily amongst the market stalls and delightedly picked up several bargains with the baby clothes on offer. Well pleased with her morning, and feeling pleasantly weary, she finally turned her steps homeward. She should be in time to have a cup of tea with Charlie and make him a sandwich before he set off for his daytime shift at the pub. Her back was beginning a dull ache and she looked forward to removing her cracked boots and putting her feet up for a while.

Coming towards her a young woman was pushing a baby carriage and running in front of it was a boy of five or six. He was bowling a hoop and Nan smiled at his frown of concentration as he endeavoured to propel it on the path. She paused to keep out of his way as he drew abreast of her. Then it happened.

A farm cart which was coming towards Nan was being overtaken by one of the few motor cars to be seen in Welland. As it drew abreast, the car backfired with a report like a gun. The horse reared in terror and lunged sideways on to the footpath, whilst its driver vainly tried to regain control. Pedestrians shouted and there was instant chaos.

For Nan the ensuing moments had a dream-like quality, with every action appearing to happen in slow-motion. She was aware that the horse's panic-stricken dance was bringing it ever closer to the child with the hoop;. His mother, with the baby carriage, was too far away to help, and the next downward plunge of those iron-clad hooves would be directly upon his upturned face, as he stood rooted in bewilderment at this sudden drama.

With no conscious thought, Nan instinctively flung herself forward and scooped up the child, slipped on the mud and was carried by her own momentum into the shelter of a nearby doorway. Here she lay face down, all the breath knocked out of her by the violent shock as her body met the ground. She could hear, as at a great distance, the outraged yells of the little boy who was partially buried beneath her, then the hysterical voice of his mother who had left her baby with a passer-by and rushed to gather him up.

"Oh, Jamie, Jamie, are you all right? I thought you'd be killed for sure!" As she swiftly examined him for any sign of injury, a crowd gathered round Nan's prone figure. The horse was now safely under control and had been led away round the corner by its owner.

"Are you all right, Missis?" The little boy's mother having discovered her son was unhurt, was now bending anxiously over Nan. "You saved my bairn's life, that's for sure. These wicked noisy contraptions, a body's not safe to walk the streets with them about!" As she clumsily smoothed Nan's hair back off her forehead and stroked her icy-cold hands, she was interrupted by the driver of the car. He crouched on the other side of Nan, and spoke authoritatively to the boy's mother.

"Would you allow me to examine this lady? I'm a doctor and I want to see if she can be moved safely." He smiled down at Nan, who vaguely perceived the distinguished countenance of a man somewhat older than herself, which was inclined above her.

"Can you feel any pain my dear? You must have hit the ground with quite an impact." He swiftly checked her limbs and then became graver as he discovered her swollen stomach. "I see you're pregnant – and I would guess it's due quite soon by the looks of things, is that correct?"

"Yes," Nan moistened her lips and found her voice was little more than a whisper. Her body seemed strangely to belong to someone else, and it was difficult to focus her eyes or her mind properly. "I think it should be any day now ... Oh!" That body which had been in some kind of limbo was suddenly rent by a spasm of pure agony, which had the effect of concentrating her mind wonderfully.

"Oh, doctor, I think it's happening now!" Her panic-stricken eyes met his knowing ones and she struggled to sit up. Gently he pushed her back and removed his greatcoat, which he wrapped around her.

"It's all right, Mrs ...? Tell me your name and where you live, will you? I think the sooner we get you home, the better. The quickest way will be in my car, which I'm afraid was the cause of all this trouble in the first place!"

"It's Stuart – Nan Stuart – and I live at eight Carlisle Street. It's not far away ... ahh!" and Nan groaned and doubled over as another contraction racked her body. The doctor waited till it passed and then very gently helped her to her feet before supporting her carefully through the crowd of sympathetic onlookers to his nearby car.

The little boy had stopped crying and his mother picked up Nan's shopping which had rolled into the gutter, and handed it into the car after her. "God bless you, Missis. I'll never forget what you did for my boy. I hope you're safely delivered of a fine one of your own today!"

Nan tried to smile at her as she allowed the doctor to lay her along the comfortable back seat, and wrap her up still further with his soft tartan rug. But once again reality was receding into a blur, and she was obliged to close her eyes and thankfully let it slip away.

Afterwards she found that her memories of much of the ensuing hours were also blurred – perhaps mercifully so. The doctor drove her home as quickly as it was possible to do so, trying at the same time to ensure a smooth journey over the rutted streets. It was fortunate that their arrival coincided with that of Jessie, who was paying her daily call to check on Nan's welfare.

Taking in the situation at a glance, sensibly avoiding any waste of time with unnecessary questions, she showed the doctor up to Nan's room, where he quickly carried his barely-conscious patient. Between them, he and Jessie undressed Nan and put her to bed. Jessie hastened to fetch the old china ginger beer bottles filled with hot water from the kitchen to warm the sheets and then un-asked, went below again, to boil up more kettles on the stove. She had three youngsters of her own, and had assisted at the birth of several others, so knew exactly what was required.

A neighbour's son was despatched to fetch Charlie, who had already left for the pub, and then Jessie settled down to her vigil at Nan's bedside, with the doctor in attendance. In some ways the accident might be seen as beneficial, since it certainly hurried the entrance into the world of Nan's first child. Whereas her labour might have more commonly been prolonged for many hours, this only took a relatively short time.

It was four in the afternoon when Jessie went down to the kitchen. Charlie was hunched by the fire, nails bitten to the quick, hair a wild mop where his fingers had been constantly dragged through it, as he listened to the muffled moans which alternated with sharp screams, as Nan's travail progressed. At Jessie's entrance he leapt up, his face a mixture of fear and eagerness.

"What's happened, Jessie? How is she? Is she very bad?"

"It's all right, lad, it's all over." She smiled triumphantly and went across to the fire for more hot water. "She's fine, although it's been a hard few hours for her and no mistake, and you're the father of a bonny little lass!" She put her arms round him in a motherly hug as Charlie swayed with relief and unashamedly buried his face in his hands.

"Thank God, Jessie! Thank God! I was so scared it would all go wrong and I'd lose her!"

"No fear of that, Charlie. She's a strong one is your Nan. Now I'll make a pot of tea and you can take her a cup and meet your daughter. Doctor's nearly finished with her. I suppose if you've got to go into labour in the street with a car backfiring, it's a help if the car belongs to a medical man, eh?"

When Charlie went into the room bearing the cup in a hand that was trembling with excitement, Nan was lying back on the pillows. On the doctor's instructions a fire had been lit in the normally empty grate and there was a cosy warmth in the room for the first time since they had moved into the boarding house.

The doctor had just closed his bag and was smiling down with quiet satisfaction at his two patients. In the crook of Nan's arm the baby's wrinkled visage was barely visible between the folds of the snug shawl that Jessie had knitted in readiness.

"Well, Mr Stuart, you should be a proud man today. You've a healthy, pretty daughter and a very brave wife. She's had a difficult few hours delivering her own child and she's also probably saved the life of someone else's." He patted Nan's hand reassuringly and smiled at Charlie as they passed in the doorway. "I'll be back in the morning to see how they are and in the meantime you're all in good hands with Jessie Campbell!"

Charlie crouched by the bed and gazed thankfully at Nan. Her face was haggard and drawn and her hair was still dark with sweat where Jessie had brushed it off her forehead. But the brilliant eyes smiled radiantly into his and she said proudly, "Look at her, Charlie, isn't she just the most beautiful creature you've ever seen?"

"Next to her mother, I reckon you're right, girl." His voice was husky with emotion and as his arms encircled them both, Nan allowed herself to sink back into thankful sleep. After watching her tenderly for a while, Charlie carefully lifted his daughter and put her into the small crib which he had made himself from scraps thrown away by the local timber yard.

For the next few days Nan stayed in bed, very weak after her ordeal. With the poor diet and Spartan living conditions, plus the hard work she had been doing throughout her pregnancy, her body was at a low ebb and her recovery was slow. Jessie continued as a tower of strength and Charlie was a devoted husband and father between his shifts at the pub. But Nan soon began to fret when she thought about the housework she was unable to do, which meant loss of income towards their rent.

It was on the fourth day, when she was attempting to get up that Charlie came in and found her swaying dizzily. "What the hell d'you think you're doing, Nan? Get yourself back in bed right now!" Before she could protest, he swung her off her feet and had her tucked up once more between the sheets.

"Charlie, I can't stay here any longer, there's work to be done. Mrs Wilson will want more money if I don't get the jobs done as part payment for the rent. It's just a momentary weakness, I'll be all right if I take things slowly."

"You will not, my girl! Now, listen to me. Doc Harris has spoken to Mrs High and Mighty Wilson. He's told her you won't be fit for any work at all for at least a month. In the meantime he's insisting on paying her the extra rent. He had a serious talk with me about what happened the other day.

"He couldn't help his car backfiring and the horse bolting, we all know that, it was an accident pure and simple. But he says if you hadn't saved that kid from under the horse's hooves and he'd been hurt or even killed … well the Doctor would never have forgiven himself! So he's very grateful to you and wants to show his gratitude the best way he can. Don't worry, girl, he's not hard up for a bob or two, lives in some posh house out towards Niagara Falls. The few quid he's giving Mrs Wilson won't be missed."

"Oh, Charlie, that is kind of him. He's been ever so good to me already – look at those parcels he's sent round with extra food and those beautiful clothes for baby that his wife bought. Oh, people are lovely sometimes, aren't they?"

He smiled down at her and lifted her work-roughened hand between both of his. He remembered fleetingly the first time he had kissed it, during the walk they had taken on that summer evening through Alexandra Palace. Then she had been an awkward, naïve young girl, now she was a wife and a mother who had endured months of hardship and come through still smiling. It was hard to imagine that Nan would ever be disillusioned, so strong was her love of life and her belief in the essential goodness of folk.

"Penny for them, Charlie?" She was surprised to see his normally cheerful countenance wearing a strangely sober and thoughtful expression as he gazed down at her. "Not worth a farthing, girl! Tell you what though, we ought to be thinking about a name for our daughter, we can't keep on calling her 'baby' and I should register her soon. What d'you reckon?"

"I don't know, Charlie. If she'd been a boy I reckon I'd have wanted to call her after Doctor Harris, as he brought her into the world and he's been so good, but since she's a girl we can't really call her David!"

"What d'you think of Joan? That's his wife's name — I heard him mention it to Jessie when he brought the baby clothes."

"Joan ... Yes, I like that Charlie. It's nice and simple. And how about Alexandra for a second name? I always thought Queen Alexandra was a nice lady — especially the way she put up with all the old King's goings-on and all those lady friends of his! Besides, it'll remind us of the old

Ally Pally and all the good times we spent there in our courting days!"

Charlie laughed and told her she was a sentimental old softie, but she could see he was touched that she kept such happy memories of their early times together. So Joan Alexandra was duly registered as the first born of Charlie and Nan Stuart.

There was no mistaking she was her father's daughter. Even new-born she was crowned with a thatch of dark silky hair, which rapidly became a halo of enchanting curls as she grew bigger. Her eyes were huge black pools, which were the mirror image of Charlie's.

Both parents doted on her, and with Jessie as a surrogate auntie, she was constantly cuddled and cooed over. With the aid of plenty of rest and the extra nutritious food that Doctor Harris sent over regularly, Nan put on weight and regained her strength. She was back on her feet and into her usual routine of washing, ironing and housework within six weeks of Joan's birth.

For a while life seemed settled on a happy, even keel. Charlie enjoyed his work at the pub, it was not too strenuous physically to be a problem with his gammy leg, and he thrived on the jovial atmosphere keeping the customers happy with his jokes and stories. He knew he was popular and that boosted his confidence. So he had no need to drink, which meant that Nan did not have to worry about him coming home the worse for wear, having drunk away her housekeeping money.

Their relationship was happier than it had been since the summer when they first met. The awful cold of the Canadian winter was behind them and Nan felt strong enough to cope with the day to day hard work and living in the depressing surroundings of Mrs Wilson's boarding house. In fact she was even beginning to think optimistically about the future again. Then the blow fell.

Charlie came home one afternoon after his lunch-time shift with a long face that was so unlike his recently cheerful countenance that Nan knew at once he had bad news. Of course she should have guessed, before he tersely informed her that the pub landlord had told him his temporary job would be ended in another week, when the injured barman would be fit to return.

"So it's back to tramping the streets looking for work again. I thought it was too good to last." He glared morosely down at the plate of sausage and mash that Nan had waiting for him, and his shoulders slumped in defeat. As if in sympathy, Joan set up a thin wail from her crib. Nan picked her up and opened her blouse to feed her.

"Well at least the weather's better Charlie. Maybe there's more opportunities now the winter's over. Perhaps the building work will be progressing faster on the canal and they may want more men. I expect that bit of trouble you had will be forgotten by now."

"Don't you believe it, girl. Those foremen have long memories and they have their favourites. We both know my leg is never going to improve, and when they have their pick of fit, strong fellers, why would they take on a cripple like me, eh? With more immigrants coming into the country every month, it's just going to get harder."

There was nothing Nan could say. She knew Charlie was being realistic and she dreaded that he would begin to slide backwards into one of the dreadful depressed states where his only solution was in the bottom of a whisky bottle. She racked her brains for ways to economise, but found no answers.

Whereas before she had cut down on her own food when times were bad, now that she was nursing Joan, she knew it was impossible to eat less, for fear her milk would dry up. Fortunately Joan was a wonderfully contented baby, who would eat and sleep and coo in her crib quite happily, so that Nan was able to get her work done just as she had before the birth. But there was no way she could earn enough to support the three of them.

Jessie was the only one in whom she could confide her worries, but even Jessie had no real answer to the problem. "It's hard, lassie, but that man of yours will just have to keep walking the streets for as long as it takes to find something. I know he's a proud man who hates to be seen as unfit and unable to support his wife and bairn, but there are plenty more like him, and if it means he has to go cap in hand to some of the foremen on the canal gangs, then that's what he'll have to do.

"He's got to realise that you and little Joanie are more important than losing face and apologising for what happened before. They're not that hard these foremen, they have wives and families of their own probably, so I'm sure they'll give him another chance if he just approaches them in the right way."

But Nan knew that Charlie was so stiff-necked, he would find it next to impossible to apologise or beg for work. That was the way he was, and she was realising that even the responsibilities of being a husband and father would not change him. Sadly there was a weakness in

Charlie where he refused to admit his own shortcomings and was unable to face up to unpalatable truths. The more difficult life became, the more he seemed to run away from it and seek oblivion in the bottle.

Nan's only escape was when she found the odd hour to walk Joan out of the town into the surrounding countryside. She longed to see more of the Canadian farmlands and forests and visit the spectacular Niagara Falls. It was possible to hear the thunderous roar that the huge volume of water made, and when the wind was in the right direction, the spray could be felt for surprising distances.

One afternoon, she was walking home after a rare outing with Joan, when Doctor Harris's car pulled up beside her.

"Mrs Stuart, how are you getting along?" He stepped out and smiled down at Joan. "Your daughter is obviously thriving," he looked at Nan keenly. "But you appear a little tired. Not doing too much, I hope?"

"I'm all right, Doctor. It's just that things are a bit difficult at the moment." She hesitated, not wanting to be disloyal to Charlie, but tempted to confide in this kind, gentle man, who she felt might be able to offer some sensible advice.

"Is Charlie having problems at work?" He intuitively understood her reluctance and immediately guessed the source of it. Thankfully Nan explained that Charlie's job at the pub had finished and he was finding it difficult to get another.

"It's not fair, Doctor. He's a really hard worker and only wants to look after Joan and me. But his bad leg makes it difficult to get a labouring job, with so many fit and strong immigrants arriving all the time. And he doesn't have any education to speak of, so he's not qualified for anything else."

"Yes, I can understand the problem. What about working outside the town? Would he think of a farm job perhaps? I know that can be physically demanding, but not in quite the same way as being on a labouring gang."

"Oh, Doctor, that's what he's always wanted! When we first talked about emigrating, his dream was to get a place in the country. We thought we'd be able to work for someone else at first and then maybe one day get a property of our own. But since we've got here we've just never seemed to do anything about it. His friend Don, who persuaded Charlie to come out with him, had said we might get a place together, but he's doing fine on one of the gangs, making good money, and Charlie hardly sees him nowadays."

"Well leave it with me, Mrs Stuart. I have one or two patients among the farming community and it may be that they'll have an opening for a man like Charlie. Give me a day or two and I'll get back to you."

"Oh, thank you Doctor Harris! You've been very good to us already, but I would be so grateful if you did hear of something in the country. I would love to have a place to bring Joan up in the fresh air. The boarding house is so confined and being in that damp, steamy kitchen, with all the washing and ironing that I take in, can't be healthy for her."

"Don't worry, my dear, I'll be in touch." He raised his hat with his usual old-fashioned courtesy and drove away, leaving Nan more cheerful than she had been for days. But she was careful to say nothing to Charlie, as she was afraid of raising his hopes falsely. Besides, he was so touchy these days, his pride having taken such a beating, that the idea of his wife talking to another man, even Doctor Harris, and organising their lives without him, would probably have driven him into one of his ever more frequent rages.

The doctor was as good as his word and also extremely tactful with it. A note arrived addressed to Charlie from him, advising that a farmer patient who lived on the road to Niagara, had a vacancy for a labourer. A cottage with a fair sized plot of land went with the job, so the tenant could grow much of his own food to supplement his wages.

Charlie rather painfully perused the letter, his lips forming the words as he read them. At the end he gazed at Nan with fresh hope dawning in his eyes. "This sounds a bit of all right, girl. A job in the country with a cottage thrown in. The Doc says he thought I might like to consider it so we could bring Joanie up in more healthy surroundings than we've got now. Says he hopes I won't mind him taking the liberty of mentioning me to the farmer! Mind! It's the opportunity we dreamed about when we first decided to come out! What d'you say, girl?"

"Charlie it sounds wonderful! I can't wait to see the place! Have you got to speak to the farmer soon?"

"Better than that! The Doc says he'll stop by tomorrow morning and give me a lift over there as he's visiting the farmer's little lad who's got a twisted ankle. He's a good 'un, the Doc, and no mistake!"

Nan smiled as she reflected what a lovely, tactful man Doctor Harris was, and forbore to mention the conversation she'd had with him herself. She hastened to get out Charlie's "good" clothes and brushed them thoroughly and pressed fresh creases in the trousers, while he lovingly polished his best boots, whistling cheerfully as he did so.

One look at Charlie's face when he burst through the kitchen door the following afternoon told her all was well. Exuberantly he swung her off her feet and then waltzed her round the room. "Get your bags packed, woman! This time next week we'll be living in Maple Cottage, in the heart of the country!"

"Oh, Charlie! Did it really go all right then?"

"Couldn't have been better girl! Mr Gilmour, the farmer, seems a really decent chap and I reckon the Doc gave me a good reference. I'm going to be doing general work around the farm and filling in for the stockman or the dairyman when they need me.

"The cottage has three rooms upstairs and a big kitchen and scullery downstairs. You won't know where you are with all that space, girl! There's a big garden, so we can grow our own veg and there's even a hen coop. New laid eggs for our Joanie, eh? What d'you think of that Mrs Stuart?"

The next few days passed swiftly as they packed their meagre belongings and searched through second-hand shops and market stalls for the basic necessities of furniture. On the day of the move, Mr Gilmour sent his farm cart to collect them, and it was laden with all their worldly possessions. Nan perched up front beside the driver, Bob the stockman, with Joanie in her arms, warmly wrapped up against any breezes. Charlie made a great joke of tucking himself in between the various bags and boxes on the back of the cart, whistling loudly *My old man said follow the van*, as they finally drove away from Carlisle Street.

Nan had no regrets about leaving the dingy boarding house and the hard-faced landlady, but she had a lump in her throat as she waved farewell to the warm-hearted Jessie who had come to wish them good luck.

It was a bumpy ride out of the town and along the country roads, but eventually they turned into the lane that wound through the Gilmour property and then stopped at the gate of Maple cottage. From her first sight of it, Nan fell in love with their new home. It was like a dream come true, she thought.

With Joan tucked under her arm, she moved excitedly from one room to the other as Charlie and Bob unloaded the cart. Downstairs the main room had two windows overlooking the front garden, which, although it was overgrown since the occupation of the previous tenants, Nan immediately visualised as a flowering picture. At the back of the cottage, the good-sized scullery held a sink, with cupboards and a tiled larder under the stairs. The staircase itself was in another cupboard and led up to two big bedrooms and a small box room above

Investigating outside the back door, Nan discovered an earth closet and a shed to house the fuel for the kitchen range. The latter was already stacked with logs and kindling, which were part of the perks that went with Charlie's job. An overgrown path leading past an empty hen-house, in need of an overhaul, and a large patch of ground for growing vegetables, ended at a small copse of mixed fruit trees and currant bushes.

"Oh, Joanie, we are going to be so happy here! Your dad and I will get this garden all neat in next to no time. We'll grow lots of lovely veggies and I'll bottle fruit and make jams and we'll have some nice friendly clucking hens to lay eggs for your tea! You are going to grow up big and strong in this wonderful country air and Daddy will make you a swing from that lovely old apple tree and we are going to be the happiest family in all of Canada!" Nan smothered the tiny, beaming face with kisses, and thought she would burst with the wonder of their good luck.

As the next months passed it seemed that Nan's prophesy was being realised. All through that first summer life was sweet for her and Charlie. He enjoyed his outdoor life and quickly became popular with the other farm workers. Nan worked hard clearing the weeds from the land and planting flowers and vegetables. Between them they decorated the rooms in the cottage and Nan delighted in making new curtains from cheap remnants she found in the market.

Charlie stained the floorboards and she made rugs to brighten them. There were always pots of flowers to decorate the windowsills and a jug of them on the table. Nan took a delight in polishing their few sticks of furniture and black-leading the range, so that it positively gleamed. Everything about the cottage spoke of her loving care and the happy life they lived under its roof.

Charlie mended the chicken coop and they soon invested in half a dozen hens. It was one of Nan's favourite chores to go out each day, clucking cheerfully to

102

encourage the birds to come for their food, whilst she would delightedly gather the eggs.

Joan was a joy to behold as she spent her days outside in the sunshine, her arms and legs becoming sturdy and strong, her smooth skin healthily tanned and a wide smile lighting her beguiling eyes. In later years Nan would look back on that first Canadian summer and recall it as one of the happiest times of her life.

It was hard to imagine the drab surroundings of her family's home back in Holgate, and although she looked forward to the occasional letter that she would receive from Emily, it seemed impossible that she had ever shared that depressing lifestyle.

Indeed Emily had little news of any importance to send out to Nan. Fred had of course come out of the army, but was, sadly, a broken man. Physically his lungs had been badly affected by the dreaded gas attacks and emotionally he suffered the terrible after effects of shell-shock. Emily described tersely how he would sit for hours on end either by the kitchen fire or up in the bedroom he had once shared with Jack, gazing hopelessly out of the window, waiting for his dead brother to come round the corner.

Although Nan was eager to tell her family of her own happy existence, she felt guilty when she compared her lot with theirs. So she glossed over the comforts of the cottage and the joys of living off their home-grown produce, and contented herself with extolling Joan's virtues and singing the praises of motherhood.

Ruby would occasionally send a misspelt, badly written note along with Emily's, which usually told of outings to the West End with her friend Vi, or some success she had enjoyed with one of the local Lotharios during a dance at the town hall. She had left her job at the café and realised her ambition of working in a dress shop in London, but she accused the other girls of being "snooty" and Nan suspected Ruby's own airs and graces would not make her popular.

The Canadian autumn or "Fall" was every bit as beautiful as Nan had expected, and she loved walking Joan in her baby carriage along the country lanes. Sometimes Charlie would borrow a trap from the farmer and take them on longer excursions, particularly to Niagara Falls, of which Nan never tired. The sight and sound of that tremendous volume of water would thrill her soul and she would be riveted by its majestic beauty.

When the winter came life was not so rosy. As the snow blanketed the countryside and the awful cold made temperatures plummet, Nan fought a constant battle to keep herself and Joan sufficiently warm. Each day it was necessary to go outside to the woodshed and bring back armfuls to fuel the kitchen stove. Joan would be snug in her winter woollens that Nan and Jessie had made for her, but when Charlie came home at the end of the day, his face was more and more gloomy as he experienced the hardships of farm work during the winter.

Nan noticed also that he found the evenings, cooped up with just herself and Joan for company, more and more depressing. During the summer they had gone out for an evening stroll, or he would sometimes drive into town for a drink with his old cronies at the pub, but the winter weather made such outings more and more difficult.

Nan would rack her brains for ways to keep him occupied and happy, but she became increasingly aware that he was growing restless and dissatisfied with their lifestyle. However, his depression was fleetingly lifted when she gave him the news that she was once again pregnant. "This one will be born in July, Charlie, so by then Joan should be walking. I know I'll have my hands full at first, but it will be nice in a year or two, when they'll be real company for each other."

"That's wonderful news, girl!" He hugged her tightly and beamed down at her. "Two nippers around the place, eh? Proper domesticated I'll be getting, if I'm not careful!" Nan knew that he was joking, but as time went on, she realised that Charlie's words had been inspired by an underlying misgiving.

All his adult life he had only himself to worry about. As soon as he had escaped from the orphanage at such an early age, he had roamed the world, becoming tough and self-sufficient in the process. In an effort to hide the lasting effects of his horrifying experiences in the war, he had acquired a veneer of good-humour and bonhomie, but underneath there were darker emotions at work.

Charlie dreaded being imprisoned or tied down in any way. Although Nan was sure he loved her and Joan, she knew that he found increasingly irksome the responsibilities they represented. He had never stayed in one place for more than a few months at the most, and he had always been free to move on to pastures new. Now he was chained to his job at the farm because of Nan and Joan.

Although he had dreamed of a place in the country and the family he had always been denied, Nan could see that the realities of his situation were gradually depressing him. He was missing the noise and bustle, the laughter and excitement of life in the city and his job in the pub, and finding life in Maple Cottage more and more claustrophobic.

It was particularly noticeable during the long winter evenings. His own mental resources were few – his lack of education meant that he rarely opened a book – and although Nan did her best to keep him cheerful and distract him every way she could, playing cards or reading bits out of the local paper to him, it was not easy. Particularly as she felt tired and sick in the throes of her pregnancy, and unable to respond with any enthusiasm to his overtures in the bedroom.

A rare social event was at New Year, when they were invited to Mr and Mrs Gilmour's house to a party given for all the farm workers. Whilst there, Nan found herself talking to Doctor Harris.

"So, Mrs Stuart, how's young Joan progressing now? What is she, eight months, is it?"

"Oh, she's fine thank you Doctor. She's sleeping upstairs tonight – Mrs Gilmour kindly put her in with her own two kiddies. As a matter of fact I was planning to pay you a visit sometime soon – I'm expecting again."

"Well, congratulations! You and your husband are pleased, I take it?"

"Oh, yes, a brother or sister for Joan will be grand. It's due next July, I believe."

"I'll call in to you next week if you like. Save you having to make the journey into town in all this snow! I have one or two regular calls I make on the Niagara road, so I can easily drop by."

"Oh, that is kind, Doctor. Mr Gilmour's very good about lending Charlie one of the farm carts or traps, but we don't like to ask too often. And the journey is very cold for Joan at this time of year!"

Accordingly the doctor paid a visit to examine Nan a few days later. He was very thorough, and said little until after he had washed his hands and sat down to the cup of tea that Nan had made, along with her freshly baked scones.

"These look delicious, Mrs Stuart. And home-made jam as well! You've certainly taken to being a country wife, and no mistake!"

"Oh, it's all my dreams come true, Doctor! And it's all thanks to you, speaking to Mr Gilmour for us."

"Oh, that was nothing, my dear. Now, I have something to tell you that may be rather a shock." He smiled into her suddenly serious eyes. "I'm pretty well certain from my examination that you are carrying twins! It's rather early to be sure, but I've delivered a few sets in my time, and I think you're showing definite signs. But we'll know more in a month or two."

"Twins! Whatever will Charlie say?" Nan was stunned at the thought of two more babies, although as she became used to the idea, she was quite thrilled. But she was less certain of her husband's reaction.

"Bloody 'ell, girl! That's a turn up and no mistake!" Charlie grinned and patted her stomach. "We don't do things by halves, do we?"

It did seem that the idea of being capable of fathering twins gave Charlie a strange boost to his confidence. Nan knew that his ignominious roots and lack of education had conspired to produce in him a huge inferiority complex. He hid this very successfully with his air of good humour and casual ease of manner, but Nan was well aware of his insecurity.

Now able to boast that he was about to father not one baby but two, he felt himself the centre of attention and a subject of admiring glances among his cronies. "Trust old Charlie!" they would say, and he would grin and accept another congratulatory pint.

So the bitter cold of winter finally passed and Nan began to see the first signs of spring in the gradually unfurling buds and the nest-building activities amongst the host of birds she fed each day in the garden.

She had been increasingly concerned at the lack of news from Holgate ever since Christmas. Emily's last letter had mentioned that Will had been laid low with flu, Fred was becoming less communicative every day and Ruby was out gadding with her flighty friends every night!

Nan had tried to write a cheerful letter in response and sent a picture of Niagara Falls for Emily to hang in the kitchen. But since then, not a word had reached them. Until one day she received a very upsetting letter from her mother. It was longer than usual and Nan had to sit down as she absorbed the news it contained.

Ruby had left home in disgrace! It seemed that one of the smooth-talking fellows at the local dances had turned out to be married! Ruby professed to be wildly in love with him and told Emily that he was going to divorce his wife and carry her (Ruby) off to a life of luxury. Emily had informed her daughter that there would be no scandal of divorce in the Fisher household and she must give him up forthwith.

Whilst Ruby was arguing with her mother that she was determined to follow her young man to the ends of the earth, divorced or not, her father arrived in time to overhear these revelations. He immediately smacked Ruby's face, called her a "little slut" and told her to make up her mind her romance was at an end. Upon which Ruby had flung upstairs, packed her belongings and left the house. "Never to darken our doors again," as Emily declared in her letter.

Well, I suppose it's not really surprising, thought Nan, as she put the letter behind the clock till she had time to answer it. Ruby had never been the sort to settle down happily to the domestic life and if she found a lover with plenty of money, the fact that he was married would not trouble her moral sense unduly. Nan had no illusions that her father would relent, should Ruby wish to return home, but probably Emily might be willing to help out if needed.

"Don't worry your head about her, girl," Charlie said after she told him the news that evening. "She's a survivor, that one. Whilst she's still got looks and youth on her side, she'll never starve!" And Nan had to acknowledge that this rather cynical judgement was doubtless correct.

Summer was upon them now, and Nan found her pregnancy increasingly exhausting. Carrying twins in this hot weather was a terrible drain on her strength and Joan, now able to toddle about quite quickly, was a little imp who needed to be watched constantly. The best time for

Nan to rest was in the dusk, when her lively daughter was tucked up in her cot and Nan was able to sit outside in the front garden, breathing in the scent of the flowers she had lovingly raised.

Charlie would go into town for a drink quite often, but it seemed that just knowing he could get away from his domestic life, if he needed to, was enough in itself and he rarely stayed out late. He was still devoted to Joan and treated Nan with a genuine tenderness as her pregnancy progressed.

One still, sultry afternoon the sky was shimmering with an almost metallic heat which reminded her of the day when she had first met Charlie, two years before at the cottage hospital. Nan was drowsing in a chair in the shade of one of the maple trees by the front gate and Joan was stretched out on a rug having her afternoon nap. Nan had been sewing a tiny night-gown for the twins, although the heat was very soporific and her fingers were gradually relaxing on top of her swelling stomach.

The sound of wheels along the lane alerted her and she shaded her eyes to see if it was one of the farm workers or a neighbour that would stop to pass the time of day. The sun was blinding, but she recognised Bob, driving the trap, and he had a female passenger. She was quite young, and Nan thought fleetingly it might be a friend whom Mrs Gilmour had sent him to fetch. But observing the rather over-bright colours of the tight blue costume and the hat with its ornate feather, Nan decided that this was more likely to be an applicant for a servant's job at the farm.

She gave Bob a casual wave and bent over her work again, when she realised the trap was stopping at the gate.

Bob jumped down and then shouted, "A visitor for you, Nan," before turning to hand down the girl. Nan pulled herself awkwardly upright, still dazzled by the sun, but as she walked forward the identity of the visitor became apparent.

"Ruby, Ruby, what on earth are you doing here?" Astounded, Nan clasped her sister in an ungainly embrace, whilst Bob beamed at this wonderful surprise he'd helped bring about, and unloaded Ruby's bags from the trap.

"A bit of a shock am I, Nan?" Ruby laughed and batted her eyelashes at Bob, although he was old enough to be her father. "If it hadn't been for Bob here, I'd have been traipsing round Welland still. Quite a knight in shining armour, Bob's been! Carrying me off in his horse and carriage as well!"

"Well ... pony and trap, more like!" Bob grinned bemused at this painted butterfly who had fluttered so unexpectedly into his life. "I was talking to Jessie Campbell in Carlisle Road, near the boarding house where you used to live, Nan, when your sister came along. She was asking your old landlady how far it was to your new address, and of course Mrs Wilson wasn't being very helpful."

"No, I can believe that, Bob."

"So Jessie hearing your name mentioned pricked up her ears, and when Ruby told her who she was, 'course I said I'd be glad to give her a lift out here."

"That's very civil of you, Bob. Won't you come inside for a cup of tea, or something cooler?"

"No, you're all right, Nan. I'll just take these bags into the house and then I must get on to the farm. If I see

Charlie, I'll tell him he's got another good reason to come home tonight!"

Ruby giggled and simpered till Bob had put down her luggage in the kitchen and driven off, before she turned pettishly to Nan. "Well, you might offer me a cup of tea, Nan. I'm quite exhausted in all this heat. What a journey I've had! And these shoes are killing me!" Looking at the spindly, high heels with the tight straps to fasten them, Nan thought that was hardly surprising, but forbore to comment.

Ruby had swept unasked into the cottage, pulled off shoes, jacket and hat and flung herself in the only armchair. Nan checked that Joan was still fast asleep and went to boil the kettle. When they were both settled with cups of tea, she said quietly, "Right, Ruby, let's hear what you've been up to then. And the truth mind, because I've already had a letter from Mum about your goings on!"

For the next hour Ruby poured out her tale of woe in Nan's appalled ears. She had always known that Ruby was self-centred, and suspected her morals were questionable, but it was not pleasant to hear just how shallow her standards really were. In her own eyes, of course, Ruby was very much the injured party.

She had no compunction in admitting that she had been conducting a liaison with a married man that she had met at a town hall dance. She had been dazzled with his tale of being a high-powered business man with a mansion in Muswell Hill. He had given Ruby a good time, wining and dining her in restaurants in London, where he met her after she finished work. He bought her several items of jewellery, which later turned out to be paste, and of course he soon expected her to pay a price for all this outlay.

She was invited to visit his luxurious home one evening, "when the servants were out" and there he seduced her. At this stage she had actually not known he was married. But he eventually told her about his wife, who was older than him and of course "didn't understand him". He promised Ruby that very soon he would be able to leave, once certain important business deals had been completed, and then he would whisk her away to the south of France.

"He told me he really hated his wife and that he was definitely going to divorce her so we could get married Nan. And I honestly believed him!" Ruby shook her head as she reflected on the perfidious treatment she had undergone at the hands of handsome George.

"Next thing I know, Mum's found out, because that old cow, Mrs Flint, saw us together at Lyons Corner House! She actually used to work for George's wife at one time as a charlady, so of course she recognised him. Couldn't wait to tell Mum, could she?"

"So that was when Dad overheard you and Mum rowing about it and you had the big bust-up?"

"Actually smacked my face, he did! Can you imagine? Well, I wasn't going to put up with that! I packed up my bags and left that night."

It transpired that having fled to George's mansion, where she expected comfort and succour, Ruby was quickly disillusioned. George's wife was fortunately out at her bridge club, but when the servant girl admitted Ruby and she poured out her tale to him, George was appalled and terrified.

Apparently the wife who was so lacking in understanding was not lacking in money. It was she who owned the mansion and she who had financed all George's business ventures. She was considerably older than him, and George knew there was no way she would be prepared to condone his little affair with Ruby. His only recourse was to buy Ruby off, using his personal allowance from his wife to do so.

Ruby made it plain that she was unable to return to the family home, so it was decided he would finance her trip to Canada where she might make a "fresh start" with her elder sister – unbeknown to the said elder sister!

"I had a terrible journey out here, Nan. George only bought me a steerage class ticket, and we were cooped up in tiny cabins and the heat was something shocking!" Ruby poured herself, unasked, another cup of tea. "Of course I had to buy myself a few bits and pieces of clothes before I left – I'm sure you can't have any decent shops out here in this wilderness! – so I've hardly a penny left now!"

Nan gazed thoughtfully at her younger sister and sighed. You came halfway round the world and still the family responsibilities followed you, she thought. "So what exactly are you planning to do now, then?"

"Well of course I thought you'd be only too pleased to take me in!" Ruby stared innocently back at Nan. "I'm sure you'll be glad to have some help, what with little Joanie and twins on the way! I should think I'd be the answer to all your prayers, Nan!"

"H'mm." Nan walked outside to pick up Joan who was now awake and preparing to wander off round the garden, picking flowers as she went. Remembering her younger sister's former lack of domesticity and total disinterest in babies, Nan certainly did not envisage her as the ideal household help. And whatever will Charlie think, she wondered, as she took Joan to meet her aunt.

Charlie took Ruby's arrival in good part. He thought it was a huge joke that strait-laced Will's daughter had sought refuge with the unwelcome son-in-law who had been responsible for her elder sister's hasty marriage. "That's going to really put the cat among the pigeons, when he finds out she's come to us for help, girl. Really stick in his throat that will!"

"Well, I dare say Mum'll be relieved to know she's safe. No matter how bitter she sounded in that letter, Ruby is still her daughter and she must care what happens to her."

"I wouldn't bet on it!" Charlie grinned cynically and put his arms as far as he was able round Nan's enormous bulk. "You're such a soft touch my sweetheart, you think everybody's nice deep down, but they're not you know!"

Nan ignored him and went to sort out some bed linen to put on the mattress that Ruby would have off their own bed, on the floor in the box room. Next time Charlie took the farm cart into town, he would have to pick up a second hand bed for her, thought Nan. Another expense they had not planned for!

If Ruby had thought that she could have a lazy holiday at Nan's expense, Charlie quickly disillusioned her. He made it very plain that she was expected to pull her weight doing a good share of the housework, especially as Nan reached the final, exhausting stages of her pregnancy. Ruby fortunately seemed to get on well with Joan, who was very placid and easy to manage, so Nan was pleased to send them off for walks about the countryside, with Ruby pushing her gurgling niece in the baby carriage.

It was on her return from one of these outings that Ruby found Nan doubled up in front of the sink, where she had been washing some of Joan's outgrown baby clothes, in readiness for the new arrivals.

"What is it, Nan? Is something wrong?" Ruby stood there, looking like a fashion plate as usual, in her spotted cotton dress, bobbed hair and straw boater.

"What d'you think's the matter?" Nan glared at her and then doubled over once more. "This isn't just something I've eaten that's disagreed with me! I'm nine months pregnant and about to give birth to twins! And if you stand there gaping for much longer, you're going to be delivering them yourself on the kitchen floor! Ahh ..."

"Oh, Nan! Oh dear! Oh, what shall I do?" Ruby looked about in panic, suddenly horrified that she might be expected to take charge of the situation, when Nan was usually the one so totally in control.

"Help me to get upstairs, then wheel Joan up to the farm and ask Charlie to go for Doctor Harris. When you've done that come back here and start boiling water ... ahh ... and whatever you do, take care of Joanie."

Nan's labour was no worse and no easier than the majority of women's. Doctor Harris arrived to find Charlie bathing her face. Ruby was in the kitchen feeding Joan with jam sandwiches, which seemed to be the height of her culinary prowess, whilst boiling endless receptacles of water. Each time an anguished moan was heard from overhead, her face would pucker in distress and she would glance at the door, as if desperate to escape from these unpleasant, basic realities of life.

The hours went by and Charlie and Ruby kept vigil together in the kitchen. Joan had long since been bathed and put to bed by her distracted father, and he had also finally lost his temper with Ruby as she had asked for the umpteenth time, "She will be all right, won't she Charlie?"

"You stupid cow! How should I know if she'll be all right? She's having twins for gawd's sake, in a cottage in the back of beyond! If anything goes wrong it's miles to the nearest hospital ... But Doc Harris is reckoned to be good at his job, so we'll have to hope he knows what he's doing. If anything happens to Nan ..." Charlie clenched his fists as he paced the floor, beads of sweat starting on his forehead at another long-drawn out moan from above.

Ruby gazed in surprise at his obvious distress – Charlie always appeared so in control of his life, and able to greet any crisis with a joke. This was a different side she was seeing. Ruby opened the door in a bid to find some cooler air on this sticky summer night, and mentally resolved to make very sure that she personally never went through the drama being enacted overhead.

Little Joanie was quite sweet of course, especially when she was newly bathed and powdered ready for her bed. But weighing that against the innumerable occasions when she was sticky or needed her nappy changing, not to mention the times she was yelling for attention in the middle of the night, Ruby decided that the doubtful joys of motherhood in no way compensated for the appalling ordeal her sister was suffering above. And it ruins your figure! Ruby turned to look in the glass above the fireplace and admired the golden tint that the Canadian sun had given her skin. Kids? Who needed them?

It was in the early hours of the morning when a dozing Ruby and a grim-faced Charlie were aroused by the plaintive cry of the new-born. Before they could speak, it was immediately echoed by an identical one.

"Thank God! It's over!" Charlie opened the door to the cupboard where the stairs wound upward and listened raptly to the wailing duet from above. Shortly afterwards Dr Harris appeared with a tired smile on his face.

"Alright, Charlie. They're fine. You have two more healthy daughters and Nan is well, although worn out as you'd expect. Ruby, make your sister a cup of tea, and Charlie you can go up and see them. I think I'll take a breath of fresh air – it's been a long night!"

Charlie bounded upstairs and paused in the doorway to gaze at Nan. She was haggard and too exhausted to speak above a whisper, but she managed a tremulous smile, as Charlie carefully gathered her in his arms, his eyes full of tears.

"Nan, girl, you've had a rough night, I reckon. I know I have!"

"Oh, Charlie! You're never serious, are you?" She shook her lead lovingly at him, and then gestured towards Joan's old crib, which had an identical, newer one beside it. "What d'you think of your new daughters then? Properly outnumbered you're going to be now!"

"Petticoat government, eh?" Charlie smiled as he gazed down at the two wrinkled, red faces, each crowned by a few wisps of damp, blonde hair. Two pairs of unfocussed eyes struggled to open and Charlie noticed that one set was blue and the other green.

"Not identical, then? Different coloured eyes – that'll make it easier to tell them apart!"

"Doctor Harris said the same. Don't take after us for their looks do they, Charlie?"

"That's true." He picked up a brush from the dressing table and gently smoothed back the chestnut hair from her forehead. She put up a hand and fleetingly stroked his own black curls. But the effort was too much and she thankfully allowed him to pull the covers round her shoulders.

"Reckon I'm going to have to watch you more closely my girl. Which of the farmhands round here has got straight, fair hair then? Maybe I've been leaving you on your own too often, eh?"

"Oh, Charlie, you are terrible!" Nan's eyes closed as she smilingly murmured, "My granny had lovely white hair, but Mum reckoned it was like spun gold when she was a girl. Mum took after her too, although her hair's so grey now, you'd never know. Mum's got blue eyes, but Granny's were green. I thought we might call them Rita and Irene. Rita with the blue eyes and Irene with the green. I've always liked those names." Her voice faded and the lines of weariness and pain gradually smoothed as her face settled into repose.

"We'll call them whatever you like, sweetheart." Charlie softly dropped a kiss on her cheek and tiptoed past his now sleeping daughters. Nan might not want that cup of tea, but he certainly did! And maybe the Doc would join him in a small tot of rum that he'd been hoarding against this very day.

Nan found she had to get back on her feet quicker than Doctor Harris would have liked. It was a busy time on the farm, getting in the harvest, so Charlie was out till all hours working. Joanie was more demanding with each passing day, developing an insatiable curiosity for exploring her surroundings as her unsteady legs became stronger and faster.

The twins were like any other babies – and of course twice the work. Life was an endless round of feeding, changing, washing, cooking and cleaning. Ruby showed less and less interest in domestic life and made excuses whenever she could to escape the cottage. At least she never objected to doing the shopping, thought Nan dispiritedly as she pegged out the nappies and rubbed her aching back.

She would be up at six these mornings to give the twins their early feed and see Charlie off to the farm. If she could settle the twins down quickly, she managed to do some washing before Joan was awake and ready for her breakfast. Then there was the housework; food to prepare for everyone's dinner; the hens to feed and eggs to collect; more twins' feeds, ironing; attending to Joan – the duties were endless.

Ruby never actually refused to help, but Nan quickly discovered it was easier to carry out the jobs herself. By the time she had explained what needed doing, and overseen Ruby doing it ineffectually and disinterestedly, it was much less strain to work on her own. But after the harvest was gathered there were all the jobs of a country wife that she had looked forward to doing, which now seemed an unbearably heavy extra burden.

There was fruit and other produce to be bottled or salted down for the winter. Jams to be made, herbs to be dried, bunches of onions to be lifted and hung in the kitchen, carrots to be pulled and buried in buckets of sand to keep till needed – the chores seemed endless. Nan laboured from dawn till dusk, and then there were the children to bath and settle for the night, and always a basket of mending to occupy her evenings, if she could keep her eyes open.

She was constantly worried that being so tired her milk would dry up and she would no longer be able to feed the twins herself. When it finally happened she was nagged by an irrational sense of guilt. She became thinner than before and it was an effort to drag herself up the stairs to bed at night.

Charlie was sympathetic at first, but as the winter months brought the usual bitter cold and the first falls of snow, the morose part of his nature took over. Ruby was appalled at what she thought of as primitive conditions, when she discovered just how gruelling the Canadian weather could be. Nan found her presence, forever complaining as she huddled over the fire with a blanket about her shoulders, an added hardship to bear.

It was therefore with great relief she greeted Ruby's ecstatic news when she returned from the weekly shopping trip to Welland. Charlie had taken her in the farm cart to fetch all their domestic supplies, along with those for the farmer, and Nan had been glad to have the cottage to herself.

Now Ruby was transformed from the recent peevish madam into a laughing, excited young girl, again. "Isn't it wonderful, Nan? I've got a job in the big store in the high street, and it pays quite well. I'm going to be working in the hat department – imagine, they may want me to help design some of the new ones! They think I must know all about fashion, when I told them I worked up West, back home!"

"Good news, eh girl?" Charlie grinned at Nan as he pulled off his great coat and held out his feet in their hand-knitted socks towards the fire. "She can stop moping around this place, under our feet. Be nice to have our home to ourselves again, eh?" He dug Ruby in the ribs, as she lifted her hands to unwind her headscarf and she squealed delightedly.

"Get off, you great bully!"

Nan watched abstractedly as they playfully struggled together, and then said worriedly, "But how will you manage that journey twice a day, Ruby? Especially during the winter. Sometimes the road is impassable for ages."

"Oh, I shan't be living here any more Nan! A lot of the girls live in at a boarding house behind the shop. It's like a proper department store, you know. The lodging goes with the job!"

"Well, I suppose in that case ..." Nan saw the transformation in her now vivacious younger sister, and decided thankfully that the prospect of living in a town again, mixing with plenty of other young people, had seemed such an enticing prospect that Ruby was quite reconciled to giving up her easy, lazy, lifestyle in the cottage.

So the following weekend Charlie drove Ruby once more back to Welland, this time with all her luggage behind

122

her. "You will keep in touch, won't you Ruby?" Nan hugged her tightly, before watching Charlie hoist her onto the seat and wrap her up tightly in rugs. "You will let us know how you're getting on? And if you need anything, you've got Jessie Campbell's address, haven't you?"

"Yes, of course I have! Don't fuss, Nan. You sound like my mother!" Ruby waved airily and fluttered her eyelashes at Charlie. "Drive on, my man!"

"Yes, my lady! Your wish is my command!" Charlie touched his cap, grinned at Nan, and set the horse in motion. Nan went thankfully back into the warmth of the kitchen and decided to snatch ten minutes to write a brief letter to Emily, to give her the news of Ruby's new job.

Since Ruby's arrival she had kept her parents fully informed of their younger daughter's activities, but when they answered Nan's letters, beyond the bare acknowledgement that Ruby had arrived in Canada, they never referred to her.

The long, cold winter months passed and Nan began to feel that she had been incarcerated in the cottage for a lifetime. With three small children on her hands, it was impossible for her to set foot beyond the garden. There was no way she could take them all out in the cold weather, even though she would have liked to go for the occasional walk herself, just to get away from the same four walls.

Doctor Harris would occasionally call in on his way to visit patients in Niagara, just to check on the children's progress. Other than him, Charlie was practically her only link with the outside world these days. He would do the shopping once a week in Welland for her and bring her news of what was happening elsewhere. Christmas and the New Year passed with a brief visit by Ruby, who was very full of her new job.

She looked more of a fashion plate than ever, in a cheap, tawdry way, and regaled Nan with stories of the various young men who were forever asking her out, and the fun that she had with the other girls.

"So is there anyone you specially like, Ruby? I mean are you courting with some young fellow now? Someone you might be serious about?"

Nan watched as Ruby devoured another slice of home-made bread and jam, her lips and nails almost the same shade as the strawberry preserve. A cheap fox fur, complete with its head and tail, had been tossed on a chair, and her spindle-heeled boots – utterly useless in the unrelenting snowfalls – were lying where she had discarded them inside the front door.

"Serious? Don't make me laugh, Nan! Most of them are glorified labourers or lumberjacks that I see in Welland. Not a real gentleman amongst them! Still, what else could you expect in this wilderness? No, I've no intentions of being 'serious', thank you very much!

"Oh, they're all very keen to spend their money on a girl, and I'm not going to object, am I? But I'm going to wait until someone comes along who can take me out of this dump, and back to civilisation! Besides, they're all just bits of lads, most of them; I prefer someone more mature."

Feeling Nan's keen gaze upon her, she looked away with an awkward giggle, and said, "Hark at me, going on! Don't worry, Nan, I'm only joking!" but somehow Nan felt that Ruby had said more than she had intended. The colour had risen in her cheeks, and Nan suddenly felt a twist of unease in her stomach.

Oh dear, what was Ruby up to now? Nan was sure that she was hiding some sort of misdemeanour from Nan's disapproval. Surely she was not embarking on another affair? But the only older men that Ruby had met, to her knowledge, were farmer Gilmour and Doctor Harris. Both respectable, married men.

She mentioned her fears to Charlie the following evening after he returned from driving Ruby back to Welland. He staggered as he walked through the door and dropped his outdoor clothes carelessly around him as he discarded them in the warmth of the kitchen.

"Don't talk so daft, girl! Ruby's just having you on. Likes to shoot her mouth off and play the vamp, like the stars she sees in the films! All she does is flirt with the lads in the shop and the ones she meets when she goes out with the other girls for a night on the town."

"Night on the town! That's rich! When I think of some of the places I stopped in when I was in the navy – some of the clubs and houses of ill-repute I visited out East! The fellers from the labouring gangs and the lumber camps wouldn't know what hit 'em!"

Laughing at his memories, that he knew would probably shock Nan, if he cared to describe them in detail, he stumbled across to her chair and half collapsed on top of her as he clumsily attempted to plant a wet kiss on her upraised face, and encountered a firm hand holding him off.

"Come on, Charlie. You've had one too many again. It's time you got off to bed, or you'll be late for milking in the morning." She managed to push him away slightly and struggled to her feet.

"Not too many, Nan. Not so many I can't give my darlin' wife what she wants. Come 'ere, girl."

Awkwardly he pulled her towards him and attempted to fumble open the buttons on her high-necked blouse, and his fingers became entangled in the thick shawl she wore against the draughts from the ill-fitting doors and windows.

"No, Charlie, no! You smell of booze and you know I hate it when you're being silly in your drink. Besides I'm too tired tonight. Now come upstairs quietly will you, or you'll wake the babies."

"Silly, is it? I'll show you how drunk I am. Now come here, woman. I'm sick of hearing you're too tired. That's all you ever tell me these days!"

His hands dug painfully into her shoulders as he dragged her towards him, and thrust the hardness of his body against hers. Where once his male nearness would have produced a shiver of answering desire in Nan's own loins, now the stench of beer and male sweat along with the rough hands simply revolted her.

She threw off her weariness enough to push him violently so that he lost his balance and fell to his knees, striking his elbow on the corner of the iron fender, and cursing at the pain.

"You bitch! You're an unfeeling, frigid cow! You're my wife and I'll have my rights, whether you want me or not!"

He attempted to pull himself upright, but Nan, suddenly scared by the wild look in his eyes and the unexpected shouted abuse, turned and ran through the door and upstairs to the children's room. She hurried inside and bolted the door behind her. Trying to silence her hurried breathing and to calm her fast-beating heart, she stood with her back to the door, straining to hear Charlie's movements downstairs.

She listened to the muttered imprecations as he made his way across the kitchen, knocking over a chair and sending crockery crashing off the table in the process. Joan whimpered and turned in her sleep, and Nan bent to cover her up, murmuring soothingly as she did so. Then came the sound of Charlie's shuffling footsteps as he groped his way upstairs.

She heard him open the door of their own room, and the sound of him walking across to the bed. The springs of the mattress squeaked as he collapsed on top of the covers, and she heard the bewildered tones as he muttered, "Nan? Nan, where are you, girl?" She waited with bated breath in the lengthening silence, and then a wave of relief washed over her as she heard the rising crescendo of his drunken snoring.

After checking that all three children were snugly wrapped in their covers, Nan tiptoed back downstairs and prepared to pass an uncomfortable night in the armchair beside the fire, with Charlie's overcoat her only cover. But that was preferable to sharing the marital bed with the snoring drunk above.

In after years, Nan would recall that evening as the beginning of the end of her love for Charlie. It seemed that once he had revealed the coarse, uncaring side of his feelings for her, even though he tried to excuse himself the next morning by telling her it was "the drink talking,"

Nan's eyes gradually saw him in a more realistic and damning light.

It did not all happen at once, and when the spring came at last and as usual Charlie felt less claustrophobic at living in the cottage, for a while Nan believed that all would be well again. The children were thriving and she felt stronger herself in the renewed warmth of the sun.

But then circumstances began to catch up with them, and her illusions about Charlie gradually fell away. Firstly Doctor Harris left the district to take up a post in a hospital in Toronto, and for Nan that was a hard blow. He had always been such a staunch friend and she knew that with him she could ask advice about any problem, and he would help whenever possible.

When he came to say his farewells, he shook her hand, and hesitated, before saying quietly, "Nan, I think I should warn you about Charlie."

"Yes, Doctor? What is it? He's not ill in any way, is he? His leg isn't getting any worse, is it?" She gazed at him anxiously, but when he smilingly shook his head, and said quietly, "No, this isn't a medical matter, my dear. I'm speaking as a friend, not your doctor," she felt a rising sense of panic that she did not want to hear whatever revelations he cared to make.

"I think you should know that Charlie is sailing a little close to the wind, as far as the law is concerned. I hear things sometimes on my rounds and I know that there is quite a bit of smuggling going on at times carrying goods across the border between Canada and America, at Niagara.

"Charlie's name has come up once or twice, although no-one has any evidence against him as yet. As you probably know, Mr Gilmour is a very respectable man, and if any scandal gets round about one of his workers, that man would be out of a job very quickly. So I think Charlie had better be careful. Perhaps you might mention it to him?"

"Of course I will, Doctor. I had no idea that he was involved in anything like this. I can't think why he would be so stupid. We manage quite well on his wages, what with having this place to live in rent-free, and the land to grow so much of our own food ... I don't know why he would need to make money by breaking the law. Of course he spends a bit on drink, but not that much ..."

"Nan, sometimes it's not the prospect of making money that causes men to break the law. Sometimes it's the need to run risks, the scent of danger for its own sake. Charlie is one of a generation that spent years in appalling conditions, wondering each night whether it might be their last one on earth. We can barely begin to comprehend what life must have been like in the trenches. You tell me that Charlie was out in France longer than most – it must be very hard for him to settle down to the humdrum realities of normal family life.

"I'm not making excuses for him, but I think it isn't difficult to understand his problem. Perhaps if you have a chat with him, you can make him realise that it's not just his own freedom he's risking, but the home and security of you and his daughters." He held her hand between his own two and squeezed it gently.

"I'm sorry to burden you with this worry, Nan, particularly as I'm going away, but I really felt you needed to be warned, before it's too late."

"Don't apologise, Doctor. You've been a wonderful friend to us, and I appreciate what you're trying to do. I'm grateful that you told me, and I'll speak to Charlie as soon as I can." Watching the doctor's car driving down the lane, Nan felt a deep sense of loss. It was only now that he was leaving the district that she realised how much of a life-line her friendship with the doctor had been.

When Charlie came home that evening she waited until he had finished his meal and the children were tucked up in bed before she took a deep breath and faced him with the doctor's suspicions.

"What bloody business is it of his anyway?" Charlie glared across the kitchen at Nan. "He wants to keep his nose out. If I want to make a few extra bob on the side, that's up to me!"

"But Charlie, if you get caught smuggling Mr Gilmour will sack you straight away. You know how strait-laced he is. Always prides himself on being such a pillar of the community. If you lose your job we'll be out of the cottage as well. What about the children? How can you risk them being without a roof over their heads? It's not as though we're desperate for extra money, is it? I think we do all right, don't we?"

Charlie's glare was wiped away and he came towards her with his usual beguiling "little boy" grin. "'Course we do all right, girl. But sometimes it would be nice to have a bit more – a bit extra, you know? I'd like to be able to spend on a few luxuries for you and the kids. Any bloke wants to do the best by his family, doesn't he?"

"But Charlie, I'm quite happy the way we are. I love this cottage – it's all I've ever dreamed of, you know that. It's such a wonderful place to bring up the girls. I love the garden, and growing our own food. I just feel we're so lucky, when I think back to Holgate and that miserable, shabby house and that tiny back yard!"

Charlie knelt beside her and gazed silently into her eyes for a moment. He wore a serious, almost sad expression, which Nan did not recognise. Then he sighed as he patted her briefly on the shoulder, before standing up and moving slowly away.

"Yes, you really are quite content here, aren't you Nan? You never dream of moving on to something more exciting – expensive clothes, servants, a car, jewels or furs, do you?"

"Servants, jewels! What would I do with them, Charlie? People like you and me aren't meant for that sort of life, are we?"

"That's just it, Nan! Why should we have to scrimp and scrape all our lives, just because that's the world we were brought up in? Who knows, I might have come from anything, mightn't I? My parents could have been from the gentry for all I know!

"I want more out of life than being a farm labourer, I can tell you! And to get more, I've got to take a few chances! Don't you see, Nan? That's part of it – the thrill of taking a few risks in the hope of getting a bit more out of life!"

Nan shook her head firmly as she started to clear the table. Once again she was seeing a side of Charlie that she did not like or understand. "I think you're mad, Charlie. Endangering what we've got for ourselves and the girls, just for the excitement and some sort of ridiculous dream of riches that will never come true. For goodness sake come down to earth and make up your mind that this is the real world. Be grateful for what we've got. We've so much compared to some."

"Grateful! Grateful! You sound like those Holy Joes back in the orphanage! Well, I'm sorry, Nan, but there's got to be more to life than this. Otherwise those years in that hell-hole out in France just weren't worth it! I'm going for a drink, so don't wait up!" and he flung out of the front door.

Nan said no more about the doctor's warning, but it hung over her like a shadow. Charlie was back to his usual cheerful self the next day and life went on in its accustomed pattern. Eventually, as Nan saw no evidence of any extra income, she began to hope that Charlie had heeded the doctor's words.

However, in July her blissful ignorance was rudely shattered. She was expecting Ruby for the day on the twins' first birthday and had planned an outing for them all to Niagara Falls. Charlie had arranged to borrow the farm cart and Nan decided to take a big picnic. They had acquired a second-hand twin pram to take the babies out for walks, and Joan would perch in the middle if her legs grew tired.

Then on the morning of the proposed outing Nan woke up, aching all over, with a headache and a sore throat. By the time she had packed the food and Ruby had arrived from town, Nan was feeling worse every minute.

"You look awful, Nan. Must be this twenty four hour flu that's going around. Some of the girls in the shop have had it. I suppose that means our trip to Niagara is off? Shame – I was really looking forward to crossing the border and saying I'd been to America!"

"No need for you all to stay home because of me!" Nan sank wearily into the armchair. "The food's packed ready and the twins' feeds are made up. You and Charlie can take them if you don't mind managing without me?"

"'Course we can manage, girl! You get up to bed and take it easy. Do you good to have a day to yourself. I'll make us a hot meal when we get back, don't you worry." Charlie put his arm round Nan and dropped a kiss on her cheek. Relieved not to be spoiling everyone else's day out, she watched as Charlie stowed the twin pram with sleeping twins safely on the back of the cart and settled Ruby on some cushions beside it. Joan was perched beside him on the driver's seat, and with a cheerful wave, he drove away down the lane.

Nan made a cup of tea, laced with lemon and honey, and then dragged herself upstairs to bed. She quickly dropped into a deep sleep and the day was practically over before she woke again. Vaguely she was aware of the sound of the cart drawing up outside and then the chatter of Joan's high-pitched tones, mingling with the laughter of Ruby and Charlie. Nan still felt very groggy and allowed herself to stay put, secure in the knowledge that Charlie had promised to deal with everything.

When next she woke it was to hear him tiptoeing downstairs, so she guessed that the children must have all been settled for the night. She was feeling hot and sticky after being in bed all day, but the headache had abated somewhat, although her throat was still sore. She decided she would feel better for a good wash, and then a soothing cold drink.

There was a slight breeze coming through the open window and she slipped out of bed to close it. As she moved through the dusky room she heard the front door open below. She guessed it was probably Charlie making ready to drive Ruby back to Welland. About to draw the curtains, thinking she might call down to say goodbye to her sister, and assure them she was awake if the children should need anything in Charlie's absence, she was prevented from speaking by Ruby's voice floating up.

"Oh, Charlie, you are terrible! I thought I should die when they stopped us coming back across the border! Suppose they found out what you were doing? You'd do time for it wouldn't you? I mean smuggling's bad enough, but moonshine as well!" Ruby's admiring giggle exploded before turning into a fit of tipsy hiccoughs.

Charlie gave a low chuckle, as he hoisted his sister-in-law up on to the driver's seat. "I thought you were going to pass out after we'd gone across the border and I told you where I'd put the hooch. White as a sheet you went! Just as well I didn't tell you first, or you'd have given us away for sure!"

"When I think it was me that was pushing the pram though, Charlie! I could have been done as an accomplice! You really are a mad devil!" Ruby swayed dangerously in another fit of intoxicated giggling and Charlie put his arm round her to hold her close against his side, as he set the horse in motion.

Nan sat down stiffly on the bed, and shivered in spite of the balmy night. So Charlie was smuggling, and what was worse, it was illicit alcohol that he was taking across the border to the United States, where it was banned by the Prohibition laws. So he was committing two crimes in one!

And what had Ruby meant, when she had been talking about pushing the pram, as though that made her an accessory? Nan felt suddenly sick. Of course! The lumbering old bassinet had a deep well beneath its removable mattress, intended for storing items of baby's clothing or bottles. Charlie had indeed used it for bottles – bottles of illicit whisky that he was selling against the law in America. It would be a very hard-hearted customs officer who would want to disturb two sleeping babies, wouldn't it? The sheer audacity of the scheme was typically Charlie!

How he must have enjoyed telling Ruby that she had been pushing a pram of moonshine all unwittingly over the border! And of course Ruby would be stupid enough to show him she admired his devil-may-care ways. She would make him feel that he was doing something exciting and praiseworthy in breaking the law in such an audacious fashion!

Nan's head started to pound again and her stomach churned with fury as she thought of the heedless way Charlie was risking the home and security of his wife and three daughters. How could he be so irresponsible?

When Charlie finally returned it was past midnight and Nan was waiting for him, wrapped in a blanket in the old armchair. He was only slightly drunk when he walked through the door, but there was a jaunty swagger to his step and a big grin on his face.

"Hello, Nan. Didn't expect to find you up at this hour. Feeling better are you, sweetheart?"

"Don't you 'sweetheart' me! You selfish, criminal pig! How dare you defile our babies' pram with your filthy goings-on! How could you treat your own daughters as a way of making your dishonest money? I would never have believed it of you, Charlie. You're scum, you are! You're less than the dust and I'm ashamed to call you their father!"

Charlie swayed slightly as her hoarse voice fell silent. His black eyes glittered dangerously as she stared accusingly at him. Then he said softly, "I suppose you heard that loud-mouthed sister of yours? Well, now you know."

"Yes, now I know. I know just what a worthless, crooked no-good I married. My sister may think you're some sort of heroic criminal mastermind, but I think you're pathetic and cheap and I wish I'd never set eyes on you."

"Right, well we know where we stand, don't we? Let me tell you something now, Nan. It's entirely mutual. Because you are nothing but a millstone round my neck, d'you know that? You and those precious daughters you're so proud of. I must have been mad getting tangled up with you and landing myself with a parcel of kids. Daughters too! You haven't even given me a son I might have taken a bit of joy in! Three bloody daughters, who

136

will no doubt grow up to be just as virtuous as their working-class boring mother!

"I was a fool, Nan. I should have enjoyed what you were so eager to offer that summer and then left you to face the music on your own. Plenty of others have done it before me. But no. I had to be so gallant, the big romantic who wanted to do the right thing by the woman he loved!

"Look where it got me. A run-down cottage in the back of beyond with four mouths to feed. And a wife who is so busy being the perfect mother, she can't even make time to keep her old man happy between the sheets! Too superior to enjoy a bit of fun any more, Nan? So worried about your 'principles' you daren't bend the rules and get any thrill out of life. Look in the mirror sometime and d'you know who you'll see? Emily Fisher, that's who. Because you are turning into your own mother before my eyes, and it's not a pretty sight, I can tell you!

"Well don't worry, Nan. I lost interest in you some time ago. You see you've lost your looks, you've lost your sense of fun and you are totally boring as far as I'm concerned. So I shan't be begging for your marital favours any more. I don't need to, because there are plenty of others out there only too eager and willing to climb into bed with Charlie Stuart. I can have my pick, darlin'. And if you really want to know, they enjoy spending my ill-gotten gains with me, even if you're too high and mighty to want a share in them."

Nan could feel the tears trickling slowly down her cheeks as Charlie faced her silently across the kitchen and then turned and flung out of the house slamming the door violently in his wake. The cottage shook and simultaneously she heard Joan's voice calling "Mummy! Mummy!" as the twins both burst into a wailing chorus. Feeling as though the weight of the world had just fallen on to her shoulders, she pulled the blanket tightly round her and moved slowly towards the staircase calling "It's all right, Mummy's coming," as she did so.

It was almost dawn before Nan finally managed to get some sleep, and the twins had her awake again before seven. She felt like a zombie as she automatically coped with the morning chores around the cottage. She wondered where Charlie had spent the night. Perhaps he had gone back to Welland into the bed of one of those women who he was sure would be so welcoming. Strangely Nan felt quite unmoved at the prospect.

It seemed that yesterday's revelation about his criminal activities, combined with the painful reproaches he had flung at her, had numbed all her feelings about him. Now, she merely wondered how she might pick up the pieces of their lives, and how she could be sure that the children's future was safe. At times during the day she feared that he might have left for good, but she forced herself to act normally in front of the little ones, and prepare the evening meal as usual.

Sure enough, at his regular hour, Charlie appeared in the doorway. He nodded unspeaking to Nan and stooped down to Joan who ran towards him and clasped his knees in her customary affectionate greeting. Nan thought bitterly that her daughter was like all the other females, totally beguiled by Charlie's superficial charm. She watched as he swung Joanie up in the air, calling her "Daddy's favourite girl," and then pulled a brightly coloured top out of his pocket.

"There you are, sweetheart, see what Daddy's brought you!" He strolled across to the twins sitting up in their pram by the window, and from his other pocket produced two rag dolls, which he placed in their chubby hands.

"See, Daddy's got something for all his little treasures. That's what money's for – spending and making you happy!" He stroked the identical blonde heads and bent down to help Joan spin the top. Nan could feel the colour rising in her face, furious that he was using the children to get back at her and her "principles".

Silently she dished up their dinner and occupied herself helping Joan with her food. The little girl chattered away in the silence between her parents, and the twins gurgled happily. When the meal was over Charlie washed and changed out of his working clothes and without a word walked out of the house. And that set the pattern for the weeks ahead.

The only words they spoke to each other were those of basic necessity. They shared the same bed still, but Nan would keep as far to her side as possible, tensing herself whenever Charlie turned over in his sleep, for fear he might touch her. The thought of any physical contact now was totally abhorrent to her. The wounding phrases he had spoken still rang round in her head, and the knowledge that he had involved his own children in his criminal activities brought terrible anguish to Nan's romantic soul.

For beneath her practical, domestic self she was still a romantic. She had idolised this handsome lover who had come into her life with his humour and passion and swept her away from her mundane upbringing to this new world. She had adored him for the new freedom he had given her and for being instrumental in providing the happy life in this clean country with its wide space and wonderful fresh air. Now, to find that what had been so perfect for her had become some sort of stifling prison for him, was quite shattering for Nan.

She continued to work as a good housewife and mother, but her spirit was blighted and it felt as though a lead weight was pressing down on her heart. The hardest part was finding she still cared about Charlie.

In spite of everything, when she watched him playing with the girls, revelling in their innocent, uncritical affection, she saw again the Charlie of their early courting days. The lover who would swing her off the ground in a sudden passionate embrace, just as he would whirl Joan above his head and make her shriek for more.

Then Nan's traitorous body ached to feel his touch that was capable of arousing such overpowering sensuality. But she dreaded his making any sexual overtures. Her own "principles" she knew would resurface and she would utterly reject a man who had boasted of other women, and who had treated his family so irresponsibly. For if she once accepted him again, in her own eyes it would be tantamount to approving his behaviour, and that she could never do.

It was a golden September day when matters finally reached their inevitable conclusion. Nan had been desperate to get out for a while and decided to take a walk with the children. There was a small pond in the woods not far from the cottage, along a path worn through the trees by the deer. It was a favourite treat of Joan's to be allowed to dangle her toes in the water and fish for tiddlers with a stick, piece of string and a crust of bread. So Nan decided to spend the afternoon there.

The twins now both walked, albeit rather unsteadily, so she let them toddle about, each on a pair of reins, having parked the pram in the shade of a large pine. After a while Joan tired of sitting still and wandered off, collecting cones. Preoccupied suddenly with Rita who had wobbled over a fallen branch and managed to send Irene flying at the same time, causing them both to set up a wail, Nan's attention was distracted from Joan for some minutes.

When she did look round, the little girl had disappeared. "Joan! Joanie! Where are you love?" Total silence greeted Nan's cries, and suddenly her heart missed a beat. Frantically she swept up the twins and thrust them into the pram, all the time scanning the edges of the lake. Surely if Joan had fallen into the water, Nan would have heard a splash, or a cry of panic? Desperately her eyes searched the area, and she spied a narrow track a few yards round the lake, which lead into the forest.

Dear God, don't let her have gone far! Shouting her daughter's name ever more urgently, her voice beginning to crack with fear, she thrust the pram before her along the overgrown path, mowing down the bracken and bouncing it over fallen branches as she did so. It seemed an eternity, but was only a matter of moments when round a bend ahead of her she espied a tiny figure running along, gurgling with delight at this game of "chase".

Nan stopped. Aware of a stitch in her side and a heart that was pounding loudly in her ears as she felt suddenly faint. The path was straight now, so she was able to keep Joan in sight as she continued on her way, and pause to calm herself. When Joan realised she was no longer being pursued, she slowed down and began to pick up interesting looking flowers or bits of mossy twigs that caught her fancy.

Nan was glad to stay beneath the cool shade as she gradually recovered from her panic. The twins were looking drowsy, so she settled them more comfortably in the pram for their nap. About to call Joan and tell her they must start back, she suddenly noticed through the foliage ahead a small wooden shack. Joan had also seen it, and with her usual insatiable curiosity was trotting forward to explore.

Nan followed her and they came into a clearing. It was just a one-storied structure, which looked very run-down. Nan thought it must have belonged to a woodsman at one time. There was a well to one side and a pile of logs, but the grass was overgrown around it and some of the nearby saplings practically obscured the grimy windows. She was about to call to Joan, who was following the outline of a barely discernible path to the front door, when the sight of some smoke curling out of the chimney made Nan realise that it was inhabited after all.

Leaving the pram, she swiftly caught up with her daughter, before she could trespass any further on what must be someone's property. The little girl was practically at the door, and as Nan scooped her up a sound reached them through the crack where it had been left unfastened.

For a moment Nan did not recognise it – fleetingly she thought it the sound of a creature in pain. Then as it became louder, it was like an echo from her own past. She saw again the two figures entwined and tumbling among the covers on Mrs Leigh's bed on a sultry afternoon so similar to this. She heard again her panting moans as Charlie had introduced her to the delights and demands of her own body. She heard her own voice echoed by the one that pleaded now in her ears, "Oh yes, Charlie! Please, oh please! Charlie please ..."

Unthinking, she slowly pushed the door wider and for a second that seemed eternity gazed into the dimness of the room. Her peripheral vision took in the paraphernalia of the still which was causing the smoke she had seen, as it produced the moonshine for smuggling into America. But her whole being was focussed on the tableau spread out on the pile of old blankets in front of the fireplace.

The two naked forms were so tightly inter-linked that it was hard to make sense of their tangled limbs. Just individual impressions forced themselves on Nan's vision, to resurface in her nightmares and her waking thoughts at odd intervals for the rest of her life.

Charlie's muscular back, tanned from long hours labouring at the harvest patterned now with scratches from the strawberry-red finger nails presently being raked across it. The white scar on his leg livid in a ray of sunshine lancing through the gloom. His damp black curls tumbling between the creamy white breasts tipped with hard crimson. That other face above him, bent backward in the triumphant peak of ultimate orgasmic pleasure, a frown of concentrated delight visible beneath the glittering tumble of auburn ringlets.

Then Ruby opened her eyes. And saw ... "Nan!"

"Daddy! It's my Daddy," Joan struggled to clamber out of her mother's arms as she recognised the face of the man who stared in shock across the room.

"Don't call him that, Joanie. He's not fit to bear the title."

Her body encased in ice, her face a mask of betrayal and hatred, Nan turned and walked steadily down the track to the pram. Ignoring Joan's pleas to "go back and play with Daddy and Auntie," Nan placed her unceremoniously in the middle of the pram, and thrust hard against the handle to propel it through the trampled undergrowth back to the lake and the main path.

The rest of that day passed in a haze of agony and disbelief. She had long ago suspected that Charlie was being unfaithful to her, but her own sister! How could Ruby? The little girl that Nan had mothered and looked out for when they were both youngsters. The disgraced woman to whom Nan had given shelter when her own parents wanted nothing to do with her. Betrayal by the two people who should have cared for her more than anyone else – Nan's mind was unable to grasp the appalling reality.

When the time came and went for Charlie's arrival from work, Nan knew quite definitely that she would never live under the same roof with him again. But she would make sure he took full responsibility for his three children. Oh yes! She would confront him if necessary in front of witnesses and demand he pay for their food and clothes. With all his ill-gotten gains to spend on his tart, he shouldn't mind spending his legal wages on his family, thought Nan bitterly.

It was getting dark and she was bolting the front door when she heard footsteps outside. She had put the chain on, and stood silent when she heard Charlie's voice.

"Open this door, Nan. I've got to come in and I've no time to waste arguing with you."

"You'll never set foot in here again, Charlie Stuart. I won't have my babies under the same roof with you! I'll see Mr Gilmour tomorrow and tell him so. You can sleep in a barn for all I care! He's a decent man, he'll make sure I get the wages you earn, to take care of the girls."

"Open this door, Nan! I mean it. I'm a desperate man tonight!" There was a note in his voice that was new to Nan. He did indeed sound desperate and she backed away from the door in sudden fear. Unthinkingly she picked up the poker from the fireplace and then moved to stand before the foot of the stairs.

The sudden shocking noise of Charlie's boot assaulting the lock rent the stillness of the night. The timber shattered and he surged into the room. His breath came fast and his flushed face terrified her with its maniacal glare as he strode towards her.

"Get out of my way, woman! I've no time to waste listening to your whining."

"You're not going near my babies!" Nan barred the foot of the staircase, poker raised threateningly. Charlie snorted derisively, feinted to one side and then grabbed Nan's wrist, twisting it violently so that the poker clattered to the floor. When she attempted to struggle with him, he wrenched her arm back brutally and tossed her carelessly to one side, so that she tripped and struck her head on the corner of the table.

The room swirled blackly about her as she hit the floor, and lay semi-conscious for several minutes. She was vaguely aware of Charlie's hasty footsteps overhead, pulling out drawers and slamming cupboards, heedless of the crying twins and Joan's shouts of panic at the noise. As Nan attempted to sit up, he ran swiftly downstairs, still pushing some clothes into a bag. He went to pick up the old tea caddy from the mantelpiece where Nan kept her housekeeping, and emptied the contents into his pocket.

He paused fleetingly before stepping over her upturned face on his way out. "I'm off now, Nan, and this is the last you'll see of me. You'll be glad to know the customs men are on to me and the police will be out looking for me soon. I've no intention of being caught and put away for a long stretch in one of their stinking gaols!"

"Oh, and by the way, you won't be seeing any more of your dear sister, either. Unlike you, Ruby sticks with a man she loves, whatever he does. She's waiting for me back in Welland and we're leaving tonight. Don't expect to hear from either of us again. But I don't suppose you'll mourn our going, will you?

"Take my advice and go back to Holgate where you belong. Living out your life in that dead-end slum is all you're good for. If you're lucky you'll find a nice, respectable, boring feller to share your bed and bring up my daughters! Good luck to you all! If that's the life you want, then may you all rot there, along with your sanctimonious parents! Nice knowing you, Nan!"

With a bitter laugh that was a sad parody of his old cheeky self, he flung out of the shattered door and ran down the path. Then Nan heard the sound of hoofbeats dying away on the road to Welland.

Jessie Campbell poured out another cup of tea and pushed it across to Nan. It was the next afternoon and she was visiting the cottage. When she had arrived unannounced, Nan saw her as the answer to a prayer. The last twenty-four hours had been a sort of living nightmare that was sweeping her along in its tragic wake. The sight of a caring face was like a light in the darkness.

Jessie had gathered Nan in a close embrace and held her tightly without speaking. Then she had settled her in the armchair, bustling about chattering to Joan and the twins and making sure they were safely occupied out of earshot in the front garden, but still in view, before she sat down herself, opposite Nan.

"Before you say anything, lassie, let me tell you what I know. When I was doing my morning cleaning job at the shop, I overheard several of the girls there gossiping away over the latest juicy scandal. When I heard your sister's name mentioned, you can guess I pricked up my ears!

"So I heard that she had been carrying on, no better than she should be, for some time with a married fellow. But that now she's landed herself in real trouble because he'd been found out as a smuggler of moonshine and was on the run from the police. Apparently she had packed her bags and gone off with him late last night! Was bragging before she went that he had plenty of money from poker games he'd been playing with other low life scoundrels, and was going to take her off to a life of luxury!"

"Much good may his filthy money do her!" Nan's lips twisted in a bitter smile as she gazed into her teacup. "He's so wealthy he had to rob his wife of her last bit of housekeeping money before he left. So she hasn't a penny piece to buy food for his children's dinner tomorrow!" Suddenly the hopelessness of the whole sordid situation overcame Nan, and she dropped her cup, buried her head in her hands and howled.

For long minutes Jessie cradled her, murmuring sympathetic endearments, before offering a spotless handkerchief. "That's it, my dearie. You let it all out, and you'll be the better for it. The life that swine has led you these last months! Oh, aye, I've heard tales of his goings on – drinking and poker playing and enjoying himself with every bar-room tart that throws herself at him. Him, with three lovely bairns and a good wife who keeps his home spotless and always a fine meal on the table. What excuse anyone could find for him, I'd like to know!"

"Oh, Jessie it's been so dreadful! I had the police here searching for him first thing this morning. I think they believed me when I said I knew nothing of his plans, but they searched the house anyway. They'd already been to the shack in the woods where he kept the whiskey still. It seems that someone had tipped them off about it. But one of his friends at the pub managed to warn him in time, so he got away.

"I still can't believe he could be so stupid, to risk everything we've got here. But of course he obviously doesn't value this very highly."

She smiled sadly at Jessie. "I've been such a fool, Jessie. I love this little cottage and living out here in the country. It can be hard work, but it's all so rewarding. Seeing the girls growing up in the good, clean air – remembering how

148

different my own childhood was back in Holgate – I wanted nothing more. But Charlie wasn't satisfied. I knew that a long time ago, I think, but I kept hoping he'd settle down eventually ..."

"He's a wicked, ungrateful fool, Nan. You're worth a dozen of him. He doesn't know what he's thrown away. Now he'll be spending his life on the run from the law, and ten to one he'll get into more trouble and end up in prison sooner or later. And that hussy will bring him no comfort, that I do know!"

"But Jessie, what am I going to do now? Mr Gilmour will have to turn us out of the cottage, to make room for whoever he takes on instead of Charlie. How can I look after the girls? I won't be able to rent anywhere for us, with no wages coming in, let alone find the money to feed and clothe them. Dear God, I'm so scared for my babies! What will become of them?" and Nan dissolved once more into heart-rending sobs.

"Now, you listen to me Nan Stuart. You're a strong woman and you'll manage somehow, that I do know. For a start you can go and speak to the Gilmours this afternoon, whilst I mind the bairns for you. Best take the bull by the horns. From what I've heard he's a good, upright man, not one to throw a helpless woman and three young ones out on the street. So go and wash your face and brush your hair, and get yourself up to the farmhouse and sort it out with him. Hold you head high, Nan. You've done nothing to be ashamed of, and don't you forget it!"

Nan nodded, her natural resilience at last asserting itself. Just to hear encouraging words from someone she knew was on her side and cared about her, made all the difference. So as Jessie suggested, she tidied herself up and set off to the farmhouse along the lane.

An hour later it was a much brighter Nan that returned to find Jessie giving the twins their baths whilst Joan sat at the table eating bread and milk.

"Jessie, you were quite right. Mr and Mrs Gilmour were really kind and understanding. He said he will have to take the cottage off me for his new worker, but he offered me somewhere else as a roof over our heads. Apparently he was looking at the woodsman's old shack this morning, when he went there with the police to dismantle the still, and says that we are welcome to live in it.

"Of course it's only small and not very convenient, no running water – just the well – but he says he'll get one of his men to see the roof isn't leaking and cut back the undergrowth away from the path, so it's easy for me to get up to the lane with the pram. He'll send a cart for me to take all our bits over there next week, when it's ready. There's a piece of land around the shack that I can turn over to some vegetables if I want to, so we should be quite snug there.

"Mrs Gilmour was really nice too. She said I can go and do some cleaning at the farm a few hours each week and help with the laundry, so I'll be earning a few bob to buy some food. I can take the girls with me when I go and let them play with her own children. Oh, Jessie people are so generous sometimes!"

"There, didn't I say you'd manage? I'll get my man to come over when you're ready to move out, and he'll do all the shifting for you. My eldest, Tom, can come with him and they'll make short work of it. Don't worry, lassie, it'll all turn out just fine. You'll be better off without that swine, see if you're not!"

For a while Nan believed that Jessie's words had come true. It did seem that her life was gradually falling into some sort of normal routine again. And at least she was in charge and could make the decisions she thought were best for herself and her daughters.

It was a terrible wrench to move out of Maple Cottage, which she had come to love dearly. She had taken such a pride in keeping it clean and the garden neat, and now it would go to strangers. When the cart, overflowing with her bits and pieces of furniture and various bags and boxes of possessions, finally lumbered along the newly cleared track from the lane and halted before the shack, Nan was overcome for a moment by a wave of panic.

She relived the awful instant when she had last been here and peered through the door at her husband and sister. Bile rose in her throat and for a moment she was unable to force her limbs to move. But then Joan was wriggling to get down from Nan's grasp, and she found herself moving towards the front door. The interior of the shack was bare and had been swept clean. There was no sign of the still. It was obvious that a few repairs had been carried out on the roof. A pane of glass had been replaced in one of the windows and the undergrowth around had been cut back.

Mr Campbell and Tom quickly unloaded everything and placed the various items where Nan requested. The shack consisted of only one room plus a small lean-to scullery, so it seemed very crowded by the time they had installed Nan's double bed, Joan's little truckle bed and the twin's large cot. Add to that table, chairs, a wardrobe and two chests of drawers and there was scarcely room to move.

By the time Nan had made up the beds and unpacked enough household items to get the children a meal, she was already exhausted. Fortunately they all three were tired and ready for bed, so she was able to take her time during the evening unpacking clothes and all the rest of the household paraphernalia. With only the well for water, life was going to be more difficult, having to carry buckets back and forth for all their washing and cooking. The lighting was by oil lamps, so she would have to be frugal in their use, since oil cost money.

Fortunately she had quite a few stores put by in the way of produce that she had grown and preserved, and Mr Gilmour told her she was welcome to any milk she wanted from the farm, but of course there were plenty of other items that she had to buy in Welland.

Looking round the overcrowded shack that night, Nan made up her mind to be ruthless and sell off whatever items she could manage without. The money was needed and so was the space.

Her own bed could go for a start – she would have a mattress on the floor. The twins were getting too big for their cot, so they too could share a mattress. These could be piled against the wall during the day to make more space for the children to move about. Nan spent quite a time going through all her belongings and made a list of what she might sell. Her immediate objective must be to keep the children warm and fed and to look no further than that.

The first weeks in the shack she worked from dawn till dusk getting the place as comfortable as possible. She thoroughly cleaned the interior and then dug over a small patch outside ready for spring planting. Mr Gilmour allowed her the use of the cart once more, with Tom Campbell in attendance, so that she could take her surplus belongings into Welland to sell them off.

Whilst there, with the money at her disposal, she stocked up as much as possible on items in readiness for the winter. Mr Gilmour had offered that any future supplies she needed he would get one of his men to purchase whenever they were going into the town, so she felt that her life was now reasonably well organised.

It was certainly a lot harder work living in the shack. Looking after the children with no running water was not easy by any means. The effort of walking with them up to the farmhouse several times a week to carry out her duties, and then facing the long walk back pushing the pram with all of them piled into it, was quite overwhelming at times. When one of the twins was fretful or Joan being particularly mischievous, there were many times when Nan was reduced to tears herself.

At nights she would wearily unfold her mattress and roll herself in blankets on the floor, utterly exhausted mentally and physically. But she kept going and was buoyed up whenever she looked at the girls' healthy faces and sturdy bodies.

On the days when she was not needed at the farmhouse she spent hours gathering wood and chopping it up ready for the onset of winter, which was nearly upon them. It was something she dreaded, for remembering how bitter it had been in the relative comfort of the cottage, the prospect of coping in the draughty shack in the depths of the woods was a frightening prospect. Still she had a good stock of kindling piled by the back door and had searched the building high and low for any cracks and crannies that would let in the cold, duly stopping them up as best she could. So she was as prepared as possible to meet the force of the Canadian winter.

At first it was almost invigorating when she confronted the challenge of the first snowfalls. Each morning she would be up at dawn, energetically clearing the pathway from the back door to the earth closet. Then on the days when she was expected at the farm she would be out with the spade making a pathway for the pram along the track to the lane. The children adored the snow, and were always eager to play in it, but it was an ongoing battle to get their clothes dried off when they came back inside.

It seemed that fate was on her side to start with, and although there were some heavy snowfalls, there was little wind so she had no big drifts to clear. She never missed a day working at the farm before Christmas and managed to get a few bits and pieces together as cheap gifts for the children. She picked up a fallen branch from one of the firs and planted it in a pot and they decorated it with coloured paper for a Christmas tree. Mrs Gilmour gave her one or two discarded baubles to brighten it up and Nan cut out a cardboard star for the top.

Mr Gilmour kept any mail for her that was still addressed to Maple cottage, so there were cards from one or two friends in Welland and some from England. She had not yet had the courage to write and tell Emily what had happened between Ruby and Charlie. It was a bitter enough pill having to write that he had abandoned them and was wanted by the law, let alone admitting his affair with her sister.

Emily's reply after Nan had told her about the change in her circumstances was predictably in the vein of "I told you the sort of layabout you were marrying, but you wouldn't listen – you've made your bed, etc, etc." However Nan managed to remain optimistic in her own letters, glossing over the problems of living in the shack, praising the Gilmours for their kindness and describing the healthy progress the girls were all making.

It was only two months into 1922 when catastrophe struck once again. On the day that Nan woke to a howling gale and steadily falling snow, Joan informed her that her throat hurt and both the twins were flushed and fretful. Touching all three Nan could tell they were running high temperatures and it was obvious they were going down with some sort of flu bug. There was no way she could risk taking them out to the farm, so she had to miss her work.

The next few days were a nightmare for Nan. The only medicine she possessed was the few herbal remedies that she stored from her garden at the cottage. She knew it was important to try and keep the temperature of all three children as low as possible, which meant endlessly sponging them down with tepid water and trying to persuade them to drink as much as possible. Since every drop of water had to be fetched from the well, it seemed that Nan was making interminable trips outside.

Each time she did so, it involved bundling herself up in all her outer clothing and then, as the wind seemed non-stop, clearing a path through the drifting snow on every successive trip to the well. In after years, remembering that time, Nan herself marvelled at how she managed to keep going.

Fortunately, like most healthy children, the girls were very resilient. After three days of being really ill, on the next they were almost back to normal. Suddenly they were all hungry and longing to get outside, chafing at their enforced seclusion in the shack. By this time Nan was shocked to find that the few days that she had not been able to get along the track meant that it was blocked by huge drifts of snow. The wind had dropped by then, but the temperature had also plummeted, so that thick icicles festooned the roof and all the snowdrifts were frozen solid.

It took Nan an enormous amount of effort to reach the well and free the handle and rope on which she lowered her bucket. There was no way she could possibly clear the path up to the lane in these conditions, so she accepted that for the time being they were snowbound. It was a frightening thought, but Nan told herself to keep calm and just wait it out.

"You've plenty of kindling left, there are still stores in the cupboard and at least the girls are all on the mend. So you've just got to be patient," she told herself. But it was not easy, and over the next week became increasingly difficult.

It was terribly hard to keep the children happy and occupied in the enforced confinement, the temperature was so low it would have been impossible to take them outside. Even with the fire banked high and all of them wearing several layers of clothing they seemed to constantly shiver and Nan was at her wit's end devising games that involved them keeping active so that they kept as warm as possible.

With each day the wood pile was dwindling and she was terrified that it would run out before she was able to replenish it. She agonised over each stick she put on the fire, but when Joan would whimper, "I'm cold, Mummy, my toes aren't there any more," she would be impelled to build up a bigger blaze.

Looking out of the window on each successive morning, she hoped she might see another human being approaching. Surely the Gilmours must realise her plight? Why didn't they send some help? It seemed inconceivable that she had been totally abandoned with her babies!

When the last few sticks of kindling were brought inside to build up the fire for the night, Nan looked about her desperately and decided she must sacrifice anything else that was burnable. She took her wood chopper and in a sudden frenzy smashed up the table and chairs, carefully hoarding every last scrap of wood from them. The children were all huddled together on one mattress in an effort to keep them warmer and gazed wide-eyed at this scene of destruction.

Nan was crying quietly as she crawled in beside them and gathered them close in an effort to provide extra warmth from her own body. From nervous exhaustion she fell into a deep sleep and it was morning when she awoke to the thunderous sound of knocking on the front door.

Wrapping herself in a quilt, she dragged back the stiff bolts. Even whilst she did so she was aware of the drip-drip of snow thawing off the roof. Outside Mr Campbell stood with his son Tom, both swathed in layers of heavy coats and wearing snowshoes.

"Mr Campbell! Oh, I'm so thankful to see you!" Nan tried hard to hold back the tears of relief.

"All right, lassie, the Campbells are come to your rescue!" He and Tom unloaded bundles of wood from their backs and took off their snowshoes. Behind them she could see a path had been cleared through the huge snowdrift, so that it was now possible to get up to the lane.

"How are you all doing, then? Jessie's been real worried about you, but we thought the farmer would have sent someone to make sure you had enough supplies. It was only this morning we heard the news about him and his family."

"What news? Has something happened?" Nan realised it must be something bad from the sad expression on his face.

"Aye, lassie, I fear so. It seems that they had all gone to visit friends near Niagara and had an accident in their motor car. It skidded on the icy road and overturned into a ravine. All four of them were killed outright. It's a terrible tragedy, especially when you think of the poor bairns!"

"Oh, no!" Nan felt sick as she thought of those two kind people and their small children all wiped out at one tragic stroke of fate. She felt even worse when she recalled her own uncharitable thoughts about them over the last few days, when she believed that they had abandoned her uncaringly to her fate in the shack.

"Aye, it's an awful thing to happen. So with everyone at the farm trying to get in touch with the Gilmour's relatives and keep the place working, you completely slipped their minds. With people snowed in around the town, it was only

158

yesterday Jessie and I heard what had happened and she's been worrying herself sick all night, thinking of you and the girls cut off here, all alone!"

"Thank God for friends like you and Jessie, Mr Campbell! You've certainly saved our lives this time!"

The two men stayed for the rest of the day and by the time they left, Nan felt a different woman. They had chopped another huge pile of firewood and the three children had been able to play outside as the temperature was so much warmer. Nan cleared up the inside of the shack and took stock of what she needed in the way of supplies. While she worked she thought over her own situation in the light of what had happened to the Gilmours.

Until new people moved into the farmhouse she would have no-one to give her any work, so for the time being no wages would be coming in. She counted the pitifully small store of coins in the old tea caddy and then sorted out her few items of jewellery. Finally she drew off her wedding ring. Before he left she spoke to Jock Campbell.

"I've made a list here of the items I shall need from town, and I'd be very grateful if you could buy them and get them out to me in a day or so. At the same time, I'd be glad if you'd take these bits and pieces of trinkets and sell them for me. I don't suppose they're worth more than pennies, but my wedding ring should fetch something. I'd really appreciate it if you'd do this for me, Mr Campbell."

"Why lassie, it seems awful hard, you having to sell your wedding ring for food. I just wish Jessie and me could help you out, but you know we only just keep our own heads above water, with the rent to pay and the bairns to feed and clothe …"

"Oh, please Mr Campbell! I'm so grateful for all you've done, no friends could have been better than you and Jessie! Besides, my wedding ring has no sentimental value for me now. It only reminds me of the man who betrayed me and my children, and left us to starve for all he knows or cares! If it can put food in our mouths then at least it's doing something useful."

"Aye, I can understand your bitterness, lassie. You can be sure I'll get the best price I can." He patted her arm kindly and she felt a lump in her throat as the two good men plodded away in the now slushy snow.

There was no further news for the next few weeks from the farm. The Campbells would make a trip out to the shack every so often to undertake any shopping Nan needed, but this was less and less as her money dwindled and she strove to eke out the provisions she had stored away. It seemed the farm was going to be sold off by the Gilmour's next of kin, so until there were new owners, Nan could not offer her services.

She became thinner with each passing day as she endeavoured to eat as little as possible to save what food she had for the children. There had been no more heavy snow, but the previous falls had not all melted as the temperatures remained low. Still at least the children could get some exercise outside, which was good for their health, but unfortunately increased their appetites. Nan longed for the spring when she might walk into Welland herself and endeavour to search for work there. Although the chances of finding a job where she might live in with three children did not seem likely.

The future seemed increasingly bleak. After the long, exhausting months of winter, Nan's own reserves of strength, mental and physical, were terribly depleted. It was in the first week of March that matters came to their shocking climax.

The day had been a lot warmer and the snow was really thawing at last. The shack roof was almost bare again and outside the path was practically clear of its white blanket. Nan had been thinking about the spring planting and wondering how she could possibly afford to buy the seeds that she needed, which was just one more problem to add to the list. She resolved that the following day she would attempt the three mile walk into Welland as the roads must now be quite clear.

She could hear the wind rising as she put the children to bed, and rain was beginning to lash the windows. March was living up to its "mad" reputation she thought, and hoped the rain would have stopped by the morning.

The shack was dim in the fire's glow – oil was too expensive to burn in the lamp, unless she really needed the light – so there was little for Nan to do. She couldn't see to sew or write one of her rare letters home. In any case, she grudged the cost of a postage stamp nowadays. And her small store of books had long ago been sold off. As usual when she was unoccupied, she gazed into the fire and tried to see a way out of the terrible predicament she was now in. She must get a job to earn money to look after the children, but how could she work and take care of them at the same time?

Above the howling of the wind, she suddenly detected another sound which brought her head up as she strained her ears. Faintly she heard a voice calling her name. "Nan! Nan! Let me in for pity's sake!"

Was she having a nightmare – some sort of hallucination brought on by fatigue and hunger? Slowly Nan rose and approached the door. A terrible fear gripped her body and she longed with all her heart not to give entry to the owner of that voice which came once again, as she steeled herself to resist it.

"Nan! Don't leave me out here. I'm begging you! I need you Nan!"

Her hand reached out in spite of herself, to slowly unbolt the door and push it wide. Looking into the dark she saw nothing, and for a split second was certain her tired mind was playing tricks, and then a movement on the step drew her eyes downward. Looking like bundle of sodden rags, a form huddled there, motionless. Then a thin white hand reached out and grasped her skirt.

"Help me, Nan. Please, help me!"

The whirling, icy rain whipped into her face and galvanised her into activity. Bending she half-lifted, half-dragged the figure inside and deposited it in front of the fire. Struggling to close the door against the lashing wind, she turned and saw the upraised, tormented face of Ruby.

Before she could speak, the features contorted in anguish and her sister bent double as she moaned in agony. "Oh God, Nan! The pain! I can't stand it! You've got to help me!" As she moved in the firelight, Nan realised with deepening horror that her sister was heavily pregnant.

For long moments Nan stared, motionless. She did not need the broken murmurs of confession that Ruby made to her during the ensuing hours, to tell her the child about to come into the world was Charlie's.

Charlie who had deserted Ruby in some back-street hovel in a small town in the mid-West. Charlie who had run up debts and then, in an attempt to settle them, had lost and lost again, in poker games that he could not afford to play.

Charlie who had run away, to escape retribution from the gamblers to whom he owed a fortune, leaving Ruby practically penniless and pregnant with his child. Nan could only begin to guess at the terrible experiences of her younger sister as she sold all she possessed, including her pregnant body, in order to survive the long journey back to Canada and her only hope of sanctuary – Nan.

Throughout Ruby's labour Nan somehow forgot the pain of her sister's betrayal, and saw once again the little girl that she had always mothered. Ruby was delirious for much of the time, and Nan could tell she was running a high fever. After stripping off her wet garments she made the pathetic figure as comfortable as possible on her own mattress. She heated kettles of water in readiness and found some clean towels and tore up a sheet as an impromptu cover for the baby when it came.

The three children woke up from time to time when Ruby's cries became louder, so that in the end Nan gave her a folded handkerchief to bite down on, to try and muffle the noise, so they should not be frightened.

Nan herself, when she had time to think, was terrified. She had given birth three times so she knew what to do, but it was obvious from Ruby's stick-thin body and burning skin that she was very ill. The ordeal of walking from Welland and finding her way to the shack, after the new owners at Maple Cottage had told her of Nan's whereabouts, was the final breaking point for her exhausted frame.

Stumbling through the torrential rain, at times falling and losing consciousness where she fell, but then dragging herself onward by the animal instinct that guided her to Nan – it was all too much. The last weeks of little nourishment had already depleted what physical resources she possessed and this final horrific journey had brought on her confinement several weeks early.

Nan could do little to help, save bathe her face and hands and murmur words of encouragement. In the hour before dawn Ruby's agony reached its crescendo and with one last tormented scream that died away into a sighing moan, she gave birth to a daughter.

Nan took the tiny wrinkled form, which was crowned by a wisp of damp fluff, glistening red-gold in the firelight. Carefully she cleaned it and wrapped it before turning back to Ruby. As she laid the baby against its mother's breast, Ruby's sunken eyes opened slowly and she looked fleetingly into those of her daughter.

"She's lovely, isn't she Nan? D'you think she looks like me?" she managed to whisper.

"She looks just like you, love. She's got your colour hair, hasn't she?" Nan was conscious of the tears stealing down her own cheeks, as she watched Ruby's attempt at a smile fading away. Nan made her as comfortable as she could and then picked up the baby. It was so terribly tiny, and Nan watched the little body fearfully as it seemed to struggle for each breath, terrified it would never survive, having been born early after these last neglected weeks of pregnancy.

"You need more care than I can give you here, little one. I've got to get you to a hospital if you're going to have any chance at all." Nan rocked the pathetically small bundle despairingly. How could she leave Ruby, so terribly ill, and there were the girls to consider as well. For long moments Nan sat by the figure of her sister and was assailed by waves of panic.

What to do for the best? Dear God, help me to do the right thing, she prayed. Vaguely she noticed the first bird song outside as the fingers of the early light stole across the room. Then Ruby's eyes opened again and she looked straight at Nan.

Her voice was momentarily firmer as she said, "I'm sorry for what happened with Charlie, Nan. I truly am. But you will look after her won't you? Keep her like one of your own, please? You won't let her go to strangers, will you? Promise me?"

She attempted to brush Nan's hand feebly with her own, and Nan held it fast. The earlier heat had gone now, and the fingers were becoming icy, even as she grasped them with her own.

She knew there was no point in pretending to Ruby. So she laid the baby close beside her mother and rested Ruby's hand on the downy head.

"I promise you Ruby, I'll take care of her and she'll be a sister for my own three ..."

"Just like you've been to me, Nan. You always took care of me, didn't you?" The lips moved into a faint smile and then there was only silence as the eyes closed for the last time and the hand slipped away from the baby.

Stiffly Nan picked up her niece and wrapped the improvised shawl more tightly round her. The room was becoming lighter by the minute now, the wind was dying away and the rain no longer lashed the windows. Nan knew what she must do. Ruby was beyond her help, but her daughter must be saved, if Nan was to keep her promise.

Quietly she moved about the room, firstly covering Ruby's still form and then gathering items of clothing for the three girls and herself. She fashioned a body sling out of a folded sheet, to carry the baby. The last of the milk was heated on the fire and mixed with some bread for the children. When everything was in readiness she roused them one by one to dress and feed them.

When Joan questioned her about the still figure, she explained that auntie had come to visit them, but needed a sleep because she'd had a very long journey and was tired.

"But she's brought a new little sister for you to play with. So when you've all had your breakfast, we're going to leave auntie Ruby to have her sleep and we're going to take baby into the town to be looked after for a while at the hospital. She's very tiny you see, so she needs the nice doctors and nurses to make sure she's really well."

"But she is going to be our baby isn't she?" Joan asked anxiously as Nan pulled on her stout mittens and wound a scarf round her neck.

"Oh, yes, don't worry about that, my love. She's going to be our baby all right."

Nan tucked all three girls into the old pram which was sagging perilously these days after all its miles of bumping through snow and over fallen branches. Please don't fall apart before we get to Welland, Nan silently begged, as she pushed it through the open door. Close under her breasts there was the almost indiscernible weight of Ruby's daughter, where she had settled her in the sling, hoping that the warmth from her own body would be an extra protection.

Before closing the door she took a last fleeting glance at her sister's still form. It seemed almost an act of abandonment to leave her lying alone in the shack, but Nan knew that it was the baby who must be her first priority now. She firmly closed the door and pushed the old pram forward.

Her memory of that journey was very sketchy afterwards, and of course the girls were too young to remember anything of it in later years. She afterwards marvelled that she found the strength to make it as far as she did.

The heavy rain had turned the track into a quagmire and at one stage it had actually merged with the little stream which had become a raging torrent. Terrified that she and the pram might be swept away, Nan pushed it forward into the rushing water, bouncing it over submerged rocks and somehow gained the other side. There she paused, bent over, the air whistling in her exhausted lungs, legs trembling with exertion. Her head was swimming and when she looked up the tall shapes of the surrounding trees whirled alarmingly around her head.

Terrified that she might faint and damage the baby as she fell, she summoned her last reserves of strength and carried on. The track had never seemed so long and she felt that the end would never come into view. When it was in sight, she was puzzled to find that instead of coming nearer, the lane that it joined was receding further into the distance. Closing her eyes against the odd impressions which they were giving her, she moved on blindly, step by step.

It was only when the pram bounced as it moved off the rutted track on to the firmer surface of the lane that she realised she was there. Momentarily she hesitated in an agony of indecision. Should she turn right towards the farm, which was nearer and where she knew she would find other people in the labourers' cottages? Or should she turn left and attempt the longer walk straight to Welland and the hospital? How much time did the baby have left?

Her tears fell as the infant let out a plaintive cry and stirred a little against her breast. She felt it was begging her to make the right decision, on which its little life so perilously depended.

"I've got to get you to hospital. I've got to get you there somehow. I promised Ruby. I promised."

Slowly she turned the pram left and forced limbs that were screaming with tiredness into motion once more. All reality seemed to be ebbing away from her now. Everything was an illusion save the desperate need to place one foot in front of the other and keep the pram moving. It was as it hit a sharp rock and the springs sagged in their death throes, that Nan sank to her knees and slowly relinquished her grip on the handle.

Succumbing finally to the terrible longing to give up and lie down there in the road, all effort spent, she was vaguely aware of the sound of an oncoming car which stopped behind her. A door slammed, there were swift footsteps and then urgent hands were turning her over and a strangely familiar voice was speaking.

"Nan! Nan Stuart! What in heaven's name are you doing? You look like a corpse, woman! And what's this – dear God, it's a baby!"

"Hello, Doctor Harris. What a lovely surprise to see you ..." She smiled up at him. Delirium was fast overtaking her now and mercifully blotting out the recent horrors.

"But you're mistaken, you know. I'm not a corpse, not really. That's my sister Ruby. I had to leave her back in the shack, you see. But I've still got her baby, just like I promised. I'm taking her to hospital. But now you're here, I expect you'll see to her won't you? Oh, and my girls, of course ..." The eyes closed and Nan at last gave in to the demands of her body and thankfully greeted oblivion.

It was several weeks before Doctor Harris found her strong enough, when he visited her in hospital, to listen whilst he explained the events of the missing period during which she had been so desperately ill.

"You were very lucky to pull through, Nan. Your body was so undernourished after all the months of trying to cope in those terrible conditions out in that shack! Jessie Campbell told me how you were snowed in for days and had to chop the furniture for firewood! Then the shock of Ruby arriving on your doorstep and having to deliver her baby. That last terrible walk with the children after she'd died – Heaven knows how you managed it, my dear."

"Well I couldn't let Ruby down, could I, Doctor? I promised her you see, before she died." Nan stopped and swallowed. In her weak state, tears came very easily at present. Doctor Harris patted her hand sympathetically and handed her a clean handkerchief.

"No, Nan, you'd never let anyone down. I know that. But you nearly lost your own life in the process. By the time I got you and all the children in the car and over here to the hospital, you had a raging case of pneumonia. It was touch and go for quite a few days, I can tell you."

"What about the baby? She is going to be all right, isn't she? You are sure about that, aren't you?"

"She should be fine, Nan. The nurses here have all fallen for her and she's been thoroughly spoiled. Just as Jessie Campbell is thoroughly spoiling your three girls!"

"Dear Jessie! She has been my salvation so often since I came to Canada. And you of course, Doctor! What were you doing, driving along the lane on that particular morning, anyway? I thought you were working in Toronto?"

"So I was. But old friends had invited me over to spend a few weeks of peace and quiet." He paused and looked away out of the window for a moment, and then said quietly, "I'm afraid my wife has recently been taken ill, Nan. And my friends thought a change of scene would be good for me."

"It's not serious is it, Doctor?" Nan looked at him with concern. His eyes held great sadness as he nodded.

"I'm afraid it's a mental illness, Nan. It's not something that can be cured, unfortunately. She is in a very good nursing home, but she has gradually deteriorated over this

170

last few months, and can only get worse. It's terrible to think that she could live on for years, and she won't know anything about her surroundings or recognise anybody at all."

"Oh, Doctor, I'm so very sorry!" Nan's tears started afresh that such a tragedy should have happened to this kind, gentle man.

"Well, enough of my problems. Let's get back to your future." He looked seriously at Nan, as he nodded his head. "Yes, I know you've been lying there worrying about what's going to become of all of the children and how soon you can be up and looking after them again. So I've given the situation some thought myself.

"How would you feel about going back to England, Nan? Would you like to go home to your own family again?"

"Home? To England?" Nan gazed at him in bewilderment.

"Well, it's not going to be easy bringing up four small children on your own, you know. I believe you told me that you have a family still living in north London, didn't you?"

"Yes, there's Mum and Dad and my brother, Fred. He's an invalid, I think – a result of being out in the trenches. But I don't know what Mum and Dad would think about me going back home." Nan gazed through the window at the Canadian forest spread out beyond the town. It was hard to even imagine Holgate existing on the same planet, let alone think of living back there again.

"Well it seems to me, Nan, that this would be your best solution. If your parents have room for you all, surely your mother would be willing to help out with the little ones, after all they are her grandchildren! That would give you a chance to work, at least part-time, wouldn't it? There, you'd be in familiar surroundings and living within reach of old friends if life gets too difficult. And at least you wouldn't have to cope with the hardships of the Canadian winter again!"

"Yes, I think you're probably right, Doctor. It would be the sensible thing to do, for the children's sake, if nothing else." Then she shook her head. "But it's hopeless thinking about it anyway. There's no way I could get the fare together for all of us."

The doctor patted her shoulder comfortingly. "Don't worry about that, Nan. It's all sorted out. People around here have all been talking about your terrible time out at the shack and how you walked through those dreadful conditions with the children to save the baby's life. And nearly lost your own in the process. You even made the front page of the local paper!

"Jessie Campbell has organised a collection throughout the neighbourhood and some of my own friends have also chipped in, and there's more than enough to pay for your fare to England and get you back to London again, with a little bit left over for emergencies. So as soon as your strength returns, I'll buy the tickets for you!"

"Oh, Doctor, people are so kind!" Nan's tears welled again and somehow she ended up with her head against this chest. As David Harris gently stroked her hair, he felt a terrible pang at the thought that this indomitable woman would shortly be going out of his life for good.

She was quite unlike anyone else he had ever encountered … But he mentally shook himself for having a ridiculous romantic daydream at his age and said cheerfully, "No more tears, Nan. You've got something to smile about now. You're going home, to England."

ENGLAND 1922

"Hallo, Mum. It's me, Nan." In the dusk of the May evening, the slight figure stood in the shadows of the basement doorway. Emily gazed unrecognising for what seemed an eternity, as Nan waited to be rejected or welcomed back to the family home.

Admittedly Emily was faced with quite an astonishing tableau, from her point of view. Nan held in her arms the shawled, sleeping form of Mavis. Amongst a litter of hand luggage (the rest was in a trunk still at the station) three small figures drooped with weariness.

Joan, now three years old, was flanked by twins Irene and Rita, whose hands she clutched protectively. All the children were quite respectably clothed, thanks to the generosity of the good people of Welland, who had made such a generous collection to send them back to England. Nan herself wore her usual shabby attire, having been determined that all the charity should be directed towards the welfare of the girls.

At last Emily said in a voice that she strove to keep steady, in spite of the shock that she was experiencing, "Well I suppose you'd better come inside. Though what your father will say I dread to think. It's just as well he's out with Mr Flint at the allotment meeting."

As she herded her little family down the passage and into the kitchen, Nan was suddenly overwhelmed by an enormous sense of relief, which was oddly mixed with despair.

Strange that she should experience thankfulness at returning to these old, familiar surroundings; the drab colours of the walls and furniture; the habitual odour that was a mixture of cooked cabbage, gas lights and carbolic soap. The room looked somehow smaller than she remembered, but was otherwise quite unchanged in the three years of her absence. Momentarily she expected to see Ruby here in her usual pose before the mirror over the fireplace. Then memory of her sister's pathetic grave in the Welland cemetery rushed back and tears threatened to overwhelm her.

Emily meanwhile returned the inquisitive stares of her three granddaughters. "Well, so these are your girls then. Got a kiss for your Gran, have you?" One after another they obediently submitted to a swift embrace and quick scrutiny. They were all exhausted and beyond speech, so Emily scooped them up and settled them round the kitchen table.

"Right, you stop there and I'll warm you up some milk. Will they want feeding as well, Nan?"

"No, it's all right, Mum. We had a meal at the station in London when we changed trains. I'm sorry to arrive so unexpectedly. I did write before we left but I wasn't sure if you'd got my letter or not."

"Oh, yes, I got it. Can't say I was surprised you decided to come back. I didn't think you'd be able to manage for long on your own with these three. But when you said you'd been ill, I didn't realise you were talking about another confinement. You forgot to mention that little detail!" and she nodded towards the sleeping Mavis.

Nan settled the baby more comfortably in her arms as she thankfully sank back in the old armchair beside the fire. "It's rather a long story, Mum. Not one I wanted to write in a letter. Can we leave it till later, please? I'd really like to get the girls sorted out and into bed. It's been a dreadfully long journey, all the way by train from Liverpool and then across London to here."

"I'll get them that milk and then I'd better sort out the beds, I suppose. Fred sleeps in the room you shared with Ruby. I like to keep him next door to me in case he has one of his turns in the night. So you'd better have the boys' old room at the top of the house, with the baby, and the girls can sleep in your Gran's old room next door. The double bed's still in there that you used with that swine of a husband, so I daresay they can all make do in that for tonight."

"Thanks ever so, Mum. I'm sorry to land us all on you like this. But I will get something arranged, once I've had a bit of sleep."

"You certainly will! Because I'll tell you straight, my girl, if you think your father and I can afford to support you and that scoundrel's family, you've got another think coming!" She bustled away to the scullery, where she clattered about self-righteously, pouring milk in the saucepan and finding cups for the children. Wearily Nan allowed her eyes to close as she murmured wryly to herself, "Welcome home, Nan!"

The next hour was a blur as she drank a cup of strong tea, which put a little more heart into her, and then shepherded the girls up two flights of stairs to the top floor. The room that she and Charlie had shared for those short, early months of their marriage appeared bare and unused. Looking at the bed, stripped to the mattress, Nan fleetingly recalled the moments of passion that had been stolen at night when Charlie returned from his shift at the pub or early in the morning before Nan had dragged herself off to a day's drudgery at Mrs Leigh's.

Although they had been married, how guilty she had felt each time that she and Charlie had made love. How desperately she had worried that the rhythmically creaking bedsprings would be heard by Emily and Will, as they lay silent and untouching in their own passionless bed, in the room immediately below!

Whilst Emily bustled about with sheets and blankets, Nan searched the baggage for night-dresses for the girls, and soon had the three of them bundled together under the old patchwork quilt that had been made by her own grandmother, years previously. The twins curled up side by side, and Joan was "top to tail" with them. All three pairs of eyes closed as soon as their heads touched the pillows.

Nan went into the room next door which had once been the domain of Fred and dear Jack. This too looked bare and unused. Emily had made up one of the two beds and left one of the drawers pulled out of the chest, with some folded bedding in it to make do as a cradle for the baby.

Nan wondered if her mother had noticed the red-gold hair that crowned the small, pink face. So far Emily had asked nothing about Ruby, and Nan was dreading having to break the news. Exhausted beyond belief, she changed the baby's nappy and then thankfully curled up at last in bed. Tomorrow she would tell Emily. Tomorrow she would face Will. Tomorrow she would see Fred, the brother who was now mentally and physically wrecked by his years in the trenches. Tomorrow she would cope!

When Nan finally awoke at mid-morning with the sun pouring through the shabby curtains, she was amazed that her sleep had been so deep and dreamless. It was of course not surprising after the strain of the long, hard journey from Canada, coping with four offspring all under four. Still, she reflected, as she allowed herself the luxury of a few further moment's peace and inactivity, she had been very lucky in travelling with Mavis Kent. The latter was a young nurse coming to England for a holiday with relatives in Essex.

Nan had met Mavis in the hospital and the nurse had been very taken with Ruby's baby. Doctor Harris had managed to book her a cabin next to Nan's, and she was only too happy to help out with the children, especially when the baby was fractious. Nan's own strength was still at a fairly low ebb after her serious bout of pneumonia which had so nearly proved fatal, so Mavis had been a godsend to her. In fact, she had decided that Ruby's daughter should be called Mavis after her new friend. Somehow she thought that it was the kind of name that would have appealed to Ruby.

It had been quite a wrench when Mavis had finally said goodbye on their arrival in London. But they had exchanged addresses and Nan hoped to see Mavis again whilst she was staying in England, and even keep in touch after the nurse had returned to Canada. Nan had a vague hope that she might send on news of Doctor Harris, for whom she felt such a debt of gratitude.

Young Mavis was now waving sturdy fists in the air and demanding her overdue breakfast, so Nan hastily dressed and took her downstairs to the kitchen. Worried that she might find the girls being a nuisance to Emily, or possibly cowed by her abrupt manner and terrified into submission, Nan was pleasantly surprised.

Emily, apparently, had overseen the three of them getting washed and dressed in the scullery. She had given them all boiled eggs newly laid by the hens she still kept in the back garden, and now they were playing outside under her watchful eye as she hung up some washing in the May sunshine.

"Finally decided to get up did you?" was her predictable greeting when Nan appeared with Mavis. "You're lucky that one didn't have you up earlier than this. Usually grizzling for the next feed at that age!"

"She's very good really, I can't complain abut her. Has her feeds very regular and quite happy to sleep or lay in her cot and gurgle for hours. She's very contented, especially when you think she was born premature. But she's putting on weight all right, so I reckon she's making up for lost time."

"Premature, eh?" Emily looked Nan suspiciously up and down. "So I presume that good for nothing of a husband of yours decided to leave you with a little keepsake, before he waltzed off with some tart?"

Nan hesitated, making sure that all three girls were busily engrossed with their dolls and out of earshot in the garden. "Where's Dad, then? I thought being a Saturday he'd be at home."

"Oh, he's off up the allotment. Can't keep him away from it these days. He took it on last year, and I don't mind. It gives him an interest and the fresh air does him good. 'Sides, he grows a nice lot of green stuff up there, so it saves on my shopping bills. You know we have to feed Fred as well as ourselves, and of course he can't get a job, poor devil. Not fit for anything, he isn't."

She nodded emphatically as she put a plate of sliced bread and butter in front of Nan, and poured them both a cup of tea. "So I meant it when I said last night your Dad and me can't afford to keep you and your tribe of girls. If you think you've come home to sponge off us, you've another think coming!"

"Oh, Mum!" Nan gazed sadly across the table at Emily. "You should know me better than that. When did I ever sponge off you and Dad? I always paid my keep from the time I left school. And I'm not looking for any favours now."

She sipped her tea and took a deep breath. With Will out of the way, this was probably a good opportunity to tell Emily the whole story, but it was hard to know how to start.

"Look Mum, there's things I've got to tell you, and it's not easy. So I'll just come straight out with it."

Emily put down her cup and folded her hands in her lap. Her face surmounted by the thinning grey hair, pulled back in its customary severe bun, seemed as though it was hewn from granite. Her piercing blue eyes never left Nan's over the next few moments and not a sound escaped from her lips as she listened to the pathetic story.

Nan's own voice faltered once or twice as she briefly told of her discovery of Ruby and Charlie together, and his subsequent flight from the police, as a result of his smuggling and the illicit still. She touched lightly on her own hardships with the children in the shack and the horrors of being snowed up in the Canadian winter.

Then she was forced to relive the agonising episode of Ruby's death and Mavis's birth – her promise to care for the baby and the subsequent struggle to reach the hospital in time to save it. For a moment the mundane surroundings of the kitchen slipped away. Once more she was battling through the Canadian backwoods, with the baby clinging so precariously to life, held closely beneath her breast.

Instinctively her arms tightened round Mavis sucking the last of her bottle, and the infant whimpered in protest. Nan returned abruptly to the present and put the baby over her shoulder to wind her.

The silence between the women lengthened and Nan wondered what thoughts were passing through Emily's mind. Her expression did not change, and Nan remembered how grief-stricken her mother had been at the news of Jack's death in the trenches. True, she had shown little signs of grief since then, but Nan had known how deep his loss had been for Emily.

But obviously Ruby was different. Emily would feel that her younger daughter had been a double disgrace. Leaving home after the scandal with a married man, and then on the other side of the world committing the same sin again but even worse, with her own brother-in-law. In Emily's eyes the enormity of Ruby's transgressions, culminating in the birth of the bastard, far outweighed any sense of bereavement at the death of her child.

Nan had always felt very little kinship with her mother, had indeed wondered where her own soft, romantic side had come from, but never had Emily seemed as alien as she did now. If I could mourn Ruby, even after the wrong that she and Charlie did to me, surely her own mother should feel some regret at her passing, Nan pondered sadly.

As if in answer to her thoughts, Emily stood up abruptly. "I won't pretend surprise at what you've told me, Nan. I always feared that girl would come to a bad end, and she reaped what she sowed. My only surprise is at you taking on her little by-blow. It seems to me she'll be a living reminder of the wrong that swine did with your own sister! But you always were a romantic fool, with your head forever stuck in some book!

"I'd have thought three kids of your own and what you had to put up with out there in that wilderness would have brought you down to earth. Supporting Joanie and the twins will take enough doing, without adding another burden to your worries."

"But, Mum, I told you. I promised Ruby – when she was dying – I couldn't do anything else. And I can't go back on that now. Besides," Nan smiled down at Mavis as the tiny fingers curled round one of her own. "I already think of her as my own daughter, and the girls think of her as their baby sister. That's the way it's going to be – always."

Emily nodded as she began to clear the table. "If that's what you want, then it suits me. In fact this is going to stay between us two, d'you hear?" she pointed a finger at Nan and her voice lowered almost to a whisper.

"Don't you dare repeat any of this to your father, or anyone else, ever. I will not have the shame of this added to what he's already endured these last few years. First of all losing Jack, then seeing what the war's done to Fred ... his elder daughter having to get married and then his younger one leaving in disgrace ... if he knew about Ruby's carryings on out there, and how she died, I don't know what he'd do. The shame would probably kill him! So mind what I say Nan. This stays between us two. As far as your father's concerned, Ruby had a row and left Welland and you know no more than that. Do you understand?"

"Yes, Mum, I understand. He'll never hear it from me, I promise."

"Right then. You'd better get on with your unpacking. It's a fine drying day, so you can get the children's washing done and out on the line, while I do my shopping. Put that baby outside in the sun – she looks a bit peaky to me."

Emily marched out of the door and Nan shook her head disbelievingly. It was amazing that her mother could take such dramatic news and neatly shut it all away in her head, because she chose not to think of it. But Nan knew that once her mother had made up her mind on such an important issue she would never waiver, and in this case Nan was glad.

She had spoken sincerely when she said that Mavis would be a fourth daughter as far as she was concerned, and this way there would be no reminders to alter that. If Emily wanted to spare her husband the unpleasant truth

183

about his younger daughter, then that was fine by his older one.

The first day back in Holgate was a very difficult one for Nan. Having overcome the hurdle of telling her mother the truth about Ruby and Mavis, she next had to face her father, and of course meet poor Fred.

Going upstairs to start unpacking, Nan paused outside the door of the room that she used to share with Ruby. Emily had told her that Fred spent many hours in there by the window, gazing vacantly down the street. Emily was convinced he was looking for his dead brother to come home.

"Poor lad, he's no trouble, really. Stays up there on his own unless I bring him downstairs. He takes his meals down here with us and if it's fine I put him out the back to sit in the sun. He never speaks, hardly at all. Does what he's told like a little boy. Washes and dresses himself, eats his food – he can even do little jobs for me sometimes – but often he forgets what he's supposed to be doing in the middle of it.

"He'll sit with his forkful half-way to his mouth and forget to put the food between his lips. He might as well be a child again. I have to keep an eye on him, because sometimes he'll wander out the door if it's open. One day I was making the beds upstairs and Mrs Flint brought him back from down the road." Emily shook her head sadly as she described the pathetic state of her younger son.,

So now Nan stood outside Fred's door, summoning the courage to confront the wreck that he'd become. Physical disabilities were not so bad, but after her attack by the

184

shell-shocked soldier at the hospital, any sort of mental disorder gave her a feeling of horror.

Bracing herself she turned the handle and walked into the room. "Hello, Fred, love. Remember me? I'm your sister, Nan, come home all the way from Canada. How are you then?"

The gaunt figure in the shabby grey trousers and the threadbare woollen jumper slowly turned his head from the vigil he kept at the window. The skin was a yellowish white and the eyes were sunken in dark pits. Lines of torment were etched deeply on the thin face, and Nan scarcely recognised the younger brother she remembered.

Filled with pity that threatened to overwhelm her with tears, she put her arms tightly round him and hugged Fred warmly. But the eyes that encountered hers were void of recognition and he sat unmoving and unresponsive in her warm embrace. Nan had the terrible feeling that there was no soul left inside Fred at all. His body was a shell, a walking automaton that occasionally faltered to a halt until someone started it into life once more. Dear Lord, what a blessing our Jack can't see you like this, thought Nan, laying the slack hands on the two knees and watching the head slowly swing back in position as Fred continued his futile wait.

After she had finished unpacking, Nan took an armful of dirty clothes downstairs and set kettles of water to heat up in readiness for the laundry. Then she offered to peel the potatoes for dinner. Emily was busy rolling out pastry on the kitchen table for a bacon pie she was making. They were both occupied with these domestic chores when the door opened and Will appeared.

185

At first glance, Nan decided he had not changed at all. But later she noticed his shoulders were more stooped and, if possible, his countenance was even more dour than she remembered it.

"Hello, Dad. How are you then?" She smiled tentatively at him across the room, with the vain hope of some kind of welcome. Will's eyes met hers briefly, before he marched to his usual chair and picked up his newspaper.

"Decided that you've had enough of foreign parts then? See you've brought your troubles home with you." He nodded towards the three girls outside.

Determined not to let him rile her, Nan called brightly, "Joanie, bring Rita and Irene in here. I want you to meet your Grandad." The three small figures trotted obediently into the kitchen and Nan propelled them towards Will.

"These are the twins, Dad, Rita and Irene, they're coming up for two now, and this big girl is Joanie, she's just turned three." Nan waited for some response as her father saw his granddaughters for the first time, but after a swift glance beneath lowered eyebrows and an almost inaudible grunt, he simply rustled his paper and returned to his reading.

Nan tightened her lips in angry disappointment. Emily looked at her and shook her head silently. She knew Will, and his reaction was exactly what she would have predicted. His resentment against Charlie for seducing Nan into a hasty marriage was so deeply ingrained, that Charlie's daughters were simply another target for it.

Nan was not really surprised, so she never bothered to show Mavis to her grandfather when she woke up for her next feed and he made no comment when Nan brought her in from the garden. Presumably Emily had mentioned to him the night before that Nan had four daughters and he was determined not to show any interest in Charlie's offspring.

In the following weeks, when Nan touched on his attitude once or twice to Emily, she was given to understand that Will's animosity to Charlie had worsened when he knew that the disgraced Ruby had been given refuge by the man he already hated.

"He never forgave him for causing you to lose your reputation and bring shame on us with your having to get married. You know what they're like round here and they loved to have a sly dig at your father about it. He was always so fixed in his opinions of right and wrong, and they thought it a good laugh when his own daughter was shown up!"

She nodded accusingly at Nan. "So when Ruby disgraced us with that married man your father was destroyed by the shame of it. Two daughters going down the same crooked path! When we heard you'd taken Ruby in, that was the last straw as far as Will was concerned. He wouldn't hear Ruby's name mentioned in this house again. So it's no surprise to me that he feels resentment towards that man's children!"

So the pattern was set that first day between Will and the girls. But there was one cheerful aspect to the family gathering, when Emily brought Fred down to join them for dinner.

The three little girls were seated between Emily and Nan, the twins on either side of Joanie. Fred sat opposite, on Emily's other hand, so that she could help him with his food, if necessary. At first he ate with downcast, lifeless eyes, but as Joanie chattered away in her baby voice, it finally seemed to penetrate his dim consciousness. He slowly lifted his head and watched as Joanie pretended to feed her doll with a spoonful of rice pudding.

His own spoon stopped in mid-air, and a globule dripped on to his dish with an audible plop. Joan's giggle was infectious and she delightedly mimicked the sound, "Plop, plop, plop. Man went plop, Mummy!"

"That's right, love. And he's not 'Man', he's your uncle Fred. Now eat up your pudding, there's a good girl."

A slow smile was lighting up Fred's gaunt features, and to Emily's amazement he laboriously filled his spoon again, and gazing hopefully at Joan, he deliberately dripped the rice back in his bowl, awaiting her reaction as it "plopped" loudly.

Nan's throat tightened as her daughter rewarded him with a scream of delight and digging her own spoon into her dish she immediately copied him. Fred beamed at her as he said softly "Plop" and went through the whole routine again.

For a moment the table was in noisy disarray as the twins copied Joan's merriment and chuckled delightedly. Fred and Joan continued to play with the pudding and Emily's and Nan's eyes met in delighted surprise at Fred's reaction and participation. Will said nothing, stolidly continuing his meal, but at least he didn't rebuke the children for making a noise at table, which he would have done when Nan herself was small.

Her heart lifted a little as she cheerfully but firmly restored order with her daughters and Emily guided Fred's

188

spoon towards his mouth and quietly admonished him to finish his food so that he might sit in the garden whilst the girls played. If Fred could be stimulated by a childish amusement watching the girls' antics, maybe that would be a catalyst to set him back on the road to some sort of mental recovery at last.

That evening, when all the children were settled for the night, Nan decided she must have a talk with Emily and Will about the future.

"Look, Dad, Mum, I'd like to get a few things sorted out, if that's all right. I want to make it clear that I've no intentions of coming home to sponge off you both. But you can see how I'm placed with the four girls to bring up, and I'd be lying if I said I didn't need your help.

"If you'll let us stay here with you, and as things stand you've got the room for us, I'll do all I can to pay our way. I'm going to look for work straight off, but to do that, I'll have to rely on you to look after the girls for me, Mum.

"I wouldn't expect to leave them with you all day, of course I wouldn't. So that means I can't go out to work full-time. But I want to try and get some part-time work of an evening, if I can. They should be in bed then, and no trouble to you. I thought maybe cleaning work in an office or factory, or even in a pub behind the bar. I'll take whatever I can get.

"At the same time, if you're willing, I'll try and get some work to do at home. In Canada I used to take in washing and mending, so I could do that here. I thought I'd put a card in the local newsagents to advertise myself.

"I've got a bit put by that'll pay for our food for the first few weeks. I told you how the local people had a whip round for us, and there's some of that left. By the time that's gone, I'll hope to have some earnings coming in. So if you'll let us live here, I'll do my best to pay my share. Of course I'll do all I can to help out round the house, so we won't make any extra work, Mum, I promise."

She stopped, conscious that her voice had cracked slightly as she endeavoured to plead her case convincingly. Aware that if Emily and Will refused, she had no other options open to her.

There was a silence, and Nan's fingers tightened round the handkerchief she was twisting tensely in her lap. Her dark eyes flickered anxiously between her parents, ensconced in their usual chairs on each side of the fireplace. Emily said nothing, but waited for Will's decision. He had always been the law-giver in this house and while he lived, that was how it would be.

He had stared, unmoving, at Nan throughout her speech, no clue to his reaction showing on his grim features. Finally he stirred, knocking out his pipe against the grate, before he rose and glared down at her.

"You've said your piece, girl, and now I'll say mine. You brought shame on this family four years ago and when you left home with that no-good scoundrel I can't say I was sorry to see you go. Since then it seems I've had nothing but grief from all my children.

"Your brother is little better than an idiot, through no fault of his own. He's a burden to your mother, having to watch him like some child that's a danger to itself. Your sister's name is never mentioned in this house and I don't have to tell you why. Although you and that lay-about thought fit to give her a home, in spite of the way she shamed her family.

"Now you've been abandoned with four children of your own, which is no more than I'd have expected from that scum. You've come crawling home, half across the world, expecting your mother and me to help you, because you've no-one else who can.

"Well, I've always done my duty as a husband and a father. I always put food in your mouths and clothes on your backs and a roof over your head. No-one can deny that. You say you're not looking for hand-outs and are prepared to work for yourself and your girls."

He nodded, as he pulled on his jacket. "You want to earn your keep, and that is what you'll do. You'll get yourself whatever jobs you can to pay your way and in this house you will more than pull your weight.

"Any work those children make, you'll do it. You'll help your mother with all the cooking and housework and you'll take off her the burden of looking after that pathetic lump upstairs. You'll clean his room, do his washing and watch over him when he needs it.

"Those are my conditions and if you are prepared to stand by them, then you can stay. But keep those brats out of my way when I'm home. I want no reminders of their father.

"From the moment you met him he's been nothing but trouble and I've no doubt his daughters will bring you the same grief that mine have brought me. There's bad blood in them, and blood will out. Mark my words!" The door closed behind him and Nan gazed soundlessly at her mother, willing her to make some gesture of sympathy in the face of such implacable hatred.

The silence lengthened between them, and then Emily stood up, purposefully. "Right, that's settled then. You know your father well enough, so I don't have to tell you he means what he says. You'd better make sure those littl'uns aren't a nuisance to him.

"Now you and me'll go down in the cellar and sort out one or two things. Somewhere down there is the old pram I had for you lot, and your cot, so I daresay they'll clean up well enough to use for young Mavis. If you're all staying you'll need to take her out and she'll soon be too big to sleep in a drawer!"

So it was agreed that Nan and her children should remain in Holgate, but she knew from that first evening that it would be very much on sufferance as far as Will was concerned. Emily would take her cue from him, but Nan was sure that she would play the role of grandmother to the best of her ability, since she would see that as her duty.

Not much love, but very hot on duty was Emily, thought Nan wryly that night as she relaxed between the sheets. But at least their future was settled, and she was not going to be walking the streets with her little ones, which had been a distinct possibility in the face of Will's strict code of morals.

That first summer back in England passed quite quickly, probably because Nan was kept busy from early morning till late at night. She counted herself lucky that she had been able to find a part-time job in the first week.

Mrs Flint, their gregarious neighbour, had been eager to chat when she met Nan pushing Mavis in the pram whilst doing the shopping. The twins were perched side by side on the end, since their short legs had quickly tired, but Joan as usual was walking docilely alongside Nan, her rag doll clutched in her hand.

"Blimey, girl, you've got your 'ands full with that little lot!" Mrs Flint beamed in the pram and then poked Nan meaningfully in the ribs. "Didn't learn your lesson the first time then? Still, 'e was a good-looking lad your Charlie. Can't say I blame you for making the most of a feller like him!" Her cosy, fat laugh shook her generous form, and she mopped her amiable face which was shining with sweat in the strong sun.

"Hello, Mrs Flint. How are you, then? You're looking well. What about the family? Vi not married yet is she?"

"Not 'er, ducks. Too busy playing off all the lads one against the other. While they'll all take 'er out and spend their money on 'er, why should she tie herself down? Bit like your Ruby, our Vi is. Oops! Not supposed to mention that name are we?"

"It's all right with me, Mrs Flint. But least said soonest mended with Mum and Dad."

"I 'ear you're back to stay. Sorry to 'ear your marriage didn't work out, Nan. Left you for some flighty piece did 'e?"

"Something like that, yes." Nan patted the twins on the head, as they became restive. "I'd better get on. I'm doing the rounds looking for a part-time evening job, and then I said I'll take them for a walk to Ally Pally. They haven't been there yet and I know they'll love the wide open spaces to run about."

"Looking for an evening job are you? Why don't you get yourself down to Davis's chip shop? I was talking to old Ma Davis last week and she was saying her son, Frankie, was looking for some help in the evenings. He's opened up the room at the back and put in a few tables and chairs, so people can eat there if they like.

"His mum says her rheumatics are playing up something shockin' these days and she has to put her feet up in the evenings, so she can't help out in the shop. Frankie can't manage by himself, cooking, serving, waiting at tables and washing up, so he was going to advertise for someone. Might be worth asking, in case it hasn't gone yet."

"Thanks ever so, Mrs Flint. I'll go straight down now."

"It's a pleasure, ducks. Hope you get it. And bring those littl'uns round one afternoon. 'Ave a cuppa and tell us all about your travels in Canada. Bet you could tell a few tales, eh?"

Nan smiled and nodded, a fleeting picture of the old shack surrounded by snow drifts flashing before her eyes, obscuring the dusty, drab street in that north London suburb. She experienced an almost physical pang of longing for the icy cold air, which was so sweet to breathe and the sight of those grandiose vistas of dark forests outlined in white.

"Mummy, are we going to play ball now? Can we go to the big park like you said? My legs are tired and there's no room on the pram for me." Joan's plaintive voice recalled Nan abruptly to the present. She scooped Joanie up to ride "piggy-back" and waved to Mrs Flint. No time for day-dreaming, my girl, she admonished herself. Get off after that job, before someone else snaps it up!

Luck was with her, and Frankie Davis was glad to find a clean, respectable, sensible young woman eager to work evenings. When she explained her situation quite openly, and he understood that she had four young children to support, he knew at once she was the answer to his prayers. This was not some silly young girl likely to be giggling with the male customers and scamping her duties in order to meet a boyfriend after hours. She would work conscientiously because she had responsibilities to fulfil.

And so it proved. Nan would settle all the girls in bed before she left number thirty and arrive in the shop at seven o'clock. They closed at ten, and during those hours she would be on her feet non-stop. Serving, waiting at table, washing up and sometimes assisting Frankie with the cooking. When they finally put up the "closed" sign, Nan would help clean up the frying equipment, wipe down the tables, and sweep the shop in readiness for the next day. By the time she staggered down the steps to the basement door of number thirty, it was usually gone eleven and her back and feet were often throbbing with weariness.

Emily and Will were normally in bed, and Nan would always have a strip-off wash at the scullery sink, in the hot water Emily would leave for her on the stove. No matter how vigorously she scrubbed, Nan was afraid the pores of her skin were impregnated with the greasy smell of frying fish and chips, but it was all part of the price she paid to support her girls!

She would drag herself out of bed at six the next morning to start on the day's chores. Apart from cleaning and helping Emily with the cooking, she gradually built up a regular clientele who liked to leave washing or mending with her. She always tried to have a couple of hours working on this before the children were demanding their breakfasts.

Fred was really like a fifth child under her care, although she never resented the demands he made on her time. He now spent less of his days peering out of his window waiting for the long-lost Jack, and much more watching the antics of the girls.

Joanie and the twins quickly took it for granted that he was an overgrown playmate and they would include him in all their games. Joan was an imaginative child and always inventing activities for the other two, in which she assumed Fred would join. Much of her prattle he never understood, but he was quite content to play the passive role of wicked giant or simply stand in the garden as a "tree" for the girls to dance around or clamber up, as the fancy took them.

When they were with him, his face wore a faint, benign smile and he never tired of their company. If Nan suggested a walk to Ally Pally, as she often did during the precious hour or two in the afternoon, which she saved as "the girls' time", Fred would of course be taken along with them. Nan would stroll beside him as he proudly pushed Mavis's pram, and when Joan or the twins grew tired, he would delightedly carry them on his shoulders, or sometimes swing them up on his head in what they called "a flying angel", whilst they squealed with excitement.

His big hands always handled them gently and Nan never felt any hesitation about letting him play with the girls. Emily told her that he had improved a great deal since Nan's return, and she had to admit it was obviously because of his joy in his young nieces.

No matter what other simple chores he might forget in the middle, or how muddled he would become with them, if Nan asked him to do anything for the children his concentration was complete and he never forgot to finish a task related to them. He even spoke more often than he had, and the wheezing attacks that he suffered as an after effect of the dreadful poison gas had not happened at all since Nan had come home.

As the months passed, Nan herself gradually lapsed into a sort of automaton. Her whole world centred round the welfare of the girls, and she had little energy to think beyond their needs. If occasionally at night she spared a thought for herself and her own future, it was a bleak outlook, on which she preferred not to dwell.

Till the girls were all grown up, her life must be that of a skivvy, in order to supply their material needs. Practically every waking hour she was working, in order to support the four little ones. There was rarely a moment in the week that she might call her own. Even on Sunday nights, when the chip shop was closed, she would sit for long hours at her paid needlework, sharing the kitchen with a silent Will and Emily.

She was constantly aware that she was beholden to her mother for acting as baby-sitter, but there was no alternative, if Nan was to earn money for their keep. But of course it would be unthinkable to ask Emily to look after the girls simply to enable Nan to go out for pleasure. Besides, as every farthing she earned must be used to pay for food and clothing, there was little recreation she could afford.

Her only real pleasure was to bury herself in a book and try and escape the harsh realities of her existence. Sometimes she might snatch the odd hour on a Sunday afternoon for this, if the girls were having a nap, but often she was so tired, she would nod off herself over the unturned pages.

As the summer passed into autumn, the life they had lived in Canada took on the semblance of a dream. Nan did exchange the occasional letter with Jessie Campbell, but the latter was a poor scholar and her misspelt, one-page efforts did little to recall the wonders of that magnificent countryside, which Nan remembered at times with an almost physical pang of longing.

As the weeks passed Nan herself became more and more sunken in a sort of mental apathy. With the girls she would make the effort to be cheerful and, as the colder weather kept them indoors, would strive to invent pastimes to keep them happy and occupied. But without the stimulus of their company, she lacked any interest in life at all.

Her conversations with Emily were confined to domestic trivia and any exchanges with Will were practically monosyllabic. As the walls of number thirty became more and more claustrophobic – the onset of winter making any expeditions outside less frequent – sometimes Nan would recall Charlie's attitude in Maple Cottage, when he seemed stifled by domesticity. Fleetingly she would almost have a feeling of sympathy for him, in spite of the implacable hatred that she now nourished for the man who had betrayed her so shamefully.

One morning they awoke to find the world transformed in white, and the temperature dropping steadily. The girls clamoured to go outside and play and at first Nan refused. But by the end of the week, she decided they must all get some fresh air and planned a walk to Ally Pally.

"Well, I just hope you're prepared to dry off all their clothes when they get back. They'll get soaked through, playing in this deep snow." Emily shook her head gloomily as she tightly tied a woolly scarf round Joanie's neck.

"I know Mum, but I feel so sorry for them cooped up inside all this time. So long as we keep moving and they're well wrapped up, the cold won't harm them. It's ages since they had any fresh air. You coming as well, lovie?" She smiled at Fred who was attempting to lace up his heavy boots and finding the task beyond his clumsy fingers.

"Ally ... Pally?" Fred looked at her eagerly and she laughed, nodding and bending to tie his laces. "That's right, Fred. You can help the girls to build a lovely snowman. Then we'll see who can make the biggest snowball, eh?"

"Snow ... man ... Yes!" Fred beamed down at the twins and clasped a hand of each, as they dragged him towards the front door. Even Emily gave a grudging smile as she watched their excited departure. Nan pushed the pram, where Mavis sat up, swathed in covers, her rosy cheeks stuffed in a tight woollen bonnet. Fred and the twins skipped ahead and Joanie trotted sedately along as usual, with one hand on the pram.

Will grunted and put another log on the kitchen fire.

When they reached Alexandra Palace, the girls were entranced by the scene. The steep grassy banks in front of the impressive building itself were a hive of activity. Blanketed in deep snow which had frozen over, they were dotted with tobogganing figures. A few actually used the genuine article, which they had either made themselves or found in an attic, but many simply improvised with tin trays.

Nan kept her little party moving, as the cold was so intense, especially up here on the higher ground, where the view across the snowy rooftops of north London was quite spectacular. As they progressed towards the lake, round the corner of the palace itself, another lovely panorama met their eyes. The sheet of water was transformed into a skating rink, on which those lucky enough to possess a pair of skates were performing amazing feats of grace. Or in some cases, falling down in uncontrollable laughter at their own ineptitude!

Excitedly the girls rushed forward, dragging Fred with them. Everywhere smiling faces and happy voices illustrated the pleasure that the advent of this unusual weather had given to adults and children alike.

Strange, thought Nan, as she wheeled Mavis up and down whilst the others busied themselves rolling a gigantic snowball. In Canada the snow was simply taken for granted, an accepted part of the winter scene, but in London, because it could not be guaranteed to appear, it was regarded as some sort of magic by young and old alike.

Of course the novelty will wear off if it stays for more than a few days, she thought wryly. People will soon get disillusioned with burst pipes, delayed trains and treacherous, icy pavements. But for today at least it's bringing a smile to people's faces and a break in their humdrum lives.

The cold spell did continue for more than a week, and as Nan had predicted, it rapidly lost its charm as transport services were interrupted, fuel supplies ran low and plumbers worked around the clock. So when eventually the thaw set in, a general air of relief abounded

Will was forced to stay at home for a few days with a bout of flu, which added to the household chores, since Emily was up and down the stairs carrying his meals and acting as nurse. This was one job she was not prepared to relinquish to Nan. Once the children had been confined to the house again for a few days, they became increasingly fractious and constantly demanded another trip to Ally Pally and the chance to build another giant snowball.

"I suppose I'll have to take them this afternoon, Mum. They say the thaw's started, so the snow will all be gone in a few days. They did enjoy it so much, it would be a shame not to let them have another outing. I can't give them many treats, poor little souls."

"Huh!" Emily sniffed with derision. "You keep their bellies full and warm clothes on their backs, and they have a roof over their heads, thanks to your father and me, so they should be grateful for that! Treats indeed! You start spoiling them with treats and they won't thank you for it! The more you give to kids, the more they want! I should know!" She nodded darkly at Nan, and marched upstairs with yet another hot toddy for Will.

Nan sighed. Oh, Mum, you never miss a chance do you? Never a day goes by but you have to remind me that we're only here on sufferance. Whatever happened to family love,

I wonder? Bitterly she shook her head as she caught sight of herself in the mirror above the fire.

Her sallow skin was taut over the cheekbones and lines of strain were visible on her forehead and round the eyes, which were darkly shadowed. The lips which were once soft and full with passion, were now permanently and grimly tightened as she forced herself through each long day's labour.

But when she told the girls they were going out in the snow again, the lines were smoothed away as she laughed at their happy excitement, while they scrambled to find scarves and coats. Fred too beamed delightedly as he sat docilely beside the fire, as she knelt to knot his laces.

"Sliding ... on ... the ... lake? Play with the ... snowman?" His eyes shone into hers as he painfully brought out the few words, punctuated with long pauses as he struggled to formulate the ideas in his confused brain.

"That's right, Fred. We'll have a lovely walk and you can help the girls with their snowman. If you're very good all of you, I think we've got enough pennies to buy some hot chestnuts from the stall at the lake. Would you like that Fred?"

"Chestnuts ... yes!" He nodded his head so vigorously and for so long that his woolly balaclava slipped over his eyes, which sent all the girls into loud giggles, and Nan was obliged to restore order. "Shsh, now. Remember poor Grandad's upstairs not well. We don't want to make him worse do we?"

Soberly they agreed, and then stifling further giggles they trooped along the passage to the front door. Emily watched from the staircase.

"He says he's feeling better, so I'll help him downstairs by the fire, whilst you're all out. He can sit there in peace till you get back. Behave yourselves, you girls. And you Fred."

"Yes, Granny." "Yes, Mum." They chorused, before scampering up the area steps.

As it was a weekday, there were only a few enthusiasts enjoying the snowy slopes when they reached the Palace. When they walked as far as the lake they found it practically deserted. The girls made instantly for the man with the roast chestnuts and he smiled into their rosy faces as they clustered round his fire.

"Not so busy today then?" Nan asked as she took the money from her shabby purse.

"No, Missis. The thaw's beginning so the ice isn't safe for skating, even though it still looks solid. Another day or two and I reckon it'll all be gone." He gestured to the dripping trees. "See all the icicles are melting fast. Soon be back to normal. Only a few weeks to Christmas, but I don't think it'll be a white one now!"

The girls and Fred took their chestnuts and set off towards the drifts of snow that were still intact among the trees around the lake. Nan followed behind with the pram, talking baby talk to Mavis who chuckled responsively as usual. A rather unkempt mongrel was running backwards and forwards, barking excitedly as it ploughed into the piled up snow, and Nan watched it, smiling.

She thought that the children would love a pet, but there was no chance, she knew. Will was adamant about no animals, except the hens kept in the yard. She remembered from her own childhood. He said they were extra mouths to feed and Emily could only see the additional muddle and dirt they created.

Nan sighed remembering Maple Cottage and her own chickens. She and Charlie had talked of getting a cat and maybe a rabbit for the girls ... If things had been different ... As always, when Nan allowed herself to dwell on what might have been, she experienced an almost physical pain at the lost opportunities of the life she might have led. If only Charlie had been the man she had first believed him to be. If only ...

"Mummy, Mummy, look at the doggie. He's taken Joanie's dolly!" Rita's voice brought Nan abruptly back to the present as she registered what was happening with the girls.

The mongrel had trotted up to them, tail wagging in friendly fashion, and Joan being an inveterate animal lover had hastened to stroke him. In doing so, she had dropped her beloved rag doll, which the dog had immediately grasped and ran off with, obviously expecting a glorious game of chase to ensue.

Joan, nothing loathe, had sped after him as swiftly as her short legs would allow. Nan called out, "It's all right, Joanie. Just stop chasing him and he'll probably bring your dolly back to you. He'll think it's a game if you follow him."

But Joan was too engrossed to listen to her mother. The doll was her most precious toy and went everywhere with her. She was quite unable to settle for sleep at night unless it was safely tucked in beside her. Determinedly she followed the mongrel, who was now reaching the centre of the ice-covered lake. At this moment his owner appeared over the brow of the hill and whistled for his return.

Obediently, the dog turned and loped off, leaving the doll behind. Joan continued purposefully towards it across the ice. Nan called again, more sharply now.

"Joan, come back here! Joan, d'you hear? You're not to go any further. Come back at once!"

The little girl stopped and looked over her shoulder at her mother. "Want dolly, Mummy!"

"Never mind the doll, just do as I say!" Nan had noticed a film of water in patches on the ice, and a knot of fear was twisting in her stomach. For what seemed a very long time, she remained locked in eye contact with the child, and then Joan, who had always been a very placid, obedient child, reluctantly started walking towards the bank.

By the time she reached Nan's outstretched hand, the tears were trickling fast down her rosy, plump cheeks. So upset at leaving her doll behind, she never even noticed that once or twice the ice had actually tilted slightly beneath her feet, before she stepped on to the snow-covered grass once more.

Nan scooped her up and cuddled her tightly. The twins stood silent and sad as they witnessed their elder sister's grief. They were very aware of how dearly she had cherished the rag doll.

Deep sobs shook the small body, and Nan strove to offer comfort. "Never mind, darling. We'll ask Father Christmas to bring you another dolly, shall we? I know how much you loved her, but that ice is dreadfully dangerous now. You can see no-one else is skating today, are they? It's melting away all the time, and if you'd fallen through it ..." How do you explain to a three year old about the horrors of drowning?

Nan swallowed and wiped the little face, whose dark eyes gazed piteously into her own. "I'm so sorry, love, if I could get dolly for you, I would. But it's just not possible. Now we'll all go home to a nice, warm fire. We'll have cheese on toast, shall we? How would you like to hold Granny's toasting fork for me, Joanie? Be a big girl and help me make the tea?"

Keeping up a flow of bright chatter, Nan organised the twins to hold each side of the pram and sat the disconsolate Joan on the end, whilst she pushed it slowly across the snow towards the path. So engrossed was she in the efforts to stem her daughter's grief over this traumatic loss, that Fred had completely slipped her mind.

It was Joan, still gazing wistfully past her mother back towards the lake who suddenly exclaimed joyfully. "Look at uncle Fred, Mummy! He's fetching dolly from the ice!"

Terror gripped Nan before she even turned to catch sight of the shambling figure slipping awkwardly across the lake. "Dear God, no!" Nan swung the pram round and hurriedly began to retrace her footsteps, shouting as she did so.

"Fred, no! It's not safe, you'll fall through! Fred, come back, please!"

The figure wrapped in the shabby greatcoat paused for a second and waved to acknowledge his sister's shout. "Gettin' Joanie's dolly, Nan!" Nodding importantly he turned towards the centre of the lake.

"Leave it, Fred! Leave it!" Nan screamed, but he moved on unheeding. His black figure stood out sharply against

206

the gleaming white landscape as he managed to slither forward and grasped the doll, indifferent to the surface tilting beneath his boots and the sharp splintering sounds that echoed in the stillness of the darkening winter's day.

The moment itself seemed frozen in time. The tableau of the terror-stricken woman whose woollen gloves were locked about the handle of the old-fashioned pram; the figures of the twins flanking their mother, eyes riveted on their uncle; the chestnut vendor huddled by his fire aghast at the tragedy suddenly unfolding before him.

Fred rose to his feet and shouted once, triumphantly. "I've got it, Nan! I've got her dolly, see!" Then came the unforgettable grinding, rending of the ice and the terrible single splash, as Fred lost his balance and tumbled backwards in one movement beneath the dark surface.

"Uncle Fred! Uncle Fred!" the screams of the children mingled with one anguished shout from Nan, who made an instinctive rush forward but was stopped abruptly by the chestnut vendor, who gripped her arm.

"It's no good Missis. It's breaking up all over, see? No-one could reach him on the surface now. By the time they make a way through for a boat he'll be long gone. In that cold water he can't stand a chance, poor devil."

Nan gazed desperately about her, but she knew the man was right and there was no way to rescue her brother. Aware of the mournful sobs of the three little girls, who were joined in sympathy by the howling Mavis, she knew that she must get them away from this terrible scene. Silently she allowed the chestnut vendor to settle Joan in her own arms and lift the twins on to the pram. Then she trudged beside him as he steadily wheeled it away from the lake.

She thought fleetingly that all the happy times she had spent at Ally Pally would now be overshadowed by this tragic moment. For the rest of her life, the place would always be inseparable from memories of Fred's tragic end.

Dimly she heard the kindly tones of her companion speaking. "Me name's Billy Wright, Missis. Was the poor bloke your brother, then? I heard the littl'uns call him uncle."

"Yes, Fred was my brother." She automatically pulled Joan's scarf more tightly round her against the increasing chill of the late afternoon.

"Now I have to go home and tell my mother she's lost her second son. Strange, isn't it? He survived that hell in the trenches, even though it left him a broken man, only to die in the lake at Ally Pally. Funny really ..." she met his compassionate eyes as the tears flowed silently down her icy cheeks.

Billy Wright was wonderful. He sent a passer-by for a policeman and then he took her inside the Palace building and sat her and the children down on a seat whilst he fetched hot drinks from the café there. He waited whilst she gave the policeman her name and address, and then in a few words, explained briefly what had happened.

When the policeman offered to arrange transport for her and the children back to number thirty, he took charge of the pram, promising to see it safely back to her the next day. Finally he gave her a piece of paper with his own name and address, which was in Wood Green.

Nan moved through those hours after Fred's death in some sort of unbelieving trance. She responded automatically to the children and worried briefly that they must be late having their tea, and that Mavis by now would certainly need a dry nappy. But overall was the horror of the scene that she was already envisaging with Emily and Will. But nothing could have prepared her for the reality that was to come.

Instead of taking the children straight home, she had the presence of mind to call at Mrs Flint's house first. In a few short sentences she told the stunned old lady what had happened and asked if she might leave the girls with her for a while.

"I don't want them there when I break it to Mum and Dad. They're upset enough with what they've seen already."

"I should think so, bless their hearts! Don't you worry, ducks. Just leave them with me and I'll give them their teas. You take as long as you like. Your pore Mum! First your Jack and now young Fred!"

Walking swiftly, before she could lose the courage to do what must be done, Nan went through the door of number thirty and into the familiar kitchen.

Will was wrapped in a blanket, ensconced in his familiar armchair beside the fire, Emily laying out the crockery at the tea table. Both pairs of eyes lifted to meet her own as she paused, irresolute in the doorway.

How did she manage to utter those terrible, disjointed phrases? Words that would tear their family apart once again. "Fred ... drowned under the ice. Fetching Joan's doll ... no way to reach him ..."

Emily had gasped aloud in shock, before collapsing sideways into a chair, her legs no longer able to support her. No words left her lips, but her head moved back and forth, in slow motion, as she appeared to deny the horrific tidings that her ears were registering.

Will rose slowly, awfully, to his feet. The familiar pipe dropped from his nerveless grasp, and the faded blanket slipped down and gathered round his ankles. His dark eyes bored into Nan's with pure hatred, and she felt a thrill of fear suddenly pierce the numbing unreality which had enshrouded her emotions for the last hour.

"Are you telling me that my son, that poor brainless fool, is dead? That you let him go out on that ice to fetch a DOLL?"

"I'm sorry, Dad," Nan whispered, trembling, as he continued to gaze at her unblinkingly.

"You're sorry? YOU'RE SORRY! You were supposed to watch over that helpless lad, because he was incapable of looking after himself, and when you let him drown you tell me YOU'RE SORRY?"

"I know, Dad, I know ... It's just that Joanie was so upset about her doll – you know how she loved it – and I just didn't see what Fred was doing until it was too late. I'm so sorry. So sorry."

Nan began to sob as the awful truth of what she was saying finally began to hit her. The silent accusation of Emily's eyes were even harder to bear than Will's spoken indictment. Broken-hearted, she made to approach her mother, hoping to offer and receive some sort of comfort, only to be halted by a howl of rage from her father.

"Dear God in heaven! Will it never end? The day you brought that swine into this house, our nemesis crossed the threshold! I hope you can live with yourself, that's all. To satisfy your lust with that filth, your whole family must go on paying the consequences!"

Nan stared at him in bewilderment. He towered before her like some terrible ranting prophet. His grey hair was dishevelled, his face scarlet – from fever or rage – and the glittering eyes mesmerised her own.

"Dad, Dad you can't blame Charlie for what's happened today. It was just a terrible accident. Try to look at it differently. It's a tribute to Fred's love for Joanie that he died the way he did. He was only thinking of her ..."

"Her! That misbegotten fruit of your disgusting coupling with that scum! She was the reason you were forced into a quick marriage that shamed our family before the whole neighbourhood. Oh, yes! They all had a field day! Snide remarks behind my back wherever I went! The high and mighty Will Fisher, such an upright chap with his strict morals! Can't even bring up his daughters to stay on the straight and narrow!

"You ran off to Canada and got away from the tongues wagging and all the finger-counting when that little brat was born. And now she's cost the life of my poor lad!"

He faltered and his head sank on his chest, swaying where he stood.

"I know, Dad. I know. I wish there was something I could do to turn the clock back. I'll blame myself to my dying day, I will. If only I hadn't been distracted with Joanie crying ..."

"Crying! Oh, she'll do some crying before she's finished! If you think you're staying on under my roof with that bastard's spawn, you've another think coming! You can pack up and leave, the lot of you!"

Nan stared at him aghast. She never suspected for one moment that he would carry his hatred this far. But he was raging on, like one demented.

"Not content with seducing my elder daughter, he then cocks a snook at me, giving shelter to my younger one, when she brings more disgrace on the family. A good laugh it must have given him, when he knew both my daughters behaved like a couple of whores."

He gave Nan a twisted grimace that passed for a smile. "Still you found out your mistake after you judged him such a wonderful husband, didn't you? Dragging you across the world to some god-forsaken wilderness, and then leaving you with four of his offspring to support. Didn't enjoy the flavour of fatherhood and responsibility when it meant he had to feed all of you, eh?

"Well as you sow, my girl, so you reap. You chose to ignore all the morals you were brought up with, and look where it got you. Your life ruined, four children to slave for and your handsome husband off with some floozy to live as he pleases. There's a just reward for you. Never a truer word said – 'You make your bed and you lie on it'!"

Nan could feel waves of emotion rushing over her. The shock and grief of Fred's tragic ending. The terrible guilt that she knew would be with her always, but the sense of unfairness that Will should lay so much blame upon her. The years of silently enduring his bigotry and listening to the diatribes since she was a child, where he was always right and the rest of the world so wrong. Suddenly the purposely cruel jibe about Charlie's infidelity with the 'floozy' was the last straw.

"Yes, Dad, you enjoy your gloating over the way Charlie left me. Revel in being right. I should never have married him, he was a no-good scoundrel. But just think of this. His 'floozy' wasn't just any bar-room tart. Oh, no. She was your daughter, my dear sister."

"What? What did you say?" Will gazed at her in bewilderment. "You mean Ruby was the one he went off with? Is that what you're saying? Your own sister?"

"Yes, Dad. My sister – your younger daughter. Not only did she run off with her brother-in-law – her second married man wasn't it? – but my dear husband got her pregnant too. And then of course he left her, just as he did me. Nothing if not consistent, Charlie, eh?"

Watching the emotions of shock, horror and disgust chasing across Will's face, Nan experienced a vicious sense of triumph at finally cracking her father's granite-like composure.

"But that wasn't the end, Dad. Oh, no! Charlie was the author of one more family tragedy. Because when Ruby was abandoned, eight months pregnant, her only option was to make her way back to yours truly. After all, I'd always looked out for her when we were kids, hadn't I? You know, the ever-loving big sister! So back she came across America and turned up on my doorstep in the middle of a storm one night.

"'Course I was living in a backwoods shack at the time, so I hadn't much comfort to offer her. Which is why she died, Dad. After giving birth on my kitchen floor. So little

Mavis is yet another bastard living under your roof. How d'you feel about that? But then I suppose it won't be for much longer will it? Not if you're going to turn us all out.

"Not a lot to choose between you and Charlie in my book, Dad. He abandoned three kids, and one unborn, you'll reject one daughter and four grandchildren. Tarred with the same brush, I'd say."

Nan's words finally petered out, as all the fear and antipathy she had built up for her loveless, domineering father throughout her life, was finally purged. For an instant there was silence. The three figures remained still. Then Will started towards Nan. He lifted a clenched fist above his head and the words were ground out of him, in a sibilant whisper which reverberated through the kitchen far more effectively than his earlier bellows.

"You dare to pour out your poison comparing me to that piece of evil? Well you've had your say, my girl, and now I'll have mine. That husband of yours is not finished with you yet. Oh, no. His tainted blood runs in the veins of those four girls, and in years to come you'll know it.

"As Charlie has been a curse to me since you brought him into this house, so his offspring will bring you pain and suffering throughout your life. Bad blood will out, and they'll cause you anguish, each and every one of them. Mark what I say ... ahh!"

His forefinger thrust towards her, the malevolent words like a curse on his lips, it seemed as though the fates themselves were turning back upon him. An expression of part surprise, part agony, crossed his features and he crashed to the floor where he stood.

Nan rushed towards him, but Emily was before her. She crouched over her husband and lifted his hand between her own. Nan waited silently, already knowing what her mother would say.

"He's dead, Nan. You'd better fetch someone. But there's nothing to be done."

When Doctor Spendlove arrived, having been summoned by Mrs Flint's daughter, Vi, he pronounced Will dead of a massive heart attack. It seemed that he had seen the doctor, complaining of pains, not long before, and the sudden shock of Fred's death was given as the official reason for his death. Only Emily and Nan ever knew of that last cataclysmic encounter in the kitchen.

In the weeks that followed, Nan was too busy with practicalities to dwell overmuch on the double fatality. There were the two funerals to get through with their accompanying formalities. Mrs Flint was wonderful, especially helping out with children. Emily became even more private in her emotions and demonstrated little overt grief over either bereavement.

Nan wondered how much blame she placed on her daughter's head. For Nan experienced a personal guilt in both instances. But whereas with Fred it was very painful, being compounded with genuine grief at his sad passing, about Will's demise she honestly felt little regret. Indeed, as the months passed, she admitted to herself that number thirty was a happier place without him.

One happier note was her new friendship with Billy Wright who had been a tower of strength. As promised, he had returned the baby's pram the day after Fred's death, and on hearing of their second bereavement was determined to help wherever he could. He had been especially supportive at the inquest over Fred's accident, where a verdict of accidental death was returned.

Nan soon learned that Billy lived with his sister in a flat in Wood Green and was a very cheerful, friendly soul. He had been invalided out of the army after lung problems with the dreaded gas, but otherwise was a wiry sort of chap. He could be relied upon to help Nan in any sort of practical crisis around the house, and even Emily showed a grudging liking for him.

He told them that his work with the chestnut stand was only during the winter – in the summer he was a "Stop me and buy one" ice cream vendor with his tricycle. He had lots of friends among the local market fraternity and would often call in at weekends with some "left-overs" of fruit and other foodstuffs that he thought they could use. In return, it became a custom that he joined them for Saturday dinner.

The girls all took to him at once. Joanie was his special ally. Nan had been so worried about her after Fred's drowning, when the little girl had become very withdrawn and prone to nightmares. Nan had wondered whether to buy her a replacement doll, but was frightened it might remind her once again about the accident.

Billy solved the problem at Christmas, which was a few weeks later, by appearing with a hand-made golliwog in a bright red jacket for Joan. It seemed his sister, Dolly, was a maker of soft-toys for a local stall. She also made a couple of teddies for the twins and a rabbit for Mavis.

Joan's allegiance was instantly transferred to the new toy, that was sufficiently different from the doll to keep unhappy memories at bay, so Nan was very grateful. As time went by the little girl gradually seemed to return to her normal cheerful self, and the tragedy at the lake faded into the past.

ENGLAND 1938 – 1945

In the next sixteen years life at number thirty was that of any other working class home. Nan's financial struggles to bring up the four girls were many and varied. But her reward was to see their sturdy bodies neatly attired and to know that they were all happy.

The most difficult years were the first five, until all the girls were at school. Then the long hours of washing, ironing and mending other people's clothes, as well as the grinding hours in the hot, greasy atmosphere of the chip shop, were punishing indeed. Nan became adept at saving pennies and even farthings in every conceivable plan. She would visit jumble sales for clothes to make over into new guises for all of them. It was her great pride to watch all four girls set off to Sunday school in their "best" attire each week.

She managed to acquire a nearby council allotment which was hard work but a constant joy. It was an escape from the confines of the drab rooms and tiny yard of number thirty, and Nan was never happier than when she was growing food to supplement their meagre income. To her delight, as she grew older, Irene inherited her mother's love of the open air, and was soon assisting at the allotment.

Once the girls were at school during the day, Nan decided to look for some different part-time work and leave the chip shop. That way she could spend time with her daughters when they were at home. Strangely enough the wheel seemed to turn full circle, as she ended up in Muswell Hill once more, where years before she had been a young skivvy at Mrs Leigh's establishment.

Her new employer, Mrs Ash, was quite different. She was a doctor's wife and a little younger than Nan. Doctor Philip Ash worked at the local hospital and Nan really liked the couple. Her hours were flexible and she was always home before the girls returned from school.

The Ash's home was very modern, with various labour-saving gadgets, and Mrs Ash was a very friendly and considerate employer. "So different from that Lady Muck, Mrs Leigh," Nan told Emily, thankfully. Mrs Ash was always happy to join Nan in the kitchen for a cup of tea, and sometimes passed on clothes that she no longer required. So it was definitely an improvement after the hours spent every night at the chip shop.

Nan was eager to see her girls make something more of their lives than she had done, although none of them were academically brilliant at school. Joan was definitely the brightest and always received glowing reports as being conscientious and neat. She inherited Nan's love of reading, and her mother was quick to encourage it. It was a great pleasure to Nan, when they would each read the same library book and talk it over afterwards. An experience she had never enjoyed before.

When Joan was old enough she passed the entrance exam for the local grammar school, and Nan was so proud of her eldest when she went off each morning in her school uniform. Never mind that Nan had practically starved herself to eke out her earnings to pay for it, Joan was going to have the chance denied to her mother.

When she left school, Joan had found a clerical job in the local post office, and Nan was thrilled to reflect that this daughter would never need to scrub floors or iron other women's laundry for a living!

The twins were not identical in looks or temperament. Irene's blonde curls had darkened to a deeper gold as she grew up, and she preferred to keep them in a neat cropped style. Irene was not particularly interested in clothes and was a very practical girl. Sometimes she and Billy would undertake a model-building project together, and even designed some cold frames they built together for the allotment.

She was good at figures, but not particularly keen on books, so when she left school, she was happy to get a job in the stores of a local factory. She did her work efficiently, but Nan knew that she hated being cooped up indoors. Unfortunately, in that north London suburb, there was little outdoor employment available for a young girl. Should have been a farmer's daughter, that one, Nan would think, as she watched Irene sowing carrot and lettuce seeds in neat drills.

Rita was the heedless scatterbrain of the family. She had not a malicious bone in her body, always had plenty of giggling girl friends and never thought before she opened her mouth. She had no application for her school work and was eager to leave as soon as possible. Her main interest was the stars at the cinema, make-up and clothes. So it was no surprise when the height of her ambition was to get a job on the production line of the local sweet factory, which was where Irene helped in the stock control.

Rita's hair was a mass of bright curls and her lively, cheerful personality made her a favourite with her peers. Nan loved her dearly, but had long ago realised that this was the least ambitious of all her girls.

Mavis was similar to Rita, with her interests in clothes and make-up. She had cause to be vain of her appearance as she was extremely attractive with her vivid blue eyes and long auburn "page-boy" bob. She was quite tall and had a beautiful figure. Male heads turned when she walked by, and Mavis relished the attention.

She had not shone at school, but Nan was aware that Mavis was like her mother with a streak of native cunning in her make-up and ambitions to get what she wanted out of life. She had left school and gone to work as a junior in a dress shop in Muswell Hill, where she made herself pleasant to staff and clients alike. Nan was sure that Mavis already knew at seventeen exactly where she was going in the future.

Nan's relationship with Emily had not really changed much. The older woman had become even more introverted as she got older, and although they all rubbed along together, there was little closeness between her and her grandchildren. Billy Wright was the only person able to bring the occasional smile to her lips, and Nan suspected that he reminded her, as he sometimes did Nan, of her lost son, Jack.

In recent months, Nan had actually been worrying about Emily, as she had not seemed at all well. So one afternoon in the March of 1938, when Nan arrived home from Mrs Ash's, she was not surprised to see her mother stretched out in the kitchen armchair, with a chalk white face screwed up in obvious discomfort.

"What's the matter, Mum? You don't look very good. Is it that indigestion again?"

"Yes, I think so. I just made some bread earlier – you know how Billy likes it home-made – and I had a slice when it was warm. I've had this awful pain ever since."

"Have you tried some bicarb? You seem to be getting it a lot lately. I do wish you'd go to see the doctor. It can't be right."

"I expect it's just a bit of heartburn. Don't fuss, Nan. You know I can't be bothered with doctors – load of quacks most of them!"

"It's just that you're looking very thin as well, Mum. Perhaps you need a tonic."

"For goodness sake, girl! If it will make you keep quiet, I'll call in the chemist tomorrow and ask him to make me up something." She looked at the clock. "Time I got that washing in. Must be dry by now."

Nan was taking off her coat when she heard a sudden cry. Looking round she discovered that Emily had risen from her chair, her face was now really contorted in agony, and to Nan's shock she fell in a heap on the floor. When Nan reached her she was unconscious and a dreadful colour. Panic-stricken, the younger woman dashed along the road and shouted for Mrs Flint to fetch the doctor.

By the time the girls had all arrived home from work, Emily was upstairs in bed and the doctor had just examined her extensively. He was now closeted with Nan in the front room and the serious voices made a low murmur. Mrs Flint was presiding over the teapot in the kitchen, and quickly informed them of what had happened.

"Terrible it was, girls! Your poor gran in such a state. Practically writhing in torment she was when the doctor got here. Your mum and me got her up to bed, but how we did it, I don't know. Anyway, she's quiet now. Reckon he gave her something for the pain. He's just telling your mum what's what now."

In the next room Nan was trying to absorb the full import of the doctor's findings. "I'm very sorry, Mrs Stuart, but I'm afraid there's little to be done. Your mother has an advanced growth in the digestive system which must have been developing for some time."

"She hasn't been herself, I know. I've tried to get her to see you, but she always insisted it was just indigestion."

"Yes, they can be stubborn, the older generation!" He smiled sympathetically. "If it's any comfort, we couldn't have really done anything for her. It's just a question of time, I'm afraid. And making her last days as easy as possible. If you like, I'll see if I can get her into the local cottage hospital?"

"No, that won't be necessary, doctor. She's my mother and I'm sure she'd rather I looked after her in her own home." Nan swallowed hard, at the thought of witnessing Emily dying.

"Just as you like, my dear. If you find it gets too much, just let me know. I'm sure you'll have plenty of support from your girls, and of course Mrs Flint is always a tower of strength! I'll make sure you have the necessary drugs to ensure that your mother suffers as little as possible. That I can promise."

223

The following days at number thirty were silent and dismal. The girls moved about with hushed voices, ears alerted to activity in Emily's room. Of them all, Nan spent the most time watching by her mother's bedside, although occasionally she was obliged to have a few hours' rest lying down on her own bed.

Mrs Ash had been very sympathetic about finding a temporary replacement, though Nan quietly assured her it was not likely to be for long.

"Of course, I understand, Nan. I'll get the agency to send someone until you can come back. But don't worry, your job will be here whenever you want it." She patted Nan on the shoulder. "Nan, I am so sorry about your mother. I know how hard this must be for you." She opened her soft suede handbag and pressed some notes into Nan's hand.

"In case you need to buy any little extras for your mother. Or something nourishing to keep your own strength up, my dear."

"Oh, Ma'am, that is kind!" Nan's voice faltered, and for the first time since Emily's collapse her eyes filled with tears. People could be so lovely, she thought.

Billy and Mrs Flint were their usual towers of strength. He would call each day to ask for news and often brought a tiny nosegay of flowers to brighten the sickroom. He always had a cheery word for Nan, and the ten minutes spent in his company were a thankful respite in the long hours.

Mrs Flint would bring round a meat pie or a basin of stew. "Save you the trouble of cooking yourself, ducks."

224

Of course the girls had to carry on with their daily work – Joan assisting in the local post office and Rita and Irene in the sweet factory. Mavis, just like her mother, was a salesgirl in a dress shop in Muswell Hill.

So the long days passed until the final inevitable moment when Emily eventually slipped away. As the doctor had predicted, the strong painkillers had brought with them a blessed unconsciousness for the last few hours of her life, and she was unaware of Nan's vigil beside her.

Sometimes Nan would bathe her mother's face or gently smooth back the white hair. Sometimes she would simply sit, holding the wasted hand. Looking at the stern lines, finally relaxed in that strong, familiar face, Nan tried to analyse her own feelings.

There had never been a great bond of affection between herself and Emily. As a young girl she had feared her mother's sharp tongue and wished she might have more humour and a lighter outlook on life. But as the years had passed and Nan faced the bitter struggle to provide for her own daughters, her admiration for Emily had grown.

Emily had been a good and dutiful mother, if not a demonstrative or loving one. She had lost two sons and a daughter in tragic circumstances and had been widowed before her time. She had battled throughout her life with poverty and never given in. She had her own strict code of morals and standards of behaviour and had stuck to them, whatever the cost. She had earned her daughter's deep respect, if not a warm affection.

None of her granddaughters were devastated with grief at her passing. Soft-hearted Joan shed a few tears; Irene was her normal practical self, helping with organising the funeral tea; Rita drifted about the house with her usual lack of interest and Mavis's main concern appeared to be the choice of a black hat for the occasion.

Once the funeral was behind them, Nan had to admit a feeling of relief that the strain of nursing Emily was behind her. She busied herself turning out her mother's room, washing down paint work and opening the windows wide to dispel the musty odour of the sickroom.

She wondered which of the girls should now use it. She still slept at the top of the house herself, with Joan and Mavis sharing the room next door. The twins shared the room next to Emily's, on the floor below. Whichever pair she split up it would probably cause friction, she thought wryly.

Joan had never minded sharing with Mavis, because she was such an easy-going, placid character. But Mavis would be delighted to boast to the twins of having her own space, if Nan offered the new room to Joan.

On the other hand, Rita and Irene in spite of being twins, were not ideal room-mates. Rita was appallingly untidy, dropping clothes where she stood, and Irene was always clearing up after her, and loudly voicing her disapproval. She herself was like Nan, naturally neat and clean in all her ways.

The problem was solved by Mrs Flint as they sat chatting over a cup of tea, a few days after the funeral. Nan had offered to their old neighbour any of Emily's clothes that she might use. Although their figures were not similar, handbags, shoes, gloves or other such trifles would be very welcome, she knew.

"If I was you, ducks, I'd think about letting out that room to a lodger. It's a good size and with a lick of paint you could really brighten it up. You won't have your mum's pension now, will you? So the extra money would come in handy."

"That's true enough, Mrs Flint. I've been thinking we'll maybe have to tighten our belts a bit, without Mum's money. Of course I'll be starting back at Mrs Ash's next week, and I know when the girls get a rise I can ask them to give me a bit more. Still, a lodger might be a very good idea. 'Course it would have to be someone we could all get on all right with, especially if I was going to have them eating in with us."

"Well you could use the front room for them to eat in, couldn't you? After all, you're just the same as us, never use it except at Christmas or special occasions, do you?" Mrs Flint looked admiringly down at a pair of shiny black shoes that had been Emily's "best" and which fitted her perfectly.

"I think that's a really good idea, Mrs Flint. I'll ask the girls and see what they think. Maybe I could put a card in the corner shop. See if I get any replies. After all, if people turn up we don't like, we don't have to take them, do we?"

In the event, Nan did not need to advertise. Having ensured that the girls were all quite agreeable to the idea of a lodger, she decided she would get some cheap paint and decorate the bedroom herself. Maybe she could get some nice remnant of material at the market and make a new bedspread and matching curtains. When Billy came in for his dinner as usual on Saturday, she was full of the idea, as she cut him a slice of apple pie.

"I think it'll be good for us, having another face about the place. Give us all a bit of a lift. It'll make me bother a bit more about my cooking, if I'm doing meals for someone else, and if I advertise the use of the front basement room as well as the bedroom, I reckon I can charge a nice little rent. What d' you say, Billy?"

He looked at her thoughtfully, as he sipped his tea. "Were you planning on a lady lodger then, or would you consider taking in a feller?"

"I hadn't thought about that. I was just going to put up a card and see who replied. What d'you think?"

"I think that if you'll consider a feller, then don't bother to put up a card, because you're looking at him!"

"You, Billy! But I thought you were settled in your flat – you've been there for so many years now."

"Well since Nellie got married again and moved to Brixton I've found it very lonely at times, Nan. That's probably why I'm always on your doorstep! So if you'd take me, I'd be more than happy to move in permanent."

"Well, Billy, that sounds fine to me. It would be much easier all round to have someone we know. I'm sure the girls will be thrilled to have their 'Uncle' Billy living here. You know how they love to see you."

So it was settled and when Nan got the paint, Billy insisted on redecorating the room himself. When it was finished and she had hung the new buttercup yellow curtains and made up the bed with the matching spread, she was delighted with it all. Seeing how pleased she was, Billy casually mentioned that he really enjoyed decorating, and if she would like him to work his way through the rest of the house, a room at a time, he'd be more than willing.

228

So in the following months, number thirty gradually had a long overdue face-lift.

Billy soon fitted into the household routine without any problems at all. Although he officially paid for the use of the basement parlour, to sit in and to have his meals, it never quite worked like that. Nan knew he much preferred to eat in the kitchen with the family and although he would make himself scarce if he felt that she or the girls needed some privacy, most evenings he was happy to sit opposite her in Will's old armchair whilst she busied herself with her mending.

Nan valued his company as much as she did his friendship, which had been so steadfast over the last sixteen years. He had filled a gap that had been left by the loss of Jack and was a very necessary masculine presence in the life of the whole family.

Over the years Mrs Flint, and indeed several other neighbours, had occasionally hinted suggestively that her relationship with Billy was more than that of platonic friends, which she always firmly and swiftly denied.

Sometimes in the long hours of a sleepless summer night she had wondered a little herself if her feelings for Billy could alter, should he make any sign that he wished it so. He was a couple of years older than she was, and although not exactly handsome, he was well set up, with an open, friendly countenance topped with a thatch of unruly fair hair, and dominated by twinkling blue eyes.

He had progressed over the years from his hot chestnuts and his ice cream round, first to a greengrocery stall in the market, and now he leased a small lock-up shop in Holgate high street, where his produce sold well. Yes, he was definitely a hard worker and well-liked in the community. But although she admired and respected him, Nan had long since realised that a certain vital spark was missing from their relationship.

At Christmas or birthdays, when he would give her a hug and a friendly kiss, her pulses never raced, and the sight of his smile or the sound of his footsteps had never yet made her heart pound or her face flush. Since he had never attempted any familiarity with her throughout all the years, she could only assume that he felt the same.

She had come to the conclusion long since that her relationship with Charlie had spoiled her for other men. The passion she had felt for him had been so all-consuming, and afterwards the shock of his betrayal with Ruby had been so great, Nan believed her own capacity to love a man had shrivelled for ever.

Oh, she had had her chances. When she had left the chip shop, it had been partly because Frankie Davis had let her see that he would like to become closer to her. Some would have called her a fool. If she had encouraged him, she would have been the wife of a comfortable trader with a thriving little business. Money worries would have been a thing of the past. But Nan knew it was not to be and made her attitude very clear.

One or two male neighbours had shown an eagerness to pass the time of day, and she would stop to chat with some of the men who had plots on the allotment, near her own, but not one came even near to jolting Nan out of her emotional vacuum.

She was not, however, immune to the stirrings of sexual awareness amongst her four girls. Joan, she suspected was such a romantic, she was simply waiting for a knight on a white horse to sweep her away from Holgate's drab reality. Irene was so practical, Nan could imagine that any dreams she entertained involved the joys of domesticity and looking after a brood, of clean, tidy, well-behaved offspring.

Rita, sadly, was showing all the signs of her aunt Ruby's feckless behaviour, but with none of Ruby's ruthless streak of self-preservation. She was forever giggling with the young lads at the factory during her lunch-hour, and whenever she was late for her evening meal, Nan would know she had been dallying with one of them on some street corner.

Nan was concerned that Rita was really very sweet, but unfortunately rather a simple girl, and could easily imagine some lad taking advantage of her good nature. She had given each of the girls a sensible, straightforward talk about the facts of life when they reached adolescence and pointed out very bluntly the consequences of promiscuity.

Nan had never been a hypocrite, so felt it incumbent upon herself to point out that she had been a walking example, in her own life with their father, of just how disastrous the effects of reckless passion could be. Each of the girls had listened and reacted characteristically.

Joan had said, wide-eyed, "But you did love Dad, didn't you, Mum. I mean, that's why you and he ... you know ... before you were married?"

"Yes, Joanie, of course I loved him. I was mad about him! Mad was the right word! But what I'm saying is, because you're feeling like that about someone doesn't mean you should throw caution to the winds. Look where it got me in the end! Of course it's wonderful when you fall in love, but you must be a bit sensible and make sure it's the right sort of permanent love that will make a good marriage. One to last a life-time, not four years like mine did!"

She had few worries about Irene. It was hard to imagine this practical young woman being carried away on a tide of passion. No, Irene would find a nice, sensible young man when the right time came, and settle down with him. Nan was pretty sure of that.

Rita was a continuing worry with her giggling excitement over the latest lad to pay her a compliment and offer to take her to "the pictures".

Mavis, in theory, should have been too young to be a worry as far as the opposite sex was concerned, but her knowing looks and her way of staring any personable male up and down with her china blue eyes, was already causing Nan some misgivings.

Yes, you're your mother's daughter, right enough, Nan thought as she watched Mavis fluttering her eyelashes at Billy as he fixed the broken strap on her handbag. Another year or two and I reckon I'll need to tie you up twenty four hours a day, to keep you out of mischief!

But the worries about the girls were soon to be driven to the back of Nan's mind by a new turn of events, in two directions. One was to affect the lives of millions with the radio announcement on that momentous September morning in 1939 that war had been declared with Germany. The other was much more personal, and involved the re-entry into her life of a figure from the past.

232

Nan was carrying out her usual cleaning duties at Mrs Ash's home several days after that fateful Sunday broadcast. She was engaged in tidying Doctor Ash's study, and his wife was sorting through a number of papers on his desk.

"He's so dreadful about accumulating rubbish, he can never find anything when he needs it. He is going to a special conference next week that is being held at Alexandra Palace, and he's mislaid the programme. It's all about mental illness, and they have a number of doctors coming to lecture from overseas. Philip has always been rather interested in psychiatry, you know, and with this wretched war I should imagine that there are going to be as many mental as physical casualties if it's anything like the last one."

"Yes, Ma'am, it was terrible the effect it had on some of the young lads in the trenches. I remember what a state our poor Fred was in. Shell-shocked they said."

"Of course, Nan, if anyone knows about it you should, with your memories. Just have a look through this pile for me, would you. I'll go through some of the drawers ..."

Nan took the heap of assorted pamphlets and papers and swiftly sorted them. Half-way through she found it – "Symposium on Mental Health, Alexandra Palace." Then it leapt at her. The name of the first lecturer "David Harris, Toronto."

"Have you got it, Nan? Why, what is it, my dear? Is something the matter?"

"Not exactly, Ma'am. It's just that I think I know one of the doctors listed. If it is the same man, he just about saved my life when I was living out in Canada with my girls."

"What an amazing coincidence! Have you kept in touch with him at all, over the years?"

"Oh no, Ma'am. I exchange Christmas cards still with my old friend Jessie Campbell, and there was a young nurse I travelled over with on the boat, but since she got married we lost touch. Jessie never puts any news in her cards, just a few lines about her own family.

"But I do think this might be the Doctor Harris I knew, because his wife had become ill with mental problems just before I left Canada. He was working in a hospital in Toronto, so maybe his wife's trouble lead him into this kind of work." Nan was silent, remembering vividly the gentle, kindly man who had been such a rock for her during those terrible days. He must be well into his fifties now, she supposed, and would no doubt have forgotten her from all those years ago.

"I'll tell Philip when he comes in, Nan. If he gets a chance to meet Doctor Harris maybe he could ask him if he remembers you. Of course with all the patients that they see, it's difficult for doctors to recall individuals. And it was a long time ago, wasn't it?"

"Of course, Ma'am. But if your husband just mentions my name and reminds him he delivered my daughters and saved my life when we'd all been snowed up in the shack in the winter of 1922 near Welland, he might remember. If he does, perhaps Doctor Ash could pass on my best regards?"

"I'll tell him, Nan. Now we'd better get on. It's your day for polishing the silver isn't it?"

Nan's thoughts dwelt often on Doctor Harris over the next few days, and by association those far off times in the shack. It was hard to believe that she had actually lived through and survived that terrible time, and all of the girls had grown up now into healthy young women.

Occasionally she would talk to Joan about those days, as she was the one with the romantic imagination who appreciated the drama of their former life. "Just like something out of a book, Mum. You looking after us, all alone, frozen and starving in that shack!"

"You never froze, my girl, or starved. I saw to that, but it was a close thing I can tell you!"

But although Nan's thoughts were full of the past, everyone else was naturally obsessed with war talk. Evacuation schemes for the children were being organised, in readiness for the cities being bombed. Nan was thankful that all of the girls were past childhood now. She would have hated to make the decision to send them to strangers or keep them at home and risk the consequences.

She was also thankful that no-one in their household was liable to be called up. Billy at forty seven was too old. Reading in the papers of the first troops landing in France, all the memories of Jack and Fred came pouring back. Seeing sons of friends appearing proudly in their uniforms her heart went out to them.

The girls were all excited and thrilled by so much drama suddenly erupting in their humdrum lives. The glamour of the young men they had seen every day at work and in the shops suddenly becoming warriors marching off in a brave cause was a thrilling sight to all of them.

Irene, practical as ever, was busy planning how to maximise the food crop on the allotment, as well as helping Nan to dig up the tiny back garden for the same purpose. Billy was determined to "do his bit" and join the Local

Defence Volunteers. Nan began the first of countless garments that she was to knit for the troops.

She was occupied with her knitting one evening when, unusually, she had the house to herself. It was a Saturday and there was a dance being held at the local British Legion in aid of the war effort. All four of the girls had gone to this. Mavis had begged so hard, and in view of the fact that she had three elder sisters to keep an eye on her, Nan had reluctantly agreed. Sixteen nowadays was a lot older than when she herself was a youngster, she decided. With the way things were happening, it was probably just as well if girls matured more quickly.

Mrs Flint's grandson, Sam, who had just joined the Navy, had offered to escort the girls, along with one of his mates, and Nan was sure they were sensible lads. Let them all have a bit of fun while they can. With her memories of the last war, Nan was under no illusions about the future. There was already talk of rationing beginning in the new year and if bombing began in earnest over London, Holgate would be very much in the "front line".

Billy had gone to spend the weekend with his sister in Brixton and it seemed strange not to have his company. He was a great tinkerer, and usually busy making some model car or engine. He would sit at the table covered tidily in newspaper and they would happily enjoy some music or a good play on the wireless.

When the knock came at the front door upstairs, Nan was amazed. Nobody ever used that entrance. It was a relic from when the big old house had been owned by a prosperous family with a servant cooking and living in the basement. In those days only tradesmen had gone down the steps and knocked at the door in the "area".

But when the neighbourhood had gone downhill and the old houses were rented out to large, working-class families, the basement had been used for all daytime living purposes and all the rooms on the two floors above had become bedrooms. Nan suspected the bolts on the proper front door would probably be stiff from disuse. The last time it had been opened, she thought, was when Emily had been taken out by the undertakers.

She opened the basement door and went half-way up the area steps, calling out, "Who's there? Who did you want?" to the tall figure with his hand poised to knock once again.

The thickset figure in the dark overcoat turned and he raised his hat as he said, peering down at her. "I'm sorry to disturb you, but does a Mrs Nan Stuart live here?"

Time stood still and Nan's throat closed with an emotion she could not have described. Then as she ascended another step, her face upturned in the light of the street-lamp, the visitor recognised her.

"Nan! Mrs Stuart, it is you!" He came quickly down the steps and held out his hand. "I don't suppose you remember me – David Harris, from Welland?"

"Doctor! How could I ever forget you!" Nan let her hand rest for an instant between his two warm ones, and then hastily turned and led him inside. In a few moments his overcoat was hanging up and he was ensconced in the armchair before the fire. Nan bustled about, putting on the kettle and getting out the best crockery, conscious of her own flushed face and the pounding of her heart as she cast sideways glances at this figure from the past sitting in her own kitchen.

The doctor let her fuss about him, whilst he observed the shabby but clean surroundings. Billy had quite recently distempered the walls a fresh cream and the woodwork was a shining brown. The table was covered with a green chenille cloth, in the middle of which a tall jug of bronze chrysanthemums brightened the room.

When Nan had finally settled opposite him he was then able to examine the features of this woman who over the years had surprisingly often invaded his dreams and, unbidden, entered his thoughts.

She was still very slim, although age had added a becoming roundness beneath the hand-knitted green jumper and brown serge skirt. The dark hair shone in its neat bun, as yet untouched by grey. The generous mouth still curved easily into a smile and the wide brown eyes had not lost their luminosity, although surrounded now by a network of fine lines.

The familiar work-roughened hands tightly clasping her teacup and saucer were showing signs of ageing, and he noticed she had not replaced the wedding ring that she had sold long ago to feed her daughters. So presumably she had never replaced Charlie.

He noticed several photographs on the mantelpiece and rose to look at them. "Are these your daughters, Nan? All grown up now, of course. Do they still live with you, or are any of them married? You're not a grandmother yet, are you?"

"Bless you, no!" Nan laughed as she stood beside him and pointed to each of the figures. "That was taken last summer when we had a day out at Southend. Joan's the one with the ice cream. I expect you can tell the twins – they still look very similar, though not at all alike in temperament. That young madam in the saucy hat is Mavis!"

"And whose is the knee she's sitting on? A family friend, is he?"

"Oh that's our lodger, Billy Wright. A very steady sort of a chap. We've known him for years. The girls all think of him as their uncle. He's been very kind to all of us. Always there when we've needed him in times of trouble."

"He sounds a good man. Now Nan, tell me all about yourself and your daughters. And Mavis of course."

"Mavis is one of my daughters, Doctor. I promised Ruby she would be like one of my own and she always has been. No-one here knows any different. The only people who knew the truth were my parents, and they're both dead now."

"It must have been a hard struggle for you, Nan, bringing up the four of them, single-handed. Money must have been a constant worry to you."

"That it was, and no mistake!" Nan smiled ruefully and launched into an account of the trials and tribulations of the previous years. David Harris listened fascinated, and as always in the past, his admiration for this woman's unselfish and indomitable courage was boundless.

After she had settled them with a second cup of tea, she said quietly, "That's enough about us, Doctor. Tell me about your life. You must have done well with your job – coming all this way to lecture to other doctors an' all."

"Yes, I suppose you could say I've been moderately successful in my field. As you may remember, my wife became ill before you left Canada and sadly was in an institution for many years before she died. All that time I suppose my job was the centre of my life. I had no other outlets. I've never been a very sociable devil and my work has made me a bit of a recluse, I'm afraid."

"So it must have been a big upheaval for you, coming all this way to England? Especially the way things are, with the war, I mean."

"Yes, it has been quite an eventful time for me. But there has been growing interest in the field of mental health and I've had papers published in various medical journals and so on. I wanted to do the lectures even with the world situation being what it is. I'm addressing several conferences in England and I've arranged to take an extended leave from my hospital work. Apart from my lectures, I may be able to offer my services in some capacity to the war effort over here. Of course, I'm too long in the tooth to join up!" He smiled at her cheerfully.

"I should think we're going to need doctors just as much as fighting men, if they're right about the bombing. I dread to think what London will be like if they really try to wipe us out. It's been bad enough the last year with those blessed IRA bombs in the tube stations, but planes dropping them on top of us!" Nan shook her head as words failed her.

"I suppose your girls are all determined to join something? Everywhere the young people are full of war talk, aren't they?"

"Yes, Joan wants to join the WAFS. She works in the post office and was the best of the four at school. I reckon she'd be useful in some sort of clerical work. Irene is all set to join the Land Army – she's always been crazy about growing things."

"Just like her mother. I remember how proud you were of your little garden at Maple Cottage. All that wonderful jam you made from your own fruit. I can still taste those scones you used to give me!"

"Yes, I've always loved a garden ... Well I daresay Irene will be safe at least in the Land Army – away from the towns – although I'll miss her. She's my right hand and the most sensible one of the lot."

"What about her twin? Is Rita likely to go as well?"

"Not her! She's too fond of a good time that one! Likes the bright lights – not that we'll be seeing many of those now! No, I reckon she'll probably go into munitions. She works in the local sweet factory at the moment, so she's used to being in a crowd. I'll be glad if she stays put, where I can keep my eye on her!"

"And Mavis? Who does she take after?" He looked at Nan sympathetically, as he asked the question. When she had spoken of Ruby's daughter earlier there had been a certain nuance in her tone from which he had intuitively realised she had ambivalent feelings towards her youngest charge.

"Mavis ... What can I say, Doctor? I suppose the truth is I see the worst of both her parents in her. She has Ruby's good looks and love of a good time. She gets that from her father as well, and she also has his self-centred outlook on life. When push comes to shove, Mavis will always have an eye to the main chance and look out for herself. I'm afraid she's just like Charlie – she uses people for her own ends, and that's the truth."

"So, you've four very different girls, Nan. I wonder what the future holds for them all?"

"Once upon a time, Doctor, I'd have said I wanted them to be happy. Right now, I reckon I'd probably settle for them all being safe at the end of this war – however long it's going to last!"

"Amen to that, Nan!" He glanced at his watch. "Good heavens, I must be keeping you up. I'd no idea it was so late. It's been such a pleasure to see you again, Nan. You don't know how often I've wondered if you were alright."

"I did think of writing to you, when we first got home, but I thought you must be such a busy man, and with your wife sick ... well I hardly liked to take the liberty."

"Oh, Nan!" He shook his head, smiling, as he allowed her to help him on with his coat. "Now we've met up again, I really hope we can keep in touch, especially while I'm still in England. When Philip Ash mentioned your name and offered to give me your address, I was so delighted, and having heard about your girls, I'd love to meet them. After all, I delivered three of them!"

"And saved the life of the fourth!" Nan swallowed a lump in her throat as she looked into his gentle eyes. "Perhaps you'd care to come round and see them one Sunday. We're usually all together for our dinner. Where are you staying? Are you local?"

"I'm stopping with a colleague in Hampstead at the moment. But when I know whether I can be of any use in London, I'll probably look for something more permanent.

Rent a flat maybe. But of course, in between times I shall be dashing off to these various lectures. Oxford, Cambridge, Edinburgh and several more in London.

"Why don't I come over one evening next week and take you out for a meal? You can mention me to the girls in the meantime and ask if they'll be around on the following Sunday, so that I can be introduced. What do you think?"

"Well, I'd love to come out for a meal, but you really needn't go to all that trouble, Doctor. You must have so many other people to meet, places to visit ..."

"No-one I'd rather see, I assure you! I'll pick you up at six thirty Wednesday evening, if that's convenient?"

"Well, yes, that would be lovely. Thank you, Doctor. I'll really look forward to it."

"Wonderful. But please, Nan – stop calling me 'Doctor'. David is my name, and I wish you'd use it!"

Nan laughed as they shook hands and promised she would try to remember in future. It surprised her as she lay in bed that night, going over every moment of their conversation, how easily she thought of him already as David.

When she told the girls about her unexpected visitor the next day they were quite interested, but obviously had no personal recollections of the doctor. When they heard she was going out to dinner with him, they were certainly intrigued. Nan had never had any men friends and they all thought it a great joke to tease her about her "date".

"Don't you lot be so cheeky! It's very civil of the doctor to look us up while he's here, and just like his kindness to offer to give me dinner. He's a retiring sort of man, and I don't think he knows many people in London, so I expect he's glad of some company. He's also keen to meet all of you, seeing as he remembers you from babies, so I shall invite him to tea next Sunday, and I want you all to be here to see him. And on your best behaviour!"

"Yes, Mum!" They all chorused meekly, but she was aware of their nudges and grins and was furious to find herself blushing, especially when she discovered Billy's eyes resting thoughtfully on her as he listened to their chat.

As she peeled the potatoes for dinner and he polished his boots in the scullery later that day, he said quietly, "Sounds as though he remembered you very well, this doctor from Canada. Very close friends were you, back in those days, Nan?"

"Certainly not, Billy! He was our family doctor, but he did a lot for us. Got Charlie the job on the farm, that gave us the cottage to live in. He was there when the girls were born, and when I was very ill with pneumonia, after Charlie had abandoned us and we had that terrible winter in the shack. I really think he saved my life.

"Afterwards, when I was as weak as a kitten in hospital, he took charge of things. The local people had heard about our troubles and very kindly had a whip round for us. He organised it all and bought the tickets for our journey home, arranged for our bits and pieces to be sold and the packing done. Even introduced me to a young nurse who was travelling on the same boat, so she could help me with the children. I honestly don't know where I'd have been without him, Billy."

"So did his wife help out as well? Just as caring was she?" There was a tone in Billy's voice that Nan found odd

– out of character – and it made her feel uncomfortable. Slicing the potatoes into the saucepan she said, tartly, "I never met his wife, Billy. Of course we didn't move in their social circle at all. Besides she became very ill before we left Canada and went into a mental institution. David told me yesterday she died some years ago."

"So he's on his own now, then?"

"That's right. Which is why he's free to leave Canada for a while and come on this lecture tour. What's more, he's hoping to help out with the war effort while he's here. And I should think those in charge will be glad of every good doctor they can lay their hands on!"

"That's true, Nan." Billy gave a final rub to his boots and picked up the kettle, with one of his normal cheerful grins. "How about a cup of Rosy Lee for the workers? Then perhaps you'd like to come and show me where you reckon I should start digging for this shelter. Don't want Jerry to catch us napping, do we?"

Nan's evening out with David was filled with new, wonderful experiences for her. To her amazement he arrived to collect her in a car, which he had borrowed from his colleague. As he held open the door for her, she fleetingly remembered that first car journey with him, when she had slipped in and out of consciousness in the agony of labour before Joan was born, after the episode with the run-away horse.

If there had been any misgivings from either of them that they might be ill at ease in each other's company, in such different surroundings, they were quite unnecessary. The conversation flowed easily as they drove along, Nan asking questions about his work and he showing a very genuine interest in the life that she led in Holgate.

She had been rather apprehensive that she might be out of place or do the wrong thing in some grand restaurant, but David's natural sensitivity ensured that never happened. He took her to Lyons Corner House, which he said he had heard about and thought he would like to experience for himself.

He chatted easily with her about the menu, and when she confessed she was "spoiled for choice" suggested a clear soup for a first course, followed by Dover sole which Nan had never tasted, but thoroughly enjoyed. They finished with a fresh fruit salad and she said quite truthfully it was the best meal she had ever eaten.

After they had lingered over coffee he suggested she might like a little drive around London, and then they parked on the embankment near Cleopatra's Needle and he talked to her about the wonders of ancient Egypt, which was apparently a hobby of his.

"I remember reading in the paper all about the opening of that tomb, the year we left Canada, by that man, Carter. Supposed to have been a curse on all of them for desecrating it wasn't there? I know he died earlier this year."

"You don't believe in curses, do you, Nan?" David raised an eyebrow quizzically as he bent to tuck the car rug more warmly over her knees, for the November evening was very cold.

"'Course not!" Nan denied it stoutly, but she suddenly recalled her father's words about Charlie being a curse on their family, and she shivered in spite of the rug.

When he stopped the car outside number thirty David said quietly, "Thank you for this evening, Nan. I've enjoyed it immensely."

"Thank you, David. I can't remember when I've had such a lovely time. It was a beautiful meal, and all the tastier when you don't have to wash up afterwards!"

"I know it's late now, but I would like to come back again some other time and meet your daughters, if I may?"

"We'd be really pleased if you'd come to tea on Sunday. It won't be anything very grand, of course, but you'd be ever so welcome."

"I'll look forward to it very much, Nan." With his usual impeccable manners he opened the car door, helped her out and escorted her to the doorstep. Raising his hat, he said, "Take care, Nan. See you Sunday." And she echoed, "See you Sunday," before going inside.

Joan was sitting at the kitchen table with Billy and a young man in army uniform who, for a moment, Nan did not recognise. But when he rose with a smile and said, "Evenin' Mrs Stuart," and held out his hand to shake hers, she knew him at once. He was a handsome, muscular figure with a mop of unruly fair hair and twinkling blue eyes.

This was Mrs Flint's eldest grandchild, and the apple of her eye. His parents had married during the First War. Mrs Flint's daughter-in-law had loaned Nan the wedding outfit she had worn. Since those days, the family had moved away to Harringay.

"Harry Flint! I wouldn't have recognised you, lad! My, you do look smart in that uniform, doesn't he Joan?"

"Yes, he does." Joan blushed and knocked the teaspoon from her saucer on to the floor. Harry hastily bent to retrieve it and, as Joan did the same, they lightly knocked their heads together. Both burst into spontaneous laughter and Harry, said, "I'll bet that hurt me more than you, Joanie. Your 'Victory Roll' must have cushioned it more than my army 'short back and sides'!"

"What a pair! I see she's made you a cuppa, Harry. Any left in the pot for me, is there?"

"It's all right, Nan, I'll make some fresh. That'll be stewed by now. Enjoy your evening out, did you?" Billy's eyes took in the grey worsted dress which Nan had made for Christmas two years previously. The pattern was simple, but she had pinned a pink silk rose to one shoulder that matched the shade of the rarely-worn lipstick. Billy thought that ten years had dropped away from her and she could easily have passed for Joan's elder sister.

They stayed chatting in the kitchen till the twins and Mavis came in from a visit to the local cinema. They were full of the Newsreel which had been about the first German bombs falling, of all places, in the Shetlands. Eight hundred-odd men had also been lost when *The Royal Oak* was torpedoed in Scapa Flow.

"It'll be nice when we get some cheerful news for a change, I'm fed up with all this doom and gloom," Nan said and firmly changed the subject.

"So what are you doing round here, Harry? Just visiting your gran, are you? She keeps herself busy doesn't she, but she must miss your auntie Vi's kids, now they've been evacuated."

"Well, she'll be seeing a bit more of me for a while. I've been posted to a training barracks in north London. I'm hoping to be a wireless operator if I can get through the course all right. There's not much doing at the camp in the evenings, so I expect I'll be popping over to Gran's quite a bit. When Joanie called round with a knitting pattern I said I'd walk her back. With the black-out an' all ..."

Nan saw the way that he and Joan exchanged glances as he said this, and once again the colour rose in the young girl's cheeks. It was the first time Nan had ever seen her show any interest in a man, and Nan's heart went out to her. The world was such a dark place and the future so bleak for all the young folk at the moment, Nan thought. They ought to grasp any moments of enjoyment they could.

Impulsively, she said to Harry, "If you're not doing anything on Sunday, lad, why don't you come over for your tea? We've got a very old family friend from Canada visiting, and you'd be most welcome to join us."

She was rewarded by Joan's beam of surprise as Harry quickly accepted the invitation. Nan was sure that the friendly young man would get on easily with David, and it might make the atmosphere more relaxed having him join them.

The tea party did go very well. Nan had done her best with sandwiches and they all had a jovial time toasting crumpets over the kitchen fire. She had remembered David's words and produced a plateful of scones as well as Irene's feather-light sponge to finish the meal. Both David and Harry were generous in their praise, and Nan was delighted to see how well they mixed with the girls and also Billy.

The latter was a little subdued when talking to David, and Nan wondered if it was simply an awareness of the difference in their backgrounds and class, or was there some more personal reason? The three men chatted together at length about the war, but then Rita and Mavis made it clear they were bored with the gloomy conversation and suggested some music on the wireless.

One of their favourite bands was playing and soon the young people were pushing back the furniture to have a dance. Harry and Joan talked quietly as they circled the room decorously; Rita partnered Mavis in the more lively dance-steps and Billy jokingly asked Irene if he might have the pleasure, and they did an hilarious version of a jitterbug. Nan and David watched in amusement, and when she went through to the scullery to find some bottles of lemonade to cool them off after their exertions, he followed her quite naturally.

"They're a wonderful family, Nan. You must be very proud of them. Thank you for letting me share this evening with you all."

"It's been lovely to have you here, David. I'm afraid that Rita and Mavis can get noisy at times, but it's just their way of having a bit of fun."

"Don't apologise for them, Nan. Young people aren't going to have many opportunities for being carefree in the near future, so I firmly believe they must take the chance when they can."

"Strange, that's exactly what I've been thinking lately." They exchanged smiles, and Nan thought how wonderful it was to be so completely in tune with another person, without even needing to talk.

She knew that as 1939 was drawing to a close, millions of people were looking forward with trepidation to the horrors and separations that war would probably bring. But watching David carry the tray of glasses through to the others, as they all embarked on a sing-song, in which he cheerfully joined, she couldn't feel anything but a glowing happiness.

Moments previously he had asked if she would like to accompany him to a concert at the Albert Hall, and when she had eagerly agreed, the warmth in his eyes promised only good things for her in 1940.

Nan's own feelings of secret happiness were often to buoy up her spirits during those first months of the new year, when all about her the news was filled with unremitting gloom. The war made itself felt on the home front very swiftly when bacon, butter and sugar were rationed in January, and meat soon followed in March. In kitchens throughout the land, women were rapidly becoming more inventive in their choice of menus.

All of the family at number thirty were quickly involved in the war effort in their various ways, some more enthusiastically than others. Irene was overjoyed to leave the sweet factory and enter the Land Army and Nan cried unashamedly as she waved her off to the country. She thought her daughter looked wonderful in her new uniform of khaki breeches, shirt and tie and smart green felt hat above her golden curls.

In the months ahead she was to miss Irene badly, but always enjoyed the letters from Cornwall which were full of vivid detail about the new life she was enjoying on the farm.

"She sounds so happy, David, If the war has done one good thing, as far as I'm concerned, it's getting Irene out of that horrible factory and into the fresh air! But I can't see her coming back here to live when it's over, and that's a fact."

"Well, it's good to know she's safe down there from the threat of the bombs. They seem to be getting more widespread every night."

"I do worry about you in that flat in Hampstead, you know." Nan looked at him across the table in the small tea-rooms where they had stopped after a walk one Sunday afternoon in Epping Forest.

"There's a very good shelter down in the basement, and in any case I don't imagine Hampstead is going to be a prime target! More likely the City and the Docks."

"From what that horrible Lord Haw Haw says, Hitler's going to flatten the whole place, suburbs and all, so I don't think any of us are safe!"

"How's your own Anderson in the garden? Billy still improving on his award-winning design?" David laughed as they both reflected on Billy's determination that Nan and the girls should have every possible convenience during their sojourns outside in the shelter.

"Well, even Billy can't do much about the damp, bless him. But we can't complain. It's quite cosy really. Loads of blankets and hot-water bottles. I take out my knitting and the girls play cards. We have the wireless sometimes, and I make up a basket with sandwiches and a Thermos of soup. Bit of a picnic really! The girls and I have the four bunks, and Billy has a camp bed down the middle. Not that he's there very often – usually out fire watching or with the Home Guard."

"How's Joan getting on in the WAAF? She certainly looks very attractive in the uniform! I daresay you'll have a procession of young airmen beating a path to your door!"

"Oh, I don't think there's much chance of that. My Joanie's a real romantic and she's only got eyes for one young man."

"Harry, you mean? Where is he these days?"

"Up at Catterick, I think. He's done well with his training and so pleased he's a fully-fledged wireless operator now. With all the rumours flying around, I'm afraid he'll be sent into action very soon. I'm dreading it for Joan's sake. She doesn't say much, but they spend every moment they can together when he's got some leave."

"How about Rita and Mavis? Managing to stay out of mischief, are they?"

"Rita's gone into the munitions factory at Stoke Newington and gets on well with the other girls, I think. At weekends she and Mavis are always off to some dance or other, or else at the pictures. Every Saturday Rita seems to come home escorted by a different uniform! And Mavis is just as bad.

"She's working in the NAAFI now. She's too young to join anything else, thank goodness. Actually it suits her quite well. She's not that brainy, so cooking is a good practical skill that she'll be able to use after the war. I could never get her to do a hand's turn around the house, so at least she's learning something now!"

"Is Joan still based in London then?"

"Yes, she gets home most nights, unless she's on late duty. She does clerical work in the air ministry at the moment. Though she could be posted to an airfield somewhere, I suppose. She's learning typing and shorthand, so I'm hoping whatever she does will be in an office. I can't imagine Joan doing anything technical with engines or guns!"

"Isn't it incredible how much difference the war has made to all our lives in just a few months?" David signalled to the waitress for the bill.

"Yes, so much has changed, so quickly," Nan said quietly, when they walked outside into the April sunshine. As if he read her thoughts, David tucked her hand into the crook of his arm, saying, "I'm afraid it sounds terribly selfish, in view of all the misery throughout the world, but I can honestly say I'm happier than I've ever been, my dear."

"I feel exactly the same, David. And I refuse to believe it's wrong. Let's just be thankful and grasp it while we can. Heaven knows, happiness can be fleeting at the best of times, and now ... well ..."

"I know." He patted her hand, and said with a warm smile. "Let's refuse to talk about the war when we're alone together, shall we? Pretend it's just not happening?"

"That sounds an excellent prescription, doctor!" They both laughed and ran, like a couple of carefree youngsters, back towards the station. Trains were notoriously unreliable these days, but since David was very limited to the amount of petrol he could obtain for his personal use, outings in the borrowed car were few and far between.

254

The doctor colleague, who was younger than David, had already enlisted in the navy and his wife had gone to stay with her mother for the duration, along with their two children. So David was very welcome to occupy the Hampstead flat for as long as he liked. Nan had not been there, but hoped an invitation would be forthcoming.

Their relationship had proceeded gently but with an unspoken inevitability. The difference in their ages and background just never came into the equation. The natural affinity between their temperaments was all that mattered. Sometimes they would talk about the early days in Canada, but mostly the present was all they needed.

Nan was unfailingly interested in David's work, which at the moment was dealing with Jewish children who were refugees from Hitler's excesses in Europe. Many were orphans and had witnessed and endured terrible violence. David was gradually trying to win their confidence and endeavouring to ensure some sort of settled future for them.

"A lot of them will be sent out of England as soon as they can face the upheaval of a long journey. After their experiences they need to get right away from any threat of bombing or war talk. No doubt the Empire will take a lot – Canada especially. I've been in touch with some of my colleagues back there and I'll act as a liaison officer when it happens. But for now I'm trying to give them some feeling of security and help them start the recovery process after what they've been through."

Apart from her job with Mrs Ash, Nan was helping out in the cottage hospital wherever she could be of use. Number thirty was like every other house with its black-out curtains at all the windows, the row of gas-masks lined up in the hall when the occupants were home, and of course the shelter in the back garden.

With Irene away now, Nan was looking after the allotment herself, as well as the small area of the back garden left for growing food, now that the shelter was built. Some hens had also been installed, to replace the ones of Emily's that had gradually died off.

At the end of April a heart-broken Joan waved farewell to a determinedly cheerful Harry, after his embarkation leave. It was widely believed that his unit would be going into France or Belgium.

"You take care of yourself, lad." Nan hugged him tightly when he came to say goodbye to the family, before Joan went to have a last private word by the front door.

"Don't worry Mrs Stuart, I'm not good enough to die young! Only don't tell me gran that!"

"In that case, what am I doing letting you go out with my daughter then?" Nan pretended to box his ear, and then said more seriously, "God speed, Harry, we'll be thinking of you." He gave her a mock salute, and then went out with his arm round Joan, while Nan went into the kitchen.

Billy was polishing the buttons on his Home Guard uniform at the table. He looked up sympathetically as Nan blew her nose. "Poor little Joanie's going to need cheering up I reckon. She's really keen on him, isn't she?"

"Yes, Billy, she is. Under normal circumstances I'd be delighted, but the way things are – I feel sorry for any young couple in love."

"I daresay a few older ones won't be finding it too easy, either," Billy said quietly. Nan looked at him quickly. She knew there was little that he missed, and was sure he guessed how she felt about David. Still at least David is still in London, she thought as a sobbing Joan walked through the door. Billy tactfully went to make a cup of tea, whilst Nan took her eldest daughter in her arms, to give what comfort she might.

The ensuing weeks made it difficult to offer any words of cheer to Joan, or anyone with men away in the forces. British troops who had landed in Norway in April, were leaving in May. Then the Germans invaded Belgium, Luxembourg and the Netherlands. Every news bulletin seemed full of bad tidings with Belgium surrendering and the British Army in full retreat across France.

Joan was busy with her job in the air ministry, but the hours spent at home she simply moped about, her face drawn and pale from sleepless nights worrying about Harry.

"Supposing he's been taken prisoner, Mum. Or wounded somewhere, or even ..." her voice broke as she could not voice the awful thought.

"If the worst had happened, Joanie, we'd probably have heard by now. You know his mother said she'd send word to his gran the minute she hears anything. Mrs Flint or Vi would come straight round, you know that. Come on love, 'no news is good news' they always say.

"Oh, drat! There goes that wretched siren again. Mavis, have you got your gas mask? Rita bring the Thermos will you? Come on Joanie, back to the shelter and we'll have a game of Ludo shall we?"

Then the news changed to that of victory in defeat, with the amazing tales of heroism of the "gallant little ships" in the incredible rescue operation at Dunkirk, and spirits lifted generally. As the family sat round the wireless listening to Churchill's wonderful uplifting words on June 5th, it was no real surprise when there was a knocking at the front door and a familiar cheerful voice was heard saying, "Anyone home to welcome the bad penny then?" and Harry popped his head in the kitchen.

When the initial storm of greeting and relief quietened down and he and Joan had spent a private hour in the front room on their own, Nan was able to hear about his experiences first hand. He spoke graphically of those terrible days spent on the beach, under continual fire, waiting his turn to be taken off by one of the tiny fishing boats.

He looked a lot thinner, the bright blue eyes were darkly shadowed and there was a new strength and maturity to his face, although he was never serious for too long. Mostly for Joan's benefit, Nan suspected.

For a short time there was a respite as Harry enjoyed a brief leave and Joan managed to wangle some extra time at home, so that she might be with him every moment. Nan suggested he put up a camp bed in the front room at nights, and stay with them for the length of his leave, so the young couple did not have to waste a minute.

During the daylight hours they would go for long walks in the park or through Alexandra Palace, and Nan would leave them alone as often as possible in the kitchen when they came home at nights. Perhaps her natural sympathy for their situation was heightened by her own relationship with David.

During those summer months they spent so many happy hours together. There were visits to the cinema, walks in the country, concerts in London, snatched meals together when David's time was limited, as his work became more demanding. In addition to the refugee children, he now numbered many servicemen among his patients, after the horrors of Dunkirk.

At the beginning of September life changed again at number thirty. Joan was posted out of London and sent to take up her duties at an airfield in Kent.

"From what she says, it sounds as though she spends all her time pushing little models of planes around on maps!" Nan told Mrs Flint when they met in a queue at the butchers.

"Well, dear she's probably safer out of London. These last few nights have been terrible, haven't they? I don't know when we last got two hours sleep together! Those poor devils in the East End! There was a close one here last night, I really thought we'd copped it, didn't you?"

"I certainly did. Felt like the ground was coming up through your feet. The kitchen window smashed to pieces again. I don't know how many times that's happened. Even the hens were scared – not one egg today! But apparently it landed on the gasworks."

"I reckon our Harry'll be off overseas again soon. A lot of talk about sending more of them out to North Africa. Harry says it'll be nice to get a tan at the expense of the army! Oh, 'e's a caution that lad!"

Nan worried about Joan's reaction if she heard the rumour; she had been so devastated when they had parted last time. But as David said when she voiced her worries to him that evening over a meal at Lyons, "There's nothing you can do, my dear. Just be a shoulder to cry on when she comes home. At least she's got her work to keep her occupied now.

"From what I hear, she's right in the thick of it down in Kent. Those chaps in the RAF are doing an amazing job, and she must be at the hub of it all. So she won't have too much time to dwell on Harry's departure, will she?"

When they had finished their meal they strolled through the nearby streets. Everywhere was thronged with uniforms and there was an air of desperate gaiety. Theatres still opened in spite of the air raid warnings and dance bands played in cellars. As usual the tube stations were lined with civilians sheltering from the expected nightly bombardment.

As the fighters droned overhead and Nan watched the vivid lights of the ack ack fire, interspersed with the brilliant beams of the searchlights picking out the enemy planes, she was conscious of a feeling of total unreality. This could not be real. She, Nan Stuart, could not be picking her way along a London thoroughfare, with bombed-out buildings on either side, her arm firmly held by this distinguished Canadian doctor whom she had come to love so deeply. It was all some weird, surrealist dream from which she would awaken, to find herself back in Holgate with four small children awaiting their breakfast.

But then David was urging her towards the nearest tube station as the bombing became closer and more intense and there was no more time to indulge in soul-searching.

That night saw the turning point in their relationship. The gentle kisses of farewell and meaning pressures on her hand were exchanged for a tight embrace that swiftly gave way to passionate kisses as they took their slow walk from the local station back to number thirty in the black-out.

They paused to shelter in a shop doorway in the high street, as yet another bomb whistled earthwards and noisily found its target, and David said suddenly, "Nan I must tell you something."

"What is it?" The tone of his voice warned her that she would not want to hear the words he was about to utter.

"I have to go away, Nan. It's because of the children, the refugees I've been looking after."

"What's going to happen, David? Where are you going? Is it far?" Nan looked up at him fearfully, as she stood within the circle of his arms, for the moment oblivious to the sounds of the bombardment in the distance.

"I've got to return to Canada. We've arranged to evacuate a large number of the children out there. Some of them will be my most seriously affected problem cases. Although it's best for them to get out of London, I know the long journey, leaving the surroundings they've grown used to, will be very traumatic for them.

"Because of this I've decided I must accompany them myself. You do understand, don't you my dearest?"

"Yes, of course I do, David." Nan swallowed, hard. "Will you be leaving soon? And will you be coming back?"

"The boat is sailing this week. But I will be coming back, Nan, I promise! I shall have to stay out there for a while, settling them into their new surroundings, but I'll return as soon as I can. Don't doubt that for one moment."

"Well that's all right then." Nan tried to smile shakily at him, but failed miserably as the tears rolled silently down her cheeks. Gently, he drew her close and softly kissed the top of her hair.

"Nan, you must know how very precious you are to me. I know this is the least romantic place to broach the subject, but I don't have much more time. There's so much to sort out before I leave. I think tomorrow will have to be our last meeting."

He raised her chin with one finger and gazed into her eyes, where he could see reflected the lights from the fires blazing on the London skyline. "When I come back Nan, I want us to be together permanently. I know you're still legally married to Charlie, but I want you to be my wife. I'll take whatever steps are necessary to make you a free woman again, so that we can get married. That's if you'll have me. Will you, Nan?"

"Oh, David, you know I will!" Nan's voice rang with sincerity as she spoke from the heart. "You were always very special to me, even all those years ago, when I came to rely on you in every crisis. I never dreamed I'd ever see you again, and since you've come back into my life, it's as though I've been reborn.

"All the bitterness and anger that was locked up inside because of Charlie and Ruby, somehow it's all gone, because of you, David. Before you arrived on my doorstep that evening, I was like a dried-up husk of a woman. All my feelings seemed to have withered away and I never felt I could ever care for a man again. Never feel passion again … But with you David, it's as though I'm a young, carefree girl – in love for the very first time!"

"Oh, Nan, my dear, if you knew how wonderful it is for me to hear those words. Because it's been exactly the same for me. Ever since Joan, my wife, became ill, I'd learned to close off all my emotions and bury myself in my work. With you, I feel as though I've started living again!"

Their mouths met in a long, passionate kiss and Nan's limbs became weak at the storm of physical longing that overcame her. She knew that David was experiencing the same intense desire, as he pressed her tightly against the hardness of his own body. His voice was hoarse as he said, "Nan, my dear, I want you so very much. Dare I ask ... would you consider coming back to Hampstead tonight, instead of going home? It will be our only chance to be together before I leave."

"David, I want that more than anything. Let's go back to the station and catch the last train. I don't want us to waste a single moment, my darling."

Oblivious of the bombs that were falling widespread over the streets of London that night, they hurried, arms entwined, back to the station in time to catch the train. For once there were few hold-ups and they quickly reached Hampstead. Swiftly they moved through the blacked out streets, which were nonetheless brightly illuminated by the searchlights dancing over the heath.

Hampstead itself was relatively untouched that night, and the hours they spent in David's borrowed flat were uninterrupted by any visit to the shelter below. Nan thought afterwards they would probably have ignored any warning sirens and willingly risked dying together during those magical hours that finally sealed their relationship.

It was so different from the times she had made love with Charlie. With him the passion had been paramount. It had been overwhelming, thrilling, a voyage of discovery that the innocent young Nan had eagerly undertaken. But with David there was an added dimension of an incredible warm tenderness that she had never known with Charlie.

Physical passion was certainly there with David, in a way that Nan never suspected two older people could experience. But all the years of loneliness they had both endured was poured out in a great flood of yearning and need. It was almost light when they finally slept, closely entwined together, and Nan was happily aware of the dawn chorus serenading them.

When she awoke, it was to find David already dressed and holding a tray laden with tea and toast. "I'm sorry to have to wake you, my dear, but I'm afraid we shall have to leave very soon if I'm to have the time to drive you home before I go into the hospital."

"That's all right. I'm supposed to be at Mrs Ash's myself. Oh, David, what a treat! I can't remember ever having breakfast in bed – unless I've been ill!"

"When we are married I shall insist on this as a treat every Sunday, my darling. Oh, Nan, I keep picturing you back in my home in Canada. It's been such an empty place for so long, I know you'll bring it warmth and light again."

"Canada – yes, I'd love to go back there. To breathe that wonderful clear air again in the forests, to listen to the thunder of Niagara – will we really do it, David?"

"Of course we will! When this wretched war is over, nothing shall stop us. My solicitors will do whatever is necessary to trace Charlie and arrange the divorce. How long is it now since you heard anything, Nan?"

"I've never had a word since the day he walked out in 1921 – nineteen years ago, David."

"Then he's hardly likely to cause any problems now, is he? As soon as I come back from this trip, we'll start the legal wheels in motion. Now my darling, I hate to hurry you, but we must get started ourselves. Will you have a problem explaining your absence back home to the family, by the way?"

"Not really. I'm sure Billy understands about us already, and will be very sympathetic. I shall simply tell them all that the bombing was bad and I stayed to shelter in London last night. I think I'm entitled to spend a single night out and leave my grown-up daughters on their own for once, don't you?"

David used some of his precious petrol to drive Nan home and they arranged to have a farewell lunch the next day. When she got to work, Nan explained to Mrs Ash that a friend was leaving for overseas and she would have to take the following day off.

"That's quite all right, Nan. Is it someone in the forces that's going away? So upsetting these partings."

"No, Ma'am. He's too old for that. But he is going abroad and I shall miss him whilst he's gone."

"Of course you will." Mrs Ash smiled sympathetically at her. "All our friends are doubly precious these days, aren't they? And with travelling overseas so dangerous, it's especially hard to say goodbye, isn't it?"

"Yes, Ma'am, it is. Very hard." Nan said quietly.

She dressed herself carefully the next day in her "best" dark green coat and a matching turban style hat. Neat brown shoes, bag and gloves completed the outfit, along with the mandatory gas mask. She caught an early train into London, to allow for any disruptions. David was waiting outside the hospital gate when she arrived, exactly on time, and they walked to a small, nearby French restaurant that he liked, where he had taken her before.

Neither did justice to the vegetable soup or the mushroom omelettes, excellent though they were. "Don't reckon these were made with dried egg," said Nan, trying to smile in spite of the lump in her throat that made swallowing the food so difficult.

David had ordered wine and she tried to sip it, to make the food go down more easily. But she refused a brandy with the coffee. "I'll never find me way through the tube if I don't keep a clear head! All those tunnels lined with the boys dozing on their kit bags and the rows of bunks for people to sleep at nights, it's like a maze in the big stations now."

"I know. I wish I could drive you back, my dear. But we have a last-minute briefing this afternoon about the travel plans for tomorrow. It's going to be quite an undertaking escorting so many children, sick and well, all the way to Liverpool and then on to the boat."

"Don't worry about me, David. I'll be fine. By the way, the girls and Billy send their best wishes. Hope you have a good journey. I think Billy really likes you now, although at first he was a bit wary of someone as posh as a doctor being a friend!"

"He's a fine man and I know he's devoted to you and the girls, Nan. It's a pity he never married. He should have had a family of his own."

"Yes, I've always felt that. But from something he once said, I think that when he was in the trenches he was wounded. I knew he was invalided out because of gas damage to his lungs – he still has to be extra careful in the winter – but I believe there was something else." She gazed at David thoughtfully, her own sadness forgotten for a moment.

"I wonder if he was wounded in such a way that he couldn't ever lead a ... well ... normal ... married life afterwards. Or father children. So he would never get into a close relationship with any woman. He just hinted about it once when we were sitting up late in the shelter on our own, and I think that's why he's always been such a loner."

"How dreadfully sad. What a waste." David shook his head, and then hastily looked at his watch. "Nan, my dear, just a few minutes and then I'm afraid I have to go."

"It's all right, David. Don't worry, I promise I won't embarrass you with a big farewell scene!" Nan smiled at him with the indomitable cheerfulness that he loved so much, and he took her hand across the table.

"Before we leave, I've something for you, Nan. You don't have to wear it yet, if you think it's too soon, but at least I want you to have it as a reminder of our plans for the future." He opened a tiny box to reveal an engagement ring with a single diamond surrounded by mauve amethysts.

"David it's absolutely beautiful. And of course I shall wear it! Please put it on for me." She held out her left hand and he slipped it on the third finger. "Is that comfortable? Does it fit? I had to guess the size." He asked anxiously.

"It's perfect and I couldn't be more thrilled. I'm so proud that you want me to marry you, David. I will try not to let you down. I do know that I've never mixed with people like your friends and colleagues and I've only ever worked with my hands. But I've read a lot and I do know there are right and wrong ways of doing things. I want you to know that when we're married, I'll try really hard to be a good wife to you – not make you ashamed of me – and run your home as it should be."

"Nan, there is no way in the world I could ever be ashamed of you! I am just so grateful that you've accepted a crusty old devil like me!"

"Not so much of the 'old' if you don't mind! From what I've seen, I reckon you could show some of these youngsters a thing or two!" Nan blushed as she nodded meaningly across the table, and he smiled back before kissing her unashamedly in front of the waiter, who was bringing their bill.

Outside, the chill of autumn was damp in the air and he pulled her closely against his side as they walked slowly back to the hospital gates. Then he drew her tightly into one last long embrace, their lips pressed fiercely together as if they could never bear to be parted.

Finally Nan stepped back. "You must go, my dear, or you'll be late for your meeting." Very gently she took his face between her hands and gazed into it silently for one last moment. "Take care, my love, I'll be waiting for you." Then she turned, and head down with the tears blurring her vision, walked swiftly away. When she reached the corner, she looked back, but the upright, grey-haired figure was already inside the hospital doors.

When Nan reached home she spent an hour alone in her room, just lying on the bed thinking about David and the future they would have together. Although she was missing him already, and the weeks without him stretched ahead of her, she still nursed a flame of glowing happiness as she pondered on their commitment to each other.

I'm so lucky, she thought. It's incredible that we should have come together like this, after all those years. We have age and background differences, but they won't come between us. When I think of girls like poor Joanie, who don't know where their young men are, or when they'll be back, I'm really fortunate that David is too old to be in the fighting.

When Rita and Mavis came home for their evening meal, she proudly showed them the engagement ring and explained that David had asked her to marry him. Both seemed amazed that two older people could even think of any sort of romance, but Mavis was impressed by the obvious worth of the ring.

"He must be quite rich, I suppose. Well doctors are professional men, aren't they? Come to think of it, he's always spent plenty on you, Mum. Taking you out to meals and theatres and such like! Lucky old you! I suppose he's got a really posh house back in Canada. Right toffee-nosed you'll be when you get married!"

"I don't know what his house is like. I never saw it. But I'm not really that bothered. All that matters is we care about each other and want to spend our lives together. It will be a wrench leaving all of you, when we go to live in Canada, but that won't happen for a long time. Not till after this war is over, that's certain. By then you could all be leading different lives yourselves."

"Well I wouldn't mind coming out to Canada with you, Mum." Mavis nodded thoughtfully. "Canada's next to

America, isn't it? I've always wanted to go to New York and Hollywood."

"Mavis, America is a big country and it's a long way from the Canadian border to the places you're talking about!" Nan smiled at her. "But of course we hope you can all visit us, and no doubt we'll come back to England for trips. I expect David's work will involve him in that."

Overhead the siren wailed ominously. "Here we go again! Let's get this war over before we start making any plans, eh? Off to the shelter girls. I'll just fill the flask with some tea. It's really bitter out there tonight."

Joan came home for a weekend leave and was pleased at Nan's news, in spite of her own worry about Harry, who was now in the thick of the fighting in Libya. She did talk a little about her work at the airfield, although they were all very conscious of the catch-phrase "Careless Talk Costs Lives" even in the privacy of their own home.

"It's dreadful, Mum, to see those young boys. Some of them scarcely old enough to grow those moustaches they're so proud of! They're always larking about, off to the local pub whenever there's a delivery of beer. They boast about how many German planes they've shot down on a mission, but every night a few of their squadron are missing. In the ops room we hear them over the radio as they come back, and you know some of them won't make it. Often it's one of the lads we've been joking with earlier, the same day. It's heartbreaking to think of so many young lives being wasted!"

"I know, love. It's terrible. But if it weren't for those brave boys, I reckon London would be in an even worse state than it is. Did you hear they got part of St. Paul's the other night? Terrible to think of it."

Two days later there was more personal bad news when Billy heard that his sister's home in Brixton had received a direct hit and she and her husband were killed. Grim-faced he set off to sort out the formalities of the funeral, and Nan felt for this lonely figure, whose last relative had now gone.

We must all be especially caring towards him, she decided. What sort of Christmas is it going to be for all of us this year? Perhaps Irene may be able to get home. It's so long since we've seen her. She's the only one of us who seems to have found happiness through this war. It's given her a chance to do what she's always wanted.

But before Christmas Nan was to face a personal tragedy so overwhelming, that she afterwards wondered how she came through it. It was an ordinary morning like any other when she set off to Mrs Ash's. All unaware, she let herself into the kitchen and started washing up the dishes left over from their meal of the night before. They had had a rare dinner party for some of Doctor Ash's colleagues, so Nan had plenty to do.

When Mrs Ash came through the door, Nan turned in surprise, as it was unusual for her employer to put in such an early appearance. "Good morning Ma'am. It's bitter out there today. Better wrap up well if you're going shopping."

"Nan, I've got to speak to you. I have some news I think you should hear." Mrs Ash came across the room and from the nervous look in her eyes, and the same timbre of her voice, a shaft of foreboding stabbed through Nan's body. She stopped polishing the glass she was holding, and waited in silence.

"You know we had some colleagues of Doctor Ash's for dinner last night, and they told us some very sad news. I expect it will be in the newspapers as well, but I wanted to tell you personally.

"Your old friend, Doctor Harris – I expect you knew that he had gone back to Canada, accompanying some children who were being evacuated?"

"Yes, I did know. We met the day before he left." Nan answered automatically. A terrible sense of impending tragedy was sweeping through her whole body, and she willed the words to hasten from her employer's lips. She was filled with the desperate urge to have the awful suspense ended, yet to prolong the moment before actually hearing the dark tidings she was sure were to follow.

"Yes, I thought you had kept in touch whilst he was here. My husband mentioned he's seen you in a restaurant near the hospital on one occasion. Of course I didn't say anything, because your private life is nothing to do with me ..." Mrs Ash was speaking quickly, almost rambling, as though loath to continue with the tidings she knew she must voice.

"Well, the tragic news is that the ship they were travelling on – *The Empress of Britain* it was – they heard at the hospital yesterday that it had been sunk by German U-boats. All those poor, poor children ... and of course Doctor Harris with them.

"Such a great loss to the world of medicine. My husband tells me he was a very gifted man. I'm so sorry, Nan. This must be quite upsetting for you, as you were acquaintances – well, friends, really - from so long ago."

"We were going to be married, Ma'am." Nan's voice was devoid of expression, as was her face, which was deathly pale. Very deliberately, she placed the beautiful crystal wine glass down on the table, and then automatically untied her apron.

"If you'll excuse me, Ma'am. I have to get some fresh air. It's been rather a shock ..."

"Why, Nan, we had no idea! I'm so dreadfully sorry. Let me get you a glass of brandy. Come and sit down. You look so pale. I'm such a fool, I should have broken it to you more gently. But we really had no idea, no idea at all ..." Mrs Ash was genuinely appalled at bearing such terrible news to a woman she sincerely admired.

"No thank you, Ma'am. I'll be all right. I'll just take myself off home, if you can manage for the day. I'm sorry to cause an inconvenience." She put on her coat and knotted her headscarf, before methodically pulling on her gloves. Mrs Ash watched in helpless dismay as Nan then went out of the back door, closing it quietly behind her.

When she got back to number thirty the house was empty, with all the others out at work. She went into the kitchen and sat before the fire. After a while she drew off her glove and stared down at the glittering engagement ring. She knew now it had all been just a lovely, impossible dream.

Nan Stuart would never leave Holgate and the drab house in which she had been born and raised her family. She would end her days in these grey surroundings. She would never live in a beautiful home overlooking a dark green forest, with the sounds of roaring waters coming faintly on the breeze. She would never breathe again the icy winter air and have her eyes dazzled by the glittering expanse of winter white, or the gleaming fires of autumn maples. The rest of her days would be spent encased in a grey cocoon.

And through the rest of her life, her capacity for tenderness and passion would be locked forever within her memory. David was gone and the terrible agony of that knowledge was a physical torment that made her catch a sobbing breath, before going slowly up to her room. There she carefully removed the ring and gently placed it in its tiny box, which she laid beneath her pile of clean underwear in the top drawer of her chest. She would never wear it again.

When the others came home that evening, Nan was lying quiet in her bed. Rita came to enquire if she had a headache, and Nan said she had. "Shall I get you a cup of tea, Mum? D'you want some aspirin?"

"No, nothing thanks, Rita. Just get yourselves something to eat. Make sure Billy has some hot food inside him before he goes fire watching. If the siren sounds get yourselves off to the shelter. I'd rather stay here tonight and take my chances."

"You all right, Mum? You sound a bit odd." Rita peered at her mother across the gloomy room, which was unlit as the black-out curtain had not been drawn.

"Don't worry about me, Rita. Just leave me alone for tonight, there's a good girl. Tell the others to let me be, will you?"

"All right then. See you in the morning, Mum."

"See you in the morning." Nan turned her face to the wall, and wished that tears would come to release the pain of a burning grief that seemed to consume her innermost self. But her eyes remained dry through all the long hours of that sleepless night.

In the next morning's newspaper there was a lengthy piece about the appalling horror of the U-boats sinking the *Empress of Britain* with its cargo of children being evacuated to Canada. Nan read it through, dry-eyed, and then left it on the table for the others.

"You'll see from the paper that David has gone. I don't want to talk about it. So please let's leave it like that." Nan addressed these words to Rita, Mavis and Billy and then walked out of the house to work. The three of them read the article in silence, and then Rita said tearfully, "Poor Mum, whatever will she do? She'd set her heart on marrying him and going back to Canada. You could see that. Poor Mum!" and she began to sob into her hanky, for Rita was a tender-hearted girl, even if rather a shallow one.

"Yes, your poor mother." Billy shook his head as he stared down at the paper, His voice was husky and he swore uncharacteristically in front of the girls. "Those bloody German U-boats! Bloody savages! Sinking innocent kids. What sort of war is this anyway?" And he violently crumpled the paper into a ball and hurled it into the heart of the fire.

"Well, you know Mum. She'll cope. She's a survivor if ever there was one." Mavis looked thoughtfully at Billy. She had always suspected his feelings for Nan were a lot more complex than they appeared. "Anyway, she's still got his ring. That must be worth a bob or two. And who knows, he may have left her something in his will, and we'll be able to go to Canada after the war!" Mavis checked her lipstick in the mirror and strolled out of the door. Had she but known it, she was a carbon copy of Ruby at her age.

Billy shook his head in disgust at her words and wondered how a sensitive, selfless lady like Nan had ever mothered such a stony-hearted, selfish little bitch. "Must be her father's daughter," he muttered.

During the weeks before Christmas Nan moved through the days like a ghost. She spoke when necessary, performed her duties automatically and would sit unspeaking beside the fire or in the shelter, during the raids. Billy did his best to help her cope with the inner torment, but knew he was making little progress. Even the daily news of the appalling bombing losses sustained not only in London, but in towns such as Birmingham, Liverpool and Bristol, brought no real reaction from Nan.

At least the family were together on Christmas Day, apart from Harry of course, who was believed to be fighting somewhere near Tobruk. Irene had managed to arrive late Christmas Eve, after the usual appalling wartime journey by train from Cornwall.

She was laden with treats sent by the kind farmer and his wife, to whom it seemed she was becoming a surrogate daughter. "I hope all this stuff is still edible, Mum. There's a chicken and some butter and cheese, bacon and home-made jam. I know it all weighs a ton!"

"I'm sure it's very good of Mr and Mrs – Tregaron, is it? I'm so glad to know you're happy down there Irene. You're one person I don't have to worry about." Nan gave her a remote smile as she went to pack away the food in the larder.

"Mum looks awful, Uncle Billy," Irene muttered to him as he sat preparing sprouts in readiness for Christmas dinner the next day.

"I know, lass. You never saw her with Doctor Harris, but his death has hit her really hard. I think it would be better if she could bring herself to talk about him, but she's simply closed herself off inside. She's just like a zombie, going through the motions, but no feeling there."

"Poor old Mum. What with her, and Joan worrying all the time about Harry out in the desert, a jolly old festive season we're all going to have!"

"Well I daresay there's a lot of people across Europe tonight who are feeling a deal worse than us. There aren't many families who haven't suffered a loss of some sort."

"Oh, Uncle Billy, I never thought! Of course you lost your sister and her husband. I was ever so sorry to hear about that." Irene gave him a hug, for she was very fond of this old family friend.

The months of 1941 ground on with news of battles in many foreign lands. Places which had just been geography lessons at school were filled with personal meaning, when much-loved husbands, sweethearts or fathers were involved in a life and death struggle in those far off war zones.

Day to day living became more of a survival course in itself, with power and water being subject to cuts because of bomb damage. Food shortages were more widespread as the blockade of Britain tightened with the U-boats more and more active. Nan found that frustrating hours were wasted in lengthy queues at the shops.

She, Billy and Rita were the ones who noticed dietary deficiencies most; for Irene (as she put it) was living on the fat of the land, Joan said the food provided in the WAFS canteen was quite adequate by comparison with home shortages, and of course Mavis always managed to wangle a few extras in the NAAFI.

But in June there was much anguish voiced by both Mavis and Rita, when clothes rationing was introduced. "I'll swear that's the first time in this war, they've really got upset!" Nan said to Billy with a flash of humour, which was rare indeed these days.

Joan suffered dreadfully with no news at all from Harry for weeks on end and was convinced he had died in the desert fighting, but by the end of the year she was delirious with happiness when she heard that he was among troops being relieved from Tobruk. Her joy knew no bounds when he arrived home on leave in time for Christmas.

This year Irene was not home, although she had paid them a short visit during the autumn. But her absence was no surprise to Nan because her daughter had often included in her conversation and letters the name of the Tregaron's son, Robert, who was in the navy. He was on a corvette, escorting the convoys of supplies that braved the German blockade, and Irene had met him when his ship was berthed quite often at Falmouth and he was able to visit his parents on brief leaves. Nan could see from the expression on Irene's face that this young man was rapidly becoming very important in her life.

"It seems his ship is in for repairs over the Christmas holidays and he's got a longer leave, so of course she'd rather be with the Tregarons. I don't blame her at all, Billy.

Who knows how much time the young people have got together?" Nan fell silent and Billy briefly let his hand rest comfortingly on her shoulder before he bent to replenish the fire.

Harry helped enliven Christmas for everyone, with his irrepressible good humour, and on Boxing Day they were all invited to spend the evening next-door-but-one with the whole Flint family. Nobody was surprised when Harry and Joan suddenly announced that they were engaged.

"We've decided not to wait to get married, with me probably being sent off abroad again. So if it's all right with Joan's mum, we want to get a special licence so we can do the deed next week." Harry was serious for once as he turned to Nan.

"I know it means Joanie won't have time to sort out a big wedding with all the trimmings, which is what she deserves, but I hope you understand, Mrs Stuart?"

"Of course I do, lad." Nan held him tightly for a moment as she whispered in his ear, "Make the most of what time you have, Harry. I know you'll make my Joan happy and I couldn't wish for a better son-in-law."

"Thanks ever so, Mrs Stuart. I promise I'll always take care of her."

"I know you will. But please, Harry, no more of this 'Mrs Stuart', eh? Call me 'Nan', or 'Mum' if you like. You're going to be family now."

"Right you are, Ma!" Harry grinned his cheeky grin and for a moment the depression and pain lifted from Nan's heart as she looked at the radiant young couple. Surely the world was not totally empty when your child was about to embark on this great new adventure. Please God, thought Nan, her marriage is nothing like mine!

But then, Harry was not really like Charlie. They might share the same impudent charm, but there was a simple ingenuousness about Harry, with not a devious bone in his body, and his devotion to Joan was utterly sincere.

So the Flint and Stuart families rallied round during the next ten days to organise a whirlwind wedding, like so many others during those war years. Brides were allocated extra coupons and old Mrs Flint, as well as Nan, willingly donated their own to Joan. So she managed to find some white artificial silk that Nan made into a long, simple wedding dress, with straight lines and pointed sleeves. A veil and head-dress were borrowed from a friend of Rita's at the munitions factory.

Irene somehow got home for forty eight hours so that she, Rita and Mavis could be bridesmaids. Outfits for them were more difficult to find, but the kindly Mrs Ash stepped in and offered to lend three of her own "smart" afternoon frocks.

"Of course they're all different colours, a pink, a green and a blue, but Joan says it's going to be a 'rainbow' wedding, and if she's happy, that's all that matters," Nan said to Billy, as she diligently stitched the hem on Joan's own dress.

"Lovely job you're making of that, Nan. Pretty as a picture she'll be. I've sorted out with Benny down the market about the flowers. You'll have plenty to make up posies for all of the girls to carry, and some for buttonholes as well. And don't worry about the cost – that's a little contribution from me."

"Oh, Billy, you are kind! By the way, Joan's told me she's asked if you'll give her away. I am glad."

"I don't have to tell you, I'll be proud as punch, walking her down the aisle. I'm a bit worried about making a speech though!"

"Well I shouldn't be. There won't be that many guests — only as many as we can squeeze into the front room! Besides a lot of people won't be able to get home — family or friends away in the forces. Still I'm sure the neighbours will give them a good send off. They're going to stay for a couple of days afterwards at a little pub near where Joan is stationed, in Kent. Ever so pretty she says it is."

The January day was bitterly cold as Nan waited by the church door to see the four girls arrive in the taxi, along with Billy. Joan looked absolutely radiant, her dark hair gleaming beneath the wreath of artificial orange blossom. The twins each had a tiny spray of real flowers pinned amongst their blonde curls, and Mavis's auburn waves were surmounted by a froth of blue nonsense that was a borrowed hat of Mrs Ash's, to match her dress. Nan herself wore her usual "best" coat and hat, but had made a concession to the occasion by pinning a large spray of white chrysanthemums on her collar. In later years, the smell of chrysanthemums always brought back memories of Joan's wedding.

After the happy excitement of that occasion was over, life settled back into the humdrum realities of wartime existence. Now of course, since the horrors of Pearl Harbour, the United States was well and truly part of it all, and soon the American presence was making itself felt throughout the land. Mavis was ecstatic when the barracks where she worked had their intake of American servicemen. She was soon showing off to Rita about the handsome youngsters who were offering her chocolate and even nylons, in exchange for a date after work.

"You be careful, my girl. They may be showering you with stockings and their 'candy' but I don't suppose they'll be backward in expecting something in return. Men are men the whole world over, and believe me most of them only want one thing from a young girl like you!"

"Oh for heaven's sake, Mum! I'm nearly twenty-one – quite old enough to take care of myself, thank you very much!"

"I wonder how many girls who said that have ended up washing nappies nine months later?" But Nan had to admit that when Mavis brought some of her conquests home for a cup of tea after a trip to the cinema, or even for Sunday dinner, their manners were faultless.

Nan herself enjoyed listening to the delightfully different accent, which was reminiscent of her days in Canada. One private actually lived on the American side of Niagara Falls, and she was able to chat with him about her time living close by. His name was Irvin and he was obviously besotted with Mavis.

When he came for a meal he would shower Nan with goodies from the American PX – tins of spam and fruit, a bottle of bourbon whisky (which Billy enjoyed in his tea on cold nights in the shelter) and of course yet more chocolate and nylons.

Harry was back fighting in the desert and Joan tried hard to keep cheerful and live on the intermittent letters she received from him. She was busier than ever with her duties as the RAF were stepping up their own bombing activities. They inflicted heavy casualties over Cologne in May, and then commenced daylight sorties in July. In retaliation, Canterbury sustained appalling damage, and one of Joan's close friends was killed when visiting her family at the time.

Nan was giving Billy cause for concern by the middle of the summer. It seemed with Joan and Irene living away, and both Rita and Mavis so occupied with their own social lives, Nan's whole existence had become pointless to her. She was eating less and less, and any sort of conversation had become a terrible effort. Her face was gaunt and drawn and all her clothes hung on her frame.

"I wish I could think of some way of getting her to take an interest in life again. But I don't know how." Billy was confiding to old Mrs Flint as they queued for their miniscule portion of liver, which the butcher had kept "under the counter" for his regular customers.

"What she needs is a purpose in life. A need to be needed, so to speak. Nan's a born mother, and now her girls are all grown up, she feels useless, especially with no man of her own."

"Yes, I know that." Billy's lips tightened and the old lady eyed him sadly. She never missed much, and had long suspected that his devotion towards Nan went beyond that of an old family friend. She had often wondered why he had not taken matters further, but assumed that Nan had made it plain she was till mourning David. Poor Billy should have stepped in long ago. she thought sympathetically as the queue finally inched forward.

Fate took a hand soon afterwards when Mrs Ash told Nan that she and her husband were moving away from Muswell Hill. "Doctor Ash has been offered a post in a military hospital in Surrey, Nan, and we've decided it's the right thing to do. As you know, I have family in Hindhead, and we would be living quite near my mother.

"Although the bombing is more sporadic these days, I must admit it will be a relief to get right away from it all. I suppose that sounds terribly selfish, but at least I'm being honest!"

"I quite understand, Ma'am. In some ways it's more of a strain not knowing whether there'll be a raid. Back in the Blitz you knew it was going to happen every night. But I'm sorry to think you won't be needing me any more."

"Oh I will miss you, Nan! Of course we mustn't lose touch. But now you'll be free to look for something else to do. Perhaps more worthwhile as far as the war effort is concerned."

"Yes, that's true." Nan nodded, thoughtfully. She already did several hours of fire watching at the town hall, as well as running the local National Savings collections. Whenever there was a local Savings Drive, she was always in the thick of the organising, helping make placards and doing her bit in preparing refreshments (such as they were) for the local dances.

"I've been hearing some rumours that the Government are going to raise the age of conscription for single women to fifty odd soon, Nan, so that would include you, wouldn't it? perhaps it would be as well to make up your mind to join something before then. At least you could make a choice."

"I'd heard the same rumour, Ma'am. I'm sure you're right, and I'll definitely get myself sorted out as soon as you let me know when you're moving."

Nan pondered over the decision at some length. It was a novel situation – one she had never enccuntered before. She could actually make a choice about her life. As a girl she had been forced to leave school and work as a skivvy to supplement the family finances. Although she had secretly wondered if she might not have been capable of a more interesting and demanding job, her parents had never given her the option.

As soon as she had the children, her life had centred round their welfare. She had done whatever work she could to bring in enough money to support them all, and enable her to run the home and look after the family. Now the girls were grown up, two were actually living away from home, and Nan was finally her own woman.

Taking courage in both hands she went along to the local Civil Defence centre and offered her services full-time. Although her education had been quite scanty, Nan wrote neatly and her love of reading had broadened her general knowledge considerably. Backed by her practical common sense, it made her an ideal candidate for the sort of local organiser that was so much in demand. In spite of the hard life she had always lead, or perhaps because of it, she was very active for her forty eight years, so physically was quite able to move on foot around the district and help where necessary during raids.

Billy was overjoyed at the gradual change that he noticed in Nan's behaviour over the ensuing months. During the daylight hours she would be busy at the town hall, organising the relief of local families that had been bombed out, finding temporary accommodation for the homeless and making sure they were fed and comforted. She also helped with the distribution of replacement clothing and domestic items, and kept written records up to date.

There was a network of warden posts throughout Holgate and she would do her rounds of these at night, a business-like figure in her uniform dungarees and tin hat. It was important to boost the morale of the volunteers whiling away the hours of boredom over their knitting and cups of weak tea. Nightly they waited to hear the ominous wail of the siren, which was their cue to spring into action should their particular street be unlucky enough to "cop it".

There was a purposeful spring in Nan's step these days, and although Billy worried that she was probably overdoing things, and not getting enough rest, at least he felt she no longer had the time to brood over the loss of David. Even the girls were not too much of a worry at present.

Joan was kept busy at the airfield in Kent, which gave her little time to agonise over Harry's whereabouts. There was a period when she heard nothing for some weeks, which was difficult to endure, and then she was informed that his unit was one of the many taken prisoner in Tobruk. It was terrible to think of him in German hands, but at least she could cling to the fact that he was still alive.

"You know Harry, love. Nothing gets him down. I pity any Jerry that tries to give him what for! He'll probably tell Rommel where to get off!" Nan tried to comfort Joan on one of her rare weekend leaves, although she could guess how hard it must be for the young woman, so recently a bride.

"Oh, Mum, sometimes I wish I'd got pregnant before he went overseas. At least then I'd have something left if anything happens to him ..."

"Now you're not to think like that, Joanie. You're doing an important job yourself, and there'll be plenty of time after this is all over to make me a grandma! If every young bride got pregnant before her husband went overseas, where would the war effort be, eh? Can't run the RAF without all you girls pushing your little flags around on your maps can they?"

"Oh, Mum!" Joan shook her head, smiling reluctantly as she hugged Nan tightly. Whatever else fell apart, there was always Nan waiting, in her sane little world back at number thirty.

Rita still seemed relatively untouched by the horrors of war. Her job in the local munitions factory was quite hard work – eleven hour shifts – but she thoroughly enjoyed the company of the other girls. She would set off cheerfully each morning in her trousers and knitted jumpers, blonde curls tucked up in her turban style headscarf.

She enjoyed the sing-songs to the accompaniment of the radio – *Music While You Work* or *Worker's Playtime* - and there was a wholesome three-course meal in the factory canteen for one shilling and two pence. Of course she revelled in the chit-chat with her mates. This alternated between latest boyfriends and favourite cinema idols, such as Veronica Lake (whose hairstyle Rita faithfully copied at weekends) or Ronald Coleman with his famous moustache.

When not working, Rita's time was totally occupied with clothes and make-up, in preparation for her next social outing. Clothes were an ongoing problem for all young girls, with the lack of coupons available. Rita did her best to "made do and mend" like all the rest, but because she was not very skilful with her needle, it was usually Nan's aid she enlisted to produce new-looking outfits from old ones.

Shortening hemlines, turning coats into jackets and skirts, embroidering blouses, unpicking jumpers to make short-sleeved pull-overs, Nan's ingenuity was stretched to all these tasks and more. Quite often the outfits she produced were more innovative, and gave Rita more pleasure, than the sort of utility designs which were now on sale, assuming one had the coupons to buy them.

There was of course a lively trade in coupons by those who did not want them, but since they sold at two shillings and sixpence each, girls like Rita were not often financially in a position to acquire them, irrespective of the moral aspects of the "Black Market".

Apart from the terror of the raids, the war was a time of excitement for young girls, and quite often the source of a lot of fun. Scarcely a week passed without a dance being held in aid of some war effort or other – "War Weapons Week", "Salute the Soldier", "Warships" or "Wings for Victory". There were local concerts and whist drives, and of course the cinema.

If Rita did not have a male escort available, there were always similarly placed girlfriends from the factory, and they would set off in a giggling crowd together. It was a rare occasion when Rita did not return with some uniformed male in tow.

Nan did worry about her giddy daughter, but there was a childish naiveté about Rita, an aura of innocence, that belied her come-hither looks and her desperate eagerness to imitate the heroines of the silver-screen. Nan hoped that this childish outlook might protect Rita from the worst sort of predatory male, although she had her doubts.

Mavis was a different matter altogether. She had moved on from her job in the NAAFI at the local barracks and was now working in an American forces club in London. It was the answer to her dreams, and Nan had the feeling that she had no control over the youngest of her girls. She would soon be twenty one and legally of age. But Nan was aware that Mavis had never paid much attention to any authority that might be exerted over her.

Her auburn curls had been fashionably bobbed under her uniform cap, and she somehow always managed to obtain the lipstick and powder that other girls were forever eking out or hunting for in empty shops. Not for her the need to resort to painted legs, when stockings were unavailable. American escorts obligingly provided as many nylons as she required. Indeed she would, in the odd generous moment, offer a pair to Rita.

Some nights she would stay in town, "because the raids were too bad for travelling". Nan suspected that Mavis did not sleep with girlfriends in the shelter, but more likely had a male companion. She still brought some of them home for Nan's inspection, but this was more to impress the family than because she really needed approval.

Mavis had a tough streak in her make-up that she inherited from both Ruby and Charlie, and Nan was sure that the girl was one of life's survivors. It might be comforting to think she was well able to take care of herself, but it was that toughness that alienated her from Nan, who, try as she might, could not feel the tenderness and affection for Mavis that overflowed towards the other three.

In November 1942 the familiar surroundings of number thirty – such a comforting memory to Joan amidst the daily trauma of the airfield – narrowly missed annihilation. One of the sporadic bombing raids was in progress and the casualty on this occasion was number twenty eight, which sustained a direct hit.

Nan was busy doing her rounds of the warden posts, and as two other bombs fell on Holgate that night, she was rushed off her feet. It was a grim and harrowing business, listing the casualties, trying to comfort next of kin and ensure that survivors were settled in the local rest centre with sufficient bedding and a nourishing meal.

The streets of Holgate were a scene of chaos with fire engines and ambulances struggling to make their way through the debris, and the air was thick with dust and choking smoke. An incendiary had wiped out the fish and chip shop where Nan had worked for those early years when she was struggling to put food in the mouths of the four girls after her return from Canada. The shop had changed hands, but the family were naturally known to Nan, as were the inmates of three other houses totally demolished.

By the time she struggled back to Holfield Terrace, as dawn was breaking, Nan was mentally and physically exhausted. She longed to indulge in a bath, even the regulation five inches of water seemed inviting. But she knew she could not spare the fuel to heat enough water, especially when there would only be herself to use it.

Most weeks they would pick a day when the girls and Billy were all home and make it worthwhile to heat enough water for all of them to bathe one after the other. Not very hygienic perhaps, and Billy always insisted on going last, but they were no different from most other households in wartime Britain.

Head bowed with weariness, Nan plodded along the pavement, and it was not until she stepped over the first debris of scattered bricks and mortar that she lifted her eyes to view the gaping hole that had been number twenty eight. Number twenty nine was still standing, but one side had been blown away by the blast. Beyond it number thirty had every window blown out.

But Nan's first thought was for her neighbours. The ARP workers were still shifting debris, and when she went towards them they straightened up and she saw that one was Billy. Sadly he shook his head and then gently put his arm round her shoulders.

"It's a bad business, Nan. A direct hit as you can see. Poor old Mrs Flint didn't stand a chance."

"Oh, Billy! Was anybody else in there with her? What about her Vi and the grandchildren?"

"No, they were all away at Vi's in-laws in Barnet. The old girl was on her own. One thing, it would have been very quick. She wouldn't have known anything."

"Yes, they always say you don't hear it if it's going to land on you … poor old lady. Oh, Billy …" Suddenly Nan crumpled. Memories flooded back of past days when the cheerful, stout old woman, with her loud, down-to-earth humour, had been such a friend in times of crisis. All the pent-up anguish over David's loss, which she had been unable to release since his death, suddenly flooded out and her whole being was buffeted by rending sobs as her legs threatened to give way.

Billy was not a robust man, but he swung her up in his arms and marched through the door of number thirty. Thick dust coated all the furniture and plaster from the ceiling was scattered across the kitchen. Carefully he deposited Nan in the old armchair and went to put on the kettle.

"Don't you worry, Nan. We'll soon get this place put to rights. I had a look round upstairs, and apart from the windows being blown in, and some of the plaster brought down, there's no real damage. Lucky it's the weekend so the girls can turn to and help us get it cleaned up."

"The girls!" Nan's sobs abated as she tried to pull herself together. "Were they all right, Billy? They were in the shelter when it happened, weren't they?"

"They weren't even here, Nan. Rita was going to the pictures with her friend Doreen from the factory, and said she'd stay at her house in Wood Green afterwards. Save her walking home late through the blackout.

"Mavis told you yesterday she was doing a late shift at the officers' club, as they were having a special dance on. Said she was sleeping there the night. Remember?"

"Yes, of course. I'd forgotten. Well thank goodness for that. Billy, how am I going to break the news to Joan about old Mrs Flint? She's so depressed these days, worrying about Harry being a prisoner. And what about him? She'll have to write and tell him about his grandma. As if he needs bad news where he is!"

"Never you mind about all that, my dear. You just drink up your tea while I go up and clear some of the dust in your bedroom. Then you're going to get some sleep. You've had a long night, and this shock at the end of it."

"But the place is in such a mess! I must get started on clearing up." Nan struggled to rise, but discovered her legs were like jelly, and tears were trickling down her sooty cheeks.

"Do as you're told for once, woman!" Billy firmly pushed her back in the chair and folded her fingers round the cup of hot tea, in which he'd lavished much of his week's ration of sugar.

"I'll make sure the girls give me a hand when they get back and I'll see if I can telephone through to Joan's lodgings to give her the news. Just leave it all to me, will you?"

Nan nodded thankfully and accepted the large, clean hanky he offered, gladly letting him take over. It was such a relief, she found, to allow someone else to take control, after a lifetime of being responsible herself.

Like so many other homes, number thirty was cleaned up and put back to rights within a matter of hours. Billy did everything and Nan was able to get a couple of days badly needed rest, before returning to her duties, after the ordeal of old Mrs Flint's funeral. She was buried along with five other victims from Holgate's own local blitz.

After that, life continued in its accustomed pattern, except that Nan's and Billy's relationship seemed closer than ever. He appeared to grow in stature now that she had allowed herself to lean on him for a while, and they reached a new understanding. Nan knew that her feelings for him could never be anything other than a warm friendliness, but she valued his companionship during the dark evenings when winter drew in and they were both off duty together.

As they sat on either side of the fire, listening and laughing to faithful old *ITMA* or *The Brains Trust*, she sometimes thought wryly they were like an old married couple of many years' standing. The only difference was at the end of the evening he would give her shoulder a pat as he passed her chair, and she would go up to her room on the top floor and he would enter his below.

With the bitter cold of winter upon them, life became more difficult with the perennial shortage of fuel. But suddenly the war reports from Africa were more optimistic and the news was full of Rommel's defeat and the victory at El Alamein. On the wireless Churchill was telling them it was "The end of the beginning" and then Joan was ecstatically rushing through the door on a weekend leave, with the glad tidings that Harry had been released as Tobruk was recaptured.

They all hoped that was the last of Joan's anguish over her husband, but it was not to be. He was sent home for a long leave at Christmas, but only to be shipped out early in 1943 to the fighting at Tripoli.

Still, they were all determined to make the most of the Christmas gathering. Joan and Irene came home for it, as Irene's Robert was away with his ship escorting one of the convoys bringing much-needed supplies from America.

Rita invited her latest boyfriend, who was stationed nearby with a searchlight battery, and whose name was Matt. He was a ginger-haired youth, rather spotty, but had an engaging grin and a Norfolk accent. He was not very gregarious, but Nan gathered he came from a somewhat dubious background, with a family who appeared to be forever moving from one area to the next.

"He sounds to me like a blooming gypsy," said Billy as he helped Nan make spam sandwiches for Christmas tea.

"Shush, Billy! He'll hear you!" Nan shook her head, reprovingly, but she had to admit he was probably right. "It doesn't matter where he comes from, anyway. He's a nice enough lad – says 'please' and 'thank you' and obviously dotes on our Rita. Besides, it'll probably be someone else she'll bring home next week. You know what she's like. Fickle isn't the word!"

"Oh, there's no harm in her, Nan. She just likes a good time. And who can blame her these days? It's not much of a life with all the uncertainties, is it?"

"No, Billy, you're quite right. As long as she's sensible and doesn't get into trouble ..." Nan didn't finish the sentence, because as usual the sentiment reminded her of her own early mistake and she always felt a hypocrite exhorting her daughters to behave themselves. Don't do as I do, do as I say, she thought wryly.

They had all been shocked at Harry's appearance when he arrived on Christmas Eve. He looked a "bag of bones" as Nan said to Billy, and there were new lines of suffering etched on his darkly tanned face.

But the old irrepressible humour was still there beneath the changed exterior, and he was soon regaling them with hilarious stories of the mad antics of his fellow prisoners of war and the ways they found to bait their German guards. He made very light of any personal suffering and Nan was almost deceived like all the rest.

But on Boxing night when everyone had finally settled down for the night after a rousing sing-song of carols interspersed with such favourites as *Bless 'em All*, *Roll out the Barrel* and *There'll always be an England*, she found herself unable to sleep. After tossing and turning for an hour or more, she decided to go downstairs and make herself a hot drink.

When she entered the stygian darkness of the blacked out kitchen, she was startled by the tiny glow of a cigarette's light. At her entrance, there was the gasp of an indrawn breath, and then a familiar voice said, "Is that you, Ma?"

"Harry, what are you doing up, son? Can't you sleep either?"

She lit the gas and found him hunkered down beside the burnt out fire. He was shivering, and looking down at his gaunt face, a lump rose in Nan's throat.

She quickly poked the embers into a tiny blaze, and then went to put on the kettle. She busied herself making some cocoa for them both, and when it was ready came back and settled herself beside him in the armchair. He remained crouched before the fireplace, his arms clasped round his knees. He reminded Nan of a small, woebegone lost child.

"What's the trouble then, Harry? Is it a problem with you and Joanie? You don't have to tell me, if it's private, but you know I'm always ready to listen if you need me."

"No, Ma, it's not Joanie, bless her. She's the one thing that's always right for me. I don't know what I'd do if anything did go wrong between her and me!" He shook his head and drew deeply on his cigarette.

"It's just the memories, Ma. You know? I lay in bed beside her and I suddenly remember what it was like. All those months shut up, the filth, the heat, the hunger, your mates dying of dysentery and malnutrition, and nothing you could do to help. Sometimes I used to think I'd go mad, Ma ..." His voice broke and he buried his face in his hands.

Nan bent forward and wrapped her arms around him, rocking him gently whilst she crooned comforting words, as she might to a frightened child. Eventually he groped in his trouser pocket for his khaki hanky and blew his nose loudly, before wiping his eyes and giving her a brave attempt at his usual cheeky grin.

"Sorry about that, Ma. Making a bloody fool of meself! Must be the Christmas spirit and all that. Blame Mavis's GI for bringing round the whisky!"

"Don't apologise, Harry. There's no need for that. You know I think of you as my own son, don't you? The one I never had! After what you've been through, no-one could grudge you a few tears, lad."

"I try not to let Joanie see, 'cos I don't want to upset her. We haven't got long before I go away again, and I know she's dreading that. I want to make this time together as happy as I can. You know what I mean? In case ... Well in case I shouldn't make it back next time."

"Don't even think that, Harry. You're a survivor and a Londoner – they don't come any tougher than that! I'm depending on you to come back and give me a whole brood of grandchildren to keep me happy in my old age, and I won't take any excuses. D'you hear?"

"Right you are, Ma!" He gave her a mock salute, and then as they both rose to go back upstairs, he impulsively drew her into his arms and held her in a close embrace. So softly, she could hardly make out the words, he whispered, "Your David would have been a very lucky bloke, Nan. They broke the mould when they made you."

They stayed motionless for a few seconds, and both were oblivious as the door noiselessly opened a few inches and Mavis peered in, before turning away with a sneering smile on her face, to walk silently upstairs.

Her current American boyfriend, a married Captain from Louisiana, had just brought her home in his staff car on illicit petrol rations, and she had been careful not to wake the rest of the household. The scene she had witnessed had been as unexpected as it had been misunderstood, and she filed it carefully away for future usefulness.

The first months of 1943 passed with the wartime privations exacerbated by the winter cold. Any news of the horrific losses being suffered on the Eastern front brought a sympathetic shiver, regardless of which side was suffering. In March Nan was pleased to hear that Joan was coming home for a forty-eight hour leave, and she looked forward to seeing her eldest daughter.

She didn't arrive until early evening, and when she finally came into the kitchen, Nan was shocked at the sight of her. Her face was chalk white, her uniform was dishevelled and filthy and there was blood on her skirt. She was shaking violently, and when Nan said, "Joanie, love, whatever is it?" she hurled herself at her mother with in incoherent cry.

Before Nan could do more than tighten her arms about her, another figure came through the door. He was tall and handsome in his RAF uniform, which just now was also dirty and blood-stained There were dark shadows beneath his eyes, and he bore a similar look of shock to Joan. When he removed his cap, his mop of curly, dark, hair reminded Nan of Charlie.

"Good evening. I'd better explain that Joan's been through rather an ordeal. You're her mother, I suppose?"

"Yes, I'm Nan Stuart. And you are?"

"Oliver Travers. I'm stationed at the same airfield as Joan. We just happened to bump into each other on the train coming on leave."

"But what is it? what's happened to upset you, Joanie? And you both look in such a state!"

"Oh, Mum, it was awful! Awful!" Joan burst into hysterical sobbing and Nan turned to the young man. He shook his head seriously and with a gesture asking Nan's permission, took off his jacket and dumped it on the floor with his cap. Then he helped lower Joan into a chair, before saying quietly, "I'm afraid we witnessed a rather horrific accident on the underground, Mrs Stuart.

"There was a bomb dropped at Bethnal Green station and people were hurrying to get below to shelter. Someone tripped on the stairs and it was like some sort of terrible stampede. More and more people pouring down and tripping over the bodies below. They just piled up and it was absolutely ghastly.

"The injured were screaming, others crying out in panic and being forced onward by those fleeing from the bombs above ..." He wiped a shaking hand across a sweating forehead, and Nan, holding the shuddering Joan, realised how deeply they had both been affected by the experience.

"It sounds really terrible. How did you manage to escape being hurt? You're not hurt are you?" She gestured to the bloodstains on their clothing, and Oliver shook his head.

"No. We were about to leave the platform and go upstairs when the panic started. We could only stand at the bottom and watch helplessly. Then we tried to help those who had been injured until the emergency services arrived. It took ages before they managed to clear a way outside. As you can imagine, Joan saw some very harrowing sights – so I thought it best if I came home with her. She insisted she had no need to go to hospital as she wasn't actually injured, but it has been an awful experience for her."

"I'm very grateful to you ... Captain Travers is it?"

"Please, call me 'Oliver'. It was the least I could do. If you wouldn't mind my cleaning myself up a bit, I'll be on my way and leave you in peace."

"I couldn't hear of it. You must have something to eat – stay the night if you'd like. We've a spare bed and you look as though you're dead on your feet!"

Joan looked up and nodded vigorously. "Please, Oliver, do stay. I'd feel much better if you would."

"In that case, I'd be most grateful for your hospitality. I was only planning on spending the night in a club in town –

thought I might take in a show – and to be honest, I'm not exactly in the mood for that now."

"That's settled then. Joanie, you go up and have a lie down, whilst I make some tea. I'll heat some water and bring it up so you can have a wash, Captain … er, Oliver. Show him up to the twins' room, love. Rita's out tonight at her friend Sandra's house – they're going to some dance or other – so he can sleep in Irene's bed. I'll make it up later on."

"Are you sure I'm not being a nuisance, Mrs Stuart?"

"'Course not, young man. I'm grateful you were there with Joan to look after her at such a terrible time."

Nan took an instant liking to the quiet, beautifully spoken pilot. She discovered later from Joan that he had been flying in bombing raids over Germany for months and the strain must have been enormous. Many of his contemporaries had been shot down – some had burned in front of him – others were lost over the sea. Joan felt sorry for him when she discovered that his parents and sister had all been killed during the blitz on Coventry.

"He doesn't talk about it much, but I think he lost a girlfriend in the same bombing. So he's really on his own now, Mum. Sometimes we walk back together to the airfield from the village pub, and he's ever so interesting when he gets chatting. He wants to be a journalist after the war. He got a degree at Oxford so he must be really clever."

"Well you can always bring him back here with you if you think he'd enjoy some home cooking – such as it is these days!" Nan clucked disapprovingly as she rolled out the pastry for yet another Woolton pie.

Billy also took a liking to Oliver, and was especially eager to talk to him in May, when they had read in the paper about the heroic "Dambusters" raids over Germany. Oliver himself had not been involved, but was obviously full of admiration for those who were.

Nan was surprised that Mavis did not attempt to flirt with the young airman, but these days she was very taken up with her American escort. She had not told Nan he was married, but Nan would not have been surprised. The similarities between Mavis and Ruby grew stronger as the former grew older.

Then in July, number thirty was rocked by the news that every family dreaded during those times. Thinking about it afterwards, Nan received the impression of history repeating itself. All the details of that dreadful moment when she realised that her brother Jack was lost forever on the battlefield of France were brought back to her.

Joan was home on leave and she and Nan were busy in the scullery making jam with some of the strawberries grown on Nan's allotment. It was a Saturday morning, so Mavis and Rita were also indoors, although both still asleep after their respective late nights out. Billy was the only one absent – working as usual in his greengrocery shop.

When the knock came at the door, Joan said, "I'll go, Mum. It's probably the second post. Maybe it'll be from Irene. You said you'd not had a letter recently, didn't you?"

Nan carried on stirring the carefully hoarded sugar into the saucepan of fruit, savouring the wonderful rich smell. Strawberries had always been her favourite fruit ... She scarcely registered the sound of the front door opening and closing and then slow footsteps as Joan came back into the kitchen.

The lengthening silence gradually impinged on Nan's consciousness and she looked at her daughter. Joan's face was a greenish white and she was staring down at the flimsy paper in her shaking hand. Her head was moving in tiny, negative gestures from side to side.

A terrible shaft of fear lanced through Nan as she swiftly crossed to her daughter. "What is it, Joanie? It's not …?"

"Mum, it's Harry. In Sicily. They say he's missing – believed … Oh, Mum, they say he's dead!" When the awful words had passed her lips, Joan's eyes searched her mother's, as though begging her to deny the truth of what she'd heard, and then when Nan simply whispered, "Oh, lovie, I'm so sorry," Joan uttered one anguished howl, and slipped to the floor in a faint.

That marked a period of dreadful torment for Nan, as well as for Joan. It was so heartbreaking to witness her daughter's suffering, apart from coming to terms herself with the loss of the cheerful, affectionate young lad, that she had come to think of as her own son.

For the first weeks Joan would cling to the thought that Harry was only believed missing. Every post that came she willed to bring a notification that he had been found somewhere. Even if he had been taken prisoner, or was injured – anything was preferable to the terrible finality of his death.

She remained at home on compassionate leave for a while, but gradually as hope slipped away and the realisation that Harry was gone forever took hold, she decided to return to work.

"I'm useless home here, Mum. You've got your own job to do, and if I go back to the airbase at least I'll be of some use. Otherwise I mope around the house when you're all out and I think I'll go mad just remembering ..." Nan held her daughter, as they both quietly cried together. She was glad that Joan had reached this decision, because it echoed her own sentiments.

They did not see Joan again for quite a while. She was working long hours as the British bombing raids on Germany were stepped up. She would write to Nan as often as possible, to assure her that she was fit and safe. Nan would reply with the day to day minutiae of her struggles with the rationing – the red-letter days when Mavis would bring in welcome contributions from her American connections; the triumph when standing in a queue for half an hour would result in the purchase of toilet paper or some razor blades as a surprise for Billy.

Rita's Matt had acquired some parachute silk and Nan had fashioned it into some glamorous French knickers and a couple of blouses, with which Rita had been ecstatic. For her birthday in July, Matt had produced some home made jewellery fashioned from bottle-tops and cup-hooks.

"Showing his gypsy background, your bloke, isn't he?" Mavis enquired with a sneer as she flaunted the rather flashy paste bracelet that her American Captain had recently given her.

Rita's normally cheerful countenance darkened as she glared at the younger girl. "You're a right cow sometimes, Mavis! Matt doesn't get the sort of money that your precious Yanks do. And at least I'm not going out with someone else's husband!"

"That's only because a real man wouldn't be interested in a brainless blonde like you! You're lucky if you get some spotty gypsy to take you to the local fleapit once a week! Personally I like my entertainment a bit more sophisticated. Aaron's taking me to the Café de Paris this weekend, after we've been to the Windmill Theatre."

Rita was unable to think of any scathing retort in the face of such name-dropping, so with a muttered "Who cares?" she flounced out of the kitchen. Nan had been listening to this interchange and as usual Mavis managed to rile her by spoiling Rita's innocent pleasure.

"That's enough showing off Mavis. I can't see the attraction, myself, in watching a lot of half-naked women prancing about on some stage. And if this Aaron is married, I'm ashamed of you. I hoped I brought you up better than that." Nan looked sternly at Ruby's daughter and reflected for the umpteenth time how like her mother she was. Shallow, vain and totally self-centred.

"For heaven's sake, Mum! Half the men in the forces are probably married and going out with other women while they're away from home. Everybody's doing it these days. There's a war on – or hadn't you noticed?" She concentrated on freshening her lipstick in the mirror over the mantelpiece, oblivious to Nan's disapproving scrutiny.

"The war shouldn't be an excuse for everyone to lose all their morals, my girl. Of course men are tempted when they're far from home and family, but that doesn't make it right for girls like you to encourage them. Especially if it's just for what you can get! You ought to be ashamed of yourself!"

Mavis turned and looked silently at Nan for a moment and then the full scarlet lips parted in a wide smile. She raised the carefully plucked eyebrows and then deliberately strolled towards the door. There she paused and looked back.

"Well, Mum, if I do encourage any of our gallant servicemen to misbehave, at least I'm not doing it in the bosom of their family – unlike some!" And she went out, quietly closing the door behind her. Nan sat open-mouthed, utterly taken aback by the knowing smile and pointed words. She gave up the puzzle when Billy came in. If Mavis was insinuating that some member of the family was misbehaving, then no doubt sooner or later she would be unable to resist accusing them in person. Nan had no patience with Mavis's posturing and soon put it out of her mind.

During the autumn months that followed the war news was full of the Allies' Italian successes. Italy had actually surrendered, but there was still bitter fighting there with the Germans.

Mavis's American, Aaron, had been posted to the battle front out East, but although she paid lip service to being devastated at his departure, she soon renewed her previous acquaintance with Irvin, her first American boyfriend. Nan was highly relieved, as she knew he was at least single, and she had liked his company when Mavis occasionally brought him into number thirty.

Nan missed Joan a lot. Her letters were brief – censorship forbade any mention of topics related to her work – and Nan wondered if the pain over Harry's loss was any easier. She tentatively suggested she might try and spend a weekend in Kent, so that at least they could have a few hours together when Joan was off duty. However, Joan proved rather evasive about the arrangements, claiming it was difficult to predict when she would be free, even at weekends, so Nan gave up the idea.

Even at Christmas Joan seemed different from her old, open self. Nan was prepared for her daughter to be still mourning for her husband, but when she mentioned the subject, Joan always hastened to speak of something else. There was an awkwardness between them, and Nan could not understand why.

Eventually she tried to broach the subject on the night before Joan's departure. The Christmas had been the most miserable of the war for all of them. Nan missed Irene, who was unable to come home, as Mrs Tregaron was ill with 'flu, and her help was needed on the farm.

Mavis and Rita were out of the house as much as possible with Irvin and Matt, whenever they could get away from their duties, so it was left to Nan, Billy and Joan to try and instil some festive cheer into the home. Although they made supreme efforts, playing cards, listening to the wireless and even going for a walk through Ally Pally, they all knew they had failed miserably.

On Joan's last evening, Nan attempted to voice her misgivings as they sat over their cocoa before Billy returned from visiting one of his market pals.

"Joanie, is everything all right? At work, I mean. It's only that you haven't seemed your usual self this Christmas. Oh, I know that's daft, because with it being your first since Harry went, of course you must be feeling terrible. No-one could expect any different. I've just had the feeling that there might be something else that's bothering you.

"You haven't mentioned Harry at all lately, and that won't help things. It's no good bottling it all up, love. Much better to talk about him and have a good cry if you want to. I know I've cried about him myself often – such a lovely chap he was – and you must feel so much worse than I do .."

"Mum, please, don't!" Joan's face was flushed and she put out a hand as if to ward off the sympathy of Nan's words. "I don't want to talk about him. Can't you understand? He's gone and nothing will change that. I've come to realise I must get on with my life. It's the only way. When you write to me, you always mention him – how much I must miss him – how much you do yourself – and I don't want to hear it!"

"Why, Joan, love, I'm sorry." Nan stared at the young woman in confusion. "I'd no idea I was making things more difficult. But it's hard not to mention him. He was such a part of all our lives, even if you weren't married for that long. I looked on him like a son ..."

"There you go again! Can't you shut up about him, please?" Joan stood up abruptly and knocked over her cup of cocoa, splashing her old dressing gown and shattering the china in pieces. "Oh, I'm sorry, I've broken your cup, Mum. I'm really sorry. Really ..." Suddenly Joan was huddled up on the rug with her arms round Nan, and her body racked with sobs.

Nan was astounded as she automatically stroked her hair and murmured endearments. At last the storm died away, and she said comfortably. "That's better, lovie. Much better to let it all come out. Grieving always does in the end, one way or the other."

"Mum, you're wrong." Joan looked up as she wiped her tear-filled eyes. "It's no good. I've got to tell you. I know how much you thought of Harry, and you'll probably think I'm heartless, with him only gone five months. But I've been so lonely, Mum. And in the end I just couldn't go on by myself anymore. It's Oliver, Mum. You remember him don't you?"

"Of course, he was a very nice, quiet chap. Very polite when he stayed that time of the disaster at Bethnal Green. What about him, Joan?"

"You won't like this, Mum, but Oliver and I are going out together. He was very kind when I first went back to the airbase after Harry died, and it just sort of developed from that. I'm sorry, Mum, but you see, we've fallen in love with each other."

Nan stared at Joan in amazement. This was quite the last piece of news she had expected. Joan misinterpreted her mother's silence.

"I knew you'd disapprove, Mum! That's why I didn't say anything before. But Oliver and I really do love each other. I cared ever so much for Harry, of course I did. But he was the first boyfriend I'd ever had. I was always a bit shy and he made me laugh, and being Mrs Flint's grandson, I'd known him for ages. I suppose I felt comfortable with him. But it's different with Oliver.

"He's older and takes life more seriously than Harry ever did. But he likes books the same way that I do. He knows so much more than me about things like poetry and music, but we can talk about them together and we look at things in the same way …

"I feel with Oliver that there's more to life than just getting a home together and settling down to having a family. He's travelled and he tells me about foreign places so that I can really picture them. It's like we're two halves of the same whole, somehow … Oh, I can't explain myself properly!"

"I think you've explained yourself very well, Joanie." Nan patted her hand and smiled understandingly at her. "Listening to you then, it was like hearing my own feelings described when I was with David.

"When I met your father, I thought I was in love with him. He was like Harry then, with his cheeky ways. He was my first boyfriend too, and I thought it would last for ever. But as you know, it didn't work out like that. But when David came back into my life, years afterwards, I realised that my feelings for him were so much deeper – we were so alike in our way of seeing things. Just the same as you and Oliver. Two halves of a whole …"

"So you're not angry or upset, Mum? You don't think I'm being disloyal to Harry's memory?"

"Never in this world, Joan! You take your happiness with Oliver while you can. Harry loved you dearly, I know because he told me so, on that last leave of his. He would want you to be happy, the same as I do. Tell your Oliver I'm glad you've found each other. We all need someone, especially in these terrible times, and I hope you'll bring him home to see me again soon."

"Thanks, Mum. It makes such a difference knowing you understand." They held each other tightly for a few moments, and Nan thought how blessed she was to have such a caring, sensitive daughter, even though she had been fathered by the selfish, irresponsible Charlie.

During the spring of 1944 the news was full of incidents in the war out East where the Americans were steadily overcoming the Japanese. The RAF was putting more and more pressure on the Germans, with raids over Berlin and Italy. Whenever Nan read an account of these exploits, her thoughts went to Oliver and his crew, and inevitably to Joan and her fears for him.

They did pay the occasional visit to Holgate and Nan warmed towards this serious young man with his hesitant smile, noting the lines of strain already marking his young face. When his dark eyes rested on Joan, his feelings were clear for all to see. Mavis and Rita were quick to remark on it. Rita thought it was "ever so nice that Joan's got herself an airman, and a pilot at that!", but Mavis was very derogatory.

"See Joan's got herself a new boyfriend then. Hasn't exactly been the grieving widow for too long, has she?" she commented tartly, when she encountered Joan and Oliver leaving to see a show in London. It was Joan's birthday weekend and Oliver was determined to spoil her. He had mentioned to Nan that he had booked them into a smart hotel in London, as a special treat.

Oliver had just been speaking alone with Nan, before they left. "I believe that things will be getting very hectic soon back at base, and I suspect leaves will be non-existent for a while. No doubt you've heard the widespread rumours about the possibility of invading Europe this summer, so I'm not divulging any information that I shouldn't." he smiled as he accepted a slice of Nan's home-baked carrot cake.

"Yes, it's all you hear these days, Oliver. Let's hope they're right. It's about time, that's all I can say! Perhaps this time next year it really will all be over ... What will you be doing then? Got any plans when you get back to civvy street have you?"

"Well I was born in the Cotswolds – my father's family all came from that area – so I'd like to go back there to settle. Ideally, live in a small town, work as a journalist on a small newspaper, and spend my spare time writing my first novel. Which of course would be an instant best-seller and keep Joan and I in luxury for the rest of our lives!"

"Sounds like a good plan to me." Nan looked at him seriously for a moment. "You two are both determined to make a go of it after the war, then? You do want to settle down together permanently?"

"Mrs Stuart, I know Joan's talked to you about us, and I promise you I'll do everything in my power to make her happy for the rest of her life. You have my word on that."

"That's good enough for me, Oliver. So now all we've got to do is win this war, eh?"

The pre-invasion rumours were rife throughout the country, in spite of the widespread propaganda that "careless talk costs lives". But anyone who lived or travelled through the south of England that summer would have been blind not to see the enormous building up of men and weapons along the coastline.

Rita was working longer hours than ever at the munitions factory. Matt's searchlight unit had been posted out of London, and she bewailed his departure loudly. Nan suspected that maybe this time Rita's heart was really touched by the awkward gauche young boy, with the rather dubious background.

Mavis too was suddenly bereft as Irvin disappeared overnight to a destination unknown, and she was actually forced to return home to Holgate for several weekends in a row. She and Rita wrangled endlessly during their enforced proximity and Nan found it trying to listen to them. She and Billy both disappeared to the allotment as often as possible, "to get a bit of bloomin' peace and quiet" he would say laughingly.

Like every other household, they were riveted by the wireless set during those first days in June when news finally came through of the Allies invading the French beaches. Remembering the dark days of Dunkirk, when defeat had seemed so horribly close, Nan, like everyone else, wanted to sing and shout with relief. But the euphoria was not to last – especially at number thirty.

The first shock was Joan's arrival, unannounced. She walked in one evening, looking as though her legs would barely support her. Her uniform was untidy and her face bereft of make-up. Her hair was uncombed and there was a ladder in her stocking. With no preliminary greeting, she walked across the kitchen and collapsed in the old armchair.

Nan put down the bowl of peas she was shelling and knew before the words left Joan's mouth what she was going to say.

"Oliver's dead. He was shot down over the Normandy beaches two days after the invasion started. The station commander told me this morning. He was very kind – he obviously knew about Oliver and me – said I should have a few days away from the base.

"So here I am, Mum. Come running back to you, so you can make it all better. But I don't think you can this time, can you?" She smiled dry-eyed at Nan, and her mother's heart almost broke just looking at her. It had been bad when Harry went, but this time Joan looked as though something inside her had actually died for good.

For the next few days Nan tried to be a comfort, but felt she was utterly useless. Words meant nothing in the face of this silent agony. It was like watching herself in a re-run of the pain she had felt when David died. Even Mavis found nothing to say and she and Rita kept out of Joan's way. Billy as usual was rock-like with his common sense and help with practicalities, but the whole house was permeated with Joan's terrible, unspoken grief.

Nan was trudging wearily along the road one afternoon with a bagful of produce from the allotment. It was a Saturday and the shabby, battered houses drowsed in the June sunshine. She had almost arrived home, when a terrible keening sound reached her from an open bedroom window. She knew it was Joan and hastened indoors.

It was pitiful to hear the girl's distress, but in a way Nan was relived. So far Joan had been unreachable behind a silent wall of pain and her eyes had been totally tearless. It would be best for her to let it all come out, thought Nan, as she ran upstairs to tap on the bedroom door and hurry inside.

Joan was stretched out on the bed, her head rolling from side to side as if she was denying her own pain. One out - flung hand was clutching a piece of paper, which when she felt Nan's hand on her shoulder, she abruptly thrust at her mother.

"Read it! Go on, read it! Dear God I think I'm going mad!" she almost screamed, and then buried her face again in the pillow.

Nan swiftly scanned the letter which came from the War Office. Her first reading left her so bewildered she had to start all over again, forming the words aloud to try and make sense of them.

"Delighted to inform you ... Corporal Harry Flint discovered on the liberation of Rome. Being flown home within the next few days on indefinite leave.' But they said he was missing believed killed. Where's he been all this time? It doesn't make sense. There must be a mistake." Nan sat down abruptly on the bed, trying to absorb the full implications of what she had read.

"It's true, Mum. They enclosed a copy of the notice from the commanding officer. Harry was injured in the fighting on Sicily and left behind in the hills. Some local people found him and looked after him. He lost his memory for a long time. Then it started coming back and he made his way to the mainland. The partisans helped him get through to Rome when the allies liberated it.

"Harry's alive and well and coming home. And all the time he was lost and suffering, I was having an affair with

Oliver. But Oliver's dead now and that's my punishment, for being unfaithful to Harry, isn't it? Just retribution!"

Nan gazed at Joan in bewilderment. It was all too much to absorb in such a brief space of time. She found herself reading and re-reading the official notification, whilst Joan sobbed more quietly on the bed.

Eventually, Nan rallied herself. Now more than ever she must give her daughter the strength she so desperately needed. She sat beside her and gently smoothed back the dark curls form her damp forehead.

"Joan, I know it's a terrible shock, and hard to take in, but you must try and think of the future. It's no good agonising over what's happened between you and Oliver. You couldn't possibly guess that Harry was still alive, so there's no question of your being unfaithful to him. It's just one of those dreadful chance episodes that happen in wartime.

"What you must do now is think of Harry. You've lost Oliver and I know that you want to wrap yourself in grief for him but that's a luxury you can't afford now. Harry is still your husband and has been through who knows what sort of hell. It seems that he's coming home very soon and he's going to need all your love and understanding."

"But, Mum, compared to Oliver, what I feel now for Harry just isn't the same sort of love at all! I can't imagine living with him again as man and wife for the rest of our lives. I just can't!"

"It's no good crossing bridges too soon, Joanie. You don't know how things will work out with Harry in the days ahead. It's all too close to your relationship with

Oliver at the moment. Give it time. You still care about Harry, now that you know he's alive, don't you?"

"Of course I do! But in comparison with my feelings for Oliver – Harry seems more like a brother than a husband."

"That's a start. You care about him and you must try to build on that. Whatever experiences he's gone through may well have changed his whole personality. Who knows? When this war is over lots of marriages are going to have to weather all sorts of strains, but for the time being you owe it to Harry, as your husband, to give him a loving welcome and all the support you can manage.

"As time goes by, if you find you can't settle down together again, then you'll have to think about alternatives. But at least make an effort to welcome him home as he deserves, love."

"Yes, of course I must. You're right, Mum. It's no good looking too far ahead. If I decide the marriage won't work out, at least I must wait until Harry's back on his feet and recovered from the ordeal he's been through. I will be strong, if I can, Mum. I owe him that much."

Nan held her tightly, a lump in her throat. "I'm so proud of you, Joanie. And you know I'm here when you need me. I'll have a word with Rita and Mavis, and make sure they understand the situation. If you decide to tell Harry about Oliver in the future, it's only right it should come from you, not through some sarky comment of Mavis's, or Rita putting her foot in it!

"Now you've had a nasty shock – well no I shouldn't say that, because it is wonderful that Harry's alive, of course it is! But it is a shock for all that, especially on top of Oliver … So I want you to get yourself into bed. I'll get you a hot water bottle. I know it's summer, but you're shivering, my girl. I'll get you a nice hot cuppa as well and then you must try and sleep. That's always the best medicine, I reckon."

"Oh, Mum, you are such a tower of strength! I don't know how I'd get through without you." Joan smiled tearfully at Nan, who patted her shoulder with a show of briskness designed to cover her own emotions, which were now threatening to overwhelm her.

It had just hit her that Harry, her "lovely lad" was alive after all. She could hear his cheerful whistle, as he put his head round the door with the familiar "Hello Ma!" and realised how much she had missed him. She had liked Oliver very much – admired his sensitivity and his learning – but Harry she had understood and loved like a son.

Please God, let him and Joan manage to work things out in time, she thought as she went down to put on the kettle. Only a supreme effort on Joan's part would get her through the first difficult encounter, Nan knew. Joan was such a romantic, she believed that love should be the most important issue in life, but Nan knew from bitter experience that sometimes love was not as important as kindness or consideration between husband and wife.

When she gave the news to Rita, Mavis and Billy they all reacted more or less predictably. Billy pursed his lips in a soundless whistle and said quietly, "That's a bit of a facer, and no mistake!"

Rita's green eyes opened wide as she exclaimed, "Well, there's a turn up for the book, Mum! Just think of him being alive all the time! Joanie must be so excited! Ooh, but what about her Oliver? I mean she really liked him as well, didn't she? D'you think she'll still be upset about him dying, now that she'll have Harry again? And what about Harry? Will she tell him about Oliver?"

"Not if she's any sense, she won't!" Mavis sniffed and tossed her curls. "Talk about off with the old, on with the new! What a welcome for Harry, to find his loving little wife has been having fun and games with one of our Battle of Britain heroes!"

"Now you just listen to me! Both of you!" Nan planted herself before the two girls, arms akimbo, with the look on her face that they recognised of old as meaning "no nonsense".

"It's nothing to do with anyone else what Joan does or doesn't tell Harry. She has nothing to be ashamed of, because she genuinely believed she was a widow when she became friends with Oliver. We none of us know how Harry will be when he gets back. He's probably gone through a terrible time, losing his memory and all, and it's up to Joan and all of us to help him to get over it.

"It's not up to anyone else to put their spoke in or drop any nasty hints about what's been going on while Harry's been missing." She nodded her head meaningly and looked from one girl to the other.

"Now I hope I make myself plain, you two. If I find either of you causing mischief, by accident or out of malice your feet won't touch the ground. You'll be in real trouble! Do I make myself clear?"

"Yes, Mum." Rita said nervously. Nan's emphatic tones had certainly struck home and Rita knew her mother was serious.

Mavis remained silent, with a contemptuous smile twisting her scarlet lips.

Nan said directly to her, "You do understand I mean what I say, Mavis?"

"I really don't know what all the fuss is about! I couldn't care less about Joan's boring love life, I'm sure. She'll be a lot happier with Harry – Oliver was far too intelligent and posh for her. She'd never have appreciated him! Harry will give her just the sort of miserable existence she'll understand. Life in a slum with half a dozen kids I expect."

"You can be a right little bitch sometimes, Mavis!" Nan sighed and shook her head. "I don't know how you get any pleasure from it. And I don't know what sort of wonderful life you expect to have after the war that will be so different from Joan's. Not that there's anything wrong about being happily married to a good man bringing up his children. Even if you're not living in a palace."

"Well I've got different plans, I can assure you! When this war is finally over you won't see me for dust! Irvin's father has got his own business in California and we're going to be married as soon as we can and move out there permanently. You may all be content to spend the rest of your drab lives in this depressing dump, but I've got more exciting ambitions."

"Well, thank you for letting us know, Mavis. I'm sorry Holgate isn't good enough for you. I've done my best to give you a happy home and bring you up properly all these years. But it seems I've failed somewhere. You've made that very clear. If Irvin wants to marry you, and you love him, then of course I wouldn't stand in your way. But I

320

hope you're doing it for the right reasons, and not just because you see him as a meal ticket to an idle life of luxury in sunny California!"

"Oh, I never expected you to approve of anything I do! You've always made it obvious that I don't measure up to your precious Joan or Irene. Even Rita counts for more than me, in your eyes! Well I don't need your approval, now or ever! And who are you to set yourself up in judgement anyway? Pregnant before you were married, abandoned by a husband who probably went off with the first tart who promised him a bit of excitement, because he couldn't stand the boredom of being married to a nagging domesticated saint!"

The vicious words and the tone in which they were delivered was so uncannily like Charlie's parting insults, that Nan's face paled. For a split second she was seized with a terrible urge to blurt out the truth to Mavis. That the "tart" in question had actually been her own mother, and that she, Nan, was only too glad not to acknowledge her as a daughter. But as she gazed into the scornful eyes and flushed face of her niece, she heard another echo from the past – Ruby's voice, extracting the promise that Nan would bring up Mavis as her own daughter.

Curbing the words that were about to burst forth, she merely shook her head and said quietly, "I won't even dignify those remarks with an answer, Mavis. I'm not proud of my past mistakes but I've never made any secret of them. I've tried to be a good mother to you – with little success – judging by your hurtful words."

"For pity's sake, stop being such a martyr! You'd think you never had a sinful thought in your life, with your 'holier than thou' attitude! Your misbehaviour has only been in the past has it? Don't think I don't know about your recent goings-on with Harry! Of course you're pleased he's coming back. You don't think of him as just a son, do you? You're disgusting! Fancying your own daughter's husband!"

"That's enough!" The words came in an explosive roar from Billy, who crossed the kitchen in two strides and gripped Mavis by the shoulders. "I will not hear you bad-mouthing your mother, when you're not fit to lick her boots, you little cow!" His face was scarlet with fury, and as he raised one fist above his head, Nan was terrified he was going to knock Mavis senseless.

Swiftly she intervened. "Billy, leave it. There's no need for you to fight my battles, though I appreciate the thought. As for you, Madam," she looked Mavis up and down more in sorrow than anger. "I don't know where you get your sick ideas from, but you couldn't be further from the truth.

"I've only truly loved one man in my life – what I felt for your father I know now was just a young girl's infatuation. No, David Harris is the only man I've ever really cared for, or ever shall do. The idea of anything between Harry and I is quite ridiculous, and some fantasy spawned by your nasty twisted mind."

"Don't give me that! I saw you with my own eyes that Boxing Night," Mavis hissed malevolently. "I came in late and saw you in this very room. You stood on that same spot where you are now. You were locked together and whispering sweet nothings to each other. Deny it if you can!"

322

Nan stood in puzzled silence for a moment, casting her mind back, and then light dawned. "I don't deny anything, Mavis. We were holding each other and we were whispering. It's none of your business but since you're so determined to misinterpret what you saw, I'll explain it to all of you. Just to put the record straight.

"Harry had been describing the horrors of being a prisoner in Tobruk and his very natural fears about the future. I was comforting him, and drawing some comfort form him in my turn, since I was still newly mourning David at the time. What you saw was the embrace of a mother and son, and even you can't make anything dirty of that!"

There was a short silence and then Mavis was the first to drop her eyes from Nan's. She attempted an air of studied indifference as she shrugged her shoulders, and muttering "As if I could care less, anyway," she marched out of the room, banging the door behind her.

The atmosphere immediately lightened and Rita, with a scared glance at Nan's grim face, said she was off to visit her friend Sandra, from the factory, and slipped hastily away. Nan felt suddenly giddy with the emotions of the past hour and swayed where she stood, legs suddenly unsteady.

Billy was at her side in a moment, easing her into the armchair. "You just have a bit of a rest, Nan. I'll put the kettle on – I think we could all do with a cuppa, eh?"

"Oh, Billy, it's all such a terrible mess!" and Nan's head was in her hands and she was sobbing – awful, tearing sobs that seemed to be wrenched from deep inside her. All the years of bottled up emotion over the secret of Mavis's parentage was suddenly unleashed, and mixed with the shock of the news about Harry, and the upsetting confrontation over Mavis's wild accusations, it finally broke Nan's iron self-control.

Billy knelt on the rug, arms tight round her shaking body and said nothing, wisely allowing her the time that she desperately needed to voice her innermost feelings. In broken sentences, sometimes incoherent with sobbing, she allowed herself the luxury of confessing the truth about Charlie and Ruby, Ruby's death and Mavis's birth.

Billy said nothing throughout the tragic recital and when Nan finally hiccoughed into silence, he simply handed her a large, white hanky to replace her own sopping one. Then he said seriously, "That's quite a secret to bear on your own for so many years. Did you ever tell anyone else, Nan?"

"My mother knew, and it was hearing the truth that caused my Dad's heart attack which killed him. Of course David knew, because he was there when it all happened, out in Canada. But not another living soul, until you Billy."

"Well, I reckon it's not a bad thing that you've finally let it come out, my dear. And I think you know me well enough to be certain that it will go no further than our two selves."

"Of course I know that, Billy. I'd trust you with any secret. There's never been a more steadfast friend than you!"

"Thank you for saying that, Nan. It means a great deal – more than you probably realise." He hesitated and then seemed to reach a decision. "Since we're talking long-held secrets, here's one of mine for you. Though I daresay you may have suspected it over the years.

"I love you, Nan, I've always loved you, ever since that sad day when poor Fred died under the ice. Maybe you've guessed, maybe not. I know that David was very special to you, and there could never be anyone else after him. But even before he came on the scene, I couldn't bring myself to tell you how I felt.

"Sometimes I thought you might care for me too, but even if you did, there was no way I could ask you to marry me. You see, when I was injured in the war, it wasn't just my lungs that were damaged with the gas. Some shrapnel found it's mark too, and although they patched me up ..." he paused, his face suddenly flushing with embarrassment and shame as he struggled to find the words. "I ended up less of a man, that's the truth of it. I could never be a proper husband to any woman, Nan, and much as I cared for you, I could never tell you. So now you know my pathetic little secret!" He attempted to smile, but painful tears trickled slowly down his cheeks.

"Oh my dear, I'm so sorry!" Nan cradled his head on her breast as her own dreadful memories were forgotten in witnessing his anguish. "Don't ever say you're less of a man, because it's just not true. You're everything a real man should be – strong, brave, kind and loyal. Those qualities are the ones that matter to women who have been married to the Charlie Stuarts of this world. Don't belittle yourself, Billy, because I don't want to hear it.

"You're right – I have wondered about your feelings for me over the years, and I'm a very proud woman to know that you care the way you do. You know how I felt about

David, and that I would never want anyone to replace him as a husband in my life. But I will always love you as a true friend, Billy, and if that means anything, you can count on it till I die."

"It means a great deal, Nan, and I thank you for it." He held both her hands for a moment and then very delicately kissed first one and then the other. "No more secrets, Nan. And friends, eh?"

"Friends, Billy," she whispered as she dropped a gentle kiss on his cheek.

The close relationship they cemented that afternoon was to stand Nan in good stead over the next months, as she was faced with one last tragic dilemma in the life of her eldest daughter.

Joan had been given an indefinite compassionate leave from the airbase when they knew about Harry's homecoming. She and Nan determined that number thirty should celebrate his return from the dead as warmly as possible. Rita moved in to share with Mavis, so that the young couple could have the twins' room to sleep in.

The two single beds were pushed together to make a double, and Billy somehow conjured up some distemper out of one of his market contacts and brightened the room with a blue wash for the walls. Nan picked some feathery carrot tops from the allotment and mixed them with candy - tuft that she grew in a window box by the kitchen – all the garden was given over to growing vegetables for the war effort. She placed her impromptu posy in a jug beside the bed and wished she might do more to promote a festive air in the room.

A welcome-home meal was practically impossible in view of all the shortages, but she managed a cake with some powdered egg and an assortment of sandwiches with dubious fillings. Billy and Rita had fashioned a banner that said "Welcome Home Harry" and hung it above the kitchen table. Billy had acquired a couple of bottles of beer from a publican friend who had known the Flint family from way back, and Nan hoped it would encourage the right atmosphere.

Joan had been dragging herself about the house like some pathetic ghost. The shock seemed to have taken its toll physically. She was terribly pale and some days would lie on her bed for hours gazing into space. Nan guessed she must be dreading that first meeting with Harry.

They knew which day he was expected, but not the time. Nan wished they might meet him at the station, but they had to simply wait for his arrival. Joan had made a supreme effort, dressing herself in a pre-war summer frock and applying powder and lipstick, so that at least she had a vestige of colour about her face.

When they finally heard the knock on the basement door, both Nan and Joan almost leapt off their kitchen chairs, where they had both been sitting attempting to knit. For seconds Joan remained, half out of her seat, staring in panic at Nan. Eventually her mother took the initiative and opened the door herself. Her first sight of Harry drove all other thoughts from her mind, except an enormous pity for him.

His face was painfully thin, skin stretched tightly over his cheekbones. Deep shadows underlined his blue eyes which once sparkled cheerfully, but now stared at Nan with a pathetic, strained eagerness. His uniform hung baggily about his thin frame, but Nan's gaze was instantly drawn to the left sleeve that hung, empty, at his side.

Swallowing hard, she forced a welcoming smile to lips that trembled, as she cleared a husky throat to say, "Welcome home son. You're a sight for sore eyes and no mistake!" Then she clasped his shaking figure tightly in her arms, aware that Joan had come up behind her, but giving her daughter precious moments to adjust to the first sight of the stranger that was her husband.

Finally she stepped aside, saying cheerfully, "I'd better let your wife have a look in now, I suppose. Take him up to have a rest, Joanie, he looks fit to drop after his journey. Come down in a minute love, and I'll make you a tray of tea, so you can be on your own for a bit." Then, unable to bear the sight of Joan's horror at Harry's shocking appearance and his pathetic joy at this reunion with the woman he loved, she hastened back to the kitchen.

Those first days of Harry's return were agonisingly tense for all of them. Nan and Billy pitied both the young couple. It was tragic watching Joan hiding her feelings of guilt about Oliver, as well as the grief she was still suffering over his loss, whilst she endeavoured to play the warm, loving wife to this crippled husband who had returned from the dead.

Harry in turn was an emotional wreck, who unless Joan was with him, would spend hours staring into space. Billy and Nan tried to draw him out of his inner torment by asking him questions about the months that he had been "missing" but he seemed reluctant to discuss more than the barest details. Joan told Nan that he would suffer some terrible nightmares, and when he woke up screaming, drenched with sweat, she had to hold him and soothe him like a small child, before he would finally calm down.

It was at these moments he did at last begin to open up to her about the harrowing experiences he had endured. He had been lying wounded out in the open in the Sicilian hills for days on end before the local peasants had found him. They had attempted to nurse him, but his bullet-riddled arm was already far advanced with gangrene. So one of the hill farmers had performed a hideous impromptu amputation. It was this that seemed to cause most nightmares.

"That and the terrible bewilderment of not knowing who he was for months on end, Mum. He couldn't talk for ages, and them all speaking in a foreign language confused him even more. The weather was very bad, so the village where they kept him was cut off for weeks. They couldn't even get him a doctor.

"Eventually he grew stronger and when they showed him some old English newspapers left behind by the troops, his memory gradually started coming back in dribs and drabs. He knew he was in the army but he couldn't remember his name or anything about his personal background for ages.

"They managed to get him across to the mainland in a fishing boat and in slow stages the partisans passed him along to Rome. Then he endured all the bombing by the Allies as the Germans fought a last-ditch stand against them. He reckons the shock of that finally helped bring back the last bits of his memory. So when the Allies liberated the city he was able to tell them who he was."

"He's suffered dreadfully, Joanie. I wouldn't have recognised him at first. It's going to be a long business nursing him back to normal health, but I'm sure you'll manage it. You've only got to see the way he looks at you – he can't bear to be out of your sight – to know how much you mean to him. He relies on you so much – I honestly think you'll be his salvation in the end."

Joan sighed and gazed into the heart of the fire. "I know, Mum. You're right, he loves me so much, and I know I owe it to him to get him better. But, oh it's so hard! Especially at night ..." She flushed painfully and looked at her mother sideways.

"You know what I mean, don't you? With Oliver, it was so perfect, we loved each other so completely, Mum. In comparison, when Harry and I got married we were a couple of innocent kids just finding out what it was all about. We had so little time together really – only a few leaves. But with Oliver the passion was total, Mum. Does that sound shameless?"

"Of course not, Joanie. I may be your mother, and no spring chicken, but believe me I remember what it was like with David, and in comparison with what I felt for Charlie, well you can't really compare it."

"Now poor Harry is so gentle towards me, Mum. But he's ashamed of the way he looks when he's undressed, with just the stump of an arm, and his body so thin and wasted. He's really apologetic when he approaches me in bed, and I try to be loving in return, but it's so difficult, pretending, thinking of Oliver ... and I feel so guilty all the time." Her voice broke and she buried her face in her hands.

Nan tried to comfort her with soothing murmurs and gentle caresses, searching for some helpful advice. She could imagine only too well what Joan was enduring, but she also saw Harry's desperate struggle to return to normality, with his pitiful reliance on his wife, and knew that there was no immediate answer to the whole sorry situation.

"I know it's terrible for you, love. But you've just got to keep trying. He's your husband and a good man. He needs all the loving support you can give him. He wants to get back to normal and his relationship with you is the best way of achieving that. Give it time.

"When he's stronger and had a chance to come to terms with his own disability, to get back some sense of pride in himself as a man, then if you honestly feel you can't keep on with the pretence, of course you'll have to tell him the truth about Oliver. But try and give him as long as you can, Joanie – he deserves that much after all he's suffered."

"I know, Mum. And I promise I won't give up on him, at least not until he's got his life sorted out and some sort of future ahead of him. Of course he's being discharged as unfit from the forces. But once he gets his strength back, he wants to start looking for work. I know it won't be easy though, with the arm missing." Joan and Nan sat in silence trying to see some light in the gloom of poor Harry's future.

The light, when it came, was in such an unexpected manner that at the time Nan and Joan saw it as the ultimate tragedy that would bring about the destruction of all their hopes for Harry. But as Nan said afterwards, "Things have a way of working themselves out, when you least expect it."

She had become increasingly concerned about Joan, who, as the weeks passed, looked paler and more listless every day. Once or twice she had giddy spells and no matter how hard Nan tried to work miracles with their food ration, her daughter found any food an effort to digest.

Nan decided it was probably all the emotional stress she was enduring, and suggested a tonic from the chemist. "The old man in there is ever so nice, love. I'm sure if you tell him all the worry you've had about Harry coming home, after being missing so long, he'll make you up some sort of tonic, just to put you back on your feet."

"Don't fuss, Mum! I'm a bit tired that's all. I'll be all right." Joan became irritable when Nan mentioned her ill health and Nan tried to shrug off her fears. Joan was a grown woman and old enough to make her own decisions after all.

Then a couple of days later matters came to a head. Nan came home one morning after an exhausting night dealing with the results of doodlebugs falling on Holgate. Several homes had been hit and a number of casualties ensued. Many families had started evacuating the children again, who had gradually returned after the earlier departures at the beginning of the war. Somehow these pilotless weapons were psychologically more terrifying than any normal bomb had been.

When Nan walked into number thirty all was quiet. Rita and Mavis were at work and no doubt Billy was still out helping in the clearing up process after the bad night.

Working till he practically drops, as usual, thought Nan, wearily putting the kettle on the gas stove.

As she wondered where Joan and Harry might be – perhaps they had slept late after the disturbances of the night – she heard a noise from the outside toilet. It was the unmistakable sound of someone being sick. A moment later, Joan appeared through the scullery door, looking like a ghost. Nan started to ask if she'd eaten something that had upset her, when her daughter shook her head and then crumpled in a heap at Nan's feet.

Dear God, what now, thought Nan, as she hurried to the front door. To her relief Billy was approaching, covered in dust and soot and looking quiet exhausted. But as soon as Nan blurted out that a doctor was needed, he straightened up, told her not to worry, and trotted off down the road.

Nan found Joan was coming round, so she managed to get her into bed with a lot of support and frequent rests on the stairs. Harry it seemed had gone off straight after his breakfast, wanting to try and help out after the raid.

"He said he felt so useless 'skulking' in the shelter as he called it. Said he must be able to do something, even with only one arm! Oh, Mum, I do feel bad!" Joan moaned and closed her eyes against another wave of nausea.

"I'll get you a glass of water, love. Billy's gone for the doctor. Though he may be a long time getting back. It's a shambles down the main road this morning. Burst water mains, four shops in ruins and rubble everywhere. I should think the doctor will have been out all night with the raids, but Billy will find him, don't you worry."

Nan tried to sound optimistic but inside she was very upset. Joan was so pale and thin and the exhausted look on her face frightened her mother. After all she's had to put up with, if she gets anything wrong with her, she'll have no resistance to fight it. Please God, don't let it be anything more serious than a stomach bug, thought Nan, as she went quickly to remove the surface grime from her own exhausting night.

Miraculously, Billy had encountered the doctor picking his way through the debris along the high street, having just pronounced life extinct in the final body being dug out of the ruins of the flat above the butcher's shop. When Billy humbly asked if he could possibly make a quick detour on his way home, he obligingly came back with him to number thirty.

Doctor Spendlove knew the family from years back and had admired Nan's strength in bringing up the girls alone, and her devoted nursing when Emily was dying.

He disappeared into Joan's room whilst Nan made Billy some toast and a pot of tea. "I'm so worried about her, Billy. She looks really ill and lifeless. She doesn't seem to have any willpower left in her to fight any more. Supposing it's something serious!"

"Don't upset yourself, Nan. Wait till we hear what the Doctor says, eh? Whatever it is, poor Harry will be in a state if Joan's ill, so we must try and make light of it for his sake."

"Yes, of course you're right. What a night, Billy. First all those years of bombing, and now these cursed doodlebugs. We were all so pleased at the Invasion – thought the end was really in sight – but now it makes you wonder when it'll ever be over!"

"Come on, Nan, chin up! We've got this far and not let that little painter with the moustache get us down! Keep smiling, eh?" Billy passed a cup across the table and gave her his usual loving smile, and Nan felt slightly better. Whatever else went wrong, with a friend like Billy, she would cope somehow.

But when the doctor had left, with weary instructions to keep the patient comfortable with plenty of rest, and the reassuring words, "Nothing to worry about, Mrs Stuart, your daughter will tell you herself," Nan entered Joan's room with a premonitory twist of fear in her stomach.

Joan was staring at the cracked plaster of the ceiling with an unfathomable expression on her face. Nan sat down on the bed beside her and picked up her limp hand lying on the faded blue eiderdown.

"How are you feeling, lovie? Doctor said it was nothing to worry about – just keep you comfortable. Some sort of stomach bug is it?"

"You could say that, I suppose." Joan looked at Nan, and said in an expressionless tone, "I'm pregnant, Mum."

"Why Joanie, that's wonderful news! No wonder you've been feeling poorly. Quite normal in your state. Oh, I should have guessed! But it never occurred to me! Oh, Harry will be so thrilled, love. This will do more than anything to help his recovery, I'm sure of it!"

"Help his recovery? Oh, yes, I'm sure he'll feel marvellous when he discovers his wife is two months pregnant by another man. Great for his morale that'll be!" The bitter words resounded round the still room and then died into silence. Nan sat there appalled, as the full implications of Joan's words gradually sank in.

335

What a tragedy, she thought brokenly. Her daughter mourning for the man she had loved and lost in the war, but now carrying his child. Harry, tremulously trying to mend the shattered pieces of his life in the arms of the wife he adored, now to be faced with tangible evidence of her unfaithfulness during his enforced absence. Even if he had come to terms with her relationship with Oliver, which had been wholly understandable as she had been told her husband was dead, surely he would never be able to accept the shame of another man's child in their life. Especially in view of his own sensitivity about his physical disability.

The silence lengthened between mother and daughter in the morning heat of that August day. Each was absorbed in their own thoughts. Looking at Joan, Nan had the impression that her daughter was so battered emotionally by the events of the last few months, that she was on the verge of giving up any conscious reasoning at all. Nan sensed that her daughter simply longed to turn her face to the wall and wait for life to quietly go away.

Nan sighed deeply. The events of her own life passed swiftly through her mind. She recalled the decisions she had made at certain times, which she might have made differently if she had simply had the love and support of someone stronger to rely upon. She too felt bone weary, not just with the exhaustion of the previous night's horrors and the personal effort involved in dealing with them, but all the traumatic events of these last war years. She knew that here was a daughter on the brink of a tragic decision, and she, Nan must ensure that she decided correctly. For the sake of all the family, now and in years to come.

Silently Nan stood up and walked to the window. Outside, Billy was feeding their hens. On the breeze she could faintly smell the damp earth where he had been giving the tomatoes their morning watering, against the onslaught of the mid-day heat. It was a pleasant, peaceful scene that for a moment belied the horrors of the night before, and the tragedy that was in the throes of being enacted within number thirty.

Nan made her decision.

"Joan, you loved Oliver very much, didn't you?"

"You know I did." Her daughter spoke listlessly, her eyes unmoving on the crack above her head.

"This child of his that you're carrying, would it make you happy – to have a part of him always with you? Would it help you to come to terms with his death?"

Joan slowly looked at her mother, and a weary expression crossed her face. "Yes, I suppose it would be good to have his child. A tangible memory of what we shared together. We talked about having a family – after the war – but now it's quite different of course."

"Because of Harry, you mean?"

"Of course. How can I be happy having Oliver's child and still be married to Harry? He'll be totally shattered when I tell him I'm carrying another man's baby. His self-esteem is low enough already. This will completely finish him! I suppose I'll have to leave him, but I don't know how he'll manage. He's so dependent on me now!" Joan shook her head wearily and closed her eyes again.

"Then don't tell him, Joan. It's the only answer." Nan's voice was calm and controlled and it dared Joan to argue with its complete assurance.

337

"What are you talking about, Mum? I'll have to tell him. He may not be all that bright at the moment, but I think even Harry will notice when I start bursting out of my clothes, and then a little stranger shares our room at nights!" Joan glared bitterly at Nan now, anger and fear burning out of her eyes.

"I mean, don't tell Harry that the baby is Oliver's. How long was it between the last time you saw Oliver and the first time you slept with Harry when he came home?"

"Four weeks, I think … But what difference does that make? You don't mean I should let Harry believe …"

"… Believe the baby is his? Yes, that's exactly what I mean, Joan. The more I think about it, the more certain I am. If the baby seems to be born a month premature, so what? And if it should really be overdue, then Harry will believe it's born at the right time. Your colouring is dark and so was Oliver's, so if the baby is dark as well, it will just be seen as taking after you. There's no reason anyone should suspect anything. Only you and I will ever know the truth, Joan."

"But it's such a terrible deception, Mum. How could I live the rest of my life with Harry, all based on a lie? How could I do it? It would be so dishonest, so wicked!" Joan gazed at her mother in horror, as the full import of the suggestion sunk in. Her respectable, straightforward mother actually suggesting such a devious way out of her present dilemma!

Nan looked at Joan in silence for a moment, and then she asked, "You do care for Harry don't you? You don't hate him?"

"Of course I care about him. That's what makes it so terrible, knowing how much this will hurt him. What it will do to him, in his present low state! I just don't know how I'll bring myself to tell him!" Joan's voice was anguished as she pictured the pathetic figure of a man that her once muscular, cheerful, husband had become.

"All the more reason for letting him believe the baby is his, Joan. Can't you imagine what it will do for his confidence, becoming a father? It will give him a whole new incentive to get his life sorted out. To make sure he has a future to offer his son or daughter. It will be just the boost that his confidence needs. To believe that he is fathering a child! Beside the happiness that will bring him, what does a lie matter, Joan? Surely you can see you'll be justified in keeping the truth from him?"

Joan gazed at Nan wonderingly. All her life, Nan had been such an honest woman, with standards of behaviour so clearly defined and rigorously upheld as she had brought up her family. Now she appeared to be arguing against every value she had ever instilled into them.

But as Joan mulled over her mother's words and weighed up the alternative, so the force of her argument became more valid. On the one side a happy family with Harry rejoicing in parenthood – she was sure he would make a wonderful father, he had always been so good with his nieces and nephews.

On the other hand, she could picture his desolate, betrayed expression when she told him about Oliver and their passionate relationship. There would be no option but an end to their marriage, and what would become of the poor, broken figure that was desperately trying to regain some stability in his life?

As she struggled to reach a decision, there was a sound of the street door slamming and then Billy and Harry's voices downstairs. Joan and Nan locked eyes, as Nan willed her daughter to make the right decision. Then the footsteps they were expecting mounted the stairs and a hesitant voice asked, "Joanie, sweetheart, are you alright?" as Harry gently pushed open the door and advanced towards the bed.

Nan stood up and smiled brightly at her son-in-law. "Hello, Harry, love. Trust you to be out of the house when all the excitement's going on!" She moved a chair beside the bed.

"I reckon you'd better sit down, while you listen to Joan's news. Might be a bit of a shock, eh Joan? But one he'll be pleased to hear – isn't that right, love?"

It seemed an eternity passed in that tiny instant of silence before Joan looked deep into her mother's eyes, and finding the reassurance she sought, said quietly, "Yes, I think he'll be very pleased, Mum."

APRIL 1945

The evening sunshine flooded the rooms of number thirty as the inmates prepared to celebrate the removal of the blackout at long last. It was Joan's birthday, so there was extra cause for celebration. The wireless had been full of bulletins that now contained only good news. Hitler was finally dead and the end of the war was a matter of days rather than weeks.

Nan left Rita and Joan to set the tea-table and went into the garden to savour alone the knowledge that peace was just around the corner. She sat down beside the old-fashioned bassinet that had been resurrected from the cellar and refurbished by Harry.

Billy saw her through the window and brought out a glass of sherry for her. His hair was very grey these days, and his body a lot more stooped, but his face was tranquil with the contentment of being an integral part of the family. They toasted each other silently and Billy did not say anything to interrupt Nan's reverie. But he could guess her thoughts quite easily.

She was counting her blessings as she reviewed the state of her family. Irene was coming home soon from Cornwall, but only on a visit. She had written in her last letter that she and Robert were now engaged, and on his next leave from the Navy would bring him to meet the family. Nan knew that this daughter would only be in Holgate for a brief time, before returning to the Cornwall that had now become her much loved home. But Nan could accept that quite cheerfully, certain that Irene was happy.

Rita would probably be off soon, Nan suspected. She and Matt might or might not stay together, with or without the benefit of Clergy, but Rita would always be a free spirit, and Nan knew that was the inheritance she carried from Charlie. There would be little point in fighting against it.

Her face darkened a little, hearing Mavis's loud laughter from the kitchen as Irvin boisterously teased her. Mavis would always be a source of pain to Nan. She would always feel an irrational guilt that she had not in her heart been successful in keeping her promise to Ruby. Mavis had not been, and never would be, the recipient of the same love that Nan felt for her own daughters – she was too much a reminder of the anguish that her mother had caused with Charlie.

Still, it would all change in the near future. Mavis and Irvin were already planning their engagement, and Mavis was longing to set sail for America. So Nan consoled herself that she would never learn the truth, and she had enough of both parents in her make up to be one of the world's survivors, whatever happened to her.

Billy grinned as the occupant of the bassinet stirred and yawned and then gave her grandmother a sleepy smile as Nan picked her up. Contentedly she sat rocking the shawled bundle. In her faded cotton dress, dark hair in its familiar neat bun, her face brightened by a hint of lipstick and rouge, marking this a special day of celebration, Billy decided that Nan looked more like Miranda's mother than her grandparent.

He leant across and watched as the tiny fist curled round his own little finger. "She's a lovely baby, Nan. Takes after her grandma, with those dark curls and great big eyes, I reckon."

"Or her mother, of course!" Nan smiled tenderly across at this old friend, who was so very dear to her. She knew that the girls would soon all have left, and number thirty would be very silent when they went, but she would still have Billy.

"Tea's ready, Grandma. Is that daughter of mine ready for hers now?" The laughing voice made Nan turn and watch the approach of her son-in-law.

"I've told you before, my lad. I'm her Nan, not her Grandma!"

As he gave her a mock salute, she thought what a change the last months had wrought in him. From the moment that Joan had announced she was pregnant, the old Harry had begun to emerge from the shell of the pathetic stranger that had come back from the dead.

The joy of fatherhood and the confidence it had given to Harry had literally made a new man of him. His physical recovery was now complete. He was still lean, but now wiry with it. His disability rarely bothered him, and he had started a new career in a wireless shop. Nan knew that he was already nurturing hopes of a similar business of his own some day.

He and Joan still lived at number thirty for the time being, but Nan guessed they would soon be thinking of a home of their own, and she would be pleased for them, although they would be sadly missed. But most of all she would miss the newest member of the family.

What a joy Miranda was to all of them! Throughout Joan's pregnancy, Nan had been so concerned about her daughter's health, and worrying how she would cope with the advent of Oliver's child, who must always be regarded as Harry's, that Nan had rarely thought about herself becoming a grandmother. So the delight of holding the first member of the next generation in her arms, and reliving the moment when Joan herself was born, was as unexpected as it was wonderful.

Now Joan was coming out of the house, with a smile for the tableau beside the pram. When Harry put his arm round her as they both gazed down at the baby on Nan's lap, she smiled warmly at her husband. Mother and daughter had never discussed Miranda's parentage, since the day Nan persuaded Joan against telling Harry the truth about her pregnancy. Looking at the two of them together, Nan was able to breathe a sigh of relief.

Many a night she had lain awake, worrying if she had done right influencing Joan to keep the baby's father a secret, but now she was sure it had been the correct decision. Joan might never feel for Harry the grand, heady passion she had for Oliver, but they were comfortably, sanely happy together and Miranda had set the seal on that happiness. Hopefully, one day she would have a brother or sister, and only Joan and Nan would be aware that it was Harry's first born.

Yes, Joan had reached a safe harbour with Harry, and Nan too felt that she found a new peace of her own. She still bore the scars of the anguish and betrayal that Charlie had brought and she would always mourn her beloved David. But the warmth of her friendship with Billy was an enduring life-line. It had seen her safely through the dramas of war and would be a constant support through whatever